DARK ANGEL

BEFORE
THE DAWN

DARK ANGEL

BEFORE THE DAWN

MAX ALLAN COLLINS

Based on the television series created by
James Cameron and Charles H. Eglee

BALLANTINE BOOKS • NEW YORK

A Del Rey® Book
Published by The Ballantine Publishing Group
™ and copyright © 2002 by Twentieth Century Fox Film Corporation

www.delreydigital.com

ISBN 0-345-45182-1

Manufactured in the United States of America

First Edition: October 2002

OPM 10 9 8 7 6 5 4 3 2 1

For Pam and Barb—
two dark angels . . .
. . . even the blonde one

ACKNOWLEDGMENTS

My frequent collaborator Matthew V. Clemens—who also assists me on the CSI novels and with whom I've written numerous published short stories—helped me here immeasurably. A knowledgeable *Dark Angel* fan, Matt co-plotted this tale and created a detailed story treatment from which I could develop *Before the Dawn*.

My editor Steve Saffel sought me out for this assignment, and then provided consistently strong support, which included not just rounding up materials, but adding his own creative input. Steve helped solve several problems of the sort a writer faces when creating a story that must exist within a world of existing stories.

I would like to thank the creators of *Dark Angel,* James Cameron and Charles Eglee, who are also the executive producers of the show; Debbie Olshan of 20th Century Fox; and Wendy Chesebrough of Lightstorm. I'd also like to acknowledge the producers of *Dark Angel,* Rene Echevarria and Rae Sanchini; and, at Ballantine Books, Gillian Berman, Colette Russen, and Colleen Lindsay. The support these, and others, provided was, frankly, remarkable, including prompt and helpful responses from Jim Cameron himself.

Matt, Steve, and I hope that *Dark Angel* fans will appreciate this exploration into the beginnings of this exceptional anti-heroine.

"It's my life
It's now or never."
—JON BON JOVI

"It's my life
and I'll do what I want."
—ERIC BURDON

Sometimes, when she looked back on it, Max might have been recalling a particularly vivid dream; other times, the memories had a strangely detached quality, as if these events were the stuff of a story she'd heard, things reported to her that had happened to someone else, or maybe one of those TV shows she'd seen when she'd lived with the Barretts.

But in moments of clarity, she knew the "story" was none of those things.

No matter how some inner censor tried to distance her from the pain, Max knew she had experienced what she remembered. Even though she saw herself from the outside looking in, the young woman still recognized that all of this had happened to her, really happened, the entire experience a part of her as much as the barcode on the back of her neck.

Normal people weren't marked that way, as if they were a box of frozen peas or one of the packages she delivered, in the job she'd taken, in the normal life inside of which she was hiding.

There were those who considered Max a cold one; but behind her unreadable gaze, Max still felt emotions, a flood of feelings that she wasn't supposed to possess, the humanity Manticore had tried to prune from her personality, from all of their personalities.

Closing her eyes, Max—for the millionth time, it seemed—allowed the movie to run again on the inside of her eyelids. . . .

Chapter One
COLD PURSUIT

MANTICORE HEADQUARTERS
GILLETTE, WYOMING, 2009

Her bare feet pounding, breaking the crust of ice on the snow-packed ground, her thin blue hospital-style smock hiked high over pumping legs, nine-year-old X5-unit 332960073452 barely noticed the February cold. Neither did she have any knowledge that in other parts of the United States, Valentine's Day was less than forty-eight hours away; that was part of a mundane, ordinary life as unknown to her as her controlled existence had been to the outside world.

Though she had learned much at Manticore, all the girl knew, at this moment, was that she was running for her life.

The deafening whir of choppers circling overhead did not cause her to look up, and she avoided the wide white beams of searchlights that probed, slashed the remote Manticore facility, turning the gloomy woods into a haunted house of light, dark, and shadow.

Brunette locks shaved down to a severe concentration-camp buzz cut, she was small, but not skinny—lean, lithe, wiry . . . and, though unmistakably a child, already battle-hard. Her dark olive complexion gave her a tiny advantage over some of the others, the ones so white they practically glowed when the searchlights neared them, ghosts in the haunted house. Her eyes were large and dark, and she might have been referred to as doe-eyed if there hadn't been something lethal glinting in there, something almost predatory in the way those orbs took in whole scenes and missed no detail.

Sprinting through the woods, she didn't breathe hard, didn't even sweat, as—machinelike—she pumped her arms and pistoned her knees up and down. Her hypersensitive hearing picked up—behind her, farther in the distance with each stride—the ragged breathing of her pursuers, grown-ups who, for all their own training, could only vainly fight to keep up with a genetically enhanced soldier-in-the-making.

The child knew it was true now—they were escaping, they were *really* escaping . . . though she and the others, her "siblings," could barely grasp the word's meaning. They were well schooled, these soldier kids, but their context was limited. The girl knew "escape" only as something you thought about when you had been captured, after you'd been taken prisoner.

But she and the others weren't prisoners, were they? After all, wasn't Manticore their home . . . the only home they'd ever known?

But that home had seemed suddenly a prison, when the man they trusted, the father figure to these special children—Colonel Lydecker himself—had callously shot one of them down. Eva was dead! For what? Mere defiance?

Now they knew exactly what they were—they were an experiment, an exercise in mutated genetics and military tactics; and they knew, too, what they were worth to Manticore, if that experiment failed: *nothing.* All the training, all the exercises, all the studying, nine years, her whole life, had shattered into something incomprehensible, within the blast and echo of a single gunshot.

A group of snowmobiles, their engines howling like a pack of wild dogs, flew by her flank, traveling too fast to see her as she pressed herself against a tree, the rough bark weirdly soothing, reminding her she was alive, awake, not dreaming this. The grown-up soldiers looked like futuristic monsters to the girl, in their baggy black fatigues and night-vision goggles, all with laser-sighted automatic weapons, pressing up the hill from the valley in an ominous wave . . .

She took off running again.

Cresting a slope, fleet as a fox, Max found herself in a

clearing. After a moment of indecision, she saw a head, Zack's head, rise up from behind a log.

Wordlessly, she moved to join him. As she neared, more kids in the blue-gray nightshirts and pajamas began to pop out from behind other logs and the trunks of trees, like strange, sudden night-blooming flowers. They shared not only the same form of dress, but the buzz-cut hair as well, and this sameness made them interchangeable, their individuality lost.

The last one to reveal herself was Jondy, her smile showing her relief that Max—that was the name her sibs had given her—had finally made it to the rally point. Despite Manticore's constant hammering the point that none of them was more valuable than any of the others, the two girls—who even without the hospital clothing and shaved haircuts resembled each other—had bonded, become sisters.

Behind Max, the roar of the snowmobiles plowing up the hill grew louder. As usual, Zack took charge; the boy could be cool and intense at once. Using military hand signals (a gift their instructors had given them), Zack broke the group into escape-and-evade pairs. One by one, the couples dispersed into the woods, each going in a different direction.

When Zack crisply signaled for her and Jondy to take off, Max shook her head. She didn't want to leave Zack behind; she didn't understand why the sibs were separating—wasn't there strength in numbers?

But the solemn boy again emphatically signaled for them to go. She didn't want to leave him alone, but she had no choice—their instructors had instilled obedience to team leaders—and then Jondy was grabbing her by the arm, and they were taking off into the cold night.

Once again, Max found herself flying through the woods, this time with Jondy at her side. Within seconds they reached the perimeter of the facility, where awaited a seven-foot chain-link fence wearing garlands of barbed wire.

The girls scampered catlike up the fence, eased themselves over the barbed wire—unaware they were centered in the night-vision sniperscopes of their pursuers—and as they dropped to the other side and freedom, Max paused to look back, thinking that had been too easy . . .

Sounds in the night perked her keen hearing and drew her gaze to where Zack turned helplessly at the center of an ever-tightening circle of black-garbed troopers, red laser beams sighting in on him, scarlet dots dancing.

Powerless to help, the young girl watched as Tazer darts struck the boy commander and sent him tumbling down a slope, twitching to the ground, his arms and legs writhing wildly, convulsively carving manic snow angels. She stood rooted to the spot, horrified by the sizzling sound of the electricity, until Jondy tugged on her sleeve and got her moving again.

Max knew now that Zack had saved her life by forcing them to separate; and running away from the fence line that night, she couldn't help feeling that somehow she and Jondy had failed him, possibly even betrayed him, by leaving him to face so many with so little . . .

The belligerent growl of the snowmobiles grew louder as the men on machines closed in on the girls on foot. Seeing an opportunity to slow their pursuers, the young fugitives scampered out onto the iced-over surface of a small pond. The ice appeared strong enough to hold them, but Max felt pretty sure it wouldn't support the weight of those bulky snowmobiles. Behind them, the roar of the choppers increased, like an accelerating scream, and the spotlights turned in their general direction as the gunships joined the pursuit.

They were nearly across the pond when Max sensed the ice going spongy, starting to give way beneath her bare feet, and she had just enough time to hear the sharp crack before the ice exploded under her and she found herself dropping into the frigid water beneath.

So cold it almost burned, the sloshing water stabbed at her like millions of tiny knives; but she ignored the feeling and pushed herself to the surface and gulped air.

Jondy, standing barely ten feet away, called, "Max! . . ."

"Go!" Max yelled, even as she struggled to gain purchase on the jagged edge of the tear in the ice.

"No, we stick together!"

"Go, Jondy, I'll find you. Just go."

The girl hesitated for a long moment until they saw a Humvee come crashing through the gate behind them. Max watched the vehicle chewing through the snow toward her and wondered if the driver knew the pond lay directly in his path. She turned and watched as Jondy dashed toward the forest, the snowmobiles plowing after her, the riders firing haphazardly, their bullets . . . *not Tazers, bullets* . . . tearing bark off the trees and ripping gouges in the snow.

Then Jondy disappeared into the woods.

To safety? To capture? To execution? Max could only wonder.

Turning back as the Hummer veered around the edge of the pond and just as the headlights were about to hit her, Max took a deep breath and propelled herself below the surface of the water. Through the veil of ice, she could barely make out the Hummer sliding to a stop, and two men climbing out. She couldn't tell for sure with the strange angle, blocked as she was by the partition of ice; but one of them could have been Lydecker . . .

. . . and he seemed angry.

The two men spoke for a moment, their words too muffled for even Max's hyperhearing to make out from her watery hiding place; but the pair climbed back into the Hummer and skidded off into the darkness.

Silence now.

It felt odd down here, so much of her body ashiver with the onset of hypothermia, and yet her lungs burned as if someone held a match to them. Fear still squirmed in her stomach, like a coiled snake, and she felt certain that when she broke the surface, Lydecker and the others would be waiting there to kill her.

She made a decision—such battlefield decisions were part of her training, after all, and instrinsic to her makeup. She would die fighting, rather than just give up. . . .

Max swam back to the hole and broke the surface just as her lungs seemed about to explode. She gulped air, went under again, and pushed her way back to the surface trying to suck in the precious oxygen between fits of coughing. She'd learned another thing tonight: even X5s, like herself, had their limits.

Pulling herself out of the water, she looked around, and was stunned to find herself alone in the dark. She was free. Her next thought was of Jondy, but she knew her first priority had to be taking care of herself. The flimsy gray nightshirt, now soaked with the icy water, offered no protection against the frigid night air.

She needed to find someplace warm, somewhere dry, and she needed to find it soon. Trudging off into the woods, she wandered aimlessly. Though she knew time was of the essence, seconds, minutes, and hours seemed to have lost their meaning and she had no idea how long she stumbled around in the darkness until she finally found herself standing on the edge of a two-lane highway.

The woods she had known—they had played war games there, the terrain was familiar; now she was in a world she recognized only from training videos. Still, she had been taught well—to adapt, to survive, had been instilled.

In the distance, Max could see the glow of headlights. The Manticore Humvees? Or someone else? Someone friendly? Hostile?

Ducking into the ditch, Max turned her cat's eyes in the direction of the oncoming lights and listened for the sound of the engine to grow loud enough for her to discern what it was. The vehicle wasn't traveling as fast as the Manticore Hummers would be going, down a highway anyway. Of course, they could be moving slow, to search the roadsides for her . . .

Genetically enhanced though she was, the child could feel the subzero wind knifing her flesh, sapping her strength. If she didn't find some kind of shelter soon, this short chaotic episode of life beyond the fence would be the only morsel of freedom she'd ever taste. She wondered if she should show herself if the headlights turned out to belong to a Manticore vehicle. If she returned, though the punishment would no doubt be severe, it could hardly be as bad as dying alone in the snow . . . could it?

But those had been bullets, snapping at Jondy's bare heels! Lydecker seemed to have made a decision: capture was not enough; execution seemed at least implied. . . .

Watching the lights inch ever closer, Max knew she wouldn't ever let herself be taken back. Ducking down, she listened intently to the pitch of the oncoming engine. It wasn't a Humvee—she'd heard enough of them to know this was a different vehicle.

Whatever it was, the thing lumbered along on seven cylinders, one of them obviously the victim of a fouled plug. As it topped the next hill over, Max recognized it as civilian . . . a blue Chevy Tahoe—Wyoming plates, AGT 249, not a government plate and not a government paint job.

Preparing for a fight, Max slowly eased herself out of the ditch and onto the road, nightshirt flapping in the chill wind like a defiant flag. In the distance, the sirens still wailed and the choppers still circled the woods, their searchlights oscillating around the forest in search of X5s to latch onto . . .

The Tahoe dropped into a valley, then crested beside Max, the tires sliding a little as the driver stomped on the brakes and locked them up. Max glimpsed the Wyoming plate, AGT 249, then the driver finally got control of the vehicle and pulled it to a stop, the passenger's side door right in front of her.

It swung open, like a slapping hand, and a woman in her thirties with dishwater blond hair to her shoulders and wide-set blue eyes stared down at Max.

"Get in," the woman said. The eyes were a peaceful color, the blue of a mountain stream; but they glistened with fear. "Hurry up! . . . Come on."

In 1.3 seconds, Max completed a threat assessment, reckoned the woman harmless, at least for the time being, and the child soldier climbed into the vehicle and shut the door.

"Get on the floor," the woman said.

Max responded to the command and the woman wrapped her in a gray woolen blanket—Manticore issue!

"It's all right," the woman said, responding to the flared-eyed expression of the girl. "I work for them . . . but I'm not one of them."

Keeping her eyes on the woman, Max said nothing. Better to let the woman keep talking and for Max to use the time to gather her strength. In the meantime, the girl calculated that snapping the woman's neck would be the quickest way to kill her; and Max knew she'd had enough vehicle training to operate this civilian machine. Killing her while the car was moving, however, would add unpredictable factors. . . .

The truck's heater hummed sporadically, but the air it blew into the compartment was warm, soothing the child as she considered murder methods. Even the itchy blanket felt good wrapped around her shoulders. . . .

The woman had a straight, thin nose, full red lips, and those aquatic blue eyes, all set inside a triangular face. She wore a white medical uniform that peeked out beneath a long dark overcoat. Security-cleared civilian medical personnel came and went at Manticore, Max knew.

Mistrustful but with no better option, Max huddled on the floor as the Tahoe labored up and down the snow-covered hills. The woman seemed frightened as she drove through the night—that was good; if this were one of Lydecker's people, the driver would not as likely be scared . . . not unless the woman knew just how deadly a package she was transporting.

The driver did look down at Max occasionally and offered reassuring smiles. Max couldn't figure out whether the gesture was meant for her or to help the woman reassure herself. Not that it mattered, right now.

Fifteen minutes later, the woman pulled the SUV to a stop, killed the lights, and turned off the engine.

"We're here," she said, her voice still a little too high, the words a little too fast, her tension bleeding through her forced cheeriness.

They both got out and Max followed the woman to the door of a cabin, a small, wooden structure. The rustic homeyness of the building meant nothing to a child raised in a concrete barracks, and it resembled nothing she had seen in their training films, which did occasionally depict civilian housing. This tiny building seemed more like a shed to the child—the shack would have fit inside one of the huge shower rooms back at Manticore.

The woman opened the door, but Max hesitated.

Another reassuring smile. "Come on . . . it's all right. Really. You'll be safe here."

Max wanted to believe her apparent benefactor; but then she had always believed Lydecker, they *all* had . . . and now one of them was dead. *At least* one of them. . . .

Still, Max followed the woman's generous gesture and stepped inside the cabin. Though she immediately understood its purpose, Max marveled at the fireplace set into the left wall. The heat it supplied gave the room a warm, cozy feeling she had only previously felt in her own bed, between the sheets, on exceptionally cold nights.

To the right, a door led to a tiny bathroom—imagine that, a room with one toilet!—and farther down, a sink protruded from the wall next to a small stove. A refrigerator squatted on the opposite wall, with a small dining table and two chairs in front of it. In the living room area, a daybed doubled as a sofa, and a leather chair with wooden arms warmed itself in front of the fire, an Indian-print blanket folded neatly on top. The furniture, what there was of it, was all made of warm, hard, dark woods.

To a child raised in a concrete bunker, so much warmth, so much wood, was dizzyingly unfamiliar . . . and yet wonderful.

The woman picked up the phone receiver and punched in numbers. A few seconds later, she said into the mouthpiece, "It's Hannah. . . . I need to see you."

Wondering if she was being betrayed, Max walked gingerly through the room, examining the homey touches (which to her were odd yet not off-putting) as she went.

To her surprise, and with an air of confusion, Max found herself feeling more at home within the walls of the teeny cabin than she ever had at Manticore. It was an emotion she was having trouble understanding, surging through her like a sweet sickness, as she looked at the candlesticks, books, paintings, and other objects that were so foreign to her.

"Naw," Hannah was saying. "She's just a kid . . . but she's got problems at home and needs to find somewhere safe."

Max wondered if she would ever have a place as beautiful as this, a place of her own; thinking of the cabin that way, that a person could live by herself, made its smallness seem suddenly roomy. . . .

"Look," Hannah was saying, vaguely irritated. "I'll explain everything when I see you . . . Thanks. 'Bye."

Hannah hung up the phone as Max reached out and touched the soft hem of the Indian-print blanket, relishing the texture. None of the wool blankets at Manticore had ever been so soothingly soft. . . .

Hannah stepped forward, picked up the huge blanket and wrapped it around Max's shoulders. The child immediately felt warm all over, down to her bare feet, and she sniffed deeply, taking in the woman's sweet scent, which still clung to the blanket.

"I'll be back as soon as I can," Hannah said, shrugging back into her heavy coat. "Make yourself at home."

Max said nothing, the phrase as foreign to her as if in a language she hadn't got 'round to learning yet. She and the woman locked eyes, then Hannah stepped outside into the cold night and pulled the door shut behind her.

Standing in the window, the blanket still draped around her, Max waited. She stood there, staring out the window, for what might have been hours. This was, after all, still enemy territory. She was not certain what distance they had traveled in the civilian car, but Max knew nonetheless that Manticore wasn't that far away.

She knew also that Lydecker and that vague yet specific entity called Manticore would never give up looking for her . . . for all of them.

Finally, reluctantly, Max decided Hannah either wasn't coming back or had been captured. Either way, the cabin must now be considered unsafe. She liked this place . . . had she known the concept, she might even have loved it. Human feelings deep within her had stirred—the warmth, the wood; the woman's kindness.

But she had already stayed here too long.

Opening the door, she took one last long look down the deserted lane; then she turned and took one more, even longer look into the warm cabin. Max yearned to stay, to be wrapped in warmth, to not be a soldier for a while; but she knew that wasn't possible.

Survival, adaptability, overcame these new emotions.

She dropped the blanket in a puddle in the doorway, and bounded off across the snow.

The sun rose to find Max moving at a slow trot, fatigue catching up with her; even the flapping nightshirt seemed weary.

She needed to find a place to hide during the daylight hours, another warm place. The cold had drained her strength even more than the constant running had. Sweat froze into tiny beads of white in her eyebrows, on her close-cropped hair, and stiffened the already starchy material of the smock.

Max knew that when the sun got high, Manticore would have very little trouble catching up with a barefoot nine-year-old girl wearing only a blue-gray hospital nightshirt. From her training, she knew enough about the outside world to realize that she and her siblings likely would be described to the authorities as escapees of some kind, perhaps from a mental institution.

Her special genetic gifts would provide some protection, yes; but she was beginning to lose the battle with exhaustion.

Since leaving the cabin, she had clung to the woods, only occasionally hearing the whine of snowmobiles or the roar of helicopters, as she moved south. She still had no idea where she was, much less where she was going, survival itself her only engine.

She did know she was still too close to her former "home" to achieve any reasonable sense of safety; and she needed to put as much distance as possible between her and Lydecker and the minions of Manticore.

Ahead of her, the woods trailed off and, across a scrubby clearing, there lay the expanse of a large parking lot filled with trucks, the same type of vehicles she had noticed bringing supplies to Manticore.

These she had seen at the facility, one or at most two at a time. Now perhaps as many as fifty of them sat not a hundred yards in front of her, a virtual forest of massive vehicles. Some moved out, while others moved in, taking their places in a constant parade.

Max watched for a long time as trucks parked, their drivers climbing down and disappearing into the distance toward a building of which she had only an obstructed view. After a while, drivers would come back out, check the rear doors on their trailers, climb back into the cab, then sometimes drive away, and other times just remain parked with the engines running, studying maps, reading, resting.

The child knew that even if the trailers weren't heated, any one of them would provide better protection from the elements than she had now, as well as give her a place to hide during the coming day.

They also presented a variety of potential hazards.

She might choose to hide in a truck that ended up back at Manticore; since she had no real sense of the size of the world beyond Manticore, this seemed a genuine possibility.

Or, if unable to relock the trailer from the inside, she might be discovered by one of the drivers, who would certainly call the authorities. And for all she knew, that could easily include Colonel Lydecker.

With the icy air biting into her, she was unsure what to do; but, as a soldier, she knew doing nothing was not an option.

Max watched patiently as two more trailers came and went, one at either end. Then she rose to her haunches and prepared to move. The tree line would provide cover for the first twenty yards or so . . . but after that, Max would be running over open ground, in the bright sunshine, with absolutely nowhere to hide. . . .

When the next trailer backed in and parked—a long orange affair with black trim—Max made her move. She shot forward like a runner coming out of the blocks, streaking through the last of the trees, then hit the open field, churning along at full speed.

Her eyes swept the parking lot for witnesses to her approach, but she saw none; the rear ends of the vehicles were lined up before her, making it unlikely a trucker sitting in a cab might spot her. As she neared the designated trailer, and zeroed in on its two doors, her heart sank . . .

. . . A tiny thread of metal ran through the two pieces of the lock. There was no way to open the door without breaking the metal, thus alerting the driver that someone had tampered with his rig. If she broke the seal, she'd be caught—that much she could figure out, without ever having seen the device before.

She kept moving, ducking in and crouching under the trailer, which would provide at least *some* cover; huddling like the spooked animal she was, Max tried to figure her next move.

Did the trailers *all* have these devices? After eyeballing the doors, she realized there would be no way to lock the door from the inside, anyway, and the driver would still know his load had been tampered with. *Damn it,* she thought, using the forbidden words she'd heard Colonel Lydecker use, when he was frustrated or angry.

Maybe, she decided, one of the other trailers would have a different type of door. . . .

Moving out from under the trailer, still careful to check for unwanted witnesses, she slid to the next trailer, and the next, and the one after that, until finally, at the fifth trailer, she found a single door that slid up, instead of a pair of doors that opened on hinges.

Even luckier, there was no little metal seal this time; but the driver would still know the truck had been opened when Max wouldn't be able to latch the door from the inside. . . .

She would have to risk it.

After unlatching the door, not rushing, she tried to raise it silently, but it squeaked, like a wounded beast, and she ducked under the vehicle, desperately, quickly scanning the parking lot for anyone who might have heard.

Nothing.

She eased back out, raised the door another six inches— just high enough for her to crawl under—and then took a step back. From a flat-footed position, Max leapt the three and a half feet to the lip of the trailer, landing nimbly, all but silently, and—in one fluid motion—slipped under the edge, pitching herself forward, rolling onto her side, under the door.

With the door still up, and the dull gray light from outdoors providing at least slight illumination inside, she checked out her latest home.

The back half of the trailer was empty, while, at the front end, five wooden pallets stacked with cardboard boxes nearly as tall as she, were jammed into the space. Behind them crouched a wooden crate that came almost to Max's neck. Inside, two black tractor seats faced each other.

It wasn't the cabin, but it would do.

Max pulled the door back down, careful to toss out the canvas strap attached to the bottom of the door. The unlatched door might draw attention, but leaving the canvas strap on the inside would have been a dead giveaway that the door had been closed by someone still inside.

Darkness consumed the trailer. This may not have been as comforting as a blanket and a fire, but Max certainly felt better being out of the wind. The wood-and-steel floor was cold beneath her bare feet; still, it was less wet and less frigid than standing in the snow outside. Max was not a child afraid of the dark—the tiny amount of cat DNA mixed into her genetic recipe gave her the ability to see even in pitch black.

Climbing into the crate, Max huddled low, disappearing into herself, peeking out from behind the seat back, trying to see between the slats of the crate. She stayed that way, on guard, for half an hour.

Then, from outside the trailer, she heard a man's muffled, "Son of a bitch!"

Max had heard Lydecker say those words, too.

The door pig-squealed in protest as it rose a foot or so, the driver still hanging on to the canvas strap. He was a short balding man with a sphere for a skull, little more than a disembodied head and shoulders floating above the lip of the trailer.

Wide-eyed, a peeled onion of a nose dominating his face, the guy bobbed his ball-shaped head as he looked around the trailer, saw nothing, swore some more, muttered something about "damn kids anyway," then banged the door down.

Max heard the latch scratch back into place; she allowed herself a minute smile.

A moment later she heard the driver's door slam, the transmission get shoved into gear, the engine roar, before the truck lurched forward.

Some time later (Max didn't know how long, as she'd finally gotten some sleep), she felt the truck come to a stop, back up for a long moment, and then the trailer rocked a little, as if it had bumped into something. She heard the burp of the air brake being engaged, followed by the slamming of the driver's door again. Hopping out of the crate, Max prepared herself. . . .

The latch groaned as it slipped loose, the door made its familiar squeal as it yawned open and daylight cascaded in.

Heedlessly, Max launched herself before she realized the driver and another tall man—both wore jeans and heavy barn coats—were blocking her path, a fork truck sitting behind them, its motor purring.

"What the hell?" the driver blurted, as he took a reflexive step backward, his hands coming up to defend himself, unintentionally clearing the way for her.

Max landed gracefully on the loading dock, the concrete frigid beneath her feet after the trailer's relative warmth. She took one step toward the wide-eyed men, pivoted and leapt off the dock onto the snow-covered parking lot below. Bolting across the lot, the two men yelling at her, she made for a line of trailers against the far fence.

As she pulled away, she could hear the huffing of the two men behind her; again a small smile formed: they were not going to catch her.

The seven-foot chain-link fence beyond the line of trailers proved to be even less of an obstacle than the one back at Manticore; she scampered up and over, the way a spider navigates a wall. And the pair of overweight old men pursuing her hardly compared to helicopters and snowmobiles.

She was gone before the two men were halfway across the yard. Beyond the fence lay a two-lane blacktop road, and across that what looked to Max like a factory of some sort.

Still making its morning ascent, the sun told her it was approaching noon, the sky's compass indicating that west lay to her left. For no particular reason she could discern, she chose that direction, hopped onto the road and ran for all she was worth.

Max passed business after business, trying not to allow the newness of it all to distract her, however much seeing such things in reality, as opposed to some training video, excited and aroused her. She kept arms and legs pumping and, eventually, she left the industrial park behind and moved into an area of houses.

Homes.

Once in the residential neighborhood (*Civilians live here*, the young soldier thought), she slowed down, finally allowing herself to take it all in. These structures were not much like Hannah's cabin at all. Much bigger and close together, they vaguely reminded Max of castles in Manticore texts.

Though most of the structures were white, occasionally there would be a blue one or a yellow one—a rainbow to a child raised in a blue-gray environment—and all of them seemed to be two-story and have a garage underneath one side. A few cars were parked on the street, all with license plates stenciled WYOMING, like Hannah's last night; but she saw no people and wondered where everyone was.

At the sound of a car motor, up the street behind her, a startled Max took off at a sprint between two houses. She circled the house to her left, coming back onto the place where she'd started, just after the car had passed, rolling down the street, oblivious to her presence.

The vehicle looked different than anything she'd seen at Manticore, and when she focused in on the nameplate, she could make out a word: AVALON. She had no idea what that meant. She did know the Manticore men traveled in black vehicles labeled TAHOE and HUMVEE; this white Avalon looked nothing like those.

Max wondered how far she was from Manticore, and how

far away she needed to get, to be safe. Though her sense of time was aided by the sun, distance remained vague to her. She returned to the sidewalk, but she knew her smock would draw attention to her, and that she needed to find cover again until dark . . . and the sooner, the better.

Rounding a corner, she wandered down a new street. Max had trouble telling this one from the previous one, the houses looking interchangeable, as if manufactured from identical plans; the cars looked about the same, too, and there still didn't seem to be any people around except her and the driver of the car that had passed by.

Max had gone another block or two when she spotted movement in the next block, on the other side of the street.

A child . . .

. . . about her age, playing in a yard three doors up. The sight of another kid made Max think again of her sibs, and an emotion rose in her, a caring emotion, and sad: she wondered if any of them had escaped.

She might never know what had become of Jondy and the others—Zack she feared had been killed—but she wasn't sure how she would find any of them, if they *had* gotten away.

But standing here on this corner, watching that other child play in the snow, Max made a vow that would form her in years to come: she would never stop looking for her brothers and sisters. . . .

Never.

Chapter Two

TITANIC NIGHT

Hanging suspended by a slender nylon rope, eight stories over nighttime Los Angeles, Max thought, *Piece of cake. . . .*

The line tethering her to the building felt snug against her wasplike waist. Though a chilly wind swept over the city, colder than one would expect for early March, it barely registered on Max, upon whom weather had little or no effect. Her lithe, athletic body was sheathed in black formfitting fatigues, providing warmth enough for her genetically amplified body; besides which, her Manticore training in the frigid winters of Gillette, Wyoming, had toughened her far beyond any mere meteorological phenomenon she might encounter in LA. Her silky black hair, worn long since her escape from the compound, was tucked neatly under a black watchcap, and she made an anonymous, asexual figure as she played human spider.

Like the music that had once been made here, the record company that had originally erected the pseudo-stacked-disc structure (where she would soon be breaking and entering) was ancient history. After the Pulse, gangster groups had taken the building in lieu of royalties owed, following negotiations that were rumored to have been a literal bloodbath.

The ragtag street army that moved in to the old Capitol Records Building turned the structure into a fortress that had withstood all attacks . . . until the Big Quake of 2012, anyway. After that, a building that had once resembled a stack of records came to look more like a layer cake with the top four stories smushed by the thumb of a frosting-licking God.

A second generation of gangsters dwelled in the building—known now as the Cap—and this particular batch of criminals-since-birth were the ones Max planned to rip off this evening. The Brood, as they were called, would buy, sell, or trade anything—as long as it was illegal.

For instance, right now the Brood had in their possession the security plans for the Hollywood Heritage Museum, not far outside Brood turf on Highland, a reconverted office building (once belonging to a powerful "agency," Max had been told—spies, she supposed) that held much of the remaining nostalgic artifacts of a city whose main business had once been (before the Pulse, before the Big Quake) entertainment.

Max knew the Brood planned to rip the museum off, and she and her own clan intended to prevent them from doing so . . . not out of civic-spiritedness, but to take down the score themselves.

After years of struggle, the sector police had finally fought to a stalemate with the Brood, penning them into an area bordered by the old 101 on the north and east, Cahuenga on the west, and Sunset Boulevard on the south. The Hollywood Freeway, the old 101, curved around the Cap and still occasionally bore spotty, sporadic traffic, vehicles driven by those brave (or foolhardy) enough to pass through Roadhog territory.

Hanging along the north side of the building, as casual and unafraid as a child on a backyard swing, Max looked down on the twinkling abstraction that was the 101 and watched idly as the Roadhogs chased after some unfortunate soul who'd had the bad judgment to try to run the freeway. She smiled a little, shook her head; *how reckless,* the young woman thought, as she dangled off the side of the tower.

Looking north toward Mount Lee, Max could see the fifty-foot letters that now spelled out HO WOOD, their whiteness stark even in the three A.M. darkness. The sign had read HO YWOOD when Max had arrived in Hollywood in 2013, barely a year after the Quake had decimated most of what the post-Pulse riots hadn't. This latest revision struck Max as appropriate to a city of scavengers and street tramps of every stripe.

She checked her watch: *it was time.*

Securing a foothold on a window ledge, Max lowered herself onto her stomach on the steel awning above the seventh floor. On her belly, she spun and slowly crawled to the edge, her head hanging down as she peeked into the window.

She saw nothing but darkness.

Silently, she ticked off the seconds until Moody's diversion would begin.

Moody—leader of the Chinese Clan, the group Max belonged to—had taken over in Max's life (though she had never made the mental connection herself) the father-figure position that had once been filled by Colonel Donald Lydecker.

An old man by the standards of these short-lived times—fifty-five, maybe even sixty—Moody had piercing green eyes, a trimmed gray beard and mustache that contained flecks of black, his long silver hair combed straight back, usually tied in a long ponytail. His skin tone said he rarely saw light of day; and his nose—a twisting series of hills on the plain of his face—spoke of many breakings, while the thin, pink-lipped line of his mouth kept the man's thoughts locked up tight. His black garments—black leather jacket, black T-shirt, black jeans—inspired Max to her own, similar style of dress.

The Chinese Clan were thieves, so named not because any of the members were of Asian descent, rather because they lived in what had once been Mann's Chinese Theatre, the grandest of many local, abandoned movie theaters. The Pulse and the Quake had combined to effectively kill the motion picture industry, and theater complexes across America stood empty, their design difficult for any worthwhile purpose, some being turned into flophouses, fortresses, whorehouses, and even occasionally, if clumsily, a hospital.

The self-dubbed Chinese Clan had occupied the theater

within days of the Pulse, and Moody's youthful gang had staved off every effort—from both police and rival gangs—to evict them.

Five, Max calmly thought, *four . . . three,* her large dark eyes locked on the window . . . *two . . . one. . . .*

An explosion rocked the world, a bright orange column of flame rising along the east side of the building like a fiery offering to the heavens!

The roar that followed a second later reminded Max of the artillery blasts during war games back at Manticore and, even as heat waves rolled through the building, for a second she froze, a chill slicing through her bones.

A second explosion, this one on the west side, sent flames shooting skyward, as well, orange and blue tongues licking hungrily.

Snapping out of it, Max could make out movement behind the darkened windows of the seventh floor. A door swung open, a light in the hallway suddenly illuminating the room, and Brood members poured out into the hallway, most likely believing they were under attack.

They weren't far wrong, considering those fires burning below; Moody's idea of a diversion seemed to Max to be just short of an all-out blitz on the Brood stronghold. Moving quickly now, unsure how long Moody's fireworks would keep the gangsters occupied, Max lowered herself onto the sill of the seventh-floor window and went to work. Using a glass cutter, she etched a circle big enough to accommodate her slender form, punched it in, and then held the edge to maintain her balance as she undid her tether.

The lithe thief released her hold on the rope and the window, seeming to hang there for a second, then leapt headfirst through the hole and somersaulted onto the mattresses scattered across the floor, coming up in a fighting stance.

The room was empty, unless you counted the stench left behind by a dozen unwashed souls sleeping in what had once been an office for one. Only the desk remained from the furniture that had formerly marked this room as a place of business; it sat to Max's left, one mattress on top of it and another underneath, one end stuffed under the desk so the owner's head rested where a worker's legs and feet had once been. In the Brood, this probably qualified as earthquake awareness.

Tiptoeing to the door, Max listened for any sound that might indicate she wasn't alone on the floor. The information about the security plan had reached Moody through a Brood intermediary who apparently figured the bribe he'd solicited from the Chinese Clan was worth risking the wrath of his own gang.

According to the sellout, Mikhail Kafelnikov—the formidable, legendarily sadistic leader of the Brood—kept the museum security layout in a safe on this floor, in his private office at the far end of the hall.

The building, tomb-silent, appeared to have emptied as the Brood poured downstairs to check out the explosions. Moving into the hallway, Max's hypersensitive hearing sought any sound—a creak of the floor, the squeak of a sneaker, even something as inconsequential as the breathing of a guard . . . nothing.

Nothing but the distant crackle of flames and raised voices, anyway, many floors below.

An eyebrow lifted in a little shrug, before Max took off into a short sprint that deposited her at the threshold of Kafelnikov's office.

She *really* wanted to make sure that sinister son of a bitch wasn't in—again, she listened intently, hearing nothing, then tried the door . . .

. . . locked.

Max considered picking the lock—she had the tools, and the knowledge—then decided her limited time would be better spent inside the office. Rearing back, she kicked the latch next to the knob and the door splintered with a satisfying *crunch* as it swung open.

Time is money, she thought, moving inside the empty room.

Empty of people, at least. This was a combination office, apartment . . . and arsenal. To the left, running the length of the wall, a rack displayed with pride guns, rifles, machine guns, and shotguns. Shelves above the rack held boxes of grenades, flashbangs, and a wide array of pistols. She could have easily helped herself; but ever since Lydecker had shot one of her X5 sibs that night in the barracks, Max had had an innate abhorrence of firearms. She hated the foul things then, she hated them now.

The wall opposite the guns, to Max's right, was home to a monstrous round waterbed covered with silk sheets; next to it, like a disapproving parent, stood a tall stainless-steel refrigerator. The wall itself was a huge window, moonlight flooding the room with ivory. The center of the office, in front of Max, was dominated by a massive kidney-shaped desk, behind which loomed an oversized, thronelike leather chair. A large-screen TV rose like an altar to the right of (and behind) the desk, angled toward the bed. Behind the leather throne, an oversized portrait in oil of Kafelnikov (not very good) took up most of the wall.

Surprising there's room for all this stuff, the young woman thought, and *the ego of that bastard Kafelnikov. . . .*

Moody's informant had said the safe that held the security plan was behind the painting. If the safe was as big as the portrait, Max thought, the dial ought to be about the size of a hubcap.

As she made her way around the desk, she slipped a switchblade out of her pocket and flicked the button, the blade springing open with a *click.* She found a metal wastebasket, turned it over, spilling refuse, and climbed up on it, and looked the Russian gang leader in his smug, superior face. Then, wearing her own smug smile, Max stabbed Kafelnikov in his oil-painted heart and sliced upward, the canvas ripping, as if the subject himself were crying out in agony.

The safe was where it was supposed to be, and the dial was normal sized. For as elaborate as Moody's plan had been, this seemed to the experienced young cat thief a routine heist. Putting the knife away, Max tuned up her hearing, placing her ear to the safe's metal door, and started turning the dial.

In less than fifteen seconds Max had the thing open; in five more she had found the security plans to the nostalgia museum, and in another second she had them tucked into her fatigues. A large pile of cash to the left proved too tempting, as well, and that disappeared into other pockets.

Moody needn't know about that; she would call it a bonus.

Finally, satisfied with her haul, she turned to leave. That was when she sensed the first dog.

She had heard the Brood kept dogs to deter intruders, though Moody had been dismissive about these "rumors."

But the big, black, beautiful beast, its shiny eyes and razor-sharp white teeth glowing in the moonlight, was no rumor. The dog, some kind of a Doberman mix, moved forward, in a low, suspicious approach, its muscles undulating like shadows beneath its taut skin. The animal growled low in its throat, a disquieting greeting.

"Nice puppy," Max soothed, her hand reaching out toward the dog in a slowly offered, underhand gesture of peace, showing the animal an empty, unthreatening palm.

The dog snarled.

And the canine sentry was not alone. . . .

She could hear their paws padding down the hall, and four more appeared in the hallway, and entered the room—very trained, none scrambling on top of each other—fanning out in almost military fashion, growling, holding their positions. Each was at least as big as the leader, with saliva dripping, fangs showing, the quintet snarling in unholy harmony as their leader edged closer.

Max rose to her full height. The soft approach had failed; so, making her voice loud and sharp, she said, "Sit."

The lead dog barked once, the canine equivalent of *Fuck you.*

Max let out a long breath. "Your choice. I didn't want to do this, but you're asking for it. . . ."

And cat prepared herself to meet dog, lowering into a combat crouch.

The first dog leapt and Max swiftly sidestepped it, the Doberman smacking into the wall with a yelp and a dull thud. As the second and third dogs came after her, separating to hit her from either side—a sophisticated outflanking maneuver coming from canines—Max jumped up on the desk, just as the two animals collided, and rolled away in a yelping ball of paws and claws and tails.

One of the two remaining in the military line inside the doorway flung itself at Max, who vaulted up and over, the dog's head snapping back around to try to bite her as Max soared over it, hit the floor in a tuck, somersaulted to her feet, and sidestepped as the last dog lunged.

Rushing out into the hall, Max pulled the splintered door shut behind her; with the lock snapped, the door wouldn't hold the animals back for long, and she knew the beasts would be hot on her heels. Their pissed-off barking said as much.

She ran to the elevator, wishing those doors would magically open before she got there, and . . . they did.

Only now she found herself face-to-face with Mikhail Kafelnikov and half a dozen members of his Brood. They all looked as pissed as those dogs, Kafelnikov especially.

Wait till he sees his portrait, she thought.

Tall and thin, the Russian immigrant was nonetheless well muscled, with close-cropped blond hair, penetrating blue eyes, and rather sensuous pink full lips. He wore a brown leather coat, knee-length, an open-throated orange silk shirt with gold chains, black leather pants, and black snakeskin boots.

Moody had said it best: Kafelnikov cultivated both the look and the lifestyle of a pre-Pulse rock star, which his late father had been, or at least so it was said. The son supposedly had musical talent, too, but just figured crime paid better than music, particularly in a time when the entertainment industry had gone to crap.

The Russian might well have struck Max as handsome if not for the expression of rage screwing up his features; handsome, that is, for a homicidal maniac.

"Who the fuck are you?" he asked, momentarily frozen in the elevator. Studying the small form in the watchcap, the Russian said, "It's a girl . . . just a girl. . . ." His boys surged out with him, even as he bellowed at them, "Who *is* this little bitch?"

Before she could respond in any manner (and words

would not have been her first choice), she and the Russian and his men turned their collective head toward a crunching sound down the hall . . .

. . . and the pack of dogs burst through the already ruptured office door, and galloped down the hall toward them, fangs flashing, tongues lolling, saliva flying.

Turning back to Kafelnikov, Max said, "I'm the dog walker you called for—remember?"

And he winced in confusion for half a second, before Max delivered a side kick to the Russian's chest that knocked the wind out of him with a *whoosh* and sent him reeling back into the elevator, taking his underlings like bowling pins with him.

Not sticking around to admire her handiwork, Max took off down the hall, the dogs dogging her heels. When she all but threw herself into the room she had originally entered, the lead dog was less than two feet behind her. Diving forward, arms extended in front of her, as if the waiting night were a lake she was plunging into, Max sailed through the round hole in the window, wishing she'd cut it a tad larger, the snarling dog right behind her.

She caught the waiting rope and swung in a wide arc away from the building. The dog, misjudging the hole slightly, slammed into the window pane, yiped, and reared back into the office, dropping out of sight. The other dogs, evidently having learned from their leader's misfortune, stopped short of the window, their heads bobbing up in view as they barked and yapped at Max, dangling just out of the range of their jaws. One even edged its head out and took swipes at her, biting air.

But by this time Max was shimmying up the rope, and their snarls turned to growls as they watched in impotent rage as she disappeared toward the roof.

Below her, she heard voices. Still shimmying up, she looked down, and saw Kafelnikov's pale enraged face, head sticking out of the hole in the window like a frustrated victim with his neck stuck into a guillotine.

"I'm going to *kill* you, you bitch!" he yelled.

"I don't think so!" she called down, smug, calm.

His response was nonverbal, and he hit himself in the head, possibly cutting himself on the glass.

Laughing softly to herself, she continued to climb, knowing the Russian's men were already on their way to the roof to intercept her. Looking down again, she saw Kafelnikov's face had been replaced at the window by one of the Brood members from the elevator. A skinny guy with long dark hair reached tentatively for the rope and, just as he touched it, Max nimbly kicked off the side of the building, jerking the strand away from the guy's grasp. He nearly tumbled out.

"You *bitch!*" he yelled, eyes wide as much with terror as rage.

These boys sure have a limited vocabulary, Max thought, as she kept climbing.

Beneath her, the guy ducked inside, then came leaping out into the night. He snared the rope, and his momentum threatened to rip the tether from her grasp. Surprised by his boldness, she could feel his weight at the far end of the rope, and knew the line wouldn't support both of them. . . .

"The rope won't hold!" she called down, warning him.

"Fuck you, little girl!"

That limited vocabulary seemed suddenly ominous. . . .

Feeling not so smug now, climbing even faster, she moved toward the rooftop, the guy now climbing the rope below her, chasing her toward the roof, heedless of the peril he was placing both of them in. As she looked up the last ten feet, she could see the rope straining against the twisted metal of the roof's distorted edge. Beyond that, the stars hung bright and glittering in the sky, as if lighting her way, until they were eclipsed by a face . . .

. . . Kafelnikov's.

Opening a switchblade with a nasty *click,* the Brood's leader said, "Stupid bitch . . . I told you I was going to kill you!"

"I'm getting really tired of you boys calling me that," she said. "Your manners *suck*. . . ."

With no alternative, and that weight below her, she kept

climbing, narrowing the distance between herself and the Brood members on the roof.

Kafelnikov bent down, the knife starting to slice through the thin rope. "Just be a couple more seconds . . . and then nobody'll be calling you 'bitch' again, rest assured, my dear. . . . Nobody'll call you anything but dead!"

The Russian was carving at the rope, threads popping, his face a pale terrible thing just above her, closer, closer. . . .

"Boss, *no!*" the skinny guy below her whined, but it was too late.

Kafelnikov's blade cut the rope.

Max let go, the rope and the skinny guy tumbling down out of sight, a screaming man riding a snake.

But as she let go, Max launched herself upward, spearing the lapels of Kafelnikov's coat in either hand. Just as gravity took over and started to pull them both over the edge, two members of the Brood grabbed their leader and just managed, barely managed, to keep him—and Max—from pitching to the pavement far below.

And so she hung there, holding on to his coat, Kafelnikov's face only inches from hers—they might have kissed, though she found his breath (what was that, sardines?) offensive—and the other two Broodsters strained to keep their fearless leader from falling, their grip on their superior's arms preventing him from doing anything to rid himself of Max.

Inexorably, gravity tilted them farther over the edge. In his panic, Kafelnikov fought to tear himself from the grip of his own men so he could try to pry Max's hands from his coat; but his loyal boys were just too strong, and kept trying to pull him away.

Just as it seemed the skinny Brood leader and the shapely cat burglar would tumble through the night together, Max looked up at the Russian and smiled.

Kafelnikov's eyes went wide in wonderment and rage—he might have been thinking, *If only she were one of mine!*— then Max headbutted him, breaking his nose, and almost prying him loose from his goons.

Blood sprayed and the Russian howled. Tearing one arm free, he swung wildly for Max's face; but she simply let go of him . . .

. . . and his follow-through carried him back out of sight onto the roof with his two goons in tow.

As Max fell through the night sky, a falling star, she grinned, enjoying the rush of air on her face. Not only did she have what she'd come for, she'd gotten to bloody the nose of the Brood's leader—not a bad evening's work, so far.

As she passed the seventh floor again, she pulled the metal ring on her suit that deployed the chute and a tiny turbine blower that filled the chute with warm air and provided enough updraft to give her an easy descent and a relatively soft landing.

She had hoped not to have to use the chute off the Cap, as she might land in the midst of the Brood members below who had been summoned by the explosions to the street. The plan had been to wait on the rooftop till the sidewalks were empty, as the Broodsters filed back into the building, to investigate the site of the burglary. And then she'd float to earth.

But this would do in a pinch. No help would be waiting below, however—Moody and the Chinese Clan were nowhere to be seen as she drifted toward the street; that didn't surprise Max . . . their job, after all, had been to provide a diversion. They'd done as much, and split. She floated to the pavement, touched down, turned off the blower, and wrapped up the chute.

Then she turned, to see Brood members swarming toward her, dangerous dimwits in tattered denim. The first one fell to a spinning roundhouse kick to the head, the second to a straight kick to the groin, the third to a right cross.

And then Max was running, the gangsters in pursuit. Turning the corner, she found herself flying down Vine Street with half the Brood behind her. She raced down the middle of the street, her shoes pounding on the shiny wet pavement. Just as she passed a manhole cover, Max wondered idly why the street was damp—it hadn't rained today, hadn't rained for weeks. As she heard the manhole cover slide open, Max stopped, pivoted, and dropped into her fighting stance.

Catching a glimpse of silver hair rising out of the manhole, the unmistakable nasty perfume of gasoline filling her flaring nostrils, Max suddenly knew why the street was wet. . . .

She spun away and ran for all she was worth—which was plenty—even as she heard the *whoosh* of the gas igniting. Some of the Brood screamed, but she assumed it was more out of fear than pain. Moody wouldn't let them get close enough to be caught in the fire . . . probably.

The idea was to stop the pursuit, not to incinerate the pursuers, though a few charred casualties wouldn't have Max or Moody losing much sleep. Looking over her shoulder as she ran, Max saw the wall of flame separating her from pursuers who were folding back into the night, scurrying home to their tower of broken dreams.

And she saw that Moody had disappeared back down the manhole, as if he'd not even really been there, a ghost haunting what had once been Hollywood's most famous street.

"Thanks," she said to the night, and was gone.

Less than an hour later, with the security plans to guide her, Max negotiated the electronic locks and first-floor laser guards of the former office building and current home of the Hollywood Heritage Museum. Her new goal lay at the far end of the second floor, in a locked room guarded by more lasers, mines, and a special alarm under the object itself.

Only two guards patrolled the museum at night, and one of them was already napping at the security desk on the first floor.

There wasn't supposed to be anything of real worth in the museum, strictly nostalgia on display; but Max—thanks to Moody—knew better. Many of the exhibits from the history of American filmmaking displayed objects of value only to wealthy collectors of pre-Pulse memorabilia. None of the kitschy artifacts could compare to the literal jewel that awaited her at the end of the hall.

The first floor contained many remnants of the days that the placards posted next to exhibits referred to as the "Golden Age of Silents." The cane, bowler, and black suit of a "comic" named Chaplin, some kind of Arab outfit a feminine-looking actor named Valentino had worn in a couple of "silent" movies, and even a train engine that the placard proudly stated came from a Buster Keaton movie called *The General.*

Silently climbing the last few stairs to the second floor, Max found herself prowling a hallway whose placard boasted of material from the "Golden Age of Studios." For a place with so many "Golden Ages," Max thought, there seemed to be precious little actual gold around. Creeping along the hallway, keeping close to the wall, Max's cat eyes registered the facility's other guard, a heavyset fella heading for the far end of the hall, her enhanced hearing picking up his heels clicking on the tile floor.

She kept moving, sliding past raincoat-clad figures from a "musical" called *Singin' in the Rain,* and a quartet of mannequins dressed as a lion, a crude robot, a scarecrow, and a pigtailed girl in a blue-and-white-checkered dress, holding a little dog; the latter grouping represented something called *The Wizard of Oz,* though Max couldn't see how these characters had anything mystical or magical about them, and the only wizards she knew about were Harry Potter and his friends.

What waited in the room beyond the hallway had nothing to do with the "Golden Age of Studios," but it was the most secure room in the building . . . so this, of course, was where the most valuable exhibit was housed.

Max watched from the shadows as the plump guard checked the door at the end of the hall, then disappeared into the stairwell, to continue his rounds on another floor. She waited to make her move, listening to the door click shut and the guard's footsteps—he was going down—on the metal stairs dissipate.

Then she all but soundlessly sprinted (*This is the Golden Age of silents,* she thought) the last fifty feet to the exhibit's door, circumvented the alarm, picked the numeric push-button lock, and took a long deep breath.

The lock and the alarm were the easy part. Mines, activated only when the museum was closed, lay beneath the floor, and lasers hooked to infrared beams crisscrossed the room with barely a foot between them. Taking one last look at the floor plan Kafelnikov had so thoughtfully provided, Max memorized it, tucked it away, and plotted her course of action.

She opened the door, slipped inside, and eased it shut behind her. The chamber was windowless and silent, reminding her of the solitude of the barracks at Manticore after lights-out. Half a dozen glass cases stood around the room, each bearing props from a movie called *Titanic*.

A tall display case in the corner contained a mannequin wearing an old-timey diaphanous white gown, while a similar glass case in the opposite corner held a mannequin of an attractive if baby-faced young man in a tuxedo.

Three long, flat cases were arranged in a triangle in the center of the room. One held silverware, another a model of a ship, and the third one was an arrangement of still pictures from the motion picture.

At the far end of the room, encased in a Plexiglas box, under a narrow spotlight, her prize caught her eyes: a gigantic blue diamond on a silver chain encrusted with smaller diamonds.

Max knew little of the film, which apparently was famous. Television was limited and very controlled in the post-Pulse era, and, anyway, she didn't care for fiction . . . what was the point? Few people in made-up stories lived more interesting lives than she did.

But she did know—thanks to Moody—that although everyone back in pre-Pulse days had thought the great blue diamond, the "Heart of the Ocean," was merely a film prop, it had indeed been real, a ten-thousand-dollar necklace commissioned by the director who later donated it to the Hollywood Heritage Museum.

"Its true value," Moody had told her, "is known to few—why attract thieves . . . like us? And to the public . . . those who still care about silly ancient celluloid . . . the magic of the prop is enough to make it stand on its own as a tourist attraction."

Funny, Max thought. *In this town where dreams once were manufactured, one of the most famous artifacts was a fraud of sorts . . .* because *it was real.*

Now the famed Heart of the Ocean lay only twenty-five feet across the room from her.

And if she could retrieve it, and get out of here with her skin, the Chinese Clan could fence it for enough money to set them up for years to come.

Her breathing slowed as she prepared for the final assault on her prize. She popped a huge wad of gum into her mouth and started chewing slowly, methodically. Withdrawing from fatigue pouches two good-sized suction cups with pressure-release handles, Max attached one to each hand with inch-wide nylon straps and looked up at the ceiling. She had less than two feet of open air between it and the top-most infrared beam.

The young woman leapt straight up, arms outstretched, suction cups sticking to the ceiling with a sucking kiss. Taking in a deep breath, then letting it out, Max pulled herself up until her neck was bent to one side and she held herself up with her arms akimbo.

Even for a soldier with her unique talents, the strain was severe.

Next she slowly pulled up her legs and stretched them out in front of her, as if in a ballet exercise. She now sat, head cocked to one side, hanging from the ceiling above the beams by no more than six or maybe seven inches. Moving across the room folded up like this would be no small feat.

Glancing down at the necklace, she formed half a smile. *No guts, no glory,* she thought, and that blue rock was serious, serious glory not only for her, but for her whole clan.

Releasing one suction cup, she held herself up, eased it forward as far as she dared, and attached it again with its tiny puff of a kiss. She repeated the action with the second cup and found herself a foot nearer the prize. The muscles of her shoulders bunched and burned, but with her breathing, she compartmentalized the pain, putting it out of her mind.

Few on earth could have done this. Max had had this ability since childhood.

Sweat trickled down her face, dripping onto her shirt front as she single-mindedly made her way across the room, still casually chewing the gum as she went. She had completed her action with the cups nine times now and not only did her shoulders burn, but her biceps, triceps, quads, hamstrings, and glutes were each in the middle of a three-alarm blaze of their own.

A voice in her head that sounded uncomfortably like Colonel Lydecker's reminded her that pain was the price of achievement.

Shut up, she mentally replied, and kept moving the cups forward.

Finally, after what seemed like forever but had only been six minutes, she found herself directly above—if barely able to cock her head enough to see—the Heart of the Ocean.

She had maybe a foot and a half of clearance on each side of the Plexiglas box. As if the trip over here hadn't been enough, now the job would get *really* tricky. In that tight space, she would have to remove the cubic foot of plastic, snatch the necklace without setting off the alarm, then suction-cup her way back to the door.

No problem.

Taking one hand out of a suction cup, Max snugged her knees up, then slowly rolled backward, letting her feet come up toward the ceiling as her head lowered toward the box. About halfway home, her body tucked into a sphere only slightly larger than a beach ball, she slipped her shoe into the empty strap of one of the suction cups.

Satisfied the strap had her securely, she let go with her other hand and swung her other leg up and into that strap. She now hung upside down, her head barely a foot above the necklace with its glimmering stone.

Working quickly, Max picked the locks on each side of the case, lifted the Plexi box straight up, withdrew the gum from her mouth and affixed it to the top of the lid. Then she rotated the thing so its top was down . . . and eased it toward the floor.

This was the part that worried her most.

Her arms were not long enough to reach the floor. She would have to drop the box the last couple of feet or so, and hope to hell the wad of gum held it in place and kept it from bouncing into one of the infrared beams.

Letting out her breath, Max released the box with as light a touch as possible. It dropped to the carpeting with a dull, barely audible *thud,* then rocked toward the beam . . .

. . . but righted itself, and stopped.

Step one accomplished.

Pulling a utility knife from a pocket, Max leaned in close to the displayed jewelry. Only one wire connected the necklace to the alarm, but she would have to work gently not to set it off.

Blood was rushing to her head, and she could feel her face growing hot, like a flush of terrible embarrassment . . . just a little longer and everything would be fine . . . fine. . . .

Hanging there upside down, Max wished absently that a dash of bat DNA had been added to her genetic cocktail—then maybe this stunt wouldn't make her so dizzy. Carefully scraping back the plastic coating on the wire, she exposed about two inches of gleaming brass strands, put the knife away, and pulled out a wire of her own with alligator clips at either end. Attaching the clips at both ends of the section she'd cleared, Max took out her wire cutters, slowed her breathing again, and clipped the alarm wire in the middle of the cleared section.

She held her breath for a few seconds . . . but no alarm sounded, no lasers blasted at her, and the mines didn't go off.

Releasing the wire from the necklace, Max gazed fondly at the huge blue stone, and for the first time all evening, a true, wide smile creased her face. She lifted the necklace—feeling a real reverence for its value, if not its history—and gave it a quick kiss . . .

. . . then, as if her lips had done it, the alarm sounded.

And all hell broke loose.

"Shit," Max whispered, her vocabulary of "forbidden" words far greater now than she'd ever heard from Colonel Lydecker.

The thief suddenly realized the necklace had also been resting on a pressure alarm—a security measure that had somehow not made its way into the Brood's stolen plans. The alarm siren squawked like a gaggle of angry geese, a grating, obnoxious sound Max decided she would have hated even under innocent circumstances.

As opposed to these guilty ones. . . .

The first laser drilled the stand the necklace had been on, and exploded it in a shower of wood and velvet, just as Max pulled herself up out of the way. Despite the mines in the floor, which were presumably now activated, choosing the lesser of bad options, she kicked her feet out of the suction cups, and dropped to the carpeting as lasers blasted holes in the room all around her.

At least where she'd alighted, there hadn't been a mine. . . .

Grabbing the Plexiglas shell of the exhibit, tucking it to her like a big square football, Max did a forward roll and popped to her feet just as a laser fired a blast at her face.

She dodged left, reacting with the lightning inhuman speed bred into her, though she nonetheless felt the heat of the blast as it shot past her right cheek, and she could hear her hair sizzle as her nostrils filled with the burned smell of it.

Leaping with all her considerable might, she flung herself onto one of the exhibit cases in the middle of the room just as another laser blast chewed the floor not far from where she'd been standing, setting off the small blast of one of the mines. They obviously weren't meant to kill, only to maim.

That was a relief . . . she guessed. . . .

She only had a few seconds now until the lasers would target her again. Hefting the Plexiglas box, she threw it halfway across the remaining distance toward the door. It hit, but the sound of its impact was swallowed by the explosion of another mine, and the box disintegrated, making shattering music in a cloud of black smoke.

Leaping to the safety of the crater she'd created, Max knew all planning, any strategy, had disintegrated along with that box . . . from here on out, she'd just have to stay smart and get lucky. She ran to the door, dodging and cutting all the way. To her great surprise, she wasn't reduced to a bloody mess by another explosion—the number of mines must have been minimal, to keep the building damage down.

She twisted the knob and found that the door had auto-locked when the alarm went off—another tidbit absent from the security plan.

The lasers were getting closer now, their aim improving as she stood motionless in front of the door, heat and/or motion sensors probably leading them to her. Another blast shot toward her and she sidestepped just enough for it to miss her, and blast the lock off the door, skittering halfway down the hall.

Max yanked what was left of the door open and leapt into the hallway, then ducked around the edge of the door as stray laser beams shot wildly down the corridor.

The two guards came running toward her, and Max realized they must have disarmed the mines in the hallway thinking she would be trapped in the exhibit room. Each carried a nightstick and a Tazer.

The nearest one was a muscular guy in his midtwenties, his face an angry mask. The farther one was the plump guy she'd seen testing doors, and he was older by at least twenty years and heavier by nearly a hundred pounds, and looked scared.

The muscular one aimed his Tazer and fired, but Max ducked under the dart, rolled forward, and came up, her right fist catching the guard under the chin, lifting him off the floor, and sending him sprawling across the hall, no doubt to wake up later and wonder how so small a "girl" had cold-cocked him like that.

The plump one tried to look determined but the gesture failed when his chins started quivering. He fired the Tazer without aiming, then stood in bewildered fear as Max came up to him. A voice in his head probably told him to draw his nightstick, but another may have reminded him how little he was being paid, so he just stood there motionless, shivering like gelatin.

Max patted his cheek, and smiled sweetly.

Then she scurried off down the hall.

The thief could hear sirens in the distance when she threw open the museum's front door, but by the time the cops got here, she'd be long gone . . .

. . . and the Heart of the Ocean was tucked safely inside her fatigues. Max couldn't wait to get back to the theater to show the prize to Moody.

She would have felt like a king of thieves, if she hadn't been . . . "a girl."

Chapter Three
A HOME FOR MAX

THE ROAD
CASPER, WYOMING, 2009

As she watched from the corner, the nine-year-old Max—a foreign figure in this residential neighborhood, her thin blue-gray Manticore smock flapping in winter wind, her bare feet planted on the cold concrete of a sidewalk—tried to comprehend what the young child was up to. . . .

But the genetically bred soldier-in-the-making simply had no idea what the female child was doing, rolling a ball of snow across the white yard, making a bigger ball of it with her every step.

Focusing in, Max looked closely at the child across the street—a girl whose long black hair peeked out from beneath a red stocking cap. A little older than Max, at least a year or two, the girl had full lips, a short nose, and wide-set blue eyes beneath long, butterfly lashes.

Mesmerized, as if witnessing a dream, Max watched as the girl rolled the ball of snow back the other way. The round white thing came up almost to the girl's waist now, and Max still couldn't figure out what this kid thought she was doing.

After backing up to the corner and ducking behind a car, Max watched the girl for a moment, then slipped across the street, a blue-gray shadow. Now on the same side of the block as the girl, Max edged behind the corner house without being seen, and took off across the backyards, heading for the third house, in the front yard of which the girl was playing. This snow-rolling behavior Max had never seen before—what sort of strategy was this?—and she needed a closer look.

When Max rounded the third house and crept up to a spot behind a large evergreen to watch, the girl was still at work in the snow. To Max, her nightshirt and bare feet seemed suddenly inconsequential, compared to the wild-colored clothes of the other girl: red stocking cap, green mittens, pink parka, blue jeans, and canary yellow boots.

Max stared in rapt fascination as the girl in the red stocking cap decided this ball was big enough, abandoned it in the middle of the yard, and moved down near the sidewalk to start another. The girl packed snow onto the new ball until it was too big to hold, then she rolled it as she had the last one.

When the child was finished, the second sphere of snow was only slightly smaller than the one next to it, and it too came nearly to her waist. The girl tried to lift it up to set it on top of the first ball, but couldn't quite get it off the ground.

Knowing she should retreat and avoid any contact, well aware she needed shelter, food, and warmer apparel, wanting to keep moving, Max nonetheless remained frozen with something other than the cold: something about this girl kept her here, kept Max watching. . . .

No matter how hard the girl in the red cap tried, it seemed, she couldn't raise the second ball on top of the first. Without really realizing what she was doing, Max stepped out from behind the evergreen and moved in to assist the other child.

One of the few human instincts that remained strong in her, despite Manticore's best efforts, was the need to help her "brothers and sisters" . . . and this girl, so close to her own age, touched that sibling cord within the X5-unit.

When Max appeared, the girl in the red cap stood up straight and her mouth fell open in obvious surprise. Max didn't say a word, just moved to the other side of the ball and put her hands underneath it. The snow felt cold against her hands, yet it was oddly bracing, not unpleasant at all, and the bare skin on her arms, where the sleeves of the nightshirt rode up, began goose-pimpling.

The girl in the red cap grasped the plan immediately and moved to help. Together, the two little girls—for Max was, for all her training, despite the genetic tampering, a little girl, too—lifted the new globe of snow up on top of the first one.

"Hold it there for a minute," the girl in the red cap asked, panting, not able to keep up with Max, "willya?"

Max nodded dutifully, keeping her hands on the ball to keep it from rolling off.

Catching her breath, the girl in the cap said, "I've . . . I've got to . . . pack some snow around it . . . to keep it from falling off. Y'know?"

Max nodded again, even though she had no idea what was going on. Finally, she asked, "What is the object?"

The girl in the cap looked at Max curiously. "Huh?"

"What are you doing here? What purpose is served?"

"Purpose? . . . We're building a snowman, silly."

"Oh. A kind of . . . decoy?"

The little girl frowned. "Does Frosty here look like a duck to you?"

"No! . . . Is this is a statue?"

The other little girl obviously had never thought of it that way. "Well . . . yeah. Sort of."

"But the statue will melt. It is impermanent."

"Of course he'll melt, someday. But not while it's this cold."

"If the statue will melt, what's the purpose?"

"It's fun!"

This word had been heard before by Max, but represented a foreign concept; such was the nature of much Manticore training.

"Aren't you having fun, helping?" the girl in the cap asked, her breath pluming. "What's your name, anyway?"

"Max."

"Max? Isn't that a boy's name?"

"No. I'm a girl."

"Duh! I can see that. . . . I'm Lucy. Lucy Barrett." The girl kept packing snow as they conversed, smoothing and securing the snow orbs. Max, a quick learner, imitated the action.

"Lucy is your name. Hello, Lucy."

"Hello, Max. Aren't you cold?"

Max shrugged again. "A little."

The girl in the cap explained that "Frosty" now needed a head; Max pitched in and they fashioned a smaller ball.

"Are you sick, Max?"

"Sick?"

"You look like you walked out of a hospital or somethin'."

"Oh. No. I am well."

"Good," Lucy said, putting finishing touches on the third ball. "You live around here?"

Max shook her head, helping lift the "head" onto the snow statue.

"Are you staying with relatives, too, Max?"

"Relatives?"

"Where's your mom? *My* mom would be really mad if I came outside without my coat, my boots, my mittens, or my stocking cap."

"Mom?" Max braced the final ball as Lucy patted it into place, until it felt more solid, like it wouldn't move if she were to let go. Max didn't let go, though.

"You do have a mom don't you? Or do you live with your dad?"

"Dad?"

Lucy removed a carrot from one pocket of her winter coat and two lumps of coal from another; she made a face out of them—Max understood that instantly—and then they stood and looked at their work of art, considering it carefully.

The older girl looked carefully at Max, too, and seemed only to be half kidding when she asked, "You aren't a refugee from a loony bin, are you?"

"Loony bin?"

The girl in the cap frowned. "Listen, are you from another country?"

"I'm an American." Max knew that much.

"Well, don't you have a mom?"

"I never had a mom."

"How can that be?"

"Lucy . . . I don't even know what a mom is."

The girl in the cap began to laugh.

"Did I say something funny?" Max asked, a little irritated, but not knowing why.

Lucy's laughter caught in her throat. "You're . . . you're serious? You don't know what moms are?"

Suddenly feeling very ignorant, Max said, "Uh, no."

"Well . . . how do you think you got here?"

Max wanted to say, *I escaped from Manticore, stowed away on a truck, then . . .*

But she didn't say that; she might be unschooled in the ways of the outside world, but Max nonetheless knew that this wasn't what Lucy meant.

Lucy had another question, faintly mocking: "You were *born,* weren't you?"

Another question Max had no answer for.

Now Lucy stepped forward, patting the snow, smoothing the statue. "Is that why you're dressed like that? 'Cause you got nobody to take care of you?"

Max wondered how she could have received so much training in the last nine years, learned so much, studied so hard, and yet still this girl in the red cap could come up with all these questions, the answers to which Max had no idea.

They moved to the shoveled cement front steps of the house and sat down. Lucy asked, "You aren't from around here, are you?"

Finally, a question she knew the answer to. "No."

"Me neither. My mom's inside visiting with my aunt. We've been here since yesterday. I like it here, 'cause Dad isn't along. . . . But we'll be leaving for home soon."

Max said, "An ant is an insect."

Lucy laughed. "Not that kind of ant! Are you kidding? . . . Aunt Vicki is my mom's sister." Again the laughter was re-placed by a look of concerned curiosity. "Max—did you run away?"

"Uh . . . yeah. I ran away." The questions seemed to be getting easier now.

Lucy pulled off her mittens. "Here—you take these."

Gratefully, Max tugged on the mittens. They were wet from the snow, but they still were better than nothing, and she appreciated the warmth of Lucy's gesture, even more. "Thanks."

"So, Max . . . you don't have a home." It was a statement, not a question.

"No, Lucy."

"And I don't have a sister."

"I have sisters. And brothers."

"Really? Where?"

"We . . . we're all split up."

"Broken home, huh . . . I know a lotta kids in your situation."

Somehow Max doubted that.

Lucy was looking toward the house, a split-level with a large picture window in the living room upstairs; then her eyes returned to Max, and a new excitement was glittering there. "You don't have any clothes, or anywhere to stay, or anything to eat, right?"

Again Max found herself at a loss for words. But now that her hands were warmer, she started to realize how cold the rest of her had become. She started shivering and had to work to keep her teeth from chattering.

"Max, my mom is a real softie. She wanted me to have a sister, but she and Dad couldn't."

"Why?"

"I don't know. But I do know one thing: my mom could help you."

Frustrated, Max said, "Lucy, I still don't know what a 'mom' *is*," shaking her head, not liking where this seemed to be going.

Looking confused now herself, Lucy pondered that for a moment. Absently, she rose from the steps and went back to work on the snowman, smoothing it as she considered the problem. Max joined her, standing as silent as Frosty.

Finally, still filling in gaps in the snowman, Lucy said, "Mom is the person who gave birth to me, and you, too."

"Yours mom gave birth to me?"

Lucy laughed again, stopped herself, shook her head. "No, not my mom. . . . *Your* mom, whoever she is, or maybe . . . *was* . . . gave birth to you. You have a belly button, don't you?"

"I don't know."

"A navel?"

"Of course I have a navel."

"Well, that's where you used to be connected to your mom, when you were born. That proves it. Whether you know her or not, you had a mom, all right." Lucy shrugged. "Everybody does."

"So . . . moms are always girls?"

"Women," Lucy said seriously, seeming to take this teacherly responsibility to heart. "When we're older, we'll be women, and moms, too."

Max didn't like the sound of that much. "Do we have to?"

"Well . . . why do you have to ask such hard questions, Max?"

That there were things Lucy *didn't* know seemed oddly comforting to Max; made her feel less ignorant.

"Anyway," Lucy was saying, as she appraised Frosty one last time, "my mom can help. She can give you food and maybe Aunt Vicki's got some old clothes. . . ."

More people—that was bad . . . wasn't it? Suddenly, Max feared she never should have stopped, never should have spoken to this little girl.

"No," Max said. "That's okay. I fend for myself. I adapt and survive."

"Huh?"

"Don't tell anyone you saw me, okay?"

Lucy seemed perplexed.

"Lucy, please. Don't make me . . ."

"Make you what?"

Kill you, Max thought.

Lucy's eyes brightened with realization. "It's 'cause you ran away, isn't it? You're afraid Mom would send you back!"

Slowly, Max nodded. She touched the girl's arm; held it firmly. "Promise me, Lucy?"

Lucy's bare hand touched Max's mittened one. "Max—were they mean to you? I mean, where you ran away from . . . were they strict?"

In her mind's eye, Max saw Eva fall dead from Lydecker's bullet.

"They were strict," Max said.

"They were mean to you there?"

"Very mean."

Lucy forgot about her mom as she became captivated with the notion of Max's dilemma. "Gee—what did they do?"

"They took me away from my mother," Max said, stating her own sudden realization, "and then told me she never existed."

"They really did that?"

A car, one block over, rolled by, Max looked up, saw the car, and ducked back behind the evergreen, Lucy hot on her heels.

"They really did that?" Lucy repeated.

"Oh yes," Max said. "And they're chasing me now. You could be in danger, too, just being with me. . . . That's why no one can know that I'm here."

Lucy seemed to understand, yet the danger Max had mentioned only seemed to excite the child. "Listen, Max . . . I've got an idea. We can hide you. You can go with us. We live far away, *really* far away. . . . Whoever's looking for you would never think to look there."

A warm feeling came into Max's chest, something she'd never felt before: hope. "But if we do that, won't you have to tell your mom?"

"Trust me—she'll want to help you."

Max shook her head vigorously; she had trusted Lydecker. . . .

"Mom likes kids, she'll help you and keep away the people chasing you. Look, she tried to adopt a sister for me and they turned her down."

"Adopt?"

"Take in a kid whose mom was dead or something. But my dad . . . they said he wasn't 'suitable,' or . . . anyway, she'd give anything for me to have a sister."

Unconvinced, Max said, "Thank you, but I better get going." She tugged off the mittens and handed them back to Lucy.

"You can't leave—you'll freeze in those jammies! You're shivering."

Max shrugged. "I would rather freeze to death than go

back." She turned and started to walk around toward the rear of the house.

Catching up with her, Lucy put a hand on Max's arm. "How about if it's just *our* secret, you and me?"

Skepticism etched Max's face.

"Honest," Lucy said. "You can hide in the car and when we get home, you'll be miles and miles away."

"Really?"

"Nobody will ever have run away better! . . . We can do it, Max, if you can stay quiet."

Max shrugged. "I'm always quiet."

"You kind of are. Deal?"

Lucy stuck out her hand; this was a gesture Max knew, from Manticore: she shook the other child's hand.

Sneaking another furtive glance at the house, Lucy led the way out front to where a tired old SUV sat in the street. When they got to the far side, Lucy said, "When I open the door, you get in quick. There's a blanket in the back . . . crawl under it and stay on the floor by the backseat. Quiet as a mouse, now!"

"I can be quieter." To Max's ears, mice were terribly noisy.

"Mom always makes me sit in the back," Lucy was saying, "with my seat belt on. If we're quiet, we can whisper . . . and if I can get a snack from Aunt Vicki for the road, we can share it. I'll sneak you some!"

"Snack?"

"Food, Max. You *do* eat, don't you?"

A smile slipped out despite her fear. "Yes—and it's been a long time since I did."

Lucy nodded. "Okay, I'll get ya something. . . . This is exciting! This beats building a snowman all to shit!"

Max's eyes widened, hearing the forbidden word from this kid.

"Now get inside the SUV," Lucy ordered, "and get under the blanket."

Lucy opened the door and Max, trained to follow her group leader, did as the other girl had instructed. The inside of the truck was technically cold, but so much warmer than the outdoors. At least she was finally out of the wind and, with the blanket, Max started to get warm almost immediately.

Less than an hour later, the back hatch door flipped up and Max nearly panicked . . . but Lucy's mom didn't look twice at the blanket when she shoved two suitcases into the storage area . . . one of them awfully close to Max's nose . . . and slammed the door again.

Max listened as the mom said good-bye to Aunt Vicki, who also said a loud good-bye to Lucy.

"Get your seat belt on," Mom said.

"Yes, ma'am," Lucky answered, her weight dropping heavily onto the seat just behind Max.

Shoving the suitcase away a little, Max silently rolled over and took stock of her small world: the seat Lucy was in sat high, with an unused storage area beneath. Max crawled under the high seat, her head hugging the floor; she looked up to see Lucy looking down at her. The other girl had to cover her own mouth to keep from squealing in delight. What to Max was an exercise in survival was to Lucy a great adventure.

"You okay, Luce?" Mom asked.

"Fine. Just fine."

The engine turned over and the SUV coughed to life. "It'll warm up in here soon, dear."

"Good. I am kinda cold."

"Catch your death making that silly snowman."

"Didn't you like Frosty, Mom?"

"He was very handsome, dear."

After a while, the heater was putting out admirably, and Lucy looked at Max, who gave her a little nod. "We're warm enough now, Mom."

"We?"

"My new friend . . . uh . . . Max . . . uh . . . can't you see her? She's sitting right next to me."

Mom let out a little laugh. "Another invisible friend?"

Lucy shrugged.

"Honey, aren't you getting a little old for that?"

Another shrug. "Max'll be the last one."

The banter went on like that for a few more minutes, Lucy

slipping Max cookies when Mom was watching the road, Max chewing as quietly as possible. As Max listened to the conversation between mother and daughter—a conversation nothing like the talk between adults and the X5 kids at Manticore. . . . the Mom seemed . . . *nice*—the young stowaway realized just how alien a universe she was entering.

Finally, the talking quieted, and music from the car radio played the country western Max was used to, from the Manticore night staff's boombox. Eventually, Lucy went to sleep, and not long after her, Max drifted off as well.

When Max awoke, the SUV wasn't moving.

Tensing, she peeked out from beneath the seat, and saw no sign of Lucy's feet hanging down. Crawling back into the rear of the vehicle, she discovered that the suitcases were gone, too. She listened, but all she heard was silence punctuated by traffic and night sounds.

Max was alone again. Slowly, she crawled out from under the blanket. A glance out the window told her it was the middle of the night; she determined that the Barretts were probably behind the numbered door in front of the SUV, which was parked in a stall indicated by white lines painted on black paving.

Getting out of the vehicle, with all the caution her training had bestowed her, nine-year-old Max climbed down and stretched her tired legs. Being folded up under the seat had taken its toll on her muscles and bones; but on the bright side, she was warm and dry, and judging from the inner calm she felt, Manticore was far behind her. She really didn't require this much sleep, but the girl was sort of . . . saving up, not knowing what awaited her. Making sure she was unobserved, she began exploring a little, keeping the SUV in sight at all times.

The weather here was slightly warmer than in the place they'd left, and the snow had practically disappeared, just patches here and there. The SUV sat in the parking lot of a two-story U-shaped concrete building, with the Barretts' numbered door right in the middle of the bottom of the U. Only twenty or so cars occupied the large lot, and most of them had license plates from the state of Utah.

The girl found a glass door marked LOBBY, peered through and saw lights on, inside. She tried the door and found it unlocked; but when she opened it, a buzzer buzzed. Ducking back outside, behind a parked vehicle, Max watched through the window as a young blond man in a white shirt and tan pants came out of a rear room, looked over the counter at the door, shrugged, then went away again.

Beyond the counter, in the center of the lobby, Max saw a table with a large bowl of fruit in the center. Her stomach rumbled with anticipation. She looked again at the door with that annoying buzzer.

Her training had taught her that no obstacle was unconquerable. She considered the problem for what felt like a long time, her eyes darting to the fruit more often than she would have liked; she should have better control. What was she, a child? Finally, she decided there had to be another way in, and she started around the building to find it.

At the far end of the left upright part of the U, she found what she wanted: another door, this one accessible only by the insertion of a keycard; it didn't seem to have a human guard, and that alone would make it easier.

She retraced her steps to the Barretts' SUV, and searched the inside, looking for what she needed. She didn't find a screwdriver, but in the glove compartment she did come upon a small pocketknife.

That should be adequate.

Five minutes later she had the front cover off the keycard box, had crossed the wires and accessed the hall, then followed it to the lobby where her reward waited in the fruit bowl. After ducking back down the hall with the entire bowl, she quickly devoured two bananas and an orange, leaving the peels as evidence of the hungry animal who'd scavenged here.

Then Max explored long enough to find a bathroom and get a drink of water from the sink, before making her way back to the SUV, a banana and two apples still tucked in her arms.

She nibbled her fruit until finally Lucy and her mom

showed up and Max slipped under the blanket, and then they were on the road again.

Lucy wanted to whisper, but Max shook her head, not wanting to risk it. Her belly full, this strange world seeming to the X5-unit surprisingly easily dealt with, Max disappeared under the blanket and slept, contentedly.

Eight hours later, when the vehicle finally stopped for good, and Lucy and her mom had disappeared again, Max climbed out of her hiding place to find herself in a land of sunshine, warmth, and palm trees.

Training videos had shown her country like this before, but it had been an abstraction—she'd never seen anything like it in person. As she stood outside the SUV, she let the sunshine bathe her face, hands, and legs. She couldn't recall ever being so warm in her life, and she loved it.

Max was standing before a small frame house, smaller than the one where she'd met Lucy; parked in the yard was the SUV, which stood between her and the street, a long, blacktop road with one-story houses lining either side for as far as she could see.

Though they were out of her view, Max heard kids laughing, somewhere. Thinking Lucy might be with them, she took one step before the sound of a woman's voice stopped her.

"You must be hungry."

Max whirled to see Lucy's mom standing behind a screen door. "Uh . . ."

A kind adult face, with echoes of Lucy's, bestowed a smile nearly as warm as the sunshine. "It's all right, honey—Lucy told me about your trouble."

Max's first instinct was to run, just run; but the only other adult female she'd ever spoken to outside the gates of Manticore—Hannah—had helped her. And, like Hannah, this woman didn't seem upset with her—had called her "honey," an apparently affectionate designation that the woman had also granted her daughter.

Right now, in fact, the woman held open the screen door for Max—held it open wide.

"Wouldn't you like to come in?" Lucy's mom asked, displaying a wide toothy smile. "Maybe get something to eat?"

Tentatively, Max approached the woman; getting her first close look at the "mom," Max couldn't help wondering if all moms looked like this. Perhaps five foot five inches, and 125 pounds, with dark brown brown hair piled high, Lucy's mom had her daughter's wide blue eyes, full lips, and those same long eyelashes. She wore a pale blue dress with small pink flowers on it.

"I shouldn't," Max finally managed.

"Look, Max. . . . It is *Max,* isn't it?"

Max nodded.

"Is that short for Maxine?"

"I don't think so."

The woman's smile lessened but did not disappear, and she still held that door open. "Look . . . Max. Lucy's told me you have nowhere else to go, and that the people you were staying with before will hurt you if they find you. Is that right?"

Another nod.

"Then you need a new place to live, don't you?"

Max looked down the street as if the answer might be there somewhere; but why would these almost identical houses hold any better answer than this one?

Finally, Max nodded a third time.

"Then . . . would you like to stay with us?"

She shrugged. She didn't know how to respond to that.

"Well, come in, dear . . . have some food, and we'll talk. Work it out."

Max looked the other way, up the street, and found no potentially better answers in that direction, either. Haltingly, she took a step toward the house. With the screen door open, she could smell the aroma of roast beef as it wafted through the home, curling its finger invitingly. . . .

The desire for a real meal overcame her misgivings and Max strode into the house.

The living room was small. Though bigger than Hannah's, this one was less immediately inviting. The smell of old cigarettes hung in the air; the source seemed to be a worn-looking overstuffed chair to her left, which had a couple of empty beer cans sitting on a table next to it, no doubt adding to the stale odor of the room.

Still, the aroma of the beef beckoned, overcoming the to-bacco odor, and Max followed Lucy's mom into a small din-ing room to a wooden table with four matching chairs. Though the food looked the same as what she'd received at Manticore, it smelled much better: roast beef, carrots, mashed potatoes and gravy, and fresh-baked biscuits.

Lucy, looking guilty and perhaps apprehensive, sat on the far side of the table, and her mom moved toward the far end, pulling out the near-side chair for Max as she went by.

"Lucy's dad won't be here for dinner tonight," the mom said. "He's working—he's a truck driver."

Max nodded. She wondered if that meant he was like the man whose truck she'd hidden in.

"He'll be home tomorrow. Do you like roast beef, Max?"

Swallowing saliva, Max said, "Yes, very much."

"Well, dig in. Lucy, give her a hand. . . . Plenty to go 'round."

Piling her plate high, Max dived in and thought that she'd never eaten anything that tasted this good.

"So, dear—were you born in Casper?"

Max turned toward the mom. "Casper?"

"You know—the town where you met Lucy?"

"No, I wasn't born there." She said this with assurance, though inside herself, Max had doubts: since she'd known nothing of mothers and births before yesterday, who could say?

"Judging by what Lucy says," the mom said, "and from that smock you're wearing, you escaped from an institu-tion . . . an orphanage?"

"What's an . . . orphanage?"

"A place, dear, where children without parents live."

"Yes. Yes, it was an orphanage."

"And they were cruel there, dear?"

"Oh yes."

Lucy's mom moved her food around on her plate with a fork, but didn't eat anything; her eyes were damp, and mov-ing side to side, in thought.

Then the mom said, "We tried to get a nice girl like you, through . . . official sources. But they wouldn't let us. My husband . . . has a drinking problem. I guess you have a right to know that."

Why would anyone have trouble drinking?

Then the mom blurted, "Would you like to stay with us?"

Still chewing, Max just looked at her.

"You and Lucy could be like sisters."

Max glanced over at Lucy who was nodding emphatically, a wide smile on her face.

"We can't have any more children, Lucy's dad and I, and God knows, we could use another hand around here."

Max held the woman's gaze. "Would anyone have to know?"

The mom's eyes flared. "No! They couldn't know, dear . . . or you'd be taken back to where you ran from."

Max shook her head, violently. "I wouldn't want that."

"You're my late cousin's Beth's girl."

"I am?"

The mom smiled. "You are now. . . . We're your foster family. Will you stay with us, Max?"

Knowing what the woman wanted, Max slowly nodded. Then and there, just that easily, she had a new home.

Lucy spoke for the first time since they'd sat down. "Will it be all right with Dad?"

"I'll convince him. Don't you girls worry. He can be . . . difficult . . . but he'll know what this means to me. And as long as Max is willing to work around here . . . you are, aren't you Max?"

Max nodded.

"Well, then, we won't have any trouble. In the meantime, I'm going to see to it you get plenty to eat, and then we'll get you some new clothes."

Glancing down at her soiled nightshirt, Max knew that wasn't a bad idea.

The mom beamed at her. "Now, you make sure you leave room for pie—it's lemon meringue."

Max had never had this exotic dish before, and it was incredibly, deliriously delicious.

The next night, Max found out what a dad was, and it wasn't near as good as a mom: a dad (this one anyway) was a burly bully with stringy graying hair, putrid breath, a foul mouth, and a vicious temper. Oh, the dad could be nice, but only when he hadn't been drinking.

Which wasn't often (and it didn't take Max long to learn what a "drinking problem" really was).

After just ten minutes with Jack Barrett, Max knew she'd been wrong thinking Lydecker was mean. Lydecker was only businesslike, cold but not brutal; Lydecker was monstrous—this "dad" was a monster.

That first night, Mr. Barrett had come in the door, brushed past his wife with the greeting, "Get me a beer," and then he dropped into his recliner, lit up a smoke, and turned his eyes toward Max (in a pink T-shirt and jeans), who stood next to Lucy at the side of his chair. "Who the hell is this?"

Popping the top on his beer, Mrs. Barrett said, "This is Max. Say hello to Mr. Barrett, Max."

"Hi, Mr. Barrett."

The dad ignored Max. "What the fuck is that war orphan doing here?"

How could he know she was an orphan? And a soldier?

Rubbing her hands on the front of her apron, Mrs. Barrett said, "Be nice, Jack. . . . She needs a place to stay for a while."

He turned to glare at Mrs. Barrett. "Another goddamn mouth to feed?"

"Jack, I want this."

"Joann, I—"

"I put up with a lot, Jack. If you don't like it, you'll come home to an empty house—no meals, Jack. No laundry. Even get up and get your own beer."

He was gazing at her like his wife was on fire. "Don't get mouthy. . . ."

"You can hit me, Jack . . . but I'll go. I'll leave. I really will this time. *You know what this means to me.*"

He turned away. Clicked on the TV with his remote and gulped his beer.

Mrs. Barrett turned and walked off in a huff. "Come on, girls."

"Not so fast!" Mr. Barrett bellowed. He turned to Max again. "You!"

"Yes, sir."

"Well . . . you're polite, anyway. Kinda scrawny . . . maybe you'll fill out like Lucy, in a year or two. . . . You gonna help around here, earn your keep?"

Max nodded.

"This one," he jerked a thumb toward his daughter, "don't do squat, half the time."

Lucy said, "I always do—"

Mr. Barrett swung around in his chair and slapped his daughter—the crack rang in the small house, like a gunshot.

Lucy's mouth was tremblingly open, as tears rolled down her face, but no sound came out.

"Don't talk back to your father."

Between gulps of air, Lucy managed to say, "Yes, sir."

"That's better."

Max took a step forward. "Don't hit her."

Jack slapped Max even harder, the pain shooting through her jaw, her teeth, through every fiber of her being. She resisted the urge to strike back; maybe this was how families behaved. She could always kill him later.

"You want to stay here," Jack yelled, "you want three squares and a bed? You keep your fucking mouth shut unless you're told to speak."

Her cheek still throbbing, Max stood there silently, glaring at Jack Barrett.

He slapped her again. "Don't stare at me, and when I tell you something, you show me the proper goddamn respect. Stick with that 'Yes, sir' shit, and we'll get along just fine."

Pain shot through her body again and this time a tear welled in her eye, but Max willed it not to fall. "Yes, sir."

"Then she can stay, Jack?" Mrs. Barrett said.

"Kid can stay. For now."

"Oh Jack, thank you." And she kissed her husband on the cheek, and he brushed her away.

Mom (as Max had now begun to call her, and think of her) escorted Max to the bedroom she was sharing with Lucy.

"Stay on Jack's good side," Mom advised, "and don't talk back when he's . . . in a bad mood."

Later Lucy said, "I hope . . . I hope you don't think this is worse than where you escaped from."

In her own warm bed, Max was weighing that. Getting slapped was better than getting shot.

"It's fine," Max said.

That had been February. There were more slaps and even some outright beatings in March, April, and May. Sometimes Mr. Barrett would enter the room in the middle of the night and take Lucy away with him; the girl would look scared, but when she returned, she'd say at least her dad hadn't hit her.

Max had been too sexually naive at the time to really understand what was happening; but she knew it was something bad. As for the beatings, they were commonplace around the Barrett house; and Max, in an effort to fit in, had only fought back one time.

That had been in early March. Jack (as Max now thought of him, never coming to think of him as, much less call him, Dad) had waxed her pretty good, and when Max had gotten to her feet and he reached out to slap her again, she'd side-stepped the blow, caught his hand in hers, and broken two fingers before he'd wrenched it back.

But hurting Jack had been a mistake.

Max was forced to go without food for a week, which only bothered her a little—she'd had deprivation training, after all—but when he'd come home from the emergency room, he'd beaten Lucy so badly the girl couldn't walk for two days.

"If you ever, *ever* raise a hand to me again," Jack told Max, "your sister pays."

From then on, Max had done as she was told; and Jack had been smart enough not to lay his hands on his new "daughter." At least until that day in June, when the whole world changed forever. . . .

June 8, 2009, had seemed like any other day—school had gotten out the week before, and Max and Lucy were settling in for a summer of no schoolwork. Max had fit in surprisingly well at school, mostly keeping to herself, though the seizures that were a side effect of her genetic breeding caused a share of embarrassment, until the school nurse finally provided an unlikely nonprescription medication—tryptophan—that would curtail and control them.

Jack kept them busy enough around the house, and of late he'd been even angrier than usual. The Dodgers—the only thing he truly loved in this life—had been losing, and the skid had only served to give him more reason to beat on Lucy and Mom.

On this June evening, the sisters were steering him a wide path. He was parked in his recliner guzzling beers and chain-smoking, as he watched the Dodgers fall behind early, 3–0. Mrs. Barrett had taken refuge in the bedroom, leaving Max and Lucy to fulfill Jack's needs and receive the brunt of his rage. Jack had already raised his hand to Lucy once tonight, and the girls hovered in the background, being careful to not rile him again.

Finally things started to look up a little: the Dodgers had men on second and third and only one out. Max had learned some baseball from being forced to watch the games while she waited on Jack, and she recognized the beginnings of a rally when she saw one. For their own safety, the girls had become Dodgers fans, too. If the team did well, Jack was less apt to slap them around.

When the electricity went out, just after nine, Max grabbed Lucy's hand and led her to the basement where the two girls hid under the stairs while Jack went berserk. As they huddled there—tears running down Lucy's cheeks, and Jack tearing the house apart looking for them so he could "beat their asses"—Max made a decision.

Once these people had all gone to sleep for the night, she was out of here. As things turned out, no one went to sleep that night, but they still managed to miss the beating. . . .

Tired of searching for them, his anger subsiding as he remembered the impending Dodgers' rally, Jack Barrett staggered back upstairs and turned on a portable radio, which relied on batteries. Jack was pissed when he couldn't find the game on the dial, but when his alcohol fog cleared some, his anger disappeared and he called Mrs. Barrett and the girls to his side.

"Something terrible's happened," he said, his voice suddenly sober, and not at all hateful.

In fact, he sounded frightened, like a scared kid.

Soon they had all gathered around the radio to listen.

"This is the Emergency Broadcast System," a voice said. "At twelve-oh-five A.M., eastern time, terrorists detonated a nuclear instrument over the Atlantic Ocean. This has triggered an electromagnetic pulse that has destroyed virtually every electronic device on the eastern seaboard."

Mrs. Barrett hugged Jack and gathered the girls to her, as well.

"All communications are down east of the Mississippi River, and there is currently no timetable for the reestablishment of contact with those areas. The threat of another terrorist attack in the western half of the country is still a possibility, and all citizens are asked to remain in their homes until further notice."

The little family huddled together like that for the next two and a half hours. The EBS continued to broadcast the same message over and over, with no new information. Finally, Jack grew bored and restless. He pulled Lucy away from her mother.

"Get me a beer," he growled.

Lucy went to the kitchen and came back with a fresh beer, popping the top for him; but the can slipped out of her hand as she tried to give it to him, and landed upside down in Jack's lap, soaking his crotch.

He jumped up and stood before them, his face reddening in anger, the can bouncing across the room, his pants looking as though he'd just wet them.

Max laughed.

The livid Jack took a step toward her, his hand shooting out; but Max had already decided to leave, so there was no reason to endure the abuse anymore. As the dad reached for her, she ducked, kicked out, and swept his feet from under him, dropping him to the floor in a heap.

He howled in rage and, as he tried to get up, she delivered an elbow that broke his nose and knocked him flat again.

Jack shrieked in pain.

Finding the sound strangely satisfying, Max backed off then, moved toward the door; but the fight wasn't out of Jack yet and he crawled after her. Spinning, she delivered a kick to the side of his head that dropped him one last time and left him lying on the floor unconscious.

With one last look back at an astonished Lucy and Mrs. Barrett—her sister and Mom didn't seem to know whether to be upset or elated—Max whispered, "Thank you."

And she walked out of the shabby little house for the last time. She didn't know where she was going, but she did know she wasn't coming back here—ever.

In the days to come, Max—like everyone—learned from the remnants of the media what had occurred.

The Pulse had screwed up everything but good. Every electronic and motorized device from New York to Des Moines bought the farm when that thing detonated. Within seconds, power grids, telecommunications networks, transportation systems, banking systems, medical services, and emergency systems had become museum relics.

One minute, the United States of America was a superpower where everybody had jobs, money, food, all their needs met. The next, the American tapestry unraveled and left the country reeling. . . . No jobs, no money, no food, people forced to start fending for themselves.

No more drive-up, no more New York Stock Exchange, no more school . . . the entire eastern half of the country came to a grinding, screeching halt. Everything people were sure of yesterday was in doubt today, and there was no telling how long . . . or even *if* . . . the country could recover from such a catastrophe.

Even though, on the night Max left the Barrett home, the effects of the Pulse hadn't yet reached California, the X5-unit found herself in the same leaky boat as everybody else. Genetically enhanced or not, a nine-year-old could do only so many things in an upside-down world; so Max quickly turned to petty theft. She did fine for a while on her own, stealing enough to eat, sleeping wherever she could find a place.

Though the East's destruction had been nearly instantaneous, the West took longer to feel the effects; but as the West Coast economic depression caught up with the upheaval in the East, the pickings for foragers like Max became more and more sparse.

Still, Max had managed to build a loner's life for herself there in Los Angeles. As the people around her broke up into smaller groups in order to protect themselves, she continued to live the outlaw life, finding herself a remote spot within the confines of Griffith Park, from which she ventured only when she needed supplies. To Max, the three years she lived in the park were like an extended Manticore field exercise.

With one important difference—she was free.

Whenever she started to get down about the state of her life, that one thought could bring her back up. But she wondered if the others—if there were any still outside the wire—missed her as much as she missed them . . .

. . . defiant Eva, shot by Lydecker, the catalyst for their escape, dead for sure; Brin, the acrobatic one; Zack, their leader and her older brother; Seth, the boy who'd been caught that night and dragged back by the guards; and her best friend and sister Jondy. . . .

These and other sibs seemed to constantly occupy her thoughts; yet she kept going. Getting bigger, stronger, smarter, Max knew these things would help her to find her sibs in this postapocalyptic America, no matter where they were.

Those were the goals that needed to be met, not spending her time worrying about what *might* be. If she could make herself good enough, finding the sibs would take care of itself.

They weren't the only ones she missed, though. Lucy, and the situation Max had left her in, still bothered Max—her other sister, back in Jack Barrett's house, his world. Then, in the spring of her twelfth year, when she finally returned to the Barrett home to rescue Lucy, she found the house abandoned.

All the way back to her home in the park, tears streamed down her cheeks, as she realized that Lucy was probably out of her life forever. Finding her siblings would be difficult enough—locating a normal child like Lucy? Next to impossible.

Three weeks later, early May, the Big Quake hit.

Measuring 8.5 on the Richter scale, the quake struck in the middle of the night, killing thousands in their beds, taking far many more lives in California than the Pulse had. Fires raged for weeks, buildings collapsed, houses slid down the sides of mountains, overpasses fell, crushing late-night drivers.

Max's small sanctuary in the park survived, but with literally millions homeless now, the job of protecting her niche, and still trying to forage enough for her own survival, was becoming hopeless. She lasted a year that way, but with supplies getting harder and harder to find, she was forced to scavenge farther and farther from home.

And like so many young girls had in that time just before hers, Max made her way to Hollywood, although in her case it wasn't to star in the movies: her journey ended up being more of a simple migratory path . . .

. . . a path that led her straight to Moody and the Chinese Clan.

Chapter Four
BLAST FROM THE PAST

THE CHINESE THEATRE
LOS ANGELES, CALIFORNIA, 2019

When Max strode across the cracked cement patio and into the former Mann's Chinese Theatre, a pacing Moody was waiting for her just inside the doors. She would have liked to think his anxiety was for her, but knew better: the Heart of the Ocean was the root of his worry.

The lobby still possessed the glass concession counters from the old days, but now, instead of food, they served up sleeping quarters for some of the younger kids. The carpeting had at one time been red but now was worn to a threadbare pink. Severely cracked by the Quake, the high ceiling had held for seven years now, and no reason to think it wouldn't last seven more, anyway. The walls were decorated not with posters but graffiti, some—like old cave drawings—representing Clan history, others just obscene.

"Are you all right, child?" Moody asked, his voice soft and smooth, but with a tinge of excitement in it.

His long silver hair was tied back in its customary ponytail and he wore a black sweatshirt, black slacks, black socks, and running shoes.

"You mean, did I get you your bauble?"

"Do you think so poorly of me, child? . . . Well—*did* you?"

"That's why you sent me, isn't it?"

A wide wolfish smile opened his face to reveal large white teeth (his grooming, by post-Pulse standards, was remarkable).

Before the conversation could progress, Fresca popped through the double doors that led to the old theater's main auditorium.

Thirteen or so, Fresca was tall and skinny for his age, with long, straight red hair and pale flesh swarming with freckles. He bounced over to them in his ancient WEEZER T-shirt (no kid in the Clan had any idea what the word represented, but it amused Fresca), and tattered jeans that were more white than blue.

"Whassup, Max?" Fresca asked, ever chipper.

The boy had enough energy zapping around in that gangly body to light a small city. Stillness took him only when he slept, and only then because he had the upper bunk, the top of the concession stand, a precarious perch: if he moved at all in his slumber, he'd end up on the floor.

"Gotta check in with the Moodman here," she said easily, "then I'm gonna chill, Fresca—maybe get something to eat."

"Great! Can I come? Can I?"

The kid wasn't even on drugs.

"Who said I was going anywhere?" Max said, trying not to smile, and failing.

Fresca grinned in response, and dug the toe of his tattered sneaker into the carpeting. She was well aware he was in love with her, and probably had been the moment he met her, when he joined the Clan a year ago.

Having been with Moody for most of the last six years, Max was an old-timer, the Moodman's chief lieutenant and the best thief in the Clan ("A master of the forgotten art of cat burglary," Moody would say), which was no small feat, considering all twenty-eight members were street-savvy thieves themselves.

"Why, Fres," Max asked, "you wanna go out?"

Fresca lighted up a ciggie and started to jitter. "Max, that would be great . . . that would be perfect. Been up all night waitin' for you to get back!"

She nodded. "Moody and me, we gotta go take care of a couple of things. . . . Then we can blaze, okay?"

"I'll wait right here," the redhead promised.

Moody—standing patiently through all of this (Fresca was

one of his favorites, too)—led the way. Just before he got to the double entryway of the auditorium, he opened a side door at left and ducked up the stairs, obviously heading to Max's crib, in what had once been the grand old theater's projection booth.

Max wondered why they were going there. Moody usually conducted business in his own quarters, the former manager's office; not that he hadn't dropped by Max's crib before . . . but this just seemed unusual.

Then again, the Heart of the Ocean was an unusual prize.

The tall man in black turned the knob and entered as if this were his room, not hers. Max's door was always unlocked—living with a building full of thieves made locks unnecessary if not outright absurd—and, anyway, Max knew of no one who might enter that she couldn't handle.

The young woman followed her mentor into the modest chamber and he closed the door behind them. Other than Moody's office/living quarters, this cracked-plaster-walled room was the biggest private room in the place. The dead projector had been shoved into a corner, a decaying museum piece unworthy of the institution Max had just looted. This provided Max a window into the auditorium where most of the Chinese Clan slept.

Down there, the rows of seats—except for the first half a dozen rows—had long since been removed and replaced with items better suited to the needs of the Clan: cots, jury-rigged walls, small camp cookstoves, and other paraphernalia, scattered around the huge room in little living-quarter pockets. The movie screen—with CHINESE CLAN! emblazoned in huge orange spray-paint graffiti—still dominated the wall behind the stage, and Moody used this platform when he addressed his shabby but proficient troops.

The projection booth itself was the biggest room Max had had to herself in her entire life. Her earliest memories were of the Manticore barracks; then she'd shared a room with Lucy, after which she lived in a hole in the ground barely big enough for one, back in Griffith Park.

Ten by sixteen, with its own bathroom, the booth seemed huge to Max, a suite all to herself. Of course, the bathroom would have been a greater luxury if the plumbing worked on a more regular basis. The theater had been abandoned because of the quake cracks in the ceiling, and had even been scheduled for demolition by the city, except someone had stolen the work order and—with all the other troubles in the city—Mann's seemed to have been lost in the shuffle.

The plumbing, which only worked some of the time in Hollywood anyway, worked even more infrequently within the theater—usually only after Moody had laid some green on local power and water reps.

Max's bed—rescued from the rubble of the old Roosevelt Hotel across the street—was a luxurious queen-sized box spring on the floor, mattress on top. A Coleman camp lantern, a prize from her days of living in Griffith Park, sat at the head of the bed near a short pile of books, mostly nonfiction (subjects Moody wanted her to study), and a dog-eared paperback copy of *Gulliver's Travels,* the one novel she owned, also provided by Moody. Her new motorcycle, a Kawasaki Ninja 250, leaned against one wall, and a padded armchair, also lifted from the Roosevelt ruins, squatted near the projection window. Her only other possession, a small black-and-white TV, sat on a tiny table to the left of the chair.

Moody gazed down at the books. "Traveling to Lilliput again, Maxine?"

Moody knew full well that Maxine wasn't her name: it was just an affectionate nickname.

She smiled. "Can't help it—I like the guy."

Her mentor chuckled. "You and Gulliver—your lives are not that dissimilar, you know."

"Yeah, I'd noticed that."

Moody eased his lanky frame into the chair; Max remained standing.

"So, Maxine . . . the score—was it difficult?"

Max recounted the evening, draining it of any excess melodrama; still, Moody seemed impressed.

Shaking his head, he said, "Mr. Kafelnikov will be . . . displeased with you."

"I hope he doesn't know who borrowed his security plan. That poor traitor would die slow, I bet."

"Very slow . . . but our Russian adversary may well have made you, you know."

"How could he I.D. me? I never met the guy before."

"You underestimate your renown within certain circles."

Max frowned. "What circles? I don't know any 'circles.' "

Arms draped on either side of the chair, as if it were a throne and he a king (the latter was true, in a way), Moody arched an eyebrow. "You think the other clans don't talk to each other? You think these . . . superhuman feats of yours have gone unnoticed?"

"I don't care," she said with a shrug.

"Perhaps you should. You've given them all one sort of trouble or another over the years, haven't you?"

A slow smile crossed Max's full lips. "Girl's gotta do what a girl's gotta do."

Moody's eyes seemed to look inward. "That security plan meant a great deal to the Brood. They meant to obtain the bauble in your pocket—and they won't take this defeat lightly. Kafelnikov will search long and hard to find out who wronged him."

Finally, casually, she withdrew the necklace from her pocket. "This old thing?"

Moody's eyes went as wide as the stone. "My God, Maxine. . . . It's even more breathtaking up close."

Max held the stone to the dim light and studied it for a long moment. "It's pretty cool, I guess." With another shrug, she handed it over.

"Pretty cool," Moody said, taking the stone. "If they connect you to us . . . and they will . . . we'll have a real enemy."

"They try to storm this place, we'll hand their asses back, with change."

Turning the stone over and over in his hands, Moody seemed not to have heard her. "The necklace alone would feed the Clan for a year."

"That was a good plan you had—'cept for those dogs. For rumors, they had *some* teeth on 'em."

He shook his head, ponytail swinging. "My apologies. . . . Anyway, a plan is worthless without proper execution. That was key . . . and the only one in this city who could have executed it was you. . . . Which, my dear, you did."

"No biggie," she said, with yet another shrug.

Rising, he tucked the stone into a pocket as he moved to her. Putting an arm around Max, Moody kissed the girl's cheek, as he had many times before . . . only now, his lips perhaps lingered a moment too long. "You did well, my dear . . . you did very well."

"Thanks," Max said, feeling suddenly uncomfortable. Oddly, the image of Mr. Barrett entering the bedroom after midnight, to fetch Lucy, flashed through her mind. "I . . . I better get Fresca—he's probably wet his pants by now. I promised to get something to eat with him, y'know."

Moody didn't move, his arm still around Max's shoulders. "If they come . . . if the Brood dares breach our stronghold . . . God help them when you reveal your powers of battle."

"Thanks." Sliding away, not wanting to anger him, but still feeling that something wasn't quite right, she made another mumbled excuse and slipped out of the room and down the stairs. She could hear Moody on the steps behind her, but didn't turn to see where he was.

Fresca was sitting like a gargoyle on the edge of the concession counter, already wearing his rumpled Dodgers jacket. His prize possession, the jacket was Fresca's only tie with his old life . . . whatever that had been. The clothes he'd been wearing when he joined the Clan had been burned, his old name forgotten, his new name adopted from the menu behind the concession stand. Only that faded blue Dodgers jacket remained.

The Clan rule—instituted by Moody and embraced by them all—was that the past didn't matter, didn't exist; time began the day you joined the Clan.

"Let's bounce," Max said as she walked past him.

Fresca jumped down and, following her suggestion, bounced along next to her, a puppy excited to be in his master's . . . mistress's? . . . presence.

They swept out of the theater across the remnants of old-time movie star handprints and cement signatures and onto Hollywood Boulevard, to be greeted by the rising sun. Max had never been near Hollywood Boulevard before the Quake, but some of the area's denizens she'd spoken to over the years told her that the Boulevard was the one part of the city that the Quake hadn't changed all that much.

"Where we goin'?" Fresca asked.

"Where do you want to go?"

"How about that waffle place over on La Brea?"

"Sure. Waffles are good. I got nothing against waffles."

Fresca giggled at that, as if Max were the soul of wit; she smiled to herself and they walked along.

The Belgian Waffle House was on the corner of La Brea and Hawthorn, a healthy but doable walk from Mann's. The place had once been all windows, but the Quake had destroyed them, and the plywood hung to replace them temporarily had become permanent. Littered with graffiti, the plywood was now the waffle house's trademark, and customers were provided with markers to add to the decoration while they waited for their food. The booths were still vinyl-covered, but wear and tear had taken them beyond funky into junky. Sparse early-morning traffic meant that only nine or ten other patrons were in the place when Fresca and Max strolled in.

They took two seats at the counter so Fresca could watch the wall-mounted TV adjacent to the food service window from the dingy kitchen.

The Satellite News Network, with headline stories in half-hour cycles, was at this hour about the only choice in a TV market that had gone from a pre-Pulse high of over two hundred cable channels to the current half dozen, all of which were under the federal government's thumb. The SNN and two local channels were all that was left out east, and in the Midwest, they got SNN and scattered local channels; so the West Coast remained, by default, the center of the television world. . . . it was just a much smaller world.

"I'm gonna make a leap here," Max said, "and have a waffle."

Fresca grinned. "You buyin'?"

Max favored him with a wide smile. "What have you done lately, to deserve me buying you breakfast?"

"Uh . . . I just figured . . . you were on some big score, and wanted to, I don't know, celebrate. Maybe share the wealth."

"Why would I want to do that?"

Fresca seemed hurt by her kidding. "I don't know . . . I just . . . kinda hoped . . . you know . . ."

She reached over and patted his hand. "Relax, mongrel. You know I won't let you starve."

He brightened and, as if keeping up Fresca's end of the conversation, his stomach growled.

A waitress came up to them with all the urgency of a stroke victim using a walker. She was in her late forties, early fifties, skinny as a straw, with a tight, narrow face. She was not thrilled to see them. "Save me a trip—tell me you don't need a menu."

Fresca shook his head. "I don't need one! I'll have two waffles and a large chocolate milk. Oh, and some bacon too."

"We been out of bacon for a week now."

"You got sausage?"

"Link."

"Okay! Double order."

Max looked sideways at him. "How big a score you think I pulled off?"

His face fell. "Uh, Max, I'm sorry, I, uh . . ."

"Kidding. I'm kidding."

"Chitchat on your own time, honey," the waitress said, and she wasn't kidding. "You need a menu?"

"Waffle, sausage, coffee with milk," Max said.

The waitress sighed, as if this burden were nearly too much to bear, turned and left. Max and Fresca settled in to watch the news. Max was not particularly interested— Moody had made it clear to her that the news was controlled, and not to be believed—but Fresca enjoyed the clips of fires and shootings and other mayhem.

While Fresca sat riveted to the screen, waiting for the next disaster, Max reconsidered her meeting with Moody. He seemed to be pushing her to take a step she wasn't ready to take . . . a step into a personal relationship. Seemed the king of the Clan was in the market for a queen. . . .

Oh, he'd been subtle about it—no direct mention; but she could read the man . . . she could feel the pressure.

Over and above that, she knew he was right about Kafelnikov, the Brood, and some of the other gangs she'd ripped off over the years: she was building a reputation, attracting attention, and this made her uneasy. Maybe it was time to move on. . . .

Although the Clan had become her family, she would get over it. She'd lost family before; sometimes, it seemed losing families, and moving on, was the only thing she did with any regularity . . . that the only thing permanent about her life was its impermanence.

She glanced at Fresca. Her leaving would break that red-headed, oversized ragamuffin's heart; but eventually he would get over it and find someone his own age to fall in love with. And besides, if her being gone took some heat off the Chinese Clan, that probably wouldn't be a bad thing, either.

The waitress showed up with their food, glancing at them as if disgusted by their need to eat, and Fresca immediately drowned his two waffles in syrup and butter, and dug in, scarfing the stuff like he hadn't had food for weeks. *Maybe the waitress is right,* Max thought; *Fresca eating* is *a little disgusting.* . . .

Max sipped her coffee and picked at her food; she was never very hungry after a big score. Fresca chugged his chocolate milk and asked the waitress for seconds. On the TV, a series of commercials ended and a news cycle started. The doe-eyed Hispanic woman reading the headlines had straight black hair, high cheekbones, and wore a sharply cut charcoal business suit.

"And in Los Angeles, with the sector turf war between the Crips and the Bloods escalating, Mayor Timberlake assured residents that he would double the number of police officers on the street by the end of the year."

Max glanced up to see video of the curly-haired mayor speaking to a gathering of citizens in front of City Hall, delivering the same old b.s. Max, like every other resident of southern California, knew he was talking through his ass. The clans and gangs had the police outnumbered nearly three to one and the city's only hope was to declare martial law and call in the National Guard.

And maybe that would finally happen . . . which was just one more reason to hit the road, she thought.

The Hispanic woman started a new story. *"Police in Seattle are stepping up their efforts in the search for the dissident cyberjournalist known as 'Eyes Only.' Well-known for breaking into broadcasts with his pirate 'news' bulletins, 'Eyes Only' is wanted by police on local, state, and national levels."*

Max watched idly; politics bored her.

"This amateur video shot in Seattle just last night," the newswoman continued, *"shows a suspected Eyes Only accomplice, doing battle with officers. The police are searching for this young rebel as well."*

Courtesy of amateur video, Max watched as a brown-haired young man in jeans and a denim jacket—surrounded by Seattle police officers—suddenly sprang to life.

A straight kick to the groin dropped the cop in front of him and, even before that one fell, the young man did a back flip that took him easily eight feet into the air before nailing a landing behind the officer who a moment before had been facing him. When the officer turned with nightstick raised, the young man hit him with a straight right to the throat that dropped him.

One of the remaining three rushed at the rebel with a Tazer, and the young man leapt out of the way at the last second, so that the cop shot one of his fellow officers. As the officer who had fired the Tazer stood in astonishment, the young man spun and kicked him twice in the face before the officer fell.

The remaining cop drew his service pistol and emptied the clip at the young man, whose response was to cartwheel, spin, and dodge until the officer's pistol was empty. When the last round missed him, the young man stepped forward and hit the cop with half a dozen alternating lefts and rights, before he mercifully let the public servant drop to the ground unconscious.

Max sat as wide-eyed and amazed as the boy's victims.

Even though she'd only eaten a tiny amount of her breakfast, the food began to roil in her stomach. She had just witnessed superhuman feats that few on the planet could have accomplished: and the only humans she knew of capable of such things had been bred and trained at Manticore. . . .

The video was grainy, shot from a distance, and she was reasonably sure it wasn't Zack; but the young man who took out the five cops could definitely have been one of her sibs. He looked vaguely like Seth, but Seth hadn't made it out that night . . . had he? The picture was so lousy, even with her enhanced vision, she couldn't tell much of anything, for sure.

This gifted guy just had to be one of her sibs . . . didn't he? Who else could do what they could do? Or were there other places like Manticore, turning out supersoldiers?

"Max. Max!"

She turned to look numbly at Fresca. "What?"

"Why . . . why are you *crying,* Max?"

She blinked. She didn't know she had been, but those were tears, all right, running down her cheeks; the streaks of moisture felt warm. "It's nothing, Fres," she said. "How you doing with your chow?"

"I'm gonna blow up soon."

"Then why don't you stop eating?"

"After you treated me to this feast? I would never insult you that way, Max!"

She couldn't help but smile through the tears. As she sat watching the boy shovel in the food, she knew her course was clear: a girl had to do what a girl had to do.

But she knew when she left, she'd miss Fresca most of all.

"You ready to go then, waffle boy?"

He slurped down the last of his second chocolate milk. "Yeah, yeah, I'm ready to blaze. . . . And thanks, Max. I haven't eaten like this in days. . . . You sure you're okay?"

"Just somethin' in my eye," she said. "I'm great, now."

"You're always great, Max."

The waitress came over as they rose and Max paid their bill, including tip.

"Be sure to come back," the waitress said; it seemed vaguely a threat.

As they walked back to the theater, with considerably less urgency, Max's mind was nonetheless racing.

She'd always wondered how she'd go about finding her siblings, and now, at breakfast, one of them had practically dropped into her lap. How long would it take her to get to Seattle, and how would she get past all the checkpoints? What would Moody think about her leaving? He had all but suggested it before, hadn't he?

Or had Moody wanted her to stay with him?

The bike's gas tank was full, more or less; but would she be able to get fuel on the road? Even if she could, the price of the stuff would eat through her bankroll. The questions engulfed her like swarming insects.

As they neared the theater, Fresca again asked, "You sure you're okay, Max?"

She wrapped an arm around his shoulders and kissed him on the cheek, taking her good sweet time, the *smack* of her lips like a sweet slap. When she let him go, Fresca flushed red, his thousands of freckles merging into one big glowing blotch. She knew instantly that he was thinking the same thoughts about her that she'd been thinking after Moody's lingering kiss on the cheek . . . only Fres didn't seem weirded out like she had been: he seemed pleased, even . . . excited.

Uh oh. . . .

Her motivations had been purely innocent, which made her wonder if maybe Moody's had been, too. . . .

Mann's was slowly coming awake, Clan members stirring and lining up to use the bathrooms, the smell of breakfasts cooking on hot plates wafting pleasantly. Max deposited the still-beet-faced Fresca next to his concession-stand berth and headed into the auditorium in search of Moody.

The sloping floor was scattered with sleeping bags and beds appropriated from the Roosevelt wreckage, while blan-

ket "walls" were draped from clotheslines. Despite the breakfast odors, the smell of stale sweat and unwashed souls hung
in the air; and yet very faintly lingered the olfactory memory
of buttered popcorn.

It was a motley crew Moody lorded over, but they were a
family—Max already was viewing them with a sort of nostalgia—and they loved the old man.

Moody's second-in-command, Gabriel—an African
American in his late twenties—was rousing the kids when
she came in.

"Moodman in his office?" she asked.

Gabriel had a shadow's worth of black hair, brown eyes,
and an ostrich neck. He cocked his head toward the movie
screen. "Yeah, and he's happy as a clam. What the hell you
pull off last night, Maxie?"

"Little score. Same-o same-so . . . save-the-day kinda
thing."

He harrumphed, but grinned. "Ain't it the truth. Don't
know what we'd do without you 'round here, girl."

Max felt a twinge of guilt.

Gabriel was looking down at Niner, a sixteen-year-old
newbie girl who'd been with the Clan for about a month.

"Get your scrawny ass outa the sack," Gabriel growled.
"There's work to be done in the real world."

Continuing on toward the looming screen, Max thought
about Niner. Nice kid; reminded her a little of Lucy. Max
hoped that once she was gone, maybe Fresca and Niner
could hook up. Might be good for both of them.

Max took a doorway to the left of the screen, into an area
where a single guard, Tippett, blocked the hallway that led to
Moody's quarters. Six-four, maybe 240 pounds of tattoos
and piercings, Tippett had been a linebacker back in the pre-
Pulse days. Now, nearly fifty, he still had a black belt in
karate and was the only person in the Clan who could hold
his own with Max. When they'd sparred once, he'd lasted
eight seconds, easily the record for a match with her. Only
now that Max knew the man's moves, he'd go down in five.

"Hey," Max said.

Tippett smiled, showing a thin line of tobacco-browned

teeth. Big and pale with an incongruous Afro, he scared the shit out of everybody . . . except Max and Moody. Even Gabriel gave Tippett more than the average amount of space.

"Cutie pie," he said. "Wanna go a few rounds?"

"No. You?"

"Hell no. You must wanna see the man."

"I need to see the man."

"Girl whips my ass don't have to ask me twice." The guard stepped aside.

The hallway had an incense odor, always pleasant to Max after the fetid sweat smell of the auditorium. Moody's office was the second door on the left of the pale-blue cracked plaster walls, an unmarked one just after another labeled MOODY—OFFICE. The latter led into a tiny empty room; but the important part of that "OFFICE" door was the four ounces of C4 wired to it.

She knocked on the second door, said firmly, "Max!"

The door replied with a muffled, "Come!"

She found Moody seated behind his desk, on his cell phone; he waved for her to enter and take a chair across from him, which she did.

The wall to her left, the one that abutted the booby trap room, was loaded floor to ceiling with sandbags to protect Moody's office should the trap be sprung. The desk was an old metal one accompanied by three unmatching metal-frame chairs, one for Moody and two on the other side. The wall to the right had a doorway carved into it, and a curtain of purple beads separated Moody's private quarters from the office. A few of the ancient movie posters—Sean Connery in *Goldfinger,* Clint Eastwood in *Dirty Harry* (both meaningless to Max)—salvaged from somewhere in the theater, were tacked here and there.

"Don't insult me," he snapped into the phone, but his face revealed calm at odds with his tone. He glanced at Max, rolled his eyes, made a mouth with his fingers and thumb, and opened it and closed it rapidly: *blah, blah, blah.*

Perhaps fifteen seconds later, Moody told the phone, "I know it's a bloody depression, but this is a diamond bigger than that one good eyeball of yours, you ignorant, cycloptic son of a bitch." He hit the END button. "That's what I've always hated about these damn cells," he said, his voice as blasé as if he were ordering tea, "you can't slam a receiver into a hook, and put a nice period on a sentence."

Max's head was cocked. "Was that? . . ."

"That was someone who, if I've done my job correctly, will be calling right back." Five seconds later the cell phone rang and Moody smiled. "Got him."

Max had watched Moody negotiate before and knew he usually got what he wanted. The man had charm and cajones and a tactical sense second to none.

"Yes," Moody said into the phone.

He listened for a few seconds.

"Well, that may indeed be true about my mother," Moody said, "but then we'll never know, will we, since she passed away some years ago . . . but one thing is certain: my price is a *fair* price."

He listened again, tossing a twinkling-eyed smile at his protégée.

"Splendid," he said finally. "Where and when?" Moody jotted something on a pad. "A pleasure, as always. I like nothing more than a smooth transaction." He hit END again.

Max's eyebrows went up. "How much is fair?"

That white smile of his could have lighted up a much larger room than this. "Don't concern yourself with details, Maxine. Suffice to say the Clan can move somewhere where we don't have to worry about the ceiling falling in on us . . . though it *will* be hard to leave here. However shabby, it has come to be home, after all."

That she understood.

"My dear . . . you're not smiling. Is something wrong? Is the notion of leaving this palace a sad one to you?"

Suddenly, Max seemed unable to speak. All the way back from the restaurant she had rehearsed the speech, and now came time to let it out, and she couldn't find a damn word.

"Do you believe you've earned a bigger share? Perhaps you're contemplating heading up your own subclan?"

Max took in a deep breath and let it out slowly, just as she had in Manticore training. This felt a lot like defusing a bomb, though she would much rather be doing that. Centering herself, she started again. "Moody, I have to take off."

He rocked back in his chair, tented his fingers, smiled gently. "For where, my dear, and for how long?"

Looking at the frayed carpeting on the floor, Max said, "I think for good."

Moody's smile disappeared. "Please don't tease me, Maxine. Things are just about to turn around for us. You can be a queen here."

She lifted her eyes to his. "I'm sorry. I'm grateful to you—you've taught me so much, but . . . I just never wanted to be a queen. I only wanted to be . . ."

"What?" he asked, his voice edged with irritation and something else . . . disappointment? "You just wanted to be what?"

This was getting hard again, emotions surging through her, stress gnawing at her guts.

"Free," she finally managed.

His displeasure accelerated with the volume of his voice. "You're not . . . *free,* here?"

She shook her head. "Of course I'm free here. That's not it . . . this isn't about you or the Clan. It's about me. Moody . . ." She touched the back of her neck, indicating her barcode. ". . . you know I'm not the only one like me."

"Yes," he admitted, quieter now.

Max sat forward. "I came upon information this morning, about where one of my brothers may be. I'm not positive. But I need to find out for myself."

Moody's sigh was endless. "I always feared this day would come. I always . . . dreaded it."

"You do understand, then?"

His dark eyes were sad as he gave her a little shrug. "You don't have enough . . . family here?"

"I have a large family here. The Clan will always be my family, but . . ."

"But?"

Max looked at the floor, then up at Moody again, their eyes locking. "*They* were my family first. Yours was the family I adopted."

"And that adopted you."

"That's right. And you've been good to me. And I've done well by you."

He nodded slowly.

She shook her head, dark hair bouncing. "We've talked about this, Moody. You know all I've ever wanted is to find my sibs."

He looked at her for a long time. Then, wearily, he said, "I know I'm being unfair, Maxine . . . but I don't want to lose you."

"I'll be back someday. If not to stay, to visit. Visit my family."

That made him smile, but it was a melancholy thing, nonetheless. "The Clan has been strengthened by having you in it, Max."

"Thank you," she said, standing. "But with the payday you'll get for the Heart of the Ocean, everything should be fine."

Rising, he said, "That's probably true . . . nonetheless, your absence will be felt." He came around the desk and stood facing her. "Can you wait until after the exchange? I could use the backup."

She shook her head regretfully. "I think he's in trouble, my brother, and I need to find him as soon as possible."

"Where is it you're going?"

"I'm just going, Moody. Where I'm going means nothing, except to me."

Moody accepted that with a nod. "You have enough money?"

"I have a stash. It won't last forever, but it'll get me where I'm going. . . . Moody, I'm sorry."

"Maxine, don't apologize for following your heart . . . not ever. Such instincts are the only pure thing left in this polluted world."

Her smile was warm, her gaze fond. "You have been a hell of a teacher."

"Have I?" He reached for something on his desk: a photo. "Know this?"

She took it in with a glance, answered matter-of-factly, "*Trafalgar Square* by Mondrian. Piet Mondrian."

His smile was admiring—and she could tell the admiration was not just for her good looks.

Gesturing with the photo, her mentor said, "Most of the cretins who inhabit this city believe the Mondrian to be a hotel from the pre-Pulse days and nothing more. But you know his paintings, all of them . . ."

". . . Most of them . . ."

". . . *all* of them, and what they're worth, and what they can be fenced for, and where to find them."

"You taught me how to be a good thief."

"I refined you, my dear. You were a good thief when you joined the Clan. . . . Now, you are the best."

He went back around the desk, opened a drawer, and pulled out a wad of bills with a rubber band around it. He tossed it to her, she caught it, looked at it—*damn, at least five grand!*—and tossed the packet back.

"Moody, I told you—I got a stash."

An embarrassed smile crossed Moody's face. "You have some money, I'm sure; but I've always kept back part of your share . . . just in case this day ever came. To tell you the truth, I do it for all of you."

"You don't," she said simply.

"Ah . . . no. But it sounded good." He lobbed the bundle back to her. "In your case, however, I did . . . because I was grooming you to sit beside me."

More than just sit, she thought; but said, "I don't want this, Moody. Use it for the kids."

He shook his head. "You'll need it more than we will: you said it yourself, we're about to have the biggest payday ever. We'll be more than fine."

Hefting the bills, she said, "No hard feelings, then?"

His eyes and nostrils flared. "Of *course* there are hard feelings, my dear, that's what life largely is, hard feelings . . . but there's no anger, and not a little love. You go, Maxine, you find your brother, and if you want, bring him back here with you. Then you will both have a family."

This time Max was aware of the tears trickling down her cheeks. She rounded the desk and hugged Moody. They embraced for a long time.

When she finally pulled back, Max asked, "You'll tell the . . . rest of the gang?" She gestured toward the theater. "I hate fucking good-byes."

"Are you sure you don't want to?"

She shook her head. "God no! I'm crying just telling *you* . . . how do you think I'd do with them?"

He laughed gently. "Ah, Maxine, my Maxine . . . for a genetically enhanced killing machine, you don't seem very tough."

"Well then help me preserve my image. You tell the kids good-bye for me."

A smirk dug a hole in one of Moody's cheeks. "I guess this is one negotiation I'm destined to lose."

They hugged one last time.

Before she left, Max called Fresca up into the projection booth and asked him to watch it for her until she got back from "a little trip" she had to take.

"Can't I come with you?" he moaned; even his freckles seemed to droop.

"No, I need you here. You're my *guy,* aren't you?"

"I am? I mean . . . I am!"

She shrugged with her shoulders and her mouth. "Well, then, kid—watch my shit for me. All I'm takin' is my bike."

"No prob!"

She put an arm around him conspiratorially. "And I want you to do one more thing for me."

"Anything."

"Keep an eye on Niner. She seems like a good kid, but she's green . . . she needs a *man* to look out for her."

Fresca seemed to pump up a little at the thought Max considered him a man. "Count on it!"

"And here, Fres—take this." She handed him a wad of bills, about half what Moody had given her.

His eyes were like fried eggs. "Max, you're *kidding,* right?"

"Put that in your pocket, and don't tell anybody that you have it, or where you got it."

"Why?"

"Because everybody needs a secret stash o' cash . . . and that's yours."

"Rad," he said breathlessly, thumb riffling the thickness of bills.

"And always remember, Fres—you're my brother, too."

He frowned in confusion. " 'Too'? You got another brother?"

"Maybe," she said. "I'll let you know."

They hugged, then she said, "Gotta blaze."

"Better blaze then," he said.

And she walked her bike out, and was gone.

Chapter Five

WELCOME TO THE MONKEY HOUSE

THE PACIFIC COAST HIGHWAY
EUREKA, CALIFORNIA, 2019

Like poison mushrooms, they sprang up all around the country after the Pulse, these villages of ramshackle shacks where people—little more than refugees really—came to live and, frequently, die. Named Jamestowns—after Michael James, the president of the United States when the Pulse hit—the ragtag hamlets were a twenty-first-century variation on the Hoovervilles of the previous century's Great Depression, those packing-crate communities named after another less-than-stellar president.

This Jamestown, located on the east side of Eureka, California, had been around since just after the LA Quake of 2012. What had started with only a few cardboard hovels had become—following a frontier pattern hardly new to the state—an actual town over the last seven years, complete with bars, trading posts, a church, and even a roughshod school. Covering acres that used to be the Sequoia Park Zoo, the Jamestown had incorporated the zoo's animal housing for its own varied purposes.

Though most of the zoo had been converted to human shelter, the monkey house had long since become a bar of the same name, also serving humans, at least technically. Bordering the Monkey House (which had a neon sign wired to its bars) were towering ravines of stately redwoods, which most people—even the rough sort who came and went to such Jamestowns—had the good sense to avoid at night. Though the village was more or less peaceful, the woods was where the majority of the bad things around here happened: the usual . . . murders, rapes, robberies. The foliage of the forest would never lack for fertilizer, thanks to the flow of decomposing bodies.

Across the main walkway from the Monkey House, army-navy surplus tents had been pitched around the former zoo's structures, providing temporary shelter for the hundreds of travelers who stayed anywhere from a day to three or four months, depending on their ability—financial and/or physical—to move on.

For the last few weeks, the tent city had been home to a band of barbaric SoCal bikers, descendants of a notorious pre-Pulse biker gang called the Hell's Angels. The New Hellions took their name seriously, were suffused with pride in their mongrel pedigree, and tried to live up to that image every day, in every way.

Strolling at twilight through this nasty-ass post-Pulse slum as if it were a benign street fair was a slim, beautiful, busty black woman with high cheekbones, a wide nose, and huge brown eyes shaded with blue eye shadow; her dark eyebrows curved with an ironic confidence that was no pose and her large, rather puffy Afro had been dressed up with a few pink stripes for good measure.

For a woman alone in a tough town, "Original Cindy" McEachin showed no fear . . . neither did she feel any.

Her pants were a second skin of leather, jet black, with an orange, midriff-baring top so tight it hardly needed the spaghetti straps, showing off not only her flat tummy but the tops of her breasts and bare shoulders, like a dare. Not surprisingly, many males took that dare, this striking female drawing goo-goo-eyed, drop-jawed stares from the few bikers who weren't already in the Monkey House.

You damn well better *be starin',* she thought; her heels were spikes, but she couldn't have moved easier in tennies. *You ain't never seen nothin' like Original Cindy—lookee but no touchee, you barbaric bozos. . . .*

Crossing the walkway, shaking what God had given her, Original Cindy all but bumped into a biker couple exiting the Monkey House.

The burly man's automatic frown flipped into a yellow-green grin when he saw the shapely form he'd almost collided with; he had long, tangled brown hair, which may have been washed at some time or other, and wore only a ragged denim vest with his obligatory jeans and boots. Despite a hairy beer belly, the biker had arms rivaling the trunks of the surrounding sequoias, each bicep tattooed with snakes that curled around and undulated whenever he flexed.

"My bad," Original Cindy drawled.

The guy had slithered one snake arm around his date, a thin little former prom queen in jeans and a black-leather-and-chains halter, with long blond hair, puffy lips, tired blue eyes, and a sultry air about her; drugs and booze had not yet robbed her of all her appeal.

Original Cindy smiled at the woman, who smiled knowingly back.

The big drunk biker, thinking the smile was for him, said, "I jus' might accept that apology, Brown Sugar," and took a step toward Original Cindy . . .

. . . which was a mistake.

The first thing he lost was the blonde. Slipping out from under his snake-embossed bicep, the prom queen said to him, "Screw you and the Harley you rode in on," and stormed off toward the tent city, leaving the biker to stare at Original Cindy.

"Hey, baby," he said flashing that multicolored grin, his speech only a little slurred. "Three's a crowd, anyway."

Original Cindy put her hands on her hips and reared back her Afroed head. "You can't be serious, Haystack—you think I was smilin' at *your* punk ass?"

His forehead clenched as he attempted thought.

Original Cindy continued with his schooling: "I was *smilin'* at the sweet squeeze that went thatta way," one long thin finger pointing in the direction the biker's chick had gone.

His eyes widened and the grin turned upside down. "Jesus! A fuckin' *dyke!*"

He took another step toward her, a menacing one this time; but stopped when Original Cindy dropped into a combat stance.

She asked, "You denigratin' my sexual preference aside . . . you *sure* you wanna go there?"

Cindy had been making her way back to Seattle since she'd gotten out of the army, not so long ago. And a woman, veteran or not, didn't hitch her way from Fort Hood, Texas, unless she knew how to handle her ass.

The drunk biker considered backing down for a moment, but his ego got the better of him and he pulled out his switchblade. The knife opened with a *snick,* long narrow blade finding light to wink off.

But he might have taken out a kazoo and started playing "Yankee Doodle," for all the reaction it got out of Original Cindy, who merely smirked a little.

"Know what they say," she said. "Longer the blade . . ."

The biker wiped several greasy locks of hair out of his eyes. "Y'gonna *really* apologize now, bitch."

She tilted her head and appraised him, as if the biker were fine print she was trying to make out.

"You know," she said, "you done nothin' but call Original Cindy names since we met . . . the 'd' word, the 'b' word . . . and you're just about a consonant away from getting my boot in the crack of your wide honky ass."

His eyes were white all the way around now, and he blurted another epithet—finally getting around to the "c" word—and charged her.

"That's the one . . ." she said, and as he neared, she side-stepped, cracking him along the ear with the back of a fist as he stumbled past her, and kicking him in the ass.

That was the second thing the biker lost: his dignity . . . such as it was.

"God*damn it,"* he roared, one hand going to the reddening ear. "I'm gonna cut you to fuckin' ribbons, you black bitch!"

Her response to this name-calling was nonverbal: with a martial-arts jump, she delivered a perfectly placed, spike-heeled kick to his foul mouth.

The biker dropped like a bag of grain, his knife tumbling from his popped-open fingers and rolling under some bushes, as if trying to get the hell out of this. The big man tried to speak again, but the words came out a mushy mumble mixed with the teeth he was spitting up like undigested corn. Blood streaked down his chin onto his bare, hairy chest in colorful ribbons.

"Ooooh," Original Cindy said, hands on hips again, wincing in feigned disgust. "You do know how to gross a girl out. . . . You wanna call me some more names? You ain't worked your way to 'n' yet. . . . 'Course then I'd have to kill your ass."

Wobbling to his feet, his eyes narrowing with hate, the biker glanced toward the bush where his knife peeked out from under some leaves.

"Now, you don't even wanna think about going for that, do you now? Your mama didn't raise a fool, did she—surely you know when you got your ass kicked?"

The response to this diplomacy was, "Fuck you!"

She waggled her head and waggled a finger, too. "No sir, nada chance, not on your *best* day . . . not even if I got some of that sweet thing you chased off afterward."

Hysterical with fury and embarrassment, the biker lunged for the bushes where his knife awaited. Original Cindy cut off his path and met him with a side kick to the head. Again the biker dropped . . . and this time he stayed down. Breathing—a bubbly saliva-and-blood broth boiling at his broken mouth.

Turning casually toward the tents, Original Cindy thought, *Now where did that fine slice of heaven get herself to?*

But the blonde was nowhere to be seen.

"Damn," Original Cindy said to nobody. "And just when I thought we had us a moment."

Turning back, she went through the open cage doors into the bar. Two things assaulted her immediately: the raucous roar of a bad rock band in the far end of the room—almost twenty years into the twenty-first century and ZZ Top covers still ruled—and the aroma of sandalwood incense laced with monkey shit. Original Cindy decided the smart money was on breathing through her mouth—which meant she would fit right in with this group.

The joint was packed with the sort of lowlifes who made the road their home, and the combination of sweat, liquor, and bad breath was an invitation to be somewhere else. *But Original Cindy ain't no quitter,* she reminded herself, and besides . . . Cindy was parched. She'd been looking forward to a brew even before she worked up a thirst kicking biker ass. So she elbowed her way to the bar.

The band continued to whack away at their instruments the singer caterwauling into a frequently feeding-back mike; but Cindy knew it would take someone with a Ph.D. in classic rock to figure out which ZZ Top song they were currently butchering.

The bartender—a skinny pale pitiful-looking guy with more hair than his comb could handle and two puffy black eyes, courtesy of a dissatisfied customer no doubt—moved in front of her.

"Beer!" she yelled, over the din of the band and the crowd.

He nodded and walked away.

She wheeled to have a look at the predominantly biker crowd. Last time Original Cindy had seen this much denim and leather in one place had been at a rodeo near Fort Hood. This was nothing like that . . . thank God; even the bikers were an improvement over the shit-kicker cowboys in Texas. Original Cindy was not prejudiced, but she had little patience for rednecks.

Or for redneck bands like this one—two guitars, a bass, drums, and a druggie vocalist in search of the key; they sounded like marbles twirled in a garbage can with a couple of fornicating cats thrown in for good measure.

Original Cindy was still shaking her head in disbelief at the sorry state of her cultural and social life at this particular moment, when the shiner-adorned bartender came back with a cold bottle of beer. She got a three-dollar bill out of her wallet—President James on it, appropriately—and the bartender snatched the bill from her fingers.

"Damn!" she said. "Go on and help your damn self, why don't you?"

The bartender walked away.

"No wonder you a damn raccoon," she mumbled, then: "Keep the change, Prince Charmin'!" . . . even though she knew he'd already assumed as much.

She sipped at the beer, hoping to make it last. At these prices being sober was looking like a reasonable option. Besides, this joint with that band and these patrons wasn't worth more than one beer and fifteen minutes of her life. No one who shared her particular worldview seemed to frequent this establishment, and if she didn't want more biker run-ins, the best bet would be to drink up and get the hell out of this zoo.

She swigged her suds and, considering this was Original Cindy anyway, kept a low profile. Nonetheless, the bikers stared at her, making her more uncomfortable than she would care to admit.

She wasn't afraid—hell, nothing scared her, except maybe life itself; but thirty bikers to one black ex-soldier seemed like shitty odds. Killing the beer, she turned toward the door just as the biker she'd pounded came staggering in, drunk (more from her beating than beer), his mouth twisted in an angry snarl, blood still trailing down his chin like a sloppy vampire.

"*Now* you get yours, you black bitch," he bellowed, though the words came out slurred and mushy because he was drunk and no longer had all his teeth.

The band kept playing; but every eye in the bar had already turned to the door, and now swiveled to Original Cindy. After all, no one in here had missed her entrance. . . .

"Oh, maaaan . . . I thought I was done with your sorry ass," she said, and looked around at the other patrons, to court their support. Once a fight was finished, the fight was finished, right? Get on with your damn lives!

But the bikers were closing into a loose semicircle around her, putting the bar at her back, leaving a path for the drunk to get to her.

Again the burly biker edged toward her, and he had that damn blade in his hand again. The circle began to close in, providing a compact stage for the coming action.

So she struck first, picking up the beer bottle and smashing it over the head of the nearest biker, who collapsed in a heap. The band finally noticed that no one was listening to them and stopped playing, providing an awful, deathly silence.

Original Cindy tore a hole in it: *"You want some more of Original Cindy?"* She gestured to herself with both hands, entering the center of the circle, oozing bravado, saying, "Then come on—plenty to go 'round!"

Unfortunately for her, they took her invitation.

There was little room to maneuver, this close to the bar, and although she got one biker across the bridge of the nose with a straight right, and another in the groin with a knee, it was only a matter of time before the bikers had swarmed her, pinning her on the floor like a dead butterfly in a collector's book. They held her down, tight, spread-eagled, and took turns copping obnoxious feels until the burly bastard she'd already defeated outside now fought his way through the crowd.

"You ain't so cocky now, are ya, bitch?"

She glared up at him, playing the only card she had. "You gutless pussy—afraid to take on a girl by your ownself? Gotta have your buddies hold her down?"

He leaned over and slapped her and it sounded like a gunshot, ringing off the cement of the former monkey house, and her head exploded in pain accompanied by colorful starbursts.

"I'm about to accept your *apology*, bitch. . . ."

Spitting blood up into his face, Original Cindy said, "I *told* you to stop callin' me that!"

He reared back a snake-draped arm to hit her again, but before he could strike, a small hand gripped the biker's thick wrist.

The olive-skinned young woman in black leather jacket and pants was petite if shapely, and she had slipped through the circle of bikers without anyone thinking to stop her. Those who'd noticed merely admired her lithe yet voluptuous figure; a few others were amused to see such a little thing walk out into the center ring of this circus.

But now they all froze, including Original Cindy's antagonist, whose nostrils flared and eyes widened, as he turned to see who dared interrupt him—and who it was that belonged to the viselike grip on his wrist.

"Walk away," the young woman advised him.

"You . . . gotta . . . be . . . *kiddin,*" the biker said, upper lip peeling back over a smile that now had a few holes in it.

The young woman smiled back. From the floor where the other bikers still had her pinned, Original Cindy basked in the radiance of the stranger's smile, expecting the sweet thing to soon be joining her on the floor, where together they'd pull a horrible biker train. . . .

"Yeah," the young woman said, little smile, little shrug. "I'm just kiddin' around."

Still holding on to his wrist, the black-clad girl thrust a sideways kick that caught the biker behind the knee, and sent him to the floor, kneeling hard. From her awkward vantage, Original Cindy couldn't focus on what happened next.

The leather-clad woman became a dervish, striking, spinning, striking again, again, kicks knocking the bikers every which way. Suddenly finding herself free, Cindy jumped to her feet, catching only the blur as her unlikely rescuer threw dropkicks and fists into one biker after another, like a damn Bruce Lee movie; but that burly biker who'd started it all was getting onto his feet, that knife still in one hand.

Original Cindy slammed a small hard fist into the side of his head and sent him down, even as the girl in leather threw a casual kick sideways, knocking the knife from the man's grasp. The biker was still on his feet, but groggy; Original Cindy doubled him over with a knee in the groin, and his mouth gaped in a silent scream until she closed it for him with a hard right.

And for the second time tonight, the big biker with the tiny mind fell to the floor barely conscious, spitting teeth like seeds.

In less than thirty seconds, the only people still standing in the bar were the band, the bartender, and the two women. The others were in various stages of semiconsciousness, moaning, rolling into fetal balls, a few crawling off, looking for a corner to bleed in.

"I'm Max," the young woman said.

"Original Cindy."

Max raised a fist and Original Cindy touched it with a fist of her own; neither had even bloodied a knuckle in the brawl. The bartender was smiling—maybe whoever had given him his shiners had gone down in this melee; he handed the two victors cold-sweating beers and held his palms up: no charge.

Toasting with the brew, Max said, "You can handle yourself, girl."

"Sister girl," Original Cindy said as she surveyed the damage, "you got a move or two your ownself."

"Think maybe we should bounce?"

"Yeah, things've kinda died down around the ol' Monkey House, don't you think?"

"A little dull?"

"I don't think these people wanna party no more."

Winding casually through the casualties, the two women walked out of the bar.

"Those peckerwoods are lucky you come along," Original Cindy said, hitching her shoulders.

Max gave her an amused sideways glance. "They're lucky?"

"Oh yeah—jus' 'fore you stuck your teeny nose in, I was about to bust loose on their asses, and cause some serious harm."

Max laughed lightly. "You shoulda said somethin'—I wouldn'ta spoiled your fun."

"How did you even know to come in?"

"I don't know—I can sorta smell trouble."

"Original Cindy hears that—'specially when there's that much of it and it smells that rank."

The night seemed suddenly chilly to Original Cindy, and she hugged herself. Max slipped out of her jacket, revealing a baby blue, well-filled sleeveless T-shirt, and passed the leather garment to Cindy.

Who said, "Thanks," and pulled the coat on.

"We probably shouldn't hang around here."

"All bullshit aside, girl, we best watch our asses in this Jamestown, else we get caps popped in 'em."

Max stopped in front of a sleek black motorcycle. "This is my ride—you got wheels?"

"This is Original Cindy's wheels." She held up a thumb. "My stuff is hidden in the woods."

"Stuff?"

"You think these is the only clothes Original Cindy owns?" She grinned. "Got me some stylin' threads out there in them woods."

"Can you find your stash in the dark?"

"Does the pope shit in the woods? Is a bear Catholic?"

Max laughed and threw a leg over the bike. "Climb on, O. C.—we'll get your stash and put some distance between us and that biker brain trust."

"You don't have to tell Original Cindy twice." She climbed on behind Max, her arms locking around the middle of the leather-clad rider.

Max turned the key, gunned the bike, and, kicking a dirt cloud, took off into the forest. They picked up Original Cindy's backpack from its hiding place and hit the road. Max kept the speedometer pegged at nearly one hundred, making conversation impossible until they stopped at a small, roadside coffee shop on the far side of Redwood National Park.

Clean by post-Pulse standards, the place had six booths along one wall, a counter with a dozen or so stools, and behind the back counter a wall with a pass-through window to the tiny kitchen. At this hour, the cook and the waitress were the only people in the place; they sat next to each other at the counter, each reading a section of newspaper. Wearing a white T-shirt and blue jeans, the cook rose when they came in. A paunchy man in his late forties, with bug eyes and greasy dark hair, he moved back toward the kitchen without a word. The waitress wore tan slacks and a brown smock. She had short dark hair, a birdlike body, and a drawn, cowhide-tough face. She stayed put until the women had chosen a booth.

"Coffee, you two?" she asked as she rose.

They both said, "Yes."

The waitress moved quickly for someone in the middle of a graveyard shift and gave them each a cup of coffee and a glass of water. "You ready to order?"

"This is fine for now," Max said.

Original Cindy said, "Yeah, me too."

Nodding, the waitress returned to her seat and picked up the paper. "False alarm, Jack!"

The guy in the kitchen came back out and picked up his paper, too; this time though, he stayed on his side of the counter.

"Original Cindy just wanted to thank you for steppin' in tonight." Sitting forward, she leaned across the booth and patted Max on the hand. "A sistah coulda looked at them odds and walked the hell right back out the door."

Shaking her head, Max said, "Wouldn't do for sistahs to be lettin' each other bump uglies with the likes of those dickweeds."

"They ain't Original Cindy's . . . type anyway."

"Low-life bikers."

"Dickweeds."

Max gave her a look.

Original Cindy explained what had started the altercation with the biker—namely, the blonde. Watching Max carefully, she said, "You gotta do what floats your boat."

"None of my business," Max said, "where people put their paddles."

Original Cindy smiled and Max gave her half a smile back. They sat and sipped their coffee for a while, letting the silence grow, both of them comfortable with it.

Finally, Original Cindy sat forward again, saying, "What the hell *was* that back there, girl?"

Max shrugged, playing it low-key. "What was what?"

Original Cindy made a couple of mock Kung Fu hand gestures. "That Jet Li, Jackie Chan action—what was up with that?"

Another shrug. Avoiding eye contact, Max said, "Had some training."

The other woman waggled a finger. "No, girl, no no. . . . Original Cindy was in the army and *she* had some training, can take of herself . . . but *whew,* nothin' like what was goin' on in that bar."

Max stared into her coffee. "Let's just say I'm a good student."

"You wanna leave it at that?"

Max held her coffee cup in both hands, as if warming them. "You don't mind?"

"That's cool. That's where we leave it then."

A smile blossomed on the heart-shaped face. "Thanks."

"*You* thankin' *me?* That's whack."

"If you say so."

"Anyway, Original Cindy just wants to say she owes you big-time."

This seemed to embarrass Max, who said offhandedly, "I was just jealous, all the attention you were getting."

"Well, you my girl now—you need anything, anytime, Original Cindy got your back."

Max saluted her with a coffee cup, and said seriously, "That's good to know."

"From now on you my Boo."

Max frowned, and looked vaguely nervous. "I, uh . . . thought I made it clear I don't go that way."

Original Cindy cracked up, the laughter bubbling out of her; but Max just studied her.

"Bein' a Boo ain't about . . . *that,* Max—it's about bein' stand-up, it's about I got your back, you got mine . . . it's about bein' tight. You my Boo."

A natural smile blossomed on Max's lovely face. "Well, then . . . you're my Boo . . . too."

The rhyme came out awkward, and made Original Cindy start laughing again, and this time Max got caught on the wave, and the two young women just sat there and giggled for maybe a minute.

Then Original Cindy extended a fist, which Max bumped with her own.

The waitress brought them refills on the coffee, an act that served as a time-out. When the waitress left, the two women sipped and talked, the conversation shifting gears.

"So," Original Cindy said, "where you headed?"

"Seattle."

"No kiddin'?"

Max looked at her curiously. "Shouldn't I be?"

"No, girl, it's just . . . I'm headed home myself."

"Seattle is home?"

"One of 'em. Spent some time in the Emerald City."

Max's eyes tightened in confusion. "Emerald City?"

"Yeah, that's what the peeps used to call Seattle back before the Pulse. You know . . . like *Wizard of Oz*?"

Max got a funny expression on her face. "I've heard of that. . . ."

" 'Course you have!" Original Cindy looked at Max like the girl was speaking Esperanto. "Who hasn't seen the best movie ever made?"

"Me," Max admitted.

"Back in the old days, every kid saw that movie."

"Well . . . I had a kind of sheltered childhood."

"Oooh, Boo, we got to introduce you to the *finer* things."

Grinning, Max said, "I'm up for that."

"Look, chile, here's the dealio: Original Cindy needs a ride to Seattle . . . and you're already goin' that way."

Max looked into her cup. "I need to haul. I'm sort of . . . meeting someone there."

"Haulin' ass is fine with Original Cindy. The sooner we get there, the sooner we're there . . . right?"

Max's eyes widened but she also smiled. "How can I argue with that logic? . . . Let's blaze, Boo."

Original Cindy's face exploded in a smile. "Boo, the Emerald City ain't never been hit by a pair of witches *this* fine. . . ."

Going inland and traveling on the interstate might have been faster, but Max still took precautions to avoid any possible contact with Manticore; so they kept to the winding PCH and moseyed up the coast at a leisurely eighty-five to ninety miles per hour.

They stopped only for food and the call of nature—and to gas up the bike, which at eight or nine bucks a gallon was burning a hole in her bankroll, as Max had known it would. The roar of the motorcycle and the wind kept conversation to a minimum, but the two young women somehow knew that each had finally found the sort of friend they needed.

There weren't a lot of questions about each other's past; instinctively they both knew the other had secrets not for sharing. Nevertheless, they just sort of fell in together and the start of their friendship felt like they were already in the middle of it.

The last five hundred miles of the trip flew by and before they knew it, Max and Original Cindy were tooling through the streets of Seattle, still a striking city despite the squalor of post-Pulse life.

"Everything's so green," Max said, over her shoulder.

"That's why it's the Emerald City, Dorothy girl."

"Dorothy?"

"Boo, you ain't got no sense of culture whatsoever."

"I might surprise you, Cin. . . ."

At Fourth and Blanchard, Max eased the Ninja over to the curb in front of a place called Buck's Coffee. The sign looked as though it used to have four letters before the B, but they couldn't be made out.

"Caffeine calling," Max said.

"Original Cindy hears it, too."

Inside, the pair of striking women walked up to the counter behind which stood a heavyset man barely taller than Max, a lascivious grin forming on his fat, five-o'clock-shadowed face. At a counter behind him, a blowsily attractive blond woman about their age—wearing knee-high pink boots, a blue miniskirt, and a pink top that bared both her midriff and most of her formidable chest—hovered over a sandwich in the making.

"Ladies, don't even bother orderin' no frappes, lattes, cappuccinos," he said. Staring at Original Cindy, he added, "I serve my coffee just like I like my women—hot and black."

The blue-cheeked guy seemed proud of himself, under the illusion he had minted this deathless phrase.

Max could tell that Original Cindy was considering jumping the counter to bitch-slap the white right off this horse's ass; so Max gently said, "Come on, Boo—let's go someplace where we can get a grande."

"Yeah . . . instead of the limp mini this mope is peddlin'."

Max giggled, and the blonde toward the back giggled, too . . . but the counter guy did not laugh; in fact, he reddened and fumed.

He started to say something, but Original Cindy cut him off with a wave of a finger accompanied by a sway of the head and shoulders. "Don't hate the playah, baby . . . hate the game."

Max and Original Cindy bumped fists and the blond woman laughed out loud.

The counter guy turned on her. "You know what's really funny? A skank like you lookin' for a new job in this market, is what's *really* funny."

The blonde fell silent.

"Hey," Max said, taking a step toward the counter.

"Butt out," the counter man said. "This ain't no concern of yours. And you . . ." He turned to the blonde. ". . . you're movin' on to bigger and better things. Get your fat butt outa here!"

Max leapt the counter, landing between the blonde and the counter guy, who was startled and a little afraid by this sudden impressive move. "Hire her back."

"What do you—"

Max lifted him up by the throat; his eyes were bulging as he stared down at her, too afraid and in too much discomfort to be properly amazed by the petite woman lifting him gently off the ground, a fact neither Original Cindy nor the put-upon blonde picked up on.

The blonde touched Max's arm. "It's all right . . . he can't fire me, 'cause I quit. . . . I'm tired of workin' for this sexual-harasshole."

"Good call," Original Cindy said.

Max shrugged and put the guy down.

He was leaning over the counter, red-faced, choking, when the three women strolled out onto the street together. They stood at the curb, near Max's bike, and chatted.

"My name's Kendra Maibaum," the blonde said, extending her hand.

•

Max shook it. "Max Guevera—and this lovely lady is Original Cindy."

"Pleased," Original Cindy said and shook hands with Kendra too.

"How did you do that?" Kendra asked. "Handle Morty like that, I mean."

Original Cindy raised her eyebrows, smirking. "Girl had training."

Max at that moment realized she would have to watch herself, from now on—she had been entirely too careless around Original Cindy.

"Training but no coffee," Max said. Her X5 skills would have to be better concealed. "And we haven't even started *talkin'* about findin' a place to crash."

Kendra asked, "You guys need a place to crash?"

"We're kind of new in town," Original Cindy explained.

"Like five minutes new," Max added.

The blonde shrugged. "If you don't need a lot of space, you can stay with me. I've got a place. Room enough for two, maybe three."

Original Cindy glanced at Max, who shrugged, asking, "Why would you do that for us? You don't know us from no-body."

Kendra gestured toward the coffee shop. "You stood up for me with Morty."

"Cost you your job, you mean," Max reminded her.

Laughing, Kendra said, "Yeah, but it was worth it, seein' Morty, scared shitless . . . and, anyway, that job sucked. Besides, it wasn't my only means of income."

"Workin' girl?" Original Cindy asked, again glancing at the pink top filled to the brim and the postage-stamp miniskirt.

Kendra's hands went to her hips. "Why would you ask that?" She didn't sound hurt, exactly—more surprised.

Original Cindy's eyes widened. Max frowned at her friend, who said nothing about the former waitress's provocative attire, merely saying. "Uh . . . uh, don't know, girl, it just sounded like maybe you, uh . . ."

"Oh, I work a lot . . . but not at that. I do some translating, language training, transcription work. I've done a buncha things, but never that."

"Sorry—Original Cindy didn't mean no offense."

Kendra shook her head. "Not to worry. Anyway, 'fyou guys need a place to crash, I've got room."

"Sweet," Max said. "Where?"

"Not far."

"Walking distance? I hope so, 'cause it's gonna be a bitch gettin' three of us on my bike."

"Oh yeah," Kendra said, with a dismissive wave, "easy walking distance."

They wound up walking for most of the next hour, Max pushing the Ninja, Original Cindy lugging her backpack, but they didn't complain—after all, a roof was a roof. But Max didn't know quite what to make of Kendra. For a woman who knew languages well enough to work as a translator, the blonde seemed remarkably like a clueless airhead.

Nice one, though.

Finally, when Original Cindy gave Max a rolling-eyed look, signaling she was sure she was about to drop, Kendra said, "That's it over there! Told ya it was close." And pointed to an apartment building two doors up and across the street.

The building didn't look like much, six stories, most of the windows plywood-covered; and, as they got closer, a piece of paper tacked to the front door became all too evident.

"The place is *condemned?*" Original Cindy asked.

Kendra shrugged a little. "Not really condemned—more like . . . abandoned."

They got to the door and Original Cindy studied the notice on the door. "Original Cindy ain't no translator, but she reads English . . . and this says 'condemned.' "

Shaking her head dismissively, Kendra said, "That's just to keep out the, you know, riffraff."

Max asked, "How many people live here?"

Kendra shrugged. "Fifty or so."

"Fifty?" Original Cindy blurted. "Fifty people live in a

condemned building? Thank God you're keepin' out the riffraff!"

"Come on in, girls," Kendra said. "You'll see—it's not that bad. Really."

When the trio got to the fourth floor—up a freight-style elevator, Max walking her Ninja along—Max and Original Cindy discovered that Kendra was right. Like the building itself, the apartment was unfinished, a study in taped drywall and plastic-tarp room dividers; but the place had running water, two bedrooms, and some decent secondhand furniture. They all crashed in the tiny living room area, Kendra in a chair covered with a blue sheet, and the other two on a swayback couch covered with a paisley sheet.

"Kendra, you right," Original Cindy said, leaning back, getting comfy. "Kickin' crib."

"And nobody bothers you in here?" Max asked.

Kendra made a small face. "Well . . . there's Eastep."

"What's an Eastep?" Max asked.

"He's a cop. Who collects from all us squatters."

"He's crooked?"

Kendra smiled a little. "I said he was a cop."

"They *all* bent in Seattle, honey," Original Cindy said to Max; then to Kendra, she asked, "What's the goin' rate?"

"Too much," Kendra said, and proved it by telling them.

"Ouch," Max said, but asked, "Are there any empty apartments left in this building?"

With a shake of her blond mane, Kendra said, "None fit for humans. Hot and cold running rats . . . holes in the walls, missing ceilings . . . no water, no electricity . . . you name it, they've got the problems. All the habitable apartments have been taken."

"Great," Max muttered. She turned to Original Cindy. "Any ideas?"

"Original Cindy's got a friend she could stay with for a while." She shrugged regretfully. "But girlfriend's only got room for one more. . . . We got to think of somethin' else, Boo."

"No you don't," Kendra said. "You two have to live together?"

The two women looked at each other.

"Not really," they said in unison.

"You aren't a couple?"

"We friends," Original Cindy said.

"Just friends," Max said, overlapping Cindy's answer.

"Fine," Kendra said. "Max, if Original Cindy's got a place to crash, why don't you move in here? I could seriously use some help payin' Eastep's rent . . . and it'd be nice to have somebody to talk to. But I just don't have enough room for all three of us."

"Sounds prime," Original Cindy said. "My friend's place ain't that far from here; she was sort of expectin' me, anyway. We can still hang, Boo. No big dealio."

Max looked back and forth from Original Cindy to Kendra. Finally, she said, "Cool—let's do it."

"Next thing," Original Cindy said, "we got to find a way to get some cash."

Screwing up her face, Max said, "You mean like a job?"

"What else you gonna do, Boo . . . steal for a livin'?"

Max said nothing.

Kendra perked up, getting an idea. "We should go talk to Theo!"

The two women turned to her.

"Theo?" Max asked.

"Yeah, he lives next door with his wife, Jacinda, and their kid, cute kid, Omar. Place Theo works is *always* looking for help."

Max and Original Cindy exchanged glances—that was a rarity in this economy.

Original Cindy said, "Well, let's not keep the man waitin' . . . Original Cindy needs some money, honey, to allow her to live in the high style she's become accustomed to. . . . Luxuries, like eatin' and breathin' an' shit."

Kendra led the way and they knocked on the door to the adjacent apartment. A tiny, knee-high face peeked out, his eyes big and brown, his skin a dark bronze.

"Omar, is your daddy home?"

The adorable face nodded.

"Can we come in?"

Omar looked over his shoulder and a female voice said, "That you, Kendra?"

"Yeah, Jacinda—I've got a couple of friends with me. They're cool."

"Well, come on in, then."

Stepping back, Omar, who couldn't have been more than five, opened the door for the three women.

Max took in the apartment, which looked a lot like Kendra's. A thin black woman in a brown T-shirt and tan slacks stood in front of the couch, an Asian man—shorter than his wife, his hair black, his eyes sparkling, his smile wide—standing next to her.

"Jacinda, Theo," Kendra said, "this is Cindy and Max."

"Original Cindy," the woman corrected.

"Original Cindy. They both need jobs and I thought maybe Theo could hook them up."

The smile never faded as he waved for the women to sit down on the couch. Jacinda moved to a chair with Omar climbing into her lap, Theo standing next to them, a hand on his wife's shoulder.

"There's been a ton of turnover lately," he said. "It's a hard job . . . very physical, and you go into dangerous parts of the city, sometimes. Lots of times."

Original Cindy asked, "What kinda job we talkin' about, Theo? Repairing power lines? Filling in potholes?"

The smiling Asian asked, "Either of you young women ever been a bike messenger?"

They looked at each other and shook their heads.

Theo asked, "You *got* bikes?"

Max half grinned. "I do—Ninja, two-fifty."

Theo's smile actually grew wider. "Bi*cycles*. Either of you have a bicycle?"

"No," Original Cindy said.

"But we will by tomorrow morning," Max said.

Original Cindy looked at her disbelievingly, but Theo took it in stride, his smile unfailing.

"Excellent," he said. "You can go in with me. The place is

called Jam Pony Xpress. Normal, the fella that runs it, he's a bit uptight . . . but he's not evil. Pay's lousy, hours are worse; but the other riders are a nice, easygoing group."

"Original Cindy's up for givin' it a shot, least till somethin' better comes along."

"What is it exactly we'd be doing?" Max asked the Asian.

Original Cindy answered for him. "We ride around on bikes delivering packages to different places, what else?"

"I don't know anything about the city," Max said.

"You will, Boo, you will. Original Cindy'll show you the way. Middle next week, you be tellin' taxi drivers how to get around this town and shit."

Theo said, "Bike messengers cover the whole city. Very interesting . . . they see everything and everyone in Seattle."

That made Max smile.

"What you thinkin', Boo?" Original Cindy asked.

"I'm thinking we were lucky to meet Kendra," Max said, "and luckier to meet Theo."

But she was thinking: *Bike messenger. Ride all around town . . . an invisible person, wheeling here, there, everywhere. . . . That could work.*

That could work. . . .

Chapter Six
MONEY TALKS

Housed in a run-down warehouse, a world of dented lockers and rough wood beams and ancient brick and obscene graffiti, Jam Pony Xpress turned out to be just the sort of madhouse where Max could blend in and lie low, while she looked for her sibling.

Having had the whole trip up the coast to replay that grainy video in the theater of her mind, Max was now a gnat's eyelash away from convincing herself that the "young rebel" she'd seen kicking cop ass on that news show was indeed her brother Seth.

The X5 didn't know how long it would take to find him, but this innocuous cover was looking like it could work for the long haul: no one, not even Moody or Fresca or any of the Chinese Clan, had any idea she'd booked for Seattle. Dodging Manticore all these years had given her very few peaceful nights of sleep; but somehow here—in Original Cindy's Emerald City—Max felt safer, more underground even than in LA, where she'd drawn attention to herself and her singular abilities by her cat-burglar activities.

As Original Cindy had predicted, the bike messenger gig allowed Max to learn the city at a far faster rate than if she'd just been bouncing around on the Ninja, hoping to get lucky in her search for Seth. Living with Kendra in the off-the-books apartment was working out just fine, too, though the rent was a bitch, thanks to that greedy bent cop.

But living in a squatter's hotel was perfect: no sign of Max would appear anywhere in the city records, and amiable air-head Kendra was easy to live with and was turning into a good friend.

At the same time, Max's friendship had grown with Original Cindy, cemented by Max staking Cindy for the cost of the bike you needed to even apply at Jam Pony. The two women were spending almost every leisure moment together, with Kendra frequently in the mix.

Original Cindy had found her own pad, after only a week at Jam Pony. Not only was she more independent, her crib was closer to Max's apartment than the friend's place she'd initially crashed at. Every morning Max would hook up with Theo, then bounce over on their bicycles to pick up Original Cindy, and the three of them would ride together. They would get coffee and bagels, stop in a park on the way and eat, then wheel on in to work.

It was during these light, chatty breakfasts that Original Cindy, Max, and Theo started getting to know more about each other. Max knew she was learning a lot more about her friends than they were finding out about her, and sometimes she could feel Cindy's hurt vibe that Max was remaining overly secretive.

But since O. C. and Theo didn't seem to be genetically enhanced killing machines, developed in a supersecret government lab, they had a tad fewer secrets than she did.

A month had glided by since Max had left Moody and the Chinese Clan, and the only thing she had to complain about (to herself, that is) was that she hadn't found Seth . . . hadn't even turned up a lead. Even the news had been devoid of any mention of the "young rebel" in league with "Eyes Only."

Of course, as good as Max was at looking, Seth would be better at hiding. He'd had the same training as her, and—like Max—had been on the run a long time, knew how to cover his tracks far better than she knew how to uncover them. After years of running and hiding, Max found it difficult to turn the process around, to look through the hunter's end of the telescope.

One thing was for sure: she would never give up. A

relentlessness was bred into her—whether by Manticore or her own human genes, she could not say. She just knew she would find Seth.

The only doubt that managed to creep in, from time to time, was the notion that she might be wasting her time, chasing someone who—though a remarkable specimen, and similar to her—wasn't really an X5.

Even worse was the possibility that this might be one of Lydecker's X5s, the star of some later Manticore graduating class, doing covert work the media was playing up as the work of a "rebel." . . .

In the meantime, Max found herself in the midst of a new life, and even a new family—some of these other Jam Pony riders were all right.

The nominal boss, however, Normal—whose work moniker was an improvement over his real name, Reagan Ronald—had turned out to be just as uptight as Theo had claimed. Conservative to the bone, a fan of both Bush presidencies, the oblong-faced, perpetually distracted Normal—with his long straight nose, thin lips, and headset that seemed as much a part of him as his hands or ears—wore his brownish blond hair short and combed back, his black-frame glasses and constant frown making him look like a sad librarian.

Normal considered Max and his other employees a bunch of slacker losers, which hardly inspired the best in them. Constantly saying, "Bip, bip, bip," his secret code for "hurry up," hadn't gained him any new friends either; neither had his favorite, painful pseudo-expletive—"Where the fire truck is . . . ?" Fill in your favorite Jam Pony rider, like for example . . .

. . . Herbal Thought, a Rastafarian with a shaved head, short beard, and ready smile, a generous and philosophical instant friend. Frustratingly cheerful, he was always ready to share anything he had—even his ganja, which Max took a pass on—as well as to proselytize for Jah and the theory, "It's all good, all de time."

The other messenger who befriended Max and Original Cindy, from day one, was a scarecrow with long, lank, black hair, greasy strands of which trailed down over his dark eyes. Sketchy, they all called him—a nickname that applied more to his thought processes than any artistic ability.

More than a little weird ("He the lost Three Stooge," Original Cindy opined), Sketchy had sold himself out for experiments in a psych lab before he'd signed on at Jam Pony, and many of his friends thought that might explain his somewhat odd . . . sketchy . . . behavior.

Today, like most days, the four of them—Max, Original Cindy, Sketchy, and Herbal—were taking their lunch break at The Wall up the street from Jam Pony, a cement slab where the gang hung out, doing bike tricks and generally chilling. Here they sat and wolfed sub sandwiches from a nearby shop. Herbal passed on having a sandwich, however; his main course was a spliff he lit up—not much bigger than Max's thumb—and inhaled deeply.

"Ah, 'tis a gift from God," Herbal said, as he leaned blissfully back against the table.

"I should become a Rasta," Sketchy piped in, admiringly. "That's my kinda sacrament."

Herbal shook his head and made a *tsk tsk* at the front of his mouth. "Ah, but worshiping Jah is not about the ganja, man. Worshiping Jah is about faith . . . faith and growth."

"Growin' ganja," Original Cindy said, and they all laughed, including the Rastafarian.

The strong scent tickled Max's nose. "No wonder you think it's 'all good,' " she said.

"Hey," Sketchy said brightly, as if the idea he was about to express weren't something he suggested every day, "who's up for Crash after work?"

"Original Cindy could be up—how 'bout you, Boo?"

Max shrugged. "Guess I could hang for a while."

The nature of the job—each rider out doing his or her own deliveries—prevented them from tiring of one another's company by the end of a long day; they enjoyed gathering to tell war stories, share anecdotes about Normal, and swap tales of tricky deliveries and asshole clients.

"Cool!" Sketchy turned to Herbal. "You?"

"If my brother and sisters need me to be there, you know Herbal will indeed be there."

"Don't refer to yourself in the third person, my brother," Original Cindy said, frowning. "Original Cindy don't dig that affected shit."

Everybody looked at her, not sure whether she was kidding; and they never found out.

"Okay," Sketchy said, eyes glittering, proud of himself for organizing something that happened almost every day. "We all meet at Crash!"

"Sounds like a plan," Max said, rising, only half her sandwich eaten. "Gotta bounce—Normal's loaded me up with every shit delivery that came in today."

Original Cindy shrugged, smirked. "He jus' knows you can go into any nasty part of town, and come out with your ass in one piece."

Sketchy frowned in fragmented thought. "Wouldn't that be . . . two pieces?"

Max left them to argue that one out.

Over the course of the afternoon, she made four deliveries. The first was to a place way the hell up on Hamlin Street, by Portage Bay; the next on the way back on East Aloha Street, just off Twenty-third Avenue East; the third on Boylston near Broadway; and the last turned out to be the Sublime Laundry, downtown.

The place—a combo Laundromat and dry cleaner—looked less than sublime, and too dingy to launder anything except maybe money. The Asian woman behind the counter was about as friendly as a Manticore training officer. Shorter than Max, her black hair tied back in a severe bun, the woman had a raisin face with raisin eyes, and a mistrustful expression.

"Package for Vogelsang," Max announced.

"I take."

"I kinda don't think you're Daniel Vogelsang."

"I take."

"Mr. Vogelsang has to sign—it's marked confidential, and only Mr. Vogelsang can sign for it."

"I take."

Max glanced at the ceiling, rolled her eyes, and thought *the hell with it.* "Look, if Mr. Vogelsang isn't here, I'll just have to come back another time."

"I take."

"You *can't* take, you aren't him and you can't sign." Max turned on her heels and headed for the door, the woman's language of choice moving from English to Chinese, her vocabulary expanding considerably from the two words Max had previously heard.

Max had enough Chinese training to know that some of the names she was being called should earn the woman a chance to have her mouth washed out with soap, and even in this shithole laundry, soap wasn't in short supply. . . .

But Max was learning to choose her battles more wisely, these days—attracting attention in Seattle was not on the itinerary.

As she reached the door, a male voice behind her boomed: "Ahm Wei, what the hell's going on out here?"

Max turned to see a heavyset man with blond crew-cut hair, mild features, and a goatee on a droopy-eyed bucket head, wearing baggy slacks and a Hawaiian slept-in shirt.

"She got package," Ahm Wei said. "She no leave."

"Ahm Wei, you know when they need my signature, you're supposed to come get me. . . . Young lady! Hold up there."

Max sighed and swiveled. "You Vogelsang?"

"Could be."

"You take?" Max mimicked, her patience growing thin, holding out the package. "If you're Vogelsang, this package is marked confidential, which means it has to be signed for personally. No tickee, no laundry, get it?"

"Punk-ass mouth on you," the guy muttered. "Yeah, yeah, yeah, I'm Vogelsang. Come on in back—I don't do my business out here."

Already tired of this rigmarole, but not wanting to have to deal with Normal about the rejected package, Max let out another world-weary sigh and followed Vogelsang through double doors into a cramped office. Max's trained eyes automatically took it all in: washer parts, jugs of dry-cleaning chemicals, unidentified stacks of boxes, typical backroom stuff.

But centrally, in front of a wall of battered file cabinets stacked with more boxes and papers, a maple desk squatted, arrayed with piles of papers, the occasional Twinkie box, and empty Chinese takeout containers . . . a swivel chair behind the desk, a comfortable client's chair opposite, beige walls adorned with bulletin boards bearing police circulars and such . . . *what was this place?*

Max handed the frumpy bear of a man the signature pad, he put on reading glasses and signed where he'd been told, and she asked, "What the hell do you do back here?"

"Private investigations."

Her eyes widened a little. "You're a detective, huh? . . . What *kind* of investigations?"

He handed her the clipboard, she handed him the package, wrapped in brown paper; it was a little smaller than a shoe box.

"You know, divorces, runaways, skip trace, stuff like that." He finally tore his eyes from the package and looked up at her—in his business, even invisible people like messengers rated a once-over. "Why?"

"If I was looking for someone, you could find them."

"I could try."

Without an invitation, she eased into the chair opposite Vogelsang, hooked a leg over its arm. "So—what's something like that cost?"

Vogelsang stroked his bearded chin, the package all but forgotten; tossed his glasses on the desk and took the chair back there. "Depends."

"That's a great answer."

"Depends on who we're looking for . . . and how much they don't want to be found."

A sour feeling blossomed in Max's stomach. Already, she could see where this was heading: money. She'd been living the straight life since she and Original Cindy had landed in Seattle, hadn't pulled a single score; and to tell the truth, she sort of liked it. But she had to find her sibs.

"All right, Mr. Vogelsang—give me an estimate."

Big shoulders made a tiny shrug. "Thousand-dollar retainer against two hundred a day . . . plus expenses."

She rolled her eyes. "You high? I'm a freakin' bike messenger!"

He shrugged, putting the reading glasses back on, his attention returning to the package.

"This office isn't exactly uptown," Max pointed out. "How can you charge rates like that?"

"The uptown offices don't have my downtown connections. . . . The private eye game is a dirty one."

"So you set up shop behind a laundry."

He peered at her over the reading glasses. "Are we done here?"

"Okay, Mr. Vogelsang . . . let's say I get you the money. . . ."

He threw the glasses on the desk again. "You got that kind of cash?"

"I can get it."

"Little girl like you."

"Don't pry into *my* business, Mr. Vogelsang."

"I won't." He grinned at her; he was like a big naughty hound dog. "Unless somebody pays me to. . . ."

"If they do, I'll double whatever they give you. I'd be buying loyalty, as well as discretion."

The detective was studying her, taking in her confident manner, her youth obviously troubling him.

She brushed by that, asking, "How long to get results?"

"This is a missing person?"

"Yes."

"Without much information to go on?"

"If I had information, I wouldn't need you, would I?"

Another tiny shrug from the big shoulders. "Searching for people is not an exact science, uh . . . what's your name?"

"Max."

"Just Max?"

"That a problem?"

"Not if you pay in cash."

"Count on it."

The private eye shrugged. "Could be a day, could be never. When your retainer is exhausted, we'll talk. Decide if you're throwing good money after bad. I'm not a thief, Max."

She mulled that over for a moment. "All right," she said finally. "When can you start?"

He gave her another shrug. "When can you have the money?"

She gave him one back. "Tomorrow, the next day at the latest."

With a nod, he said, "Which is exactly when I can start. Nice how that worked out."

"Yeah—it's all good." She rose and moved toward the door. "I'll be back with a grand. Fill you in then."

Vogelsang smiled—a big teddy bear of a man who was not at all lovable. He touched his temple with a thick finger. "Got ya mentally penciled in."

She went straight from Vogelsang's to Crash, where Sketchy, Herbal, and Original Cindy had already commandeered a table and were on a second pitcher of beer.

An old brick warehouse not unlike Jam Pony, the place had been converted to a bar years ago, pre-Pulse. Round brick archways divided the three sections and video monitors, including a massive big screen, displayed footage of stock car races, dirt bike events, and skateboarding, all featuring the wild crashes that gave the bar its name.

Small tables fashioned from manhole covers were scattered around with four or five chairs haphazardly surrounding each. A jukebox cranking out metal-tinged rock hunkered against one wall, and through the nearest archway lay the pool and foosball tables. The entire wall behind the bar was a backlit Plexiglas sculpture of bicycle frames.

"Hey, Boo," Original Cindy said as Max came up.

With a tired-ass smile, Max took a seat and Sketchy poured her a beer.

Herbal said, "Ah, how goes the battle, my sister?"

Max forced the smile to brighten. "Why it's all good, my brother."

Herbal smiled and nodded, convinced he had a convert;

Sketchy handed Max the beer with his trademark stunned-baby-seal expression.

"You up for some pool, home girl?" Original Cindy asked Max, giving her a sideways look.

Sketchy shook his head and even Herbal's eyes narrowed in warning.

"O. C.'s a shark, Max," Sketchy said. "Watch your ass."

"My brother speaks the truth," Herbal said. "Our sister has already made poor men of us both."

"Yeah, but it's still all good, right?" Max glanced toward Original Cindy.

With a shrug and no chagrin, she said, "What can I say? Original Cindy's better with balls than these boys."

Sketchy thought about that, while Max grinned and said, "Well, bring it on, girlfriend, bring it on."

Leaving the guys at the table, the two young women—though familiar sights around here, they were followed by every male eye in the bar, and a few female, too—sashayed over to an empty table.

Though her analytical ability and enhanced eyesight gave her an advantage, Max still lost three straight games to Cindy.

The encounter with the private detective had been replaying in her mind ever since leaving the Laundromat. Jam Pony paid peanuts, and her bankroll from Moody had been eaten up by travel expenses and the cost of living, not the least of which was paying off that cop at squatter's row. Now she needed a cool k, in less than twenty-four hours . . . and she had no idea where she was going to get it.

"Had enough, girl?" Original Cindy asked, leaning on her cue.

Max nodded slowly and they headed back to the table.

"You okay, Boo? Your mind's on some other planet."

"Just a little distracted."

They reached the table, where Sketchy and Herbal sat before an empty pitcher, with the slightly buzzed expressions to match.

"Somethin' Original Cindy can do?"

"Just workin' out some private stuff."

"Well, you call me in off the bench, girl, when the game goes into sudden death."

Max smiled at her friend . . . maybe her best friend. "Yeah?"

"Hell yeah!"

Snatching up the pitcher, Max said, "My turn to buy," and moved off toward the bar. She was almost there when two guys in the far corner triggered her peripheral vision. Crash wasn't crowded at this hour, and two guys confabbing so far from everybody else in the place put them on Max's radar.

With a seemingly casual sideways glance, she focused in and watched as a wad of cash passed between them . . . also a package the size of a fist, wrapped in brown paper, passing the other way.

Drug deal.

Max had an instinctive dislike of hard drugs—possibly linked to the medical tampering she'd been subjected to—and suddenly, an inner smile forming, she knew exactly where the money for Vogelsang was going to come from. . . .

She had always been that kind of thief. Moody had made sure to send her after unsavory types; something about crooking a crook just . . . sat better with Max. This would be like ripping off the Brood, only minus the acrobatics—easy, profitable, and stealing from guys who weren't exactly model citizens, anyway.

The bartender gave her the pitcher, she paid, and hustled back to the table, her smile wide and genuine.

"Nectar," Sketchy said, accepting the pitcher as if an award for Best Bike Messenger 2019, and started sloshingly filling glasses.

"Just say no," Max said, holding up a hand to block Sketchy from pouring her another glass; her peripheral vision still trailed the drug dealers, who were on the move.

So was she.

"Gotta jet," she said.

Original Cindy looked at her with only partly feigned outrage. "Yo, Boo, you just got here! What can be more important than kickin' it with your homeys?"

"Just remembered an errand I've got to run . . . for me, not Normal."

"Take care, my sister," Herbal said, in benediction.

"Catch ya in the mornin', girl," Original Cindy said, picking up on Max's distracted gaze but unable to latch onto whatever Max was trained on.

Sketchy saluted her with a beer glass but said nothing, having just moved into a nonverbal state.

The two drug dealers split out different exits. Max tailed after the one with the cash—dealing the drugs was a line she couldn't cross.

Outside, the light was little better than in the bar, and Max couldn't tell much about the guy except he was tall, and so skinny he seemed lost in that expensive brown leather jacket; also, he had short brown hair, big ears, and walked with a definite slouch. Except for the short hair, from this distance, he could've been Sketchy.

She stayed with him for several blocks, on foot, on the opposite side of the street, hanging back enough to keep the guy from making her. The brown leather jacket kept moving, and half a dozen blocks melted away, as he led her into a seedier side of the city than she'd yet seen as a messenger. Max was still more than a block behind him when three figures emerged from the shadows and planted themselves in front of the guy.

They obviously planned to rip him before *she* did—and that pissed her off!

As she crept forward, she watched two of the interlopers move to either side of the dealer, leaving the third facing their mark. These were wide, tough men, buzz-cut white guys in muscle shirts who'd pumped themselves into brawny animals—blocky torsos with arms, legs, and no necks, possibly part of a local neo-Nazi group, the Swatzis, known to loot dealers and then peddle their own shit through intermediaries to minorities . . . making money off their idea of homegrown genocide.

The apparent leader, positioned in front of the dealer, stepped forward. Trimly Satan-bearded, he was smaller, still muscular, though he probably depended more on his brain than his brawn. Plus, there was that nine-millimeter auto in his hand. . . .

"Give up the money, lowlife, and you just might limp away."

Traffic was nil; Max didn't even have to look both ways when she raced across the street in an eyeblink, and sprang high; she came down in the middle of the four men as if she'd fallen from outer space, poised with catlike grace in a battle stance.

Their mouths all dropped open at once.

One at a time, she closed them.

Starting with the devil-bearded gunman: she decked him with a left, the automatic flying out of his hand and clattering to the street; then she spun, taking out the nearest would-be Nazi with a sweeping kick. Down low, she swung an uppercut to the dealer's groin, and, coming up, headbutted the last Nazi and watched him teeter, then tumble to the sidewalk, as unconscious as the cement that received him.

The scrawny, big-eared dealer rolled on the ground, his hands clutching his jewels. The Nazi she'd kicked to the pavement struggled to his knees in time for his face to halt a flying kick from Max. He, too, fell unconscious, his face a bleeding, broken mess. Scrabbling in the street to find and snatch up his pitched pistol, which he managed, the gunman turned, grinning, raising the automatic as he came.

Just as he leveled the gun, Max dropped and rolled toward him, exploding out of the roll with a vicious blade of a left hand that chopped the gun from the man's hand, then sent a chop across the bridge of his nose, which broke it, leaving him bloody and unconscious on the sidewalk near his buzz-cut companions.

"I hate guns," Max said, not winded.

Sucking air like a two-pack-a-day smoker, the dealer—his hands still protecting his crotch—made it to his knees. "You . . . you saved my life," he managed.

"That's right."

"But I think you broke my balls. . . ."

Looking down at him, she said, "Ice pack may help. Just wanted to make sure you didn't book."

His eyes were as wide as a puppy begging a bone. "But . . . why? If you were gonna rescue me . . . why? . . ."

Arms folded, Max stood amid the fallen Nazis, all of whom were slumbering, and said, "Just didn't want you to leave without paying."

The Dumbo-eared dealer's face went blank. "Huh?"

"You think I saved your life out of the goodness of my heart?"

"I was . . . kinda hoping. . . ."

Max shook her head, dark locks bouncing. "What world do you live in? . . . Hand over the wad."

The dealer's voice came out a squeak: "You're . . . *muggin'* me?"

"That's such an ugly term. Let's just say I'm claiming my reward for savin' your scrawny ass."

"But . . . I don't have any money."

"Aw, you just want me to put my hands on you," Max said. "I'm flattered . . . left front pocket. The money you made tonight at Crash? Selling whatever drugs were in the brown paper wrapper."

He winced. "You saw that?"

"I recommend a dark alley next time. Time-honored thing, y'know. Give."

His hands came off his privates and folded prayerfully; begging. "Please . . . please . . . you *can't* take the money . . . if I don't pay my connection, he'll kill my ass!"

"Here's how this works—I just gave you a reprieve. Next death sentence, you're on your own. You rather I knock your lights out, so you can wake up about the same time as the master race, here?"

"I'm not kidding, lady . . . really, he's a badass . . . he'll kill me . . . real slow."

Max sighed, shook her head. "You run with a rough crowd, son, you break a toenail now and then."

"Jesus! This is *serious shit!*"

The gunman seemed to be rousing, and Max kicked him in the head, then said to the jug-eared beggar, "If you run you might get away . . . you can start over. Find a new life, or stay a lowlife, down in Portland or Frisco."

He got himself to his feet. "What the hell with?"

"With your skin for starters. Hock the jacket." She pulled back, ready to hit him again. "Or lights-out. . . ."

"All right, all right!" He reached into his pocket and pulled out the wad.

Taking it, Max asked, "How much?"

"Fifteen hundred. . . . Maybe you could steer your way clear to . . ."

She glared at him. "Disappear."

The dealer took her advice.

She trotted off toward Crash, where her bike waited, even as the dealer's shoes hammered the concrete as he ran-limped as far away from her as possible, making hollow echoes in the night.

The next afternoon Max found Vogelsang camped behind his desk, stuffing an Oreo into his mouth.

"Health food?" she said, stepping from the shadows.

The big man jumped—he hadn't heard her come in. His eyes shot from her toward the double doors and the front of the laundry where the Asian woman was supposed to screen his visitors.

"I found another way in," she said.

"What the hell . . . what the hell you doing here?"

"Didn't you pencil me in?" she asked, stepping up to the desk, arching an eyebrow. "You did say a thousand."

"Yeah, so?"

She tossed a thick envelope onto his desk. He looked at it as if it might bite, then picked it up, juggled it once, twice. He looked in the envelope—it wasn't sealed—and studied the thickness of green admiringly.

"That's a thousand," she said.

"It would seem to be."

"Go ahead and count it."

"Naw . . . I wouldn't insult you." He set the package of Oreos aside, wiped his mouth with the back of a hand, and sat back in his chair. "Now . . . who is it you want me to find?"

"Two people."

"But this is *one* thousand. What, are they together?"

She shook her head.

He cocked his bucket head and made the peace sign. "Max, that's two cases . . . one, two."

"Be that way," she muttered, and reached for the wad of bills. "I'll find somebody who likes my money."

"Whoa, whoa—no need to go off like a little firecracker. . . . I like your money just fine. I'll take this as a down payment, if you understand with two cases, more time is obviously gonna be involved . . . and we'll go from there."

Max didn't move for a long moment, then slowly relaxed and dropped into the chair behind her.

"Tell me about your two people," Vogelsang said, the money disappearing into a desk drawer.

"First one is male—white, about my age, athletic, badass."

"Distinguishing marks?"

She paused. "A barcode on the back of his neck."

Vogelsang looked up. "A what?"

She repeated what she'd said, adding, "Just a funky tattoo . . . you know how it goes with us weird-ass kids."

That seemed to answer it for Vogelsang, who began scrawling some notes. "Any idea where he is?"

"Here. Seattle."

"It's a big city."

"And it's your city, Mr. Vogelsang. That's why I'm hiring you. If it was easy, I'd have found him by now."

"Give me a more detailed description. More than just a badass with a barcode."

She thought about that, then said, "Six-one, one-ninety maybe, dark hair . . . I think."

Vogelsang's eyes vanished into slits. "You think?"

"Saw him for ten seconds on a crappy video feed."

She explained about what she'd seen on the news show, and that she thought she'd recognized a long-lost "relative."

"Might be able to get that clip from somebody I know at SNN," Vogelsang said, almost to himself. "He got a name, this long-lost relation?"

"Seth."

"Last name?"

She shook her head. "Don't know. He'd be using different ones. Maybe even different first names."

Vogelsang studied the pad, then looked up at her. "Anything else? This is pretty slim."

"The news story said he might be working with an underground journalist—Eyes Only?"

The detective's eyes widened, and one of them twitched at the corner; he seemed to turn a whiter shade of pale. "Is that right. . . ."

"Why? Is that gonna be a problem?"

The big man shrugged. "Could be. This Eyes Only guy, he's on the g's shit list. Politics make me nervous. Plus, this Eyes Only dude, he's messed some people up . . . doesn't like to be interfered with. Takes himself *way* too serious . . ."

Max offered the investigator a reassuring smile. "You find Seth, I'll take care of Eyes Only . . . I'll take the heat . . . *if* there's a problem."

Flipping a page in the notebook, Vogelsang said, "Okay—who's missing person number two?"

Max sighed. "Afraid this is gonna be tough, too . . . maybe even tougher: a woman, Hannah, and that's all the name I've got."

"What does she look like?"

Max considered the private eye's question, replayed that first night of freedom in her head. In her mind's eye appeared a woman in her thirties with dishwater blond hair to her shoulders and wide-set blue eyes the color of a mountain stream . . . staring down at Max in her memory, as if the nine-year-old were still on that car floor.

She gave Vogelsang the description.

"Anything else?"

The Tahoe dived into a valley, then roared up beside Max, the tires sliding a little as the driver stomped on the brakes and locked them up. Max glimpsed the Wyoming plate, AGT 249, then the driver finally got control of the vehicle and pulled to a stop.

Max told him the license number.

"That's it?"

"She may have been a nurse, or some other kind of medical personnel. Maybe for the federal government."

Vogelsang wrote that down. He looked up, his smile friendly. "Okay . . . give me a week. You got a number?"

"Pager." She gave him the number.

"Okay, Max—I'll call when I've got something."

"For a grand—you better."

Outside the Sublime Laundry, Max hopped on the Ninja and headed for her crib. She felt both closer and farther from her sibs than she ever had.

Unless the media attention had spooked him, Seth was somewhere in this city, *right now*. . . .

In the meantime, while Vogelsang did his thing, she'd be doing hers, just fitting in with her new Jam Pony family.

Funny . . . in her brief time on the planet, Max had been part of . . . and lost . . . three different families. First the Manticore sibs, then the Barretts, and finally the Chinese Clan.

She'd been separated from her siblings by a strange confluence of force and circumstance; and fleeing Mr. Barrett had been self-defense.

Still, sometimes late at night . . . and tonight would be one of those . . . she felt a twinge of guilt for abandoning Lucy, and for running out on Moody and Fresca and the others.

She wondered if the Jam Pony bunch would be just as impermanent.

Chapter Seven
THEATER PARTY

THE CHINESE THEATRE
LOS ANGELES, CALIFORNIA, 2019

Two days ago, it had begun.

A quartet of Moody's kids—ranging in age between fourteen and eighteen—had been cut down by sniper fire from the half-standing structure of the former Roosevelt Hotel. Two boys, two girls, shaken like the naughty children they were, were dropped in a mist of blood to the cracked cement squares where hands and feet of forgotten celebrities remained on pointless display.

Every attempt to leave the building, through whatever exit, had resulted in a hail of slugs flinging Moody's people to the pavement in a sprawl of death. Pinned down like this—based upon the food and ammunition on hand—Moody and his crew couldn't last longer than a week. But should be time enough to plan, to react effectively, even to wait for support from the city or the feds.

The youth of his clan, however, was a problem—even in a cavernous auditorium like that of the Chinese Theatre, a sense of claustrophobia could descend . . . that is, when you knew that stepping outside the building would end your life in echoing gunfire. Sandbags, furniture, crates, old theater seats, and anything else not nailed down had been arranged throughout the theater as little aboveground bunkers. Moody would move among them—floating like a silver-ponytailed shadow, a flowing black bathrobe loose over black T-shirt and jeans, for melodramatic effect—calming them with words and gestures, assuring them their fortress was impregnable.

"The world beyond will take note of our plight," he would tell them. "We are not forgotten—be strong till help arrives."

And his kids believed him; if only Moody could believe himself. . . .

Right now, as he looked through the glass doors of the lobby, toward the nighttime street where those four bodies were still asprawl on the patio, pools of blood dried into terrible brown scabs on the cement, the bodies grotesquely attracting flies after fifty-some hours, the charismatic leader of the Chinese Clan feared help would never come.

Outside, still unseen, their enemy had them paralyzed, as if the Clan were bluecoat soldiers in a frontier fort, facing endless Indian hordes. But as of yet their attackers hadn't shown the colors of their war paint. Attempts to send out heavily armed scouting teams—no matter which exit—had resulted in the groups getting gunned down within five feet.

The enemy knew about the building's secret exits, too, the basement catacombs that led to the sewer system, and the tunnel under the block up into the adjacent building. Pairs of kids had been directed to slip out those passages, and were eliminated to a man. That is, to a boy. . . .

Moody knew who had to be doing this: the Brood, of course. He had expected retaliation for the theft of the museum plans, and for snatching the Heart of the Ocean from their Russian leader's fingers. Such a vicious, all-out assault, however, was a surprise . . . he would never had guessed the Brood would attempt a full-on siege. . . .

After all, despite their youth, the Chinese Clan had the Brood (whose members were admittedly older) outnumbered by perhaps a third, and they were possessed of superior firepower, chiefly handguns and rifles from that Orange County armory they'd looted last year; further, their rivals would probably not be aware that the awesome fighting machine, Max, was no longer a part of the Clan. . . .

But the kind of armament the Brood had deployed in the last two days—sniperscopes, automatic weapons—made Moody wonder . . . guns like that weren't easily come by . . .

For all his tactical skills—commando training in his distant past had stayed with him—Moody simply did not know how to stop this slaughter.

And as for the "help" he assured his kids would be on the way, Moody could gather from the lack of police response so far that the Brood had bribed the cops to keep their blue noses out of the conflict. Such was not uncommon in LA gang wars: the police collected money, sometimes from both sides, and let the "real" bad guys . . . the street gangs . . . fight it out. It was an old refrain: who the hell cared if this rabble killed each other?

But what really struck Moody as disturbing, and dangerous beyond comprehension, was the lack of any federal response. In a case of carnage like this, uncontrolled by the local cops, the National Guard should be stepping in.

How could the Brood have influence on a federal level? Such a thing took more bribe money . . . and better connections . . . than that Russian scumbag Kafelnikov would ever have access to. And unless the LAPD was directly involved—cordoning off the area for the Brood, effecting a press blackout, actively cooperating with the Russian—the feds *had* to be aware that blood was running on Hollywood Boulevard.

What the hell *was going on?*

In a gray T-shirt and chinos, the lanky yet lithely muscular Gabriel—an Uzi in his hands, an ammo belt around his waist—watched Moody's back as the Clan leader peered out into the street.

Heavily armed Clan members—older, more seasoned ones, mostly male—took up their position to either side of the glass doors, as Moody nodded to Gabriel, motioning him to the concession stand, where they spoke quietly, so the nearby sentries would not hear.

"Unless they plan to starve us out," Moody told his second-in-command, "they'll strike in force—storm our battlements."

"We lost a few people," Gabriel said, and shook his head. "I seen better morale."

"Our troops will come through for us, and themselves."

Moody glanced at the half a dozen kids—none older than eighteen—in T-shirts and jeans and tennies, caps on backward, semiautomatic weapons in hand. Freckle-faced Fresca, with the new girl Niner at his side, stood with the group nearest Moody and Gabe.

"Even with the hits we've taken," Moody said, a hand on Gabriel's shoulder, "we outnumber these bastards."

"Their average age is twenty-two—ours is sixteen."

"We still have the numbers. And that gives them only two choices—mount a commando raid, send in their best people, armed to the teeth . . . and hope to outfight us. Or . . ."

"Or," Gabe finished, "they come in in force."

"In which case," Moody said, "they can't have every exit pinned down to the degree we've been suffering these last two days. With a building this size, covering every way out would drain a third of their manpower."

"So," Gabe said, thinking it through, "if we see a damn horde of these suckers stormin' in, we head for the exits."

"Fighting even as we retreat," Moody said with a nod. "And we beat them at their own game."

"How's that?"

Moody grinned wolfishly. "We head for the Cap . . . we'll trade headquarters with the sons of bitches!"

Gabe grinned wide, head shaking on that ostrich neck. "The Moodman still has moves, I see."

"Always. Now—I'll help you spread the word."

In the auditorium, Moody and Gabriel did just that, and faces brightened, morale visibly lifting, and yet the fear remained. Though he felt his plan was a good one, Moody remained uneasy, still troubled by the absence of both the local and federal authorities. How he wished Max was still here. . . . She alone might turn the tide for them, and certainly even up the fight.

His bodyguard, Tippett, looked as stoic as ever in biker leathers, his tattooed arms bared as threats, but the hulking man had removed all his piercings—he never went into battle giving opponents anything to rip from his flesh.

"You want me in the hall?" Tippett asked.

"No—let them have the hall . . . they'll try my 'office'

door and that'll tell us what they're up to. You take the back exit, over there. . . ." Moody pointed. "They may still have somebody positioned, so serpentine your ass."

"No prob. . . . I ain't had so much fun since the pigs ate my cousin Fred."

Moody found himself smiling at that. "We should have at *least* that much fun, this evening. . . ."

His black robe trailing like a cape, Moody threaded through the auditorium, passing along the strategy, continuing to build morale. Then he went upstairs to the old projection booth, where Max had kept her quarters, and knocked.

Freckle-faced Fresca answered. "Yes, sir? What can I do, sir?"

"The girl Niner in there with you?"

"Yes, sir. Just kinda . . . cooling her out, sir."

"I hope you haven't been doing anything I wouldn't do."

"Kinda doubt that, sir." And Fresca grinned.

Of all these kids, only Fres seemed unafraid under these siege circumstances—whether this was courage or naïveté, Moody would not hazard a guess.

"You and Niner go down and block the doors."

"What with?"

"Use those sandbags we stacked up against the wall, by the stairs, last night. I want them piled directly against the front entry."

"You got it!"

Fifteen minutes later, when Moody was again moving through the lobby, he saw that the freckle-faced boy and his new girlfriend had set to work.

"Don't worry, Niner," the boy was saying. Though he was several years younger than the skinny-looking newbie, Fresca spoke with the authority of experience. "You'll see."

"You really think Max'll be back?" Niner asked.

"Oh yeah—she's just off on some errand or something. She ride in on that bike of hers, and kick Brood ass!"

Eavesdropping, Moody could only wish Fresca were right.

Gabriel seemed to materialize at his side. "Them knowin' about our secret exits," Gabe said quietly, "you don't think Max sold us out, do ya?"

"Don't let Fresca hear you say that."

"What do you think?"

"I think, no. No way in hell."

Moody walked Gabriel off to one side, to make even more sure this confidential conversation was not overheard.

Gabriel, Uzi ready, was saying, "They could have grabbed her . . . tortured it out of her. . . ."

Moody just looked at Gabe. "Do you really think they could get anything out of that girl?"

Gabe's concerned expression dissolved into an embarrassed smirk. "Listen to the stupid shit's comin' outa me. . . . Guess I'm getting stir crazy."

"You'll like it at the Cap," Moody said. "End of the day, we'll come out of this with better digs . . . you'll see."

The explosion erupted through the doors in a belch of orange flame and gray smoke, hurling Fresca and his girlfriend across the room, slamming them into the concession stand in a shower of glass fragments. The girl, Niner, lay decapitated by one oversized glass shard, her head nowhere in sight, perhaps incinerated; and Fresca rested at her side, a twisted charred bloody husk with its guts trailing out, and the only mercy that neither had to witness the horror of what had taken the other from this life.

The kids who'd been standing guard duty at either end, alongside those doors, had their own share of nicks from flying glass, though none seemed to have serious injuries. But it was a bit hard to tell, since before the smoke had even begun to clear they'd started running pell-mell toward the auditorium . . . until machine-gun fire cut them down like tall grass under a swinging scythe.

Blasting away as they came, screaming unintelligible war cries, Broodsters charged up the patio toward where the doors had been, automatic weapons in hand, eyes wild, piling in over the broken glass and the small barrier of sandbags that Fresca and Niner had managed to pile there before they died. . . .

Moody and Gabriel stayed ahead of the invaders, and dashed into the auditorium. The Clan kids—with handguns, mostly, a few with rifles—had taken refuge behind their sandbag and theater-chair battlements. The two leaders circulated quickly, dispatching kids to sandbag the auditorium doors shut; then they sent small groups to try various exits, now that the Brood was attacking in full force, which would presumably open up some outlets for escape.

Each group that headed for an exit, however, opened doors onto figures . . . soldiers . . . in black combat gear, heavily armed, blocking the way.

Tippett was the first to discover this, and reported it to Moody.

"That doesn't sound like the Brood," Moody said.

"Not hardly! Some kind of damn military SWAT team. . . ."

"Any casualties?"

"No—they didn't fire on us. . . . We got back inside before they could. . . ."

Four more older Clan kids scrambled up, and reported their exits similarly blocked.

Gabriel said, "Bastards have the building surrounded! We're blocked in by these guys, while the Brood comes in to party!"

It made an awful, crazy sense to Moody: this explained the siege, the suddenly superior Brood firepower . . . the Russian had high-level support in this effort, even federal government sanction. . . .

Moody looked toward the auditorium doors, where sandbags were piled waist-high. The enemy had breached the lobby maybe five minutes ago, and had not yet made a move to rush the theater itself.

Where the hell were they?

A nearby blast, separated from the auditorium by the left-side wall—accompanied by screams—provided an answer: the explosion came from the corridor along which Moody kept both his real office and the C4-rigged door to his nonoffice. This told him two things: the enemy was filtering into the building, to come at them not just through the main auditorium doors. But it also said that his booby trap had been sprung.

He only hoped the C4 had taken a good number of them out.

Even so, in that moment, it became crystal clear to Moody that there would be no escape. They would either win or lose, live or die, right here in this auditorium . . . and Moody didn't like the odds one little bit. . . .

Right now Gabriel was shouting orders, but these children seemed scared, barely listening. Hell was knocking at the door, and pep talks weren't going to cut it.

Turning these kids into self-reliant thieves was one thing: turning them into soldiers was another. Moody had never tried to do the latter, really—kids weren't cut out for that.

The harsh metallic rattle of machine-gun fire rained down on them from the balcony—that was where the Brood made their first appearance in the auditorium—And then the doors blew open with plastic explosive charges, and members of the Brood streamed into the room, up and over the sand-bag barricades, automatic weapons blazing, eyes wild with speed, screaming like the murderous maniacs they'd become.

Moody, in his way, loved his kids . . . but this was a lost cause. He now began to wonder if he himself could survive, and get to the Heart of the Ocean, in its hiding place, and somehow slip out into the night.

Then Tippett aided him in this self-serving effort: the bodyguard threw himself on Moody and took them both down to the floor, shielding the leader with his own body. Wedged to the floor, like that, Moody bitterly watched the massacre unfold. . . .

All around him, bullets were shaking young bodies like rag dolls and then discarding them, flinging them dead to the floor. The Brood fanned out in murderous waves, gunning down anyone who moved, including those who had raised their hands in surrender. Over the gunfire, Moody could make out screams and pleas for mercy and, worst of all, crying. The acrid odor of cordite seemed to singe the air, the gun smoke creating a fog through which the Brood roamed like well-armed homicidal zombies.

Like a crazed Davy Crockett in his last Alamo moments, Gabriel swung a chair back and forth; but furniture was no match for machine guns, and Moody watched helplessly as at least thirty slugs slammed into Gabe, making him do a terrible dance, lifting him off the floor to deposit him in a bloody heap not far from Moody's face.

Gabe's blank eyes stared at Moody accusingly. . . .

The gunfire was subsiding, only an occasional *pop* now, as an occasional living Clan member was spotted, like the last few firecrackers on the Fourth of July.

In his knee-length brown leather coat and snakeskin boots, Mikhail Kafelnikov—his high-cheekboned features looking carved and cruel—seemed to glide down the incline of the auditorium floor, a wraith in a yellow silk shirt emerging from the gun-smoke fog. He surveyed the carnage—they were all dead now, the Chinese Clan . . . almost all, anyway. . . .

One of the Brood, a skinny clear-eyed lieutenant, came up to their leader, who batted the snout of the automatic weapon away.

"Sorry," the lieutenant said. "No sign of the girl."

"Check all the corpses—careful! If she's alive, and playing dead, you'll have a wildcat on your hands. Remember the briefing!"

The mention of Max inspiring him, Moody suddenly revealed himself, by pushing his bodyguard off and getting to his feet, (while surreptitiously slipping a knife from his boot, keeping it tucked in his palm and half up his sleeve).

Several Broodsters, eyes glittering with gore and drugs, moved in quickly, raising their guns, but Kafelnikov shouted, "No! You were told!"

Two burly Brood boys latched onto Tippett's arms and hauled him to his feet. The big former linebacker had no fight left in him—his eyes were on the floor . . . the sight of the slaughtered kids, all 'round, appeared too much for him.

Slowly, Moody approached the Russian, planted himself a few feet away, folded his arms, the knife out of sight. He said, "You told them not to kill me. I'm not surprised."

"And why is that, Moody?"

The Clan leader ignored the question, saying, "I always suspected you were a barbarian." He glanced around the room at the dozens of dead kids, their blood streaming down the slope of the theater floor like spilled soft drinks. "You've confirmed it."

The Brood leader let out a small chuckle. "Bravado to the last. . . . I appreciate that, Moody. I'd almost say you've earned a quick death."

A bitter smile etched itself on the well-grooved face. "You're not about to kill me, Mikhail . . . not yet."

An eyebrow arched, an amused half smile formed. "You're right. After all . . . we have business."

Looking around at his slaughtered family, Moody asked, "Really? And why would I bother doing business with a butcher?"

"Because you are at heart a man of self-interest, Moody . . . despite the the 'loyalty' drivel you fed your 'family.' And you have two things that interest me."

"The necklace," Moody said.

"Yes, and . . ."

"The girl. Max. I heard . . . why?" Moody's eyes narrowed and he studied the Russian's narrow, handsome face. "Revenge? Did she embarrass you on your home turf? How sad for you."

Kafelnikov snapped his fingers. A circle of Broodsters formed around them—automatic weapons everywhere Moody looked. Not much he could do with the knife . . . perhaps slash the Russian's throat, and maybe try to claim leadership. . . .

Somehow he didn't think that would play, even in a movie theater.

"Where," the Russian asked, "is the necklace?"

"I'm sorry to disappoint you . . . but I've already sold it. That deal is done. And the money is not on the premises. It was a Swiss bank transfer, and—"

Kafelnikov nodded once and the two burly Broodsters holding on to Tippett released him, stepping away from the bodyguard. Moody frowned, wondering what that was about. . . .

The Russian's hand came up and an automatic was in it; he fired, to the left of Moody, where Tippett stood.

The bodyguard's scream echoed even as the shot rang in

the auditorium, as Tippett grabbed for his leg, a red flower blossoming between the fingers that clutched at his right knee.

Moody's fingers tightened, now white around the handle of the hidden knife. He took a tentative step but froze when he heard several guns cock. Tippett was quiet now, his hands still holding his shattered joint.

"I'm okay, Moody," the bodyguard managed. "Don't you worry 'bout me."

"You were saying?" the Russian said to Moody.

"I was saying . . . I already dealt the Heart of the Ocean . . . but I can lead you to the buyer. You can get it back from him . . . kill his ass, for all I care."

Again Kafelnikov raised the gun, fired, and Tippett screamed as another report reverberated in the auditorium and crimson petals bloomed from the other knee. Tippett went down hard on the cement, and he whimpered there, like a whipped dog.

"Moody," the Russian sighed, "I don't underestimate your intelligence . . . why do you do me the disservice of insulting mine? I know who your *potential* buyer was . . . he negotiated a better price with me, at the same time he was negotiating more time from you, supposedly to raise sufficient funds to meet your outrageous fee. So . . . I need to deliver the Heart of the Ocean to him . . . where is the diamond, Moody?"

"Tell me, Mikhail," Moody asked. "Don't your men find that yellow shirt a bit . . . effeminate?"

The Russian frowned and fired, bullets stitching across Tippett's groin and thighs and the bodyguard now rolled around in agony, screaming for them to kill him, go ahead, kill him; but no one moved.

"Where is the *necklace?*" Kafelnikov asked over the screams, his voice more brittle now.

By way of an answer, Moody spun and hurled the knife . . .

. . . into his bodyguard's chest.

Tippett whispered, "Got some moves, Moody," closed his eyes, and slipped away.

Kafelnikov leapt forward, and slapped Moody with the automatic.

A gash ripped in his cheek, Moody went down on one knee, as if about to be knighted by the Russian, who instead grabbed Moody's silver ponytail and yanked him down, smashing the older man's face into the concrete floor. Moody made only a tiny moan as he pushed himself up, his nose broken, blood streaming down the front of his black shirt.

"If you won't tell me where the necklace is," Kafelnikov said, "at least tell me where the girl is."

"Who . . . who the *fuck* . . . is helping you?"

"*I* ask the questions. Tell me, and I'll let you live, and we'll go partners on the necklace. You can be my second-in-command, Moody. . . ."

Moody's mind, clouded by pain, tried to parse that: *what made Max suddenly more valuable than the Heart of the Ocean?*

"Where is she, Moody? Or do you start losing kneecaps?"

Moody swallowed blood, then sputtered, "Gone. The girl's . . . gone."

"Don't lie to me, goddamn it!"

"Do you . . . see her? She's gone, I tell you. . . ."

"Where?"

"She . . . she didn't say. Quiet, that one. . . ."

Kafelnikov again slammed the man's head into the floor. Blood exploded in an arc around Moody's face.

That was when Moody, barely hanging on to consciousness heard footsteps—hard soles on the cement floor. Someone new had entered; someone was on the periphery . . . watching. . . .

"Your last chance, Moody—*where is she?*"

Through broken teeth and bleeding lips, Moody managed to say, "Don't worry, Kafelnikov . . . once she finds out what you've done to her family . . . you won't have to look very hard. . . . She'll turn up."

The boot-heel footsteps started up again . . . moving closer.

Moody turned his head sideways and saw a man in black

combat gear approach—blond, late forties, with a face that might have seemed boyish if the slitted eyes weren't those of a snake.

And Moody knew, just *knew:* he could smell the black-ops military on the man; no doubt at all—*this was the devil Kafelnikov had made his deal with.*

"This is the leader?" the blond man asked. "This is Moody?"

Kafelnikov rose, leaving Moody in his bloody sprawl.

"Yes, Colonel Lydecker," Kafelnikov whispered. "What's left of him, anyway. But he says—"

The blonde and the Russian stood near Moody; no one else heard the sotto voce conversation. . . .

Lydecker's mouth twitched in an otherwise impassive face. "I heard what he had to say, Mikhail."

Looking up sideways, Moody saw the blond in black. smiling innocuously down on him. "If you know where the girl is, and tell us . . . I'll see that you live, and even let you keep your necklace."

Moody felt unconsciousness trying to move in and take him. He managed, "If I knew . . . I'd tell you. . . ."

Lydecker studied him like a lab specimen. "But you don't?"

Moody shook his head, and flecks of blood spattered the cement. "No . . . much as I'd . . . love to see her . . . kick all your sorry asses. . . ."

Holding out an open palm, Lydecker knelt over Moody, and said to the Russian, "Your gun, please."

Kafelnikov filled the colonel's palm with the automatic.

Lydecker asked Moody, "Are you a religious man?"

"No."

"Then you won't need time for a prayer."

But Moody sent up a quick one, anyway, for Max's safety, in the moment before the colonel fired the automatic, sending a bullet through Moody's left temple, crashing through his right, burying itself in the floor.

"Goddamn it!" the Russian blurted, rushing over. "What's wrong with you!"

Lydecker took Kafelnikov by the arm and whispered, as if

to a lover, in the man's ear: "What's wrong with *you,* Mikhail? You made me dispatch him: *He heard you call me by name.* I wasn't here . . . remember?"

Then, lip twitching with disgust, Lydecker placed the automatic back in the Russian's hand and shoved the man away from him.

Brood members, looking on, exchanged glances, surprised to see their leader take such abuse without protest.

As Lydecker walked toward the exit, the Russian called, "With him dead, how the hell am I supposed to find the stone?"

Without turning, Lydecker said, "It's probably somewhere in the building. Look for it yourself. . . . You have several hours before any police show . . . I've seen to that."

The Russian said, "*You've* got manpower! At least pitch in—"

From the doorway, Lydecker bestowed a mild smile on the Russian. "You've got all the help from me you're going to get today. . . . Let me know if you get a lead on the girl."

Then the blond man in black glanced around at the dozens of dead Clan members, who lay like discarded candy wrappers on the theater floor.

"Terrible thing to do to a bunch of kids," Lydecker muttered.

And was gone.

Chapter Eight

ART ATTACK

Under the cover of a dense fog, Max made her way across Puget Sound in a small battered motorboat, the outboard chugging like a tired vacuum cleaner—she had "borrowed" it from a nearby group of similar craft designated for tourist rental, and a sleeker, faster number would have been preferable, of course . . . but the absence of such a boat might have raised too much attention.

Such tactics were second-nature to the X5-Unit. The night air was windless but cool, almost cold. Vashon Island, her destination—home of her target—lay somewhere in the mist off the port bow. In her black turtleneck, black slacks, and rubber-soled boots—and the new black leather vest with pockets for all her toys—she might have been (but was not) a commando mounting a one-woman raid. The ensemble had been expensive, but even a bandit could be stylin', right?

That brittle chill in the air promised a deeper cold to come, and Max was glad she hadn't had to swim. Just because she'd been genetically engineered to ignore such trivialities as freezing her buns off, she saw no reason to embrace hardship.

As the boat putt-putted into the fog, Max kept the throttle down on the motor, both for safety's sake, on this pea-soupy night, and so as not to advertise her approach. It was possible there was security, in this wealthy part of the world, that she had not anticipated.

Some security she *could* anticipate. The Sterling home, a secluded multimillion-dollar castle on Vashon Island, sat on Southwest Shawnee Road behind a tall brick-and-concrete wall and would undoubtedly boast a state-of-the-art system. Main access to the island was provided by toll ferries—one running to the northern end, one to the southern tip—though Max knew they were not the only avenues of approach.

The precious object she sought might be covered by video, infrared, pressure alarms, and God only knew what else; but Max still had to smile. With no mines and no lasers trying to dissuade her, this time around, a simple home invasion would be a walk in the park . . . or anyway, cruise on the lake.

Even now, as she moved through the fog with single-minded purpose, Max remained in something of a personal fog. She was disappointed that her straight life had required this crooked side trip; she wished that the straight-and-narrow path could have stretched endlessly on for her. . . .

She liked the idea of *not* being a burglar; even relished the notion of becoming just another straight in a world of straights. But she could only kid herself so long: she was not normal, not straight, merely hiding in that world, behind that facade.

Keeping gas in her Ninja, when fuel was over eight bucks a gallon, having the occasional meal and now and then a beer—and paying off-the-books rent, even with Kendra's help—was about all her pitiful messenger wages covered. And a normal person—a straight person—could put up with that, make do with eking out an existence.

But when you added in buying tryptophan off the street, to control her seizures—one of the genetic drawbacks of her Manticore breeding—and in particular factored in funding her efforts to find Seth and her other siblings . . . well, maybe Max had known all along it was only a matter of time before she'd have to turn back to what Moody had taught her—maybe crime was her true calling.

She just wished it hadn't come back around so soon.

In particular, keeping that private eye on the trail of Seth (and Hannah) would soon require more cash. Sure,

Vogelsang may have been a trifle seedy, but Max needed that. An investigative agency higher up the food chain would have cost even more, might have lacked the P.I.'s usefully shady connections, and might be too tied in with the upper-echelon of the city, the very radar she was trying to fly under.

Since arriving in Seattle, Max had been reading the local papers on line, borrowing Kendra's laptop, in an attempt to find out more about Eyes Only and, she hoped, Seth. But in more recent days, she had turned her Moody-trained eye toward potential scores, as well.

Frustratingly, she hadn't learned anything substantial about Eyes Only—he was a "menace," according to the mayor, and "awards for information leading to yada yada yada"—and had come up with zip on Seth, also . . . no coverage since that scrap with the cops that SNN had covered.

But she *had* stumbled across a story about a billionaire art collector—and political contributor—named Jared Sterling.

The focus of the recent press attention was Sterling's latest "major" acquisition, an original Grant Wood painting called *Death on the Ridge Road*. Color photos showed Sterling in his late twenties, not bad looking . . . thick blond widow's peaked hair with a well-trimmed beard, and piercing blue eyes, short, straight nose, thin decisive line of a mouth, turning up in a sly smile, in this photo, anyway.

Good looking and loaded, she'd thought as she stared the LCD screen; *maybe I oughta give up burglary and go on the sugar-daddy hunt. . . .*

In several of the photos—shown next to Sterling—the painting was a vaguely cartoony illustration of an antique red truck bearing down on a black car turned sideways on a twisting road . . . painted in 1935, the cutline indicated.

Max didn't know the painting, but—thanks to Moody's schooling—she certainly knew Grant Wood, and recognized the distinctive style. And she knew as well that Wood works were fetching as much as ninety to a hundred thousand, now that so much Americana was being sold off.

Due to her particularly warped upbringing, Max had little sense of what America had once meant; but she knew Moody had been disturbed by such things. With the Baseball

Hall of Fame sold and moved to Kyoto, Japan—not to mention the Statue of Liberty, purchased by the Sultan of Brunei—it was obvious that America (Moody would rant), and all her possessions, were for sale "to the highest goddamn bidder."

To Max, however, what this painting meant was one thing: with proper fencing, it would cover Vogelsang's expenses for a good, long while. . . .

Max knew a great deal about art, artists, jewelry, antiques, collectibles . . . hell, she even knew the value of baseball cards. Moody had taught her well—not for altruistic reasons, or to broaden her human horizons (at least that had not been the main purpose).

Rather, her Fagin-like mentor knew that LA was a city of collectors, that even after the Pulse, and after the Big Quake, the town brimmed with valuable artifacts. Anticipating this—knowing the Chinese Clan might from time to time encounter any number of priceless objects on their various larcenous forays—Moody had made sure he was trained to recognize the finer things, and—as he was more and more not accompanying his kids on their capers—had methodically passed this knowledge along to Max.

A quick study, Max had devoured the material given her by Moody and sought out even more; she told herself her motivation was practical, but art nonetheless stirred something within her.

And it got to where she could walk into any antique shop in LaLa-land and know, in a glance, what was worth stealing and what wasn't. She had known, just looking at it, that the Heart of the Ocean was no fake; the level of security alone would have been a tip-off, but the stone itself had spoken to Max, telling her it was the real deal.

She'd done her on-line homework on Jared Sterling, the painting, and the place where Sterling now kept it; much of the information could have been discovered by anyone with a Comsat link. But to a Manticore-trained hacker like Max, the cyberworld was an oyster coughing up one Internetted pearl after another. . . .

Fittingly enough, it seemed Sterling had made his money

in resurrecting the post-Pulse computer infrastructure. Almost singlehandedly, ol' Jared had gotten the Internet up and running again, on the West Coast. Only a shadow of its former self in many areas at first, the Net was up, thanks to Sterling, and progress was quickly made.

Being in the right place, at the right time, with the right technology, had given Jared Sterling wealth comparable to the Bill Gates (pre-Pulse, before Gates went famously broke, of course). The hard-hit East Coast states had come sniffing around Sterling, trying to convince him to help them get back into the on-line world; but when they wouldn't (or perhaps couldn't) meet his price, and his terms, he'd left them on the outside looking in.

Sterling's hard-nosed way of doing business—he was often a vicious target of liberal op-ed writers—meant that once the eastern states *did* come crawling back, to avail themselves of his product and his services, the price would double, if not triple. Sterling had a legendary mean streak, and the country's major left-wing political magazine, *Hustler,* had not long ago made him their "Post-Pulse Predator of the Month," accusing him of having no conscience.

"A lot of businessmen have been called sharks," publisher Laurence Flynt III opined, "but Sterling is the real thing. Rumor has it, he even has slits tailored into in the back of his thousand-dollar suits, to accommodate his dorsal fin."

Politics were a blur to Max, of course—all she knew was, Manticore was tied to the federal government; therefore, federal government . . . bad.

As for the painting, Max already knew *Death on the Ridge Road* had been created by Wood in 1935. What she found out online was that the work was oil on a Masonite panel, thirty-two by thirty-nine inches . . . which made it kind of big and unwieldy, for a cat burglar. But the paycheck would more than make up for the hassle factor.

In 1947, Cole Porter, a twentieth-century songwriter, (the online info listed several "famous" song titles, none of which rang a bell for Max) had given the painting as a gift to the Williams College Museum of Art in Massachusetts.

After the Pulse, however, *Death* had disappeared for ten years before turning up, unharmed, on that easel next to Sterling.

The Net magnate only laughed when the media asked where he'd purchased the painting, and waved off any suggestion that it might be stolen property. Such ownership issues had become something of a moot point, after the Pulse, of course.

"I acquired it from a private collector," was all he would say.

Although none of the media had made a thing out of it, two days after Sterling's picture had appeared with the Grant Wood, a Miami collector named Johnson washed ashore in the Gulf of Mexico, the victim of an apparent boating accident.

This Max had not discovered online. In fact, that particular piece of information came courtesy of one of her *other* interests . . . when, at Jam Pony, as she and Original Cindy were waiting for their next assignment, an Eyes Only broadcast had interrupted SNN headline news on the break-area TV. . . .

"This cable hack will last exactly sixty seconds," the compelling voice said, as strong, clear eyes stared out from between bands of red and blue at the screen's top and bottom, over which moving white letters (STREAMING FREEDOM VIDEO) were superimposed. *"It cannot be traced, it cannot be stopped, and it is the only free voice left in this city."*

" 'Cept for Original Cindy," Original Cindy said.

Sketchy leaned in. "I dig this guy—he's intense."

"He's just another scam artist," Max said, pretending to be unimpressed.

"The mainstream media considers this small news. But Eyes Only wonders if there is a connection between the death of art dealer Harold Johnson and the very much alive-and-well art collector, Jared Sterling. . . ."

After driving the boat onto the sand, sliding it up into some bushes, and securing it, the young woman in black made her catlike way up a rolling landscaped lawn to the wall of Jared Sterling's estate. The fog hadn't dissipated any, in fact was clinging to the earth like a cloud that lost its way; this would make Max harder to detect on video.

The wall—seven feet of brick topped with video cameras at every corner—proved to be little challenge to Max. She jumped to the top, easily got her footing, hopped down, and landed gently on more grass. Listening closely, she heard only silence, saw merely the general shape of the castlelike house in the fog.

Edging low along the wall, she avoided the cameras even though she felt sure they couldn't catch her in this soup unless she was on top of one. It was a hundred yards across a pool-table green lawn—no slope, now, nice and flat—to the looming tan-brick house, and Max covered the turf quickly, making time an Olympic runner would have envied.

She had half expected dogs, but she sensed no animal presence: canines would have made her cat's nose twitch. Her only other real fear . . . make that, apprehension . . . would be motion detectors that might trigger yard lights. Nothing. And the only lights on in the entire immense house were in two windows on the first floor in the back.

Security room, Max thought.

Up close, the three-story house seemed huge. An article in the on-line *Architectural Digest* said the place had seven bedrooms, two kitchens, and four bathrooms; a carriage house on the opposite side of the estate housed Sterling's full-time ten-man security team (this fact she had hacked from the security company's Web site, having learned their I.D. from info lifted from the Sterling Enterprises official Web site). Eight-foot evergreens stood between the windows like giant green sentinels. Centered on the near side of the house were French doors with two windows on either side, the whole thing wired to that security room in the back of the mansion.

She wouldn't be going in this way.

Most home invaders avoided the one point of entry that wouldn't start sirens screaming and or bells clanging, the moment it got popped: the front door.

That was only because most home invaders lacked Max's singular skills.

Even here, behind the security-up-the-wazooed walls of a paranoid ka-zillionaire like Jared Sterling, Max would have a good thirty seconds to punch in the correct security code, before the ten-man team came scrambling after her. The keypad and its pin did make this a little tougher than taking candy from babies.

A little.

Four wide concrete stairs, with a huge concrete lion presiding over either side, led to a small landing in front of a formidable green door (it looked to Max like a big dollar bill) with a fancy brass knob and above that a centered, ornate brass knocker. Thankfully, the porch light was not on.

Large dark-curtained windows, each about thirty inches wide, bookended the door, and for a brief second Max considered just breaking one, climbing in, and kicking the shit out of those security boys . . . just for practice . . . just for fun. . . .

Pleasing though the notion was, Max thought of Moody ("Only amateurs take unnecessary chances on a score"), and she withdrew her switchblade from her jacket pocket and eased its tip into the latch of the big green door. Less than ten seconds later, that oversized dollar bill yawned open, and Max silently started to count.

Thirty, twenty-nine, twenty-eight . . .

She stepped inside the entryway, and was swallowed by the darkness of the slumbering house; her night vision would kick in soon. She folded the knife, slipped it away, the world in here so silent she heard only the ticking of a few clocks, her own breathing, and the counting in her head.

Twenty-five, twenty-four . . .

The keypad was on the wall to her right, each touchpad conveniently aglow, a red light shining in the right bottom corner, a green light in the left, with a copper-colored window to display the code above the numbered pad. She'd been correct: ten digits. Typically, a four-number code.

Twenty-two, twenty-one . . .

Her extraordinary eyesight determined which of these keys—four of them: 1, 3, 7, 8—had wear; the code would be twenty-four combinations thereof. . . .

Sixteen, fifteen, fourteen . . .

Her hands flew over the keyboard, her eyes, ears, and

brain working in concert at a pace only nanoseconds slower than a computer.

Ten, nine . . .

Eleven combinations tried.

Eight, seven . . .

Seventeen tried.

Six, five, four . . .

Finally the correct combo kicked in and the red light blinked green. Thinking, *It would have been more fun to just break a window,* she smiled nonetheless with satisfaction, touched a button marked IN, and the light blinked back red.

The house was secure . . .

. . . at least that's what Jared Sterling's security staff would be thinking.

Max's night vision was in full force now. She was in a foyer larger than most homes. The floor was marble (pale yellow in the photos on-line), the walls plaster, and the furnishings here, and elsewhere in the house, were Mission-style, some of them vintage pieces, including some Frank Lloyd Wright originals. She had entered a starkly beautiful, masculine world where every item, however mundane, might be a valuable objet d'art.

Straight ahead a staircase wide enough to accommodate ten people abreast led to an upper floor where a long hallway would extend to either end of the house. Glancing up at the landing, Max could make out a couple of dark wood doors, ironically making the second floor, with its plaster walls, look like a hallway in an inexpensive hotel.

On the left side of the staircase, maybe halfway up, was a small wall-mounted video camera trained on the entryway.

To Max's left and right, closed doors led to living rooms and billiards rooms, dens, and a few other rooms whose functions were not spelled out in her online research. She had tried to find plans for the house, but even with her hacking of both the security company and Sterling's own firm, plus the web site of the architect who'd built the castle, the plans for Sterling's home remained elusive, apparently guarded as if they were a government secret. What she did know, Max owed *Architectural Digest. . . .*

The curtains on the windows bordering the front door were heavy masculine maroon brocade. *Pretty fancy,* Max thought, *but then my digs run more to taped drywall and sheet plastic.* Sterling could afford to live well, and his quality of life was reflected in the quality of his things. If she'd been able to, Max would have backed a moving van to that front door, and spent the rest of the night hauling enough swag out of this joint to retire at nineteen.

Hugging the walls, she worked her way around the foyer till she was on the left side of the staircase, near the camera. Staying low, she climbed the stairs to the camera, got behind it and carefully unscrewed it from its mount, then unscrewed the coaxial cable from the back, all the while listening for the sound of pounding feet, a sure sign she'd been spotted.

She heard nothing. Just those same few clocks . . . and of course the steady beat of her heart.

Next, from a vest pocket, she took out a device much like a small Tazer, touched it to the cable, fired it, sending a high-voltage burst through the cable. This should short out the entire video system.

Now she heard feet pounding through the house, voices, too, whispers so as not to alert any intruder too quickly. She replaced the camera on its wall mount and hoped the security cam would look normal enough to pass a rapid inspection. Melting into the shadows behind one of the brocade curtains, she watched as four men, all in shirts and ties, converged in the foyer.

Two of these spiffy security guards had pistols drawn, .38 Colt Specials, while the other two carried automatic weapons, Heckler & Koch MP7A submachine guns. A negative wave of emotion ran through Max, momentarily breaking her remarkable self-control.

Guns made her react like that—but it was not fear . . .

. . . and she knew how to use such weapons herself, proficiently in fact; only, since her sib Eva's death, she could hardly stand to touch the damn things.

Each man wore an earphone and . . . was that? . . . She looked closer, the cat's eyes working their magic—yes, each also had a tiny microphone peeking out from the end of his sleeve. Sterling would seem to be serious about protecting his possessions: suits and ties aside, these boys were six feet tall or better, ranging from midtwenties to early forties, two white, one black, one Hispanic, apparently all in shape, their manner professional, their look hard-core, that chiseled emotionless quality you found only in career soldiers . . . or mercenaries.

Max smiled; she felt a tingle of excitement. . . .

Not that looking at the men frightened her, or intimidated her in any way. But she knew that if the master of the house had gone to this much trouble to protect something, that something must really be worth protecting . . . something more, even, than a highly valuable painting like the Grant Wood. Maybe, just maybe, she would make an even bigger haul here than she had imagined.

And, too, she kind of liked the challenge of being up against worthy opponents. . . .

Tall, with a graying crew cut, the oldest of the quartet took charge; he had narrow colorless lips, dime-sized scars on either cheek, and—like Max—he wore black from head to toe . . . his shirt and tie included.

"Maurer," the leader said, "upstairs."

One of the guys carrying the MP7As—black, broad-shouldered, clean-cut, wearing a gold shirt with a striped tie—ran up the stairs right past the camera Max had used to disable the video system.

"Jackson," the leader barked.

Also carrying an MP7A, Jackson identified himself to Max by stepping forward. Burly, white, the youngest of them, he looked like a college athlete attending an awards dinner in his too-tight white shirt and gray slacks with a red-and-blue-striped tie.

The leader said, "You start working the grounds."

Jackson said, "Yes sir," crisply military, and moved over to the keyboard, where he punched several buttons, the alarm light turning green. Once Jackson had gone outside, the fourth member of the team—a muscular young Hispanic in a light blue shirt, navy slacks, and navy tie—punched the IN button, once again setting the alarm.

Max turned her head to watch Jackson heading away from the house, holding her breath, just waiting for him to turn and look right at her, standing there in the window . . . but he did not. Soon the foggy front yard had swallowed him.

"Morales," the leader said, his voice soft, "you go right, I'll go left."

While the leader opened the door and entered the room on the left, Morales entered the room on the right. Through the second of the open doors, just before Morales closed it behind him, Max glimpsed a painting in a gold-leaf frame on the far wall.

She decided that was as good a place as any to start.

A minute ticked by. Stealing a look in the direction the leader had gone, then glancing up the stairs, Max satisfied herself neither man was headed back her way, not immediately anyway.

So she made her move.

She slipped from her hiding place and crept across the foyer; she opened the door slowly, carefully, quietly, peeked into the room . . .

. . . and didn't see Morales.

She eased in.

The room was large, almost . . . huge, more like something out of a museum than a house. High-ceilinged, with a beautifully polished hardwood floor and dark mahogany paneling, this was home to painting after painting, framed canvases covering all four walls of the windowless chamber, three and sometimes four rows of them, like fabulously expensive wallpaper. A few Mission-style chairs were positioned around the floor, but it was essentially bare, and—more important to Max—vacant.

Stepping farther into the gallery, she noted another door on the opposite wall at the far end. Morales had obviously entered, not seen anyone, and exited right out the other side, to check rooms beyond.

Max strolled up the middle of the room, gazing at the paintings on either side. Some she'd seen before in Moody's books, and in magazines and online; but others were strangers to her, though the styles were familiar and she could probably play pin-the-artist-on-the-painting. . . .

This was more than she could ever have imagined.

Again the thought of stealing enough to retire surfaced, but she wouldn't need a moving van to do it; she could cut canvas after canvas out of their frames, roll them up, and take the whole lot. If Moody's lessons on quality had served her well, then her eyes told her she wouldn't need Vogelsang to find Seth. She could *buy* an uptown detective agency; hell, she could buy *Manticore!* . . .

This fantasy blipped across her mind, and then she banished it—too much time, too many risks; in this house, with those four armed security soldiers roaming, she could spend no longer thinking about such things. She needed to get her damn painting—and maybe one or two more—and get the hell out of Dodge.

The thief found her Grant Wood halfway down the right-hand wall. She did not fool around, jumping the alarm wire, pulling the painting down, and freeing it from its ornate antique gold frame . . . which, she momentarily lamented, could have been sold for a good price, as well; but that would have made this package even more bulky than it was now.

The thirty inch by thirty-nine inch sheet of Masonite was heavy and hard, and perhaps she just should have abandoned it as her goal, and gambled on a few canvases; but this painting was a sure thing, an objective she'd researched well.

Plan and execute, Moody would say; *improvise at your own risk.* . . .

Max carefully slid the Wood into a zippered waterproof bag she'd carried in folded under her vest, and glanced around to see if she dared snatch one more prize, before the security boys came back.

As her eyes flicked from frame to frame, something in a corner at the far end of the room caught her attention—a pedestal on which perched a Plexiglas case about the size of a basketball, with something resting on black velvet inside. The only such display in the room, it had a temporary feeling, as if this had been arranged only until a better show-case could be found.

As she got closer—and finally began to comprehend just what it was she was beholding—her stomach wrenched, and she suddenly had the feeling that a nest of snakes was slithering down inside her. . . .

Sitting smugly on black velvet, much as it had back at the Hollywood Heritage Museum, was the Heart of the Ocean.

The air seemed somehow thinner now, and her breathing came in short, rapid gasps. Questions tumbled through her mind, like dominoes knocking into each other. . . .

How had it gotten here?

Had Sterling been Moody's buyer?

Or had some fence bought it from Moody and sold it to Sterling?

Sufficient time had passed, since the original theft, for either of those transactions to have taken place; and yet somehow Max couldn't understand how the necklace had gotten from Moody's pocket to this room, in this house. Something seemed . . . wrong.

Very wrong.

Her face felt hot, her stomach icy, and goose bumps of fear ran up her arms, something that had not happened since . . . *and she flashed on herself, in the woods, the night of the escape, fleeing Manticore, fleeing Lydecker.* . . .

"Beautiful, isn't it?" a warm voice asked from behind her.

And yet there was something cold about it.

In fact, the voice froze her, the zippered bag with the Grant Wood inside still dangling from her right hand, like an absurdly oversized purse.

It wasn't a voice belonging to any hired help: this was Jared Sterling's voice; she hadn't turned around yet, but she recognized it, from video clips she'd played on Kendra's computer.

Still looking at the lovely blue stone, she said, "Someone told me once . . . diamonds are a girl's best friend."

"Wrong movie. . . . You want to put the painting down?"

Max shook her head slowly. "Not really. I worked pretty hard to get it."

"As did I."

A door opened, and another voice blurted: "Sir!"

"Ah—Morales. Take over, would you? I'm just having a glass of warm milk . . . my ulcer again."

Behind her, she heard a pistol cock.

"Try not to kill her, Morales," the warm voice said. "She has a very nice ass."

Then another door opened, and footsteps echoed away.

The new voice spoke again, and it was touched with a south-of-the-border lilt: "Turn around, you . . . slowly."

She did as she'd been told—a good girl—and Morales stood in front of her now, his pistol aimed at the middle of her chest.

"Nice and easy now," he said. "I want you to set that bag on the floor, like it's your poor sweet gran'ma."

Again she did as told—even though she had no "sweet gran'ma" that she knew of.

Morales's other hand went up to his mouth and he spoke into his sleeve. "Intruder contained in the gallery, repeat, the gallery."

Rising slowly, she heard a crackily "ten-four" from Morales's earpiece.

Then the security man crossed slowly toward her and, though his face remained impassive and professional, something sexual flickered in his eyes when he said, "I'm going to have to pat you down."

"I don't think so."

"Put your hands behind your head, little girl; wing those elbows."

Morales crouched, keeping his handgun and his eyes on his captive even as his free hand reached for the zippered bag. He had begun to rise, slowly, when footsteps in the foyer drew his eyes toward the door, just long enough to give Max the opening she needed.

She swung at the waist, twisting her body as if exercising, and one of those elbows he'd requested caught Morales on the side of the head.

Pitching sideways from the blow, he got off one wild shot that buried itself in the wall, between two of those valuable pictures. She thrust her right foot into his throat, and—already off-balance—he tumbled backward, gasping for breath. Before he hit the floor, Max had kicked the gun from his fingers and it went spinning across the waxed wood floor, clattering against the floorboards clear across the room.

Morales gurgled and seemed vaguely conscious, but showed no sign of getting up.

Behind her, in that doorway Sterling had slipped out, a deep voice growled, "Freeze!"

Instead, Max did two cartwheels, and was into her back flip when the tall crew-cut leader's pistol coughed harshly, twice, both rounds missing the blur that was Max and burying themselves in a wall and a painting, respectively.

The catlike home invader landed in front of him, perhaps a yard separating them, enough room for her to kick the pistol from his hand. Then she pirouetted, back-kicked the estate's top security man in the belly, folding him up, and sent him flying across the room, where he smacked into a wall hard enough to make several pictures hang crooked.

He still had that gun, so she went to him, incredibly fast, and when he tried to rise, and looked at where she'd been, the intruder was gone . . . and he then glanced to his right, where she was now standing.

"Can't play with you," she said. "Sorry. . . ."

Her left foot caught him in the groin and he cried out shrilly and sagged to the floor again. Max was taking no chances, however, and as soon as her left foot touched the floor, her right foot came up and caught the leader under the chin, knocking him unconscious and sending him sliding across the waxed surface, like a kid on a sled.

She sprinted back to where Morales lay bubbling—he was unconscious now—and snatched up the waterproof bag. Then she smashed the Plexiglas case with a kick, and—for the second time!—grabbed the precious Heart of the Ocean, triggering an alarm: a buzzerlike bawling.

Max slipped the necklace into a vest pocket, which she zipped shut, and carried the bag with the painting in her left hand as she moved toward the door that would take her back to the foyer—she had come in the front way, she'd go out the same.

She was heading for the security keypad when she all but bumped into the black guy, Maurer, finally down from upstairs, looking a little disheveled, and sweaty, from an apparently thorough and fruitless search of the vast upper floors. The MP7A was in his hands, and he swung it up, leveling the weapon at her . . .

. . . but Max leapt high and with a martial-arts kick sent the weapon flying; when the MP7A landed on the marble floor, hitting hard, it fired off its own burst and shattered a priceless Frank Lloyd Wright chair into kindling.

Maurer was no pushover, however, and he came roaring at her with his fists raised.

"Wanna box?" she asked.

A straight right broke his nose and another landed squarely on his jaw with a satisfying crunch. Maurer fell backward, stiff-legged, and did a backward pratfall, his head smacking on the marble. The only question Max had was whether he was out from her punch, or from losing that battle with the floor. . . .

She didn't bother to Gameboy the keypad; it wasn't like they didn't know she was there. She threw open the front door, triggering the alarm—this one an annoying honking, which made an off-key counterpoint to the gallery buzzer (different sounds apparently indicated different security breach points—Max admired the strategy).

Bad move, she thought, realizing she should have taken the time to punch in the keycode; mentally, she pictured Moody frowning and shaking his head at her.

Those dueling alarms would, with honking and screeching, draw the attention not only of the rest of the security team, but cops and neighbors and anybody for at least a square mile who wasn't stone-cold deaf.

Halfway across the yard, slipping back into the fog, she suddenly saw Jackson emerging from the swirling mist, crossing toward her, his MP7A raised.

Not waiting for him to act, Max launched herself to one side, diving, rolling, disappearing into the smokelike fog.

The guard knew enough not to fire into the fog—he might shoot one of his own team—and when he pursued her, assuming she was on the move, almost ran into her.

Startled, his eyes popped open, and before he could fire, she kicked him in the side of the head, dropping him out-cold to the lawn like a toppled garden gnome.

With those alarms still blaring like dissonant horror-show music, waterproof bag tucked under an arm, Max circled the house, leapt the wall, and approached her hidden boat carefully, in case any of Sterling's security team had scouted ahead.

But only her boat was waiting, and she eased it out onto the lapping water and she, the Grant Wood, the Heart of the Ocean, and the ungainly tourist craft disappeared onto the fog-flung lake.

Not exactly a perfect heist, but the haul was good, and even with a few flubs, she knew Moody would be proud of his girl. This was a seven-figure evening, easy, enough to finance the search for Seth and allow her to slip back into the anonymity of the straight life . . . for a while anyway.

A few hours later, with the glow of the coming day already lightening the easterly sky, Max sat on the couch in her squatter's flat, staring at the necklace.

She still had no idea how Sterling had ended up with it, and now she wondered what she was going to do with it. The painting needed to be fenced, which would cover immediate expenses; unfortunately, she had no such connections in Seattle . . . yet.

She had not called Moody in LA, since getting to town and settling into this new life; she'd wanted a clean break . . . but now she *had* to talk to him. This time of night . . . or morning . . . she didn't dare bother him. But in a few hours, she'd find out what the hell was going on with the real prop of the necklace.

Dropping the stone into a black velvet bag, she hid it in her bedroom, and ambled back out to the living room to try to relax—so hard for her to get to sleep after a score. . . .

To Max's surprise, Kendra was sitting on the couch now, watching TV.

"What's up?" Max asked.

Kendra gave her roommate a coy smile. "Just got home. Had a date."

"Really?" Max sat beside her, gave her sly look. "Nice guy?"

Kendra's smile widened. "No, he was a bad, bad boy . . . in a nice, nice way."

They laughed at that, perhaps a little too much—what with Kendra a little drunk, and Max trapped in wide-awake exhaustion.

"Details," ordered Max, "details."

"No way."

"I would tell *you*."

Her mouth open wide in mock astonishment, Kendra said, "You would not, and we both know it—you are the most secretive little bee-atch on the planet . . . and you're pumping *me* for details?"

"*I* wasn't pumping you," Max said with a laugh. "What I want to know is, *who* was pumping you?"

"Oh, you're wicked. . . ."

They were interrupted by the distracting white noise of TV static; both young women quickly recognized what this signaled, and their conversation ceased as they gave their attention to the cool yet intense eyes on the screen, eyes bordered above and below by blue, with the words STREAMING FREEDOM VIDEO gliding in white letters against a red background.

"Do not attempt to adjust your set," the calm yet intense voice intoned, making the same introduction as before, a sixty-second untraceable cable hack from the only free voice in the city.

"Look at those eyes," Kendra said.

"Shhhh," Max said.

"He can hack my cable any ol' time. . . ."

"Quiet, Kendra."

"This bulletin contains graphic violence, and we are broadcasting at this hour to avoid young viewers. This

footage—banned from the media in Los Angeles where the slaughter occurred two days ago—is sobering evidence of what happens to people who stand up for freedom."

Max's eyes widened in dread as she saw the handheld footage of the outside of the Chinese Theatre.

"Official documents indicate that the gangster group the Brood was responsible," the electronically altered voice continued, *"but the media clampdown—and reports of black-uniformed, heavily armed soldiers at the scene—indicate government involvement, even collusion."*

The camera moved closer to the theater and revealed four bodies sprawled on the patio in postures of bullet-riddled death. Max's fingers clutched the cloth of the couch.

"The Chinese Clan, freedom fighters in the Los Angeles area . . ."

Freedom fighters? Max thought bitterly. *Not hardly. . . .*

The camera moved into the lobby where more bodies were flung, some of them Brood members, and she wondered if Moody's crew had been able to fight back, to hold off the onslaught, to limit the carnage. . . .

". . . were gunned down by the Brood in a dispute, allegedly over stolen goods."

And Max saw Fresca, in his worn Dodgers jacket, lying in rubble next to a headless girl . . . Niner? Fresca's jacket, originally Dodger blue, was now an ugly, blood-soaked purple.

"None of this group of freedom fighters escaped the wrath of the Brood."

The handheld was in the auditorium now. Bodies lay strewn about like abandoned, broken toys.

"Gross," Kendra said; but her eyes were glued to the screen.

Again Max felt warm wetness trailing down her cheeks, but she otherwise remained passive, simply sitting watching the video footage of her dead Clan family.

"Eyes Only sources indicate the Brood may be expanding into Seattle," the voice continued. *"If this criminal gang truly has government sanction, our city will be further enslaved."*

The camera swung around in the theater's auditorium for the image Eyes Only had chosen to make his final point: *Moody's head impaled on a spike.* On spikes on either side of him were the heads of Tippett and Gabriel. . . .

"Shut it off!" Max gasped, and turned away.

Kendra used the remote, but the bulletin was already over, SNN back on; the tears on Max's cheeks surprised her roommate into sobriety.

"What's wrong, Max? You're not the squeamish type."

"I know them . . . *knew* them."

"What?"

"I was one of them . . . the Chinese Clan. They were . . . family. Like family. . . ."

Kendra slipped an arm around Max's shoulders. "Oh, God, Max, I'm so sorry. What can I do to help?"

Max shut the grief off, as if she'd thrown a switch. "You can help me find Eyes Only, I've got to talk to him. I've got to find out more about what happened at that theater."

Kendra's eyes were big, and she was shaking her head. "Honey, I don't know *anything* about him—nobody does. He comes on the tube at will, he does his thing, he splits."

Max shook her head. "There's got to be more to it than that—there must be an underground movement in this city."

"Well, if so, I don't know anything about it. And I don't know anybody who knows anything about Eyes Only. . . . you gonna be all right?"

Nodding, Max said, "I'm fine."

"No you're not. You're holding it in—that's not healthy. If you don't let it out . . ."

"There's nothing to be done for them now."

Kendra frowned in concern. "You sure you don't want to talk it out?"

"Yeah, I'm sure."

"Well . . ." Max's roommate rose, yawned, and said, "I guess I better catch some z's . . . that is, if you're *sure*—"

"Kendra, go ahead and crash. . . . I'll be fine."

After Kendra stumbled off to bed, Max went to her own

room, where she took from its hiding place the black velvet bag with the necklace.

This stone had cost Moody and the others their lives . . . and she hadn't been there for them. . . .

She wept, quietly, her face in a hand, for several minutes; then the thoughts, the questions, began to crystallize.

Eyes Only, Seth, this necklace, the Brood, the art collector Jared Sterling, and maybe even Manticore and Lydecker himself were interwoven in the tragedy that had befallen the Clan.

But *how?*

She knew where to start. Not Eyes Only—his whereabouts, like his identity, were a mystery. Seth had given up no leads since the brawl with the boys in blue; and the necklace was a mute witness. The Brood was in LA, and Lydecker was at Manticore.

That left one option.

The ten-man security team would be ready for her next time, but she could see no other choice: Max would have to return to the scene of the crime.

Chapter Nine

EYES ONLY

LOGAN CALE'S APARTMENT
SEATTLE, WASHINGTON, 2019

Even in the post-Pulse world, the ringing of a doorbell was, generally, an innocuous thing.

Right now, with midnight approaching, the doorbell in Logan Cale's condominium was trilling the hello of an unannounced guest. The building was secure, and the lobby guard would normally call and check before sending anyone through.

But there had been no call—just the ringing of the bell.

And in the life of Logan Cale, answering a doorbell could mean his last act on earth.

First, there was the risk that someone with the government—or some "civic-minded" citizen looking for reward money—would enter and discover the not-terribly-secret home studio from which Logan broadcast the cyberbulletins of his very secret alter ego, Eyes Only.

Second, Logan was one of a long line of Americans born to wealth who developed a sense of shame—even guilt—for his life of privilege, a sentiment that had blossomed into genuine social concern. And, while his underground identity as Eyes Only seemed secure, his reputation as an aboveground left-leaning journalist was well known.

This of course did not prevent Logan from being perceived as just another fat-cat target. The Cale family had the kind of affluence that had easily weathered the Pulse and its various upheavals and problems . . . one of which was kidnapping the rich for ransom.

As in the Great Twentieth-Century Depression, this left-handed entrepreneurial pursuit had become the "racket of choice" of many criminals, from down-on-their-outers to sophisticated career criminals. And as in the Lindbergh era of "snatches," the victims usually turned up dead, even after full payment had been made.

So . . . if this caller wasn't who Logan thought it was, he just might never get to open the door again.

Logan could ignore the bell. His two-hundred-fifty-pound ex-cop bodyguard, Peter, had the night off, and—unless this was a full-scale raid, in which the door would be battered down, anyway—Logan could just continue with his research and wait for whoever-it-was to go away.

But if this caller was who Logan suspected it might be, he would prefer to take the meeting during Peter's absence. If this was someone else, well, that was why Peter very seldom got a night off, and on the rare occasions when Logan did answer his own door, he did so in the company of a shotgun.

The bell rang again.

Paranoia runs deep, Logan thought with a wry little smile, quoting a very old song as he rose from his massive array of racked computer gear—including half a dozen monitors and a networked laptop—and strode from his work space with an easy grace suggesting an acceptance of whatever might befall him in his quixotic but so-necessary crusade.

A shade over six feet tall, dark blond and blue-eyed behind wire-frame glasses, Logan Cale had rowed crew at Yale, and continued to work out, maintaining a slender yet muscular physique worthy of a college athlete; his apparel—jeans, a pullover gray sweater, and sneakers—added to an eternal-college-boy air of which he was wholly unaware.

His surroundings—the sprawling, modern condo, decorated with quality and taste (or at least he liked to think so)—were the one indulgence of wealth Logan allowed himself. With hardwood floors in each room, and the occasional area rug, the place had a stark, masculine feel; translucent panels separated the rooms, track lighting bathing his world in pale orange, peach, and yellow.

In the living room, each wall bore a different color, earth tones or a combination thereof. Two walls came together to form the corner of the predominantly glass high-rise, allowing a great deal of light into the room by day. Though the furniture was expensive—hard woods, sleek lines, designer stuff—the overall statement was minimalism. A plush brown sofa dominated the center of the room with simple white and silver end tables and a matching coffee table in front. Chairs sat perpendicular to the couch, completing the feng shui of the room.

Shotgun in his hands, Logan approached the double doors that were the front entry to the apartment; a small video screen to the right served as an electronic peephole.

About Logan's height, his visitor was a sullenly handsome young man of maybe twenty or twenty-one—short brown hair, green eyes, and a long, angular face—in a black leather jacket, dark blue T-shirt, and black jeans.

Logan opened the door.

"Take your goddamn time, why don't you?" the young man said, his voice deeper and older than his years, his barely contained rage evident.

"Why hello, Seth," Logan said. "Forgive me—from now on, I'll just sit by the door, waiting for you to stop by, unannounced."

Seth grunting a humorless laugh was his only reply.

Logan tried not to take Seth's dark attitude personally; the boy had this kind of quiet contempt for just about everybody and everything.

Logan gestured for Seth to come in, which he did. While Logan shut the door, pausing for a moment to look at the video security monitor, just in case someone had followed Seth up, the young man crossed to the couch and fell onto it with the kind of casual familiarity of a family member.

"Make yourself at home," Logan said, dryly, ambling in after his guest.

"I'd feel more at home with a drink," Seth said, a condescending smile tickling the thin lips.

Logan took a deep breath and let it out slow, fighting irritation; this screwed-up kid had a way of looking both happy and miserable at the same time, like that old-time movie actor . . . what was his name? Then Logan remembered: James Dean.

Deciding not to slap the smirk off the young man's face, Logan asked, "Scotch, I suppose?"

"I been off Bosco for a while."

What a charmer, Logan thought, went to the kitchen and came back with a glass filled with ice and clear liquid. He handed Seth the glass.

"This is water," the young man said, just looking at it.

"Can't get anything by you."

"What are you . . . my daddy now? I'd like a goddamn Scotch."

"Maybe 'daddy' doesn't feel you need your judgment impaired any worse than it already is."

Seth obviously knew immediately what Logan meant, and sipped the water, putting the glass—thoughtfully—on a coaster on the nearby coffee table.

The relationship between the two had been strained from the beginning—neither liked the other's style, or manner. But they needed each other (*codependents,* Logan thought), each offering abilities and knowledge the other didn't have. It had made for a rocky ride thus far, Seth with his gift for alienating almost anybody who came into his life—particularly anyone who got at all close—and Logan, always focused on the struggle, with little patience for those who did not share his passion.

The pair had been introduced less than a month ago by Ben Daly, a mousy middle-aged med tech who was a mutual acquaintance. Among Logan's Eyes Only efforts was a sort of Underground Railroad, and the cyber–freedom fighter had been working on securing safe passage to Canada for Daly, where the tech hoped with Cale's help to disappear into a new identity.

Daly was on the run from his former employer, a private corporation that had been taken over by U.S. government black ops. The med tech and his fellow employees had been experimenting in bio-enhancement technology, but the new covert project—Project Manticore—moved the experiment into using recombinant DNA to produce a superior combat soldier. When Manticore started using children as guinea pigs, Daly decided he'd had enough.

Another research scientist at the facility gave notice, and this encouraged Daly to make an appointment to see his boss, to tender his own resignation . . . and the next night, said research scientist was a hit-and-run fatality. The head of Manticore, the spookily soft-spoken Colonel Donald Lydecker, had said to Daly, "A dangerous world out there—what was it you wanted to talk to me about, Mr. Daly?"

So Ben Daly settled in, did his job, and waited for his chance. It wasn't until well after the Pulse that he'd gotten away—Manticore was the kind of job you couldn't quit . . . you had to *escape* from it, like the prison it was—and he'd stayed hidden for years, the last three in Seattle, working as a lowly (but alive) lab tech.

And then Daly had been tracked down by Seth. At first Daly thought the X5 had been sent by Manticore, but it quickly became apparent he was simply looking for a solution to the seizures that had afflicted him, and his siblings, since their youth. A runaway. Still, Seth's turning up gave Daly a sudden, desperate desire to leave Seattle, and find some new rock to crawl under. If Seth, a kid on the run, working by himself, could find Daly, it was only a matter of time until organization-man Lydecker came calling.

Though he hadn't been able to solve Seth's health problem, Daly had informed the renegade X5 that tryptophan—a homeopathic neurotransmitter—could help control the symptoms. In an effort to keep from getting his ass kicked by Seth for failing to end the seizures, Daly had introduced the volatile young man to Logan.

Daly, of course, was unaware that Logan was Eyes Only; but he did know that Logan was an anti-establishment journalist from a very wealthy family.

"Maybe you can track down some doctor or research scientist," Daly had said, "who can address Seth's condition . . . maybe you can network with this Eyes Only character. Who knows?"

"Who knows," Logan had said.

Logan suspected Daly didn't care if the X5 got help or not. Likely the med tech only hoped that Seth would latch onto Logan as a new target of his dark moods. If so, Daly's strategy had proved successful: the tech was in some little town on the edge of the Arctic Circle, and Seth was still in Seattle, playing a dangerous game with Logan Cale.

Sprawled on the couch, running shoes up on it, Seth might have been a patient in a psychiatrist's office. Referring to Ryan Devane—the corrupt sector chief who had been selling everything from under-the-table sector passes to minority teenagers into slavery overseas—Seth said, "Problem solved."

Few in Seattle, no matter their political persuasion, had any doubt that Devane was a bad man . . . many would have called him evil; but his position had been so well insulated, he couldn't be touched . . . except by Eyes Only.

"Solved," Logan echoed emptily.

"Did what you wanted," Seth said.

"What I wanted, and more."

"You wanted him stopped." Seth smiled over innocently at Logan, who had settled into a chair. "I stopped him."

"You killed him."

Seth shrugged, folded his hands on his tummy, stared at the ceiling. "That's pretty much the most efficient way to stop somebody."

Shaking his head, Logan said, "The most efficient way isn't always the best way."

"I agree . . . but in this case, it was. You're not going to lecture me on that ends-don't-justify-the-means b.s. again, are you? They taught us ethics at fuckin' Manticore."

"I'll just bet they did. They teach you anything about justice?"

The younger man thought about it for a long moment. "Justice was served. . . . What's next?"

"Never mind what's next," Logan said, rising, propelled by rage. "How the hell do you figure 'justice' was served by murder?"

Seth glanced over with an expression of mock innocence. "Any children sold into slavery lately?"

"That doesn't justify—"

"Sure it does. Bastard got what he deserved."

Logan began to pace, hands in the pockets of his slacks. "Seth—that's not justice, that's revenge."

"Same difference," Seth said, and swung into a sitting position, leaning back, arms outstretched on the back of the couch.

Logan said, "I wanted to stop him—expose him, entrap him—"

"Whoa, whoa, whoa—isn't entrapment illegal? I thought the ends didn't justify the means?"

"When law enforcement itself is corrupt, certain extreme measures have to be taken. It's a matter of degree, Seth— some laws go beyond politics. These are laws that have to do with society, with civilization, even religion."

"Oh, shit, you're not gonna go *religious* on my ass, now!"

"No . . . no. But 'Thou Shalt Not Kill' is part of the social contract, Seth. You can't—"

"Bullshit! The social contract got ripped up when the Pulse went down—where was the social contract when Manticore was makin' *me,* like instant soup in a damn test tube?"

Logan stopped pacing. He sat down next to Seth. "Don't make me regret taking you into my confidence."

Seth's grin was a terrible thing. "Thought you had a supersoldier to play with, didn'tcha? And now you're afraid all you got is a loose cannon . . . am I on to something, 'Eyes Only'?"

"Seth . . . please . . . We have the opportunity to be a team. To make a difference. . . ."

"We're already making a difference!" Seth sprang to his feet; now he was the one pacing, but there was a raving and ranting quality to the words that accompanied it. "Logan, you were unhappy when a corrupt official was ruining lives and selling children into slavery . . . and now you're telling me you're *still* unhappy, even though we stopped the mofo!"

"I'm not unhappy he's been stopped—"

"But you *are* unhappy this blight on society is dead? Are you fuckin' *high?*"

Logan sighed. "You were acting as my . . . agent. I feel responsible for that man's death. And I don't like it, not one little bit."

Seth stopped in front of Logan and put his hands together in a prayerful gesture. "How touching . . . but your liberal guilt doesn't negate the fact that the mission was accomplished and we saved maybe hundreds, who knows, maybe even thousands of kids from being sold into slavery."

Logan could see he wasn't going to prevail in this debate. And he feared the moral complexities would continue to elude this kid—the supersoldier genetic makeup perhaps had made Seth a literal killing machine.

Maybe over the long haul, Logan could convince Seth that justice didn't necessarily mean the summary execution of everyone they went after. He only hoped he could control and shape Colonel Lydecker's nasty lab rat into something positive for society.

Now Seth plopped down in a chair opposite the couch. A tiny, almost naughty smile formed on the sullenly handsome face. "I think it's time."

"Time?"

"Time we went after Manticore."

Logan sighed again. "It is *not* time."

"Well, *I* think it is."

That was the level of their discourse, Logan thought: *Is too,* is not, *is too,* is not. . . .

Meeting the young man's unblinking gaze with his own, Logan said, "We don't know enough. Really, we don't know anything. We still don't know where their headquarters is, we don't know where you were raised, other than the Wyoming mountains somewhere. . . ."

Seth exploded out of the chair. "What have you been doing while I been risking my ass?" Seth gestured with both hands, his arms wide in frustration. "What are you doin' with those fancy-ass computers? Downloading porn? Hitting the cybercasinos?"

"These things take time."

Bouncing on his heels, Seth said, "You've had what—

three, four weeks? Enough time for me to take out Devane, and you haven't found out *anything?*"

Seething inside, Logan resisted the urge to tell Seth to use his abilities to take a spectacular flying fuck, and said, "I've started looking into old factories, abandoned prisons, military bases. But these people are smart, and they're dangerous, and they don't want to be found. If they did, you would have found them already."

Seth seemed almost to pout, and said, somewhat childishly, "But you've had three weeks, man!"

"You've had how many years? And you haven't found them, have you, Seth?"

"I haven't been looking—I've been hiding. But now I got *you,* and your resources . . . we can take 'em on, Logan! We can take 'em down!"

"And we're going to. We *are.* And I do have a lead. . . ."

Seth's eyes widened, like a child anticipating Christmas. "What kind of a lead?"

"I take it you didn't see the bulletins on the LA Massacre—I ran it three times yesterday."

"No . . . I was . . . busy."

"I guess you were. Come with me."

Logan walked Seth to the office-cum-broadcast-center, where the main monster computer was (as always) running and each monitor had several windows open. The cyberjournalist played the X5 a video CD of the bulletin that included the grisly footage of the Chinese Theatre slaughter. At the mention of the troops in black rumored to have supported the Brood in the massacre, Seth perked up.

"That's Manticore . . . that's *got* to be Manticore."

Logan ran the VCD again, with the sound down. "What would draw Manticore into helping one side of a street gang war?"

"I'd like to know the answer to that."

"Good." Logan smiled at Seth, rather blandly. "Because that's where we're going to start . . . assuming you don't kill our target, before we find anything out."

Seth smirked. "Who is he?"

"Well, it is a him . . . but it's *more* than a him. It's a 'them.' "

"The Brood?"

"The Brood is part of it. You heard the bulletin: they're expanding to Seattle."

"Who did they send here?"

"They didn't 'send' anybody—the top man himself came . . . Mikhail Kafelnikov."

Logan brought up another picture: a muscular blond man who had the good looks of a pre-Pulse rock star, and the rap sheet of a serial killer. "He's rumored to have ordered or taken part in as many as one hundred murders in Los Angeles."

The young man studied the picture. "You made a good point, Logan—Manticore and a street gang . . . it just doesn't compute."

"Seth, back in the early part of the last century, street gangs of Italian kids evolved into the biggest, most successful organized crime syndicate in the history of man."

"And this history lesson is because? . . ."

"The Brood may evolve into something much bigger than a street gang . . . particularly with covert support from Manticore."

"So what is this . . . Haselhoff guy *up* to, in our great city?"

"It's Kafelnikov . . ."

"Whatever."

". . . and he's selling art and Americana to foreigners. Any precious remnant of our past that he can get his hands on, really, he'll sell to whoever offers the most."

Seth arched an eyebrow. "And we care, because? . . ."

"Because he's selling off priceless works of American art."

Seth was not following this. "The point being . . ."

Logan knew he could never make Seth understand how he felt, and why this battle was important.

No Americana would eventually mean . . . no America. He'd watched other countries sell the heritage that was their symbolic soul, during financial hardships since the Pulse. People needed that cultural bedrock to build their societies on, and when that bedrock was peddled to other nations, it took away a country's sense of permanence, a people's sense of home. Citizens began to feel like renters in their own land.

"I can't explain this easily," Logan said. "You were Manticore's prisoner for how long?"

"Ten years. What's that got to do with it?"

"Even though you hated it, even though you eventually ran from it, Manticore was your home. When you escaped, didn't part of you miss it?"

"You *are* high!" Seth's eyes blazed. "No, *hell,* no!"

Logan put a hand on the boy's shoulder. "You mean to say you didn't . . . you don't . . . miss your siblings? The sense of belonging that comes from being with a group you know you can trust to take care of you? That sense of wholeness? You didn't miss any of that?"

Seth looked at him for a moment, then the young man's eyes fell away and he found something on the floor to study.

Logan said, "That's what I'm talking about, with these people selling off American art. It destroys, one piece at a time, who we are . . . how we feel about the American family . . . making it easier to divide us. We're all abused children, now, Seth—and this kind of abuse to our . . . national spirit . . . well, it's one thing we don't need."

"Run for fuckin' office, why don't you? Look, this art scam—it's the first hustle the Brood's working on our turf?"

"Yes."

"Well, Logan, why didn't you say so. We got to stop the bastards."

Feeling a little embarrassed, and a bit like a pompous ass, Logan couldn't keep himself from smiling. "Kafelnikov isn't moving the stuff out of LA—somehow he's moving it out of the country through Seattle."

"And you want to know how he's doing that?"

"Yes—who's working with him, and where the deals go down—maybe we can . . . rescue some Americana."

"Groovy," Seth said, still unimpressed by the cultural flag-waving. "Any clues at all?"

Logan leaned in, used a mouse to open a window on one of the many glowing monitor screens. A picture popped up of a blond, trimly bearded man in his late twenties, next to a painting called *Death on the Ridge Road*.

Pointing, Logan said, "That's Jared Sterling."

"Looks like an upstanding citizen."

"As upstanding as they come . . . major art collector, philanthropist, and billionaire computer magnate."

"Sterling . . . Sterling—the Internet guy?"

"The Internet guy."

Seth leaned in, taking a closer look at the Grant Wood painting. "Looks like he's into, what's-it, Americana, too."

"Oh yes." Using the mouse, Logan brought up pictures of various American art pieces. "These paintings—*American Gothic* . . . *Whistler's Mother* . . . Jackson Pollock's *Key,* works by Thomas Hart Benton, Winslow Homer, and several other major American painters—have come into Sterling's hands . . . legally . . . and then disappeared."

"Disappeared?"

"Perhaps that's overstating. He acquires these pieces—sometimes with great fanfare—seems to have them for a while, loans them for a museum showing or two . . . and then they vanish into his 'collection.' As art pieces the public can appreciate, they drop out of sight, and are never seen again."

"If he owns them, I guess he's got the right."

"Well . . . I don't want to venture into ethical waters with you again, Seth. But you should know also that Jared Sterling is considered to be one of the most ruthless and, yes, unethical businessmen to emerge in the post-Pulse world."

"Even if he's selling this stuff overseas, Logan, it's no crime—he owns the shit, right?"

"Yes he owns the 'shit'—but it *is* a crime." After the Cooperstown and Statue of Liberty debacles, there had been a backlash, and a number of bills had been passed to protect what remained of America's heritage. "The American Art Protection Act, of twenty-fifteen, makes it very illegal for any paintings on the protected list to be sold outside of our shores."

Seth frowned. "There's a list of paintings like, what? Endangered species?"

"More like historic landmarks, important buildings that can't be torn down to make room for another detention center. Jared Sterling owns dozens of paintings on the Smithsonian American Masterpieces list."

"So Sterling can own these paintings, but he can't sell them?"

"Not overseas—the paintings would be confiscated, and he'd be a felon. In addition, I suspect he's moving stolen art, and some of the 'legal' transactions include such odds and ends as the original owner of Sterling's latest acquisition washing up dead on a beach."

Mention of a murder seemed to have finally caught Seth's attention. "Where would *we* come in?"

"Well, he's obviously making these transactions discreetly . . . and he may be using the same conduit to move his artwork as Kafelnikov. In fact, Sterling may *be* that conduit . . . that may be what brought the Russian to Seattle."

"So Sterling's scam will lead us to the LA guy's scam."

"My instinct is it's the *same* scam." He handed Seth a slip of paper with an address on it, and some security info Logan had hacked. "Your next stop . . ."

Seth glanced at the paper, memorized in an instant, and tossed it on the nearby computer station. "You're the boss," Seth said, with only the faintest sarcasm.

Logan walked him to the door. "And do me a favor, Seth?"

Seth smirked. "Why not?"

"Please don't kill this one right away."

"Which one you talkin' about—Sterling, or this Russian guy?"

"Either. Neither."

Seth shrugged. "Fine—but take this Russian, for example. Look at all those gang kids he massacred. Guy is an evil dude—and he's tied to damn *Manticore!* Wouldn't the world be better off without him?"

"Just gather the information, Seth."

Seth was shaking his head, truly not getting it. "If this Kasselrock is the problem . . ."

"Kafelnikov."

". . . then killing his evil ass ought to *end* the problem . . . his part in it, anyway."

Logan grasped the X5's arm. "Seth, if you kill him, we'll never know what happened to the paintings he's already smuggled . . . assuming, of course, that he's the right guy to begin with."

"If these paintings are gone, they're gone. What's the difference?"

Logan wasn't sure whether Seth was . . . teasing him, or really was this bloodthirsty; probably the former, but that he could even be considering the latter was very disturbing. . . .

"Seth, we need to know if Kafelnikov is tied to Manticore . . . and if so, how, and why. *That's* our best lead, at the moment."

"You don't mind if I let *that* motivate me," Seth said, "and not some sense of preserving 'Americana.' "

"Not at all. But watch your all-American ass, my friend. The Russian, whose name you refuse to learn how to pronounce . . ."

Proving he'd been yanking Logan's chain all along, Seth said, "Kafelnikov."

"Any way you say it, Seth, he's a dangerous man."

Halfway out the door, the X5 shrugged. "*I'm* a dangerous man."

Logan couldn't think of anything to say to that.

MANTICORE HEADQUARTERS
GILLETTE, WYOMING, 2019

Colonel Donald Lydecker sat at his desk, drumming his fingers on its Lucite-covered metal top.

Had Max been there to see him, she would have noted that he looked little different than he had when the X5s broke out of Manticore back in '09. The years had been kind to Lydecker, despite an alcoholism problem that he had kept in check during that same time span. His blond hair now contained a few straggling grays but was thick as ever. His icy blue eyes had changed only in that he now needed glasses for reading, and more "smile" lines had been etched in the corners. His body was still tight and muscular . . . it just took a little more effort these days, to keep it that way.

His office was strictly government issue, the walls and ceiling a pastel mint green, the file cabinets, chairs, desk, and computer table all standard institutional gray. Not one personal item adorned the top of his desk or any other part of the anonymous, no-nonsense office. Only his black shirt, slacks, and leather jacket were—because of his sub-rosa status—not GI.

Across the desk from him were two subordinates—a kid in his early twenties, Jensen, and an African American in his mid- to late thirties, Finch. The two men stood at attention, soldiers in civilian suits and ties, and Lydecker thought he detected a slight trembling in both.

It pleased him that they feared him—in his lexicon, *fear* and *respect* were analogous. He let his breath out slowly, calming himself, getting centered, just as he'd taught his kids.

"I've been watching video footage of one of our X5s—a male."

"Yes, sir," they said in unison.

"And where do you suppose I got that footage?"

They glanced at each other quickly, then turned their eyes front. Neither man spoke.

"Perhaps I got it from our own intelligence efforts. Do you think I got it from our own intelligence efforts, Mr. Jensen?"

". . . no, sir."

"How about you, Mr. Finch?"

"Yes, sir . . . I mean, no sir. . . ."

Lydecker sighed, just a little. "I got it from SNN."

The two men stared straight ahead; they might have been carved from stone . . . if stone trembled.

"Would someone please tell me why the Satellite News Network can find one of our kids, and we can't?"

Finch and Jensen had no answers.

"Mr. Finch, I want our people at the offices of SNN within the hour."

"Yes, sir," Finch said.

"Mr. Jensen, I want to know the source of this tape."

"Yes, sir."

"And I don't want it tomorrow. Dismissed."

The two men saluted, turned, and left.

Lydecker turned to the TV and VHS machine on a cart near his desk, and played the tape again. He watched the grainy picture as the young man leapt across the screen. He knew immediately it was one of his X5s. Judging by the athleticism of the boy's moves, Lydecker figured the young man on the tape was Zack, or perhaps Seth. The two oldest subjects, they had always been the best athletes of the X5 program.

Lydecker could only appreciate the athleticism of the young man, the beauty of his discipline. If this one was anything to judge by, these kids were growing up to be just what he and the others had dreamed they could be. Watching his creation clean the clocks of five police officers in less than forty seconds, Lydecker felt a surge of parental pride. . . .

Thirteen of them had escaped that night, the group of twelve and their leader, Zack, with Seth immediately captured but overcoming the two guards and slipping out in the confusion; and the colonel had spent much of the last ten years trying to round up this deadly baker's dozen.

He knew the higher-ups considered his recapture record less than stellar; the irony was, he had done his job so well with his young soldiers that they had made him look incompetent. Two out of thirteen in a decade did seem a shade paltry . . . he still remembered the general staring at him in contempt, saying, "You mean to say you can't recover a goddamn bunch of little *kids?*"

Little kids.

When they'd escaped, the youngest one had been seven. That meant six years of full-bore Manticore training. . . . Kavi had been the first to be recaptured and that had taken over five years. Even then, it had been luck that they'd stumbled onto him in Wolf Point, Montana.

Kavi, then twelve, had been spotted by a Manticore

operative—Finch, in fact—who'd stopped to watch some
kids playing baseball. Kavi made a throw on the fly from the
outfield fence to home plate . . . a major leaguer would have
envied that throw . . . and Finch knew immediately where
the kid had gotten the golden arm.

Two and a half years later, Vada, a female—eleven at the
time of the escape—had been surrounded in the desert outside Amargosa Valley, Nevada. She had grown into a shapely
young woman in a T-shirt and jeans and running shoes—soft
brown hair, huge brown eyes, full sensuous lips.

Noting the sexual attractiveness of one of his own kids,
Lydecker felt a twinge of something . . . guilt? Embarrassment? But the colonel could hardly fail to notice that
Vada's blossoming physique looked ready for a whole different set of sins than those she'd been designed for.

When she fought back, dropping three members of the
TAC team without losing a drop of sweat, Lydecker had
drawn his pistol, warned her once.

She cursed him and came running at him, like a wild
beast, her fists tiny hard things raised to pummel. . . .

When he put that bullet between her pert breasts, Lydecker
surprised himself with an immediate feeling of loss.

Self-defense, his mind assured him.

But it wasn't that easy: Vada was, after all, one of his own.
He had reminded himself that this was his job, and if anyone
was going to kill one of his kids, it should be him. After all,
the X5s were his responsibility.

And it wasn't like she was the first.

After the unpleasantness in Los Angeles—he'd found
dealing with the Russian and his rabble extremely distaste-
ful—Lydecker had returned empty-handed again. The amazing reports of the dark-haired young woman—Jondy? . . .
Max, maybe?—had all the earmarks of an X5.

But after aiding and abetting the slaughter at the Chinese
Theatre, Lydecker had come home with bupkus, the trail
cold, ice cold. . . .

Now, a reprieve, a real shot at getting back another of the
X5s, a male, and he didn't want to let that chance get away
like the girl in LA.

He picked up the phone to arrange transport to Seattle. No matter what his men learned or did not learn at SNN, Lydecker had a trip to take.

One of his kids had turned up in Seattle . . .

. . . and "daddy" longed for a reunion.

ENGIDYNE SOFTWARE
SEATTLE, WASHINGTON, 2019

The child Lydecker sought was creeping down the hall of the uppermost floor of Engidyne Software, the computer infrastructure company whose youthful CEO . . . and owner . . . was Jared Sterling. Seth had bypassed the alarm, opened a window in a lunchroom, and gotten inside.

This was the executive level of a steel-and-mostly-glass six-story suburban box that was otherwise primarily rabbit warrens of underpaid computer geeks. This floor, unnervingly quiet after hours, served the top echelon, half a dozen wonks who had been with Sterling from the start, millionaires thanks to Engidyne stock options. No one on this floor had to stay late to prove him- or herself, and—while a few geeks on the floors below labored into the night, seeking advancement that would never come—that left only a token security staff, about half a dozen . . . who had just finished their hourly rounds of the floor.

With its deep plush carpeting, expensive oak paneling, and gilt-framed examples from Sterling's art collection lining the walls, the executive floor felt more like the mansion of the company's owner than his corporate office. Seth moved down the darkened hallways, spidering himself to the wall, avoiding the built-in video cameras. Slick and unobtrusive, the security cams had a flaw: they were stationary, and could be maneuvered around.

Without any trouble—and with the help of Logan's info— Seth easily made his way to Sterling's office. Even without Logan, Seth could hardly have missed the egomaniacal display that was Sterling's name, embossed in gold on a black plate on the rich wood door. He picked the lock and went in.

To the right sat the desk of Sterling's executive assistant, Alison Santiago (or so said the nameplate). This reception area gave Ms. Santiago a generous space that any nerd downstairs would have given his or her pocket-protector collection for.

Stepping to Sterling's door, Seth found this inner barrier locked as well, used a pair of picks to open it in 3.5 seconds, and stepped inside, closing and relocking it. If the security guards checked while he was inside, they'd find this door locked and likely move on: all Seth would have to do to facilitate that was conduct his search in the near dark. Between his sharper-than-shit eyesight, and blinds he adjusted to let in moonlight, Seth knew that would be no prob.

He settled in for a thorough search.

Seth didn't even turn on a lamp or use a flashlight to take this unguided tour of Sterling's office. The CEO's desk was clutter-free and not quite big enough to accommodate an ice-skating competition, his computer station a second, smaller desk behind. An immense painting took up the whole wall above the computer. . . .

Seth's wide eyes traveled over severed arms, bull's heads, image upon image, screaming women, dead people . . . it was the strangest, most bizarre painting he had ever seen and he wondered what weird shit had been going on in the mind that created such a horrific, yet undeniably beautiful scene.

He also wondered what sort of a man would have a painting like this in his office—would want to live with such a violent collage of images, who might find this nightmare in oils soothing, or somehow inspiring. . . .

Slipping behind to the computer, Seth sat down, touched a key, and the monitor came alive, the flat screen glowing brightly in the dark room; the computer itself was already on.

What a thoughtful host, Seth thought, and started breaking Sterling's security.

Coming from a company so supposedly adept at computer tech, Sterling's system caved pretty quickly; on the other hand, X5s had hacker training and physical abilities that would put the best system to the test. Once in, however, Seth searched through thousands of computer files with no luck.

He did find one promising folder, though . . . an encrypted one with its own password. No matter what he tried, he couldn't open it, which was starting to piss him off (admittedly, his rage threshold was easily crossed).

Finally, giving up, Seth copied the file onto a disc, covered his computer tracks as best he could, and crept back to the door. He unlocked it quietly, slipped into the executive assistant's space, then opened the hall door a crack to peer out and down, both ways, to see a wonderfully empty corridor.

Seth was halfway back to his lunchroom entry point, on a floor where no geeks labored, when he saw a member of the security team, a heavy guy in his midfifties—probably an ex-cop or maybe somebody's uncle, passing the days until retirement. The guard had no firearm, but he did have a Tazer and a walkie-talkie on his belt.

Keeping to the shadows, Seth followed the guard down the hall toward the entry point. All the guard had to do was keep moving and Seth could slip out as easily as he'd slipped in.

But as they passed the lunchroom, the security man looked in casually . . . then stopped—*cold.*

Seth didn't think the guard could've spotted the window from that vantage point, but, damn, the guy *must* have! Here Seth was, a lean young genetically tuned engineered soldier, less than twenty feet from his access out of here . . . and this old fat friggin' guard decided to pick *now* to be on top of his job.

Fatso reached for the radio on his hip, his head swiveling as he looked down the hall in the other direction, apparently checking for more evidence of an intruder.

Seth had hoped to get in and get out without raising any suspicion; but that seemed impossible now. The guard had lifted the radio from his belt, poised to put in his call—a call that if Seth let him make meant the rest of a (presumably slimmer) security force would be on the way in seconds. But taking the guard out first would tell Sterling that his company's security had been breached. . . .

Manticore training, and life on the streets, had taught Seth long ago to pick the lesser of evils.

The guard had just pushed in the TALK button, and sucked in a breath to form the first word, when Seth chopped him on the back of the neck, and the guard folded up like a fat card table, pitching awkwardly forward, the walkie-talkie clunking to the carpeted floor and bouncing away a few feet. The guard had barely hit the indoor-outdoor carpeting when Seth had him by his collar, to drag the man away.

"Hey!"

The voice came from behind Seth, off to one side.

"What the hell?"

Another voice.

"What's going on?"

Another!

Spinning toward the lunchroom, Seth saw four more guards sitting around a big table, sandwiches spread out before them, two empty chairs, their eyes all now turned toward the boy in shock.

Shit, the X5 thought. Fatso hadn't discovered Seth's entry point—the guard had simply been calling to the last member of the security team, to invite him to join the group for their midnight lunch!

So much for getting away clean.

Seth didn't wait for them to gather their wits; he'd been trained to use surprise, and the surprise on their faces invited him to join them, in the lunchroom. . . .

As the nearest guard rose from the table, Seth jammed a fist up under the man's nose, the X5 thrusting hard, the guard unconscious, possibly dead; as the guy toppled, Seth grabbed the man's Tazer before he landed, taking the chair with him.

Seth aimed the Tazer at the guard across the table, out of the X5's reach—a kid barely his own age. The two darts flew and struck the young guard in the chest, the charge dropping the kid to do a twitching dance on his back on the floor.

"Fuckin' kill you!" another of the guards spat, a square-jawed probably ex-military boy, on his feet, going for his own Tazer; but then, like a jump cut in a movie, Seth was suddenly beside the guard, and triggered the weapon in the man's grasp, sending the shocking darts sailing down, sinking into the guard's own trousered leg, to convince him to do his own convulsing Riverdance before he dropped in a spasmodic heap, to duet with his twitching buddy.

Seth allowed himself a laugh at that, which may have been what sent the final guard's scare level into overdrive, inspiring the guy—another older, overweight waste of a security-guard uniform—to make a run for it.

The X5 merely walked quickly—running was not necessary—and grabbed the guy by the hair on the back of his head and guided him, face first, into the door frame. The guard dropped to his knees, a glistening red clown's nose in the midst of a pitiful expression.

The red-nosed guard wasn't unconscious, though, able to say, "Please," before Seth put him to sleep with a right hook that caught the guard on the side of the jaw, knocking him over like a potted plant, blocking the lunchroom door.

Seth could not cover his break-in, but he could cover the reason for it, and turn this failure into a financial success, anyway.

He vaulted over the slumbering clown-nosed guard, leaving his lunchroom exit behind; he sprinted back to the stairwell and returned to the executive floor, and that hallway where he'd seen the paintings . . . but coming through the fire exit door, on the run, he collided with the last guard.

The two of them crashed to the floor in a mutually surprised mound of writhing flesh, each yelling angrily as they wrestled for position. Seth was stronger, of course, but the guard was wiry and young and kept his head.

The guard even managed to avoid most of Seth's blows, and surprised Seth with an elbow to his groin, which sent nausea-tinged agony through his belly, and another elbow jammed into Seth's left eye, which dazed the X5 and sent the hallway spinning.

Reaching for his Tazer, the guard struggled to his feet, and—as he freed the weapon from his belt—Seth swept his feet out from under him, and the guard landed on his ass with a hard *thunk,* Tazer flying.

Seth, on his feet now, nimbly leapt out of reach when the dazed guard tried to repeat the sweeping maneuver on him.

Looking down at the fallen guard with respect, Seth asked, "Nice work—we finished here?"

The guard looked up, his eyes blinking rapidly as he tried to clear his head and understand what was happening.

"You got cuffs?" Seth asked, conversationally. "I'll cuff you and then I'm outa here."

The guard shook his head, whether in protest or to clear the cobwebs, Seth couldn't tell. Then the guard dived at Seth, and the X5 threw a hard right down, catching the man's chin, breaking his jawbone, dropping the guy into an unconscious heap.

"That's one way to get cuffed," Seth muttered to himself.

Now that he had the luxury of time, Seth studied the paintings; there had been no Moody in his life, and Manticore was rather light on arts training . . . so this X5 took down half a dozen that pleased his eye, using his switchblade to cut the canvases from their heavy frames. He rolled them up together like a carpet and took the elevator downstairs.

In the lunchroom, the guards were all still out—one or two of them might be in comas, or even dead—but Seth didn't care one way or the other. Feeling exhilarated—this had been fun!—the boy slipped out his window into the night.

LOGAN CALE'S APARTMENT
SEATTLE, WASHINGTON, 2019

Logan Cale took the computer disc from Seth, and loaded it into his computer, as the X5 filled in his benefactor on the night's adventures.

"You did what?" Logan asked.

Seth grinned, proud of himself; this was the happiest Logan had ever seen the boy.

"I made it look like a robbery," the X5 said. "With any luck, Sterling won't even notice the breach in his computer security."

That *was* smart, Logan knew; and the last time he'd dispatched Seth, homicide had happened . . . this was merely grand larceny, with assault and battery as a chaser. Maybe the team could work their way down to jaywalking.

Shaking his head, Logan asked, "What did you take?"

"Six paintings."

"Where are they, Seth?"

"Trunk of my wheels. . . . Know a good fence?"

Logan stared at Seth like the boy had gardenias growing out of his ears. "You're kidding, right? These paintings could be evidence in a case against Sterling, might even implicate the Russian."

Seth shrugged, *what the hell.* "There's plenty more where these came from. Anyway, I thought they might bring in a little pocket change."

Pocket change, Logan thought. *More like millions.* . . .

"Get them," Logan said.

"Hey, they're *mine!* I did your damn job, for free—this is, whaddya callit, a perk!"

"Seth," Logan said, "this is more important than money."

"Easy for you to say, Donald Trump!"

"Sterling may be our link to Manticore."

Seth let out a long, slow breath. "Okay . . . I'll let you eyeball 'em . . . but that's it."

While the boy was gone, Logan struggled to open the disc. This was going to take time, and a lot of concentration, which wouldn't be possible with the X5 underfoot. He set it aside; he'd deal with it later.

Seth returned with the rolled-up paintings, spread them, smoothed them out, on the sofa and on the nearby floor.

"Eyes Only" couldn't believe his eyes.

He'd known Sterling had a mammoth collection, but to think these had been on display at corporate headquarters . . . N. C. Wyeth, Charles Russell, Norman Rockwell, Frederic Remington, Jackson Pollock, and John Singer Sargent . . . he was staggered, stunned.

"Leave these," Logan said, "and I'll have an art expert go over them."

Seth's head reared back. "You're kidding, right? I mean, you're not really thinking I'm going to leave these with you, are you?"

"You need them authenticated, Seth."

"Do I look that stupid?"

"Is that a trick question? It'll help you sell them, if you know what they're worth."

Seth thought about that for a moment, but then shook his head. "You get the art expert—call my pager . . . and I'll bring the paintings back."

"All right," Logan sighed, patting the air with his hands. "All right."

Rolling up the paintings like dorm room posters, Seth said, "Do it by tomorrow night, or I'll take my own chances with a fence."

"What if I can't line somebody up by then?"

"Oh I got faith in you, Logan," Seth said, the rolled-up masterpieces under one arm. The James Dean face grinned in all its awful boyishness. "Just like you got faith in me, right?"

Seth showed himself out.

Chapter Ten
SCENE OF THE CRIME

Turning to Kendra and her closet for help, Max dolled herself up in one of those skimpy sexy frocks that she had so scrupulously avoided until now. At least it wasn't frilly or trashy—the simple black strapless minidress, set off by a rhinestone belt, displayed much of her sleekly muscular legs, plentiful cleavage, and just about all of her unblemished, bronze shoulders. Sitting on the bench in front of her roommate's makeup mirror, Max put on some black you-know-what-me pumps that rivaled any torture Manticore had come up with.

"You look good, girl," Kendra said with an appreciative, almost envious grin. "Foxy and fine."

Original Cindy, who had come over to help with the makeover, widened those big beautiful brown eyes and, with a head shake, said, "You look any better, Boo, Original Cindy'd set out to recruit you for *her* team."

That took the edge off, making Max laugh, and the other young women joined in, in a round of giggles.

Then, studying her reflection, Max rose and turned in a slow circle. "Damn, you two are really good at this—you oughta do makeovers on the tube. . . . I can't find the butt-kicking tomboy no matter how hard I look."

"Oh, she's in there," Original Cindy said. "She'll come out, anybody screw around witchoo."

"But these shoes . . ." Max winced, working to maintain her balance. "They're tighter than Normal's ass."

O. C. laughed at that, and Kendra shrugged. "Those are the best I can do—not my fault, my feet are just a little smaller than yours. . . . Cin, you got anything in your collection?"

"Hell," Original Cindy said, "my dogs are bigger than either of you. . . . But don't you the get the wrong idea: Original Cindy is *still* damn delicate!"

More shared laughter.

"The pumps're fine," Max lied, lightly. What was she going to do, pick her best pair of running shoes?

Hands on hips, Original Cindy asked, "What's your secret, Boo? How'd you get yourself an invite to some Fat Daddy Greenback's booty shake?"

Grinning, almost embarrassed, Max said, "Ain't no booty shake . . . just a cocktail party."

Original Cindy raised an eyebrow. "They gonna be tunes?"

Max felt the argument slipping away from her. "Well, yeah, I suppose."

Original Cindy raised the other eyebrow. "Gonna be all kindsa young, firm hotties with their talent hangin' out?"

Max smiled and sighed. "You know there will be."

Original Cindy turned to Kendra and in unison, they bumped hips and said, "Booty shake!"

"Would I doubt my elders?" Max asked innocently.

That got the expected feigned indignation, and after some more giggling, Kendra went to her bedside table, opened the drawer, selected something, and returned to hand it to Max: a two-inch-square foil package.

"When you accessorize," Max said, and now she was the one arching an eyebrow, "you don't kid around."

Original Cindy whooped in delight. "Aw-iiight," she said, slapping five with Kendra. "Sister girl lookin' out for ya, Boo! You gotta love it."

Max was amused and, well, touched. "I doubt I'll need this," she said, "but because you're the one givin' me the makeover, I'll take it with me—you never know what might come up."

They all laughed again. In truth, that sprinkle of feline DNA in Max's makeup had reared its furry little head again not so long ago, and Max had again found herself doing battle with her hormones. For a human being to devolve into a cat in heat, from time to time, was one of the more humiliating aspects of her test-tube development. But she was on the downside of it now.

Earlier, Kendra and Original Cindy had penciled Max's brows, taught her about eyeliner, mascara, eye shadow, blush, and lipstick . . . techniques of war Manticore had skipped, criminal methods Moody had passed over. . . .

Fifteen minutes in, her patience wearing thin, Max had asked, "Is this porn-star trip really necessary?"

Kendra looked hurt. "You want to make a good impression, don't you?"

Max smirked. "What, you mean in the guys' pants?"

"Boo," O. C. said, "you have to put your trust in the hands of those with more experience in these matters. Original Cindy and sister Kendra know the ins and outs of dressin' to kill."

The latter phrase was more to the point, but Max had of course omitted her real purpose for attending the party. All she had told her friends was that she was going to a cocktail party—which was true. And that a very rich man had invited her—which was a lie.

O. C. waggled a finger. "You catch yourself a rich fish tonight, Boo—you just remember it was your home girls help provide the bait."

Admiring herself in the mirror, a hand to her hair, surprised by how much she liked looking this beautiful, Max said, "But *I* provided the lure."

Original Cindy, rather wistfully, said, "No argument, girlfriend . . . no argument."

Kendra put her hands on either side of Max's head. "Hold still or we're *never* going to turn this pumpkin into Cinderella."

Original Cindy seemed to be thinking over that remark—something didn't seem right about it.

After that, Max sat painfully still throughout a forty-five-minute ordeal, rather amazed by the elaborateness of the makeup application when the end result made it look like she wasn't wearing any. It was at this point that she'd stepped into the little black dress and now, finally—after taking one last twirl in the mirror, delighted by the shimmer of her dark curls, and the way the dress clung to her, like an attentive lover—she was ready . . . dressed to go to work.

After her last visit to the Sterling estate—as a cat burglar in the middle of the night—Max had decided on a new strategy to gain entry into the mansion and get information from the king of the castle. She'd found out a lot more about Jared Sterling in the meantime.

For one thing, Sterling was not the upstanding, model citizen the mainstream media liked to present to the public; however hard he tried to pass himself off as the post-Pulse poster child of responsible wealth, he was no philanthropic patron of the arts.

Otherwise, Max's little home invasion would have made the news—bigtime. Her escapade would have been on SNN and front pages and all over the Net, and every other place in the so-called free world.

But there had been no mention of it anywhere.

The paper's police beat hadn't even run the usual one liner about "Officers responded to an alarm at . . ." No matter how private a person Sterling might be, the break-in should have made some kind of noise—certainly those alarms had. Police had no doubt responded, and either had been sent away by the great man, or any investigation of the break-in was kept confidential from the media.

Why?

Because Jared Sterling was up to what was commonly called *no good*.

Exactly what, Max couldn't yet say; but Sterling was clearly dirty—as indicated in spades by his possession of the Heart of the Ocean.

And if Sterling had ordered the slaughter of the Chinese Clan, in pursuit of the stone, she would kill his ass.

But she would have to be convinced of his guilt, first; if he was nothing more than a collector who bought hot property from a fence, that meant Sterling was just a link to the real villain. And with Manticore involvement suspected in the Chinese Theatre slaughter, that villain might well be Colonel Donald Lydecker himself.

On a more mundane . . . but helpful . . . level, Max had also learned that the art collector was famously single. He collected pretty women as well as paintings, and was hosting a party to show off the new Grant Wood—at his home . . . this evening.

Manticore had instilled in Max the need to take advantage of any opportunity, and this seemed like a prime chance to finally meet Jared Sterling . . . again. Her back had been to him, in their first, brief encounter, and to her knowledge her image hadn't been captured on any security-cam tapes.

Normally Max would have made her way to the ferry landing by the most economical—and most exhilarating— method: her Ninja. Her outfit made that impractical, though, and she wound up investing ten or twelve times as much to take a taxi. The ferry ride to Vashon Island wasn't free, either, and another taxi took her from the landing to the front gate of the Sterling estate.

Adding up the costs, Max rolled her eyes and understood why only the rich lived way out here—who the hell else could afford the commute?

The taxi driver—an older, skinny guy who looked like he hadn't touched solid food since the Pulse—pulled the cab up to the front gate, where a security guard in black suit with tie—dark-haired, Mediterranean-looking, not one of her playmates from the other night—approached with clipboard in hand. The cabbie waved the guard around to the back passenger's seat where Max was sitting.

Max rolled down the window.

"You have an invitation, miss?" he asked, his tone pleasant, but his dark face serious, his brown eyes on her like lasers.

"Oh damn," she said, pretending to dig through her tiny purse, "I have it *some*place. . . ." Finally, she gave up, looked up at the guard with wide and (she hoped) lovely eyes, smiling full wattage. "Guess not. . . . Such a long ride out here, too."

He leaned a hand on the rolled-down window. "Perhaps if you gave me your name, I could check the guest list."

She had selected, from the various pictures of Sterling with pretty young women (and there had been dozens over the last year or so), a petite brunette, who bore a faint resemblance to Max.

"I've been here before," she said. "A few months ago? Marisa Barton."

A tiny smile played at the corner of the security man's mouth. "Ms. Barton is already inside."

Max's smile curdled. "Look . . . I'll be straight with you. I'm a journalist, and this is my big chance." She withdrew a precious twenty-dollar bill from her purse.

But the guard, not at all mean, almost amused, just shook his head.

Max said, with a frozen smile, "You're not going to let me in, are you?"

"Worse luck for you, 'Ms. Barton'—I'm gay. You don't even have *that* going for you. . . . Tell your driver to turn it around, and we don't have to take this another step. . . . You wouldn't like that step, anyway."

"Bet not." She'd already put her twenty bucks away.

Max told the driver to turn the hack around, but before the cabbie could shift gears, the guard leaned down, like an adult talking to a child, and said, "By the way, just so you know next time—Ms. Barton's a blonde, now. . . . For a journalist, you're not so hot on details."

She smirked. "I'm savin' up for a research assistant."

The driver turned around and drove back toward the ferry. When they were out of sight of the gate, Max told him to stop and, after waiting till no cars were coming in either direction, climbed out of the cab. The street was dark and Sterling's mansion was two blocks back.

"If you're plannin' to go over the fence in that dress," the skinny cabbie said, when she came to his rolled-down window to pay him, "I wouldn't mind hangin' around to watch."

She got the twenty back out. "Here."

"Hey! Thanks, sweetie . . . that's generous."

"No—it's payment for you getting amnesia. You alert that guardhouse about me, I'll want my Andy Jackson back."

"Sure . . ." He took the bill from her, and she clamped onto his stick of a wrist. Hard.

She looked at him hard, too, and his eyes were wide and amazed and somewhat frightened.

"If you're thinking of playing both ends against the middle," she said, "you might be surprised what a girl in a dress like this can do."

He nodded, said no problem, no sweat, and pulled away.

On her walk back, Max avoided the road to the front of the castle, and the other cars she knew would be using it. She passed the place where she'd docked the boat the other night, and kept moving. Even in the short dress, the wall wasn't any more of an obstacle than it had been the first time, though that cabbie would have received quite an eyeful.

She glided around the house to the front, staying in the shadows, waiting until a larger group of six or seven people poured out of a stretch limo—their slightly drunken laughter like off-key wind chimes in the night—and breezed up the wide stairs toward the massive green dollar-bill door. As they moved up past the lions, Max just blended in with the crowd and, for the second time, entered the Sterling mansion.

A string quartet sat to one side of the foyer, their soft melodies providing unobtrusive musical wallpaper for the many conversations going on. Thanks to Moody, Max recognized the piece as Bach, though the name eluded her—it wasn't something you could steal, after all.

The last time Max had stood in this foyer, she'd broken and entered—and had felt much more at ease than in the midst of this crowd of tony people . . . chatting in little groups, sipping flutes of champagne, nibbling at canapés, courtesy of silver-tray-bearing waiters in tuxedo pants and white shirts with black bow ties, winding through the throng like moonlighting Chippendale's dancers. The male guests tended to be in their late thirties to midforties, wearing tailored suits and an air of success. The female guests often were ten years younger than their dates, and wore clingy cocktail dresses, and airs of excess.

Max fought a spike of panic—she had rarely felt more out of place in her young life, perhaps not since those early months after the Manticore escape.

Some rich people had not weathered the Pulse at all well, even spiraling into failure and poverty. For those born to wealth—or those capitalists (like, say, Jared Sterling) who saw in disaster potential for their own prosperity—it was as if there had been no Pulse. To such people, affluence was as natural as breathing; and those who'd been born to it, should they lose their fortunes, would wither and die.

This way of life was completely foreign to Max, who'd scratched for every cent she'd ever earned . . . or anyway, stolen. Oh, she'd seen her share of fancy parties and posh events in Los Angeles, of course; but she'd always been on the outside looking in, hoping to snag a bauble or snatch a purse when the wealthy left whatever function she and the other members of the Chinese Clan were staking out.

Despite the care Kendra and Original Cindy had taken to help her blend in here, that was impossible for Max; in a way, her home girls had done *too* good a job on her. Her dark exotic beauty, so fetchingly displayed in the low-cut frock, had attracted male eyes from the moment she walked in. The women took only a few seconds longer to catch onto her unique presence . . . and suddenly it seemed that Max wasn't the only female with cat genes in the room: the debutante girlfriends and trophy wives threw her looks of undisguised contempt.

A waiter paused for Max to select a champagne flute from his tray, and she exchanged smiles with him—two human beings trapped here in the Decadence Museum. Then he was gone, and she sipped, hoping the bubbly would relax her, but instructing herself to hold it to one glass: she was, after all, working. . . .

As she eased off toward the gallery, Max nodded at several of the appreciatively gazing men, thinking, *Even if I were still in heat, you toms wouldn't stand a chance. . . .*

The vast room where, not so long ago, she and a security guard had interacted now held fifty-some people, mostly milling about enjoying the artwork, murmuring appreciatively at Sterling's collection, about every third one trying to impress with his or her knowledge. Music from the foyer filtered in, but muffled, as if this were Muzak piped in.

Glancing around the room, Max saw that Sterling's people had cleaned up the mess after her visit, neatly, efficiently. The holes from the security leader's pistol shots had been patched; the Jackson Pollock ruined by Maurer's MP7A had been taken down (and replaced by a different Pollock painting!); and—much to Max's surprise—she caught glimpses of a new Plexiglas display case in the corner, where she'd found the Heart of the Ocean. But she would have to get closer, to see what new object had been put on display in the necklace's place. . . .

Not wanting to arouse suspicion—and now starting to look for Sterling in earnest—Max went down the left side of the room (the side opposite the display case), gliding behind guests lined up staring at paintings. A stunning blonde in blue velvet who must have been straight out of art school was explaining a Georgia O'Keeffe flower to her much older male companion, specifically the "powerful symbol of life and female becoming."

As Max slipped by the couple, she noticed the blonde's hand was brushing the thigh of her date, who was about as weathered as one of O'Keeffe's cow skulls. He was studying her, not the painting—though Max had a hunch the guy understood the blossom symbolism just fine.

Shaking her head a little, Max spotted, on the far wall, one of Andrew Wyeth's *Helga* pictures, which she wished she'd grabbed on her first visit. She smiled privately, moving on even as she considered the possibility of a third visit to the mansion, some night soon. . . .

Still no sign of Sterling—or, for that matter, any of his security staff. She slipped in and out of the clusters of pompous people until she stood in front of another Grant Wood, which had taken the wall space that had belonged to *Death on the Ridge Road. Spring Turning*—another oil on

Masonite, done in 1936—featured large green fields going on seemingly forever, rolling hills beneath a blue sky filled with fluffy white clouds. In the bottom foreground, a tiny man used a horse-drawn plow. At eighteen by forty, *Spring* was also a bulky painting; if she did return, she'd leave this one behind.

Again, Max slowly scanned the room for Sterling, and didn't see him. But before she'd move on to another room to continue her search, she just had to know how Sterling had filled that Plexiglas case. She waited until two couples blocking her way moved on, then stepped up and looked down at the black velvet pad . . .

. . . and its contents made her breath catch.

The Heart of the Ocean!

What the hell? . . . How could Sterling have gotten it back? There was no *way*—the necklace was hidden in her crib, and even Kendra didn't know it was there.

The necklace on display was breathtaking, and appeared to be the genuine article . . . but this was *crazy*. Her heart pounding, her palms sweaty, Max stepped closer, leaning in, trying to get a better look. A gold plate labeled the exhibit: "The Heart of the Ocean—one of two prop necklaces from the famous film *Titanic;* the other resides in the Hollywood Heritage Museum."

Just as she was forming an opinion on its authenticity, Max felt a presence—someone stepping up behind her.

"Beautiful, isn't it?"

Recognizing the warm masculine voice, Max turned to see Jared Sterling—a tall, blond man in his late twenties with intense blue eyes, a neatly trimmed, slightly darker beard; he wore a black suit with a crisp black collarless shirt, buttoned to the neck, and no tie—casual, in a formal way.

"Beautiful," she said, adding, "for a fake."

Sterling favored her with a small twitch of a smile. "Yes, a beautiful fake . . . like you, my dear."

A shiver shot through her. "I beg your pardon?"

"Is the music too loud? Can you not hear me?" He was standing right next to her now, and leaned sideways to her and, with a tone that managed to be both pleasant and rather vicious, said, "The necklace is like you—beautiful, but not what it appears."

She bestowed a smile of her own. "And what do I appear to be?"

"One of numerous beautiful young women, who were invited to my party . . . but you're not, are you?"

"Not beautiful?"

"Not invited," Sterling said with a chuckle. "What they used to call, in the old days, a party crasher."

She swiveled so they faced; they stood close together, as if contemplating a kiss, the Plexiglas dome a foot from her left hand and his right. She could smell his lightly applied cologne, something citrus and deeply inviting. The air between them seemed charged and their eyes locked.

She asked, "How do you know I don't have an invitation? Or maybe I'm here in the company of one your guests?"

"My dear," he said, with sublime condescension, "I threw this little party myself . . . and I personally okayed every invitation. No one brings a guest to my parties without clearing it first . . . unless one doesn't mind never getting invited again."

"And here I thought you were such a warm host."

"Oh I am." He nodded toward the people appreciating his paintings. "I'm friends with all these people, in fact I know everyone here . . . everyone, that is, but you. Although there is something . . . familiar about you. Have we met, my dear?"

She felt another shiver, asked, "In your dreams, perhaps?"

Another smile twitched within the well-tended beard. "If only I had that vivid an imagination. . . . Would you like a drink? More champagne, perhaps?"

She held up her empty glass. "Why not?"

"Before we do," he said, "tell me, please, why you think my famous film prop is a fake."

"Oh, it may actually be a film prop—I'm sure they had a backup for the *real* necklace, when they made that movie."

"Real necklace?" he said innocently.

"Very few people realize that the necklace in the Hollywood

Heritage Museum—which was stolen, by the way—was truly valuable, with forty-eight tiny zircons that formed the heart around the blue stone."

"That's simply absurd," he said, without conviction.

"And," she continued, with a casual, almost contemptuous nod toward the display case, "this paste job has fifty."

He looked from her to the necklace and back. "Well! . . . You're a very bright young woman. Now, do you want that champagne?"

"I'm right, aren't I?" Entwining her arm in Sterling's, Max allowed him to lead her toward the foyer.

"In a way—the necklace on display *is* a film prop . . . you don't think I would show off the original in front of guests? The more valuable of the two prop necklaces, used only for close-ups? Particularly when its . . . provenance is so . . . controversial."

"You mean, because it's stolen property. . . . So, then, the real necklace is somewhere safe—bank vault, that sort of thing."

"I wouldn't know where it is."

"Why not?"

"Don't be coquettish, my dear—you stole it. Remember?"

Their eyes met and Max's stomach did a back flip, but she said nothing; she did not think he would make a scene here—not and risk it coming out that his collection included hot property.

They got fresh glasses of bubbly from a butler and walked down one of the stairways toward the rear of the house. The crowd was thinner back here.

"Where are we going?" she asked.

"Sitting room. I have something I want to show you."

She smiled. "If it's a gun, I'm not interested. . . . If it's something else, thanks anyway—I've seen those before, too."

"You're such a droll child," Sterling said, with a chuckle. "Very engaging, but that's not what I meant. I want you to see another piece of art."

With a shrug, she said, "All right."

Sterling unlocked a door and they entered a large sitting room with a plush violet velvet sofa.

"For our privacy," Sterling said, "I need to lock the door again . . . are you comfortable with that?"

She was not afraid of him in the least. "Go ahead."

He locked the door and they soon sat side by side on the velvet sofa; the Mission style again predominated. A walnut coffee table separated them from two wing chairs and one wall was taken up by bookshelves filled with leather-bound volumes. On the opposite wall hung heavy velvet curtains that matched the sofa and presumably covered a large window that overlooked the rear of the estate.

On the wall behind the couch was what Max suspected to be the original *Night Watch* by Rembrandt. Near the locked door was a Remington painting that Max recognized as *The Snow Trail*.

"Are these the pieces you wanted me to see?"

"No." The collector sipped his champagne, then smiled again, a toothy smile that was a little too white, a little too wide. "Did you really tell the guard outside you were Marisa Barton?"

Sterling didn't seem to miss much, around here. Suddenly that locked door was starting to bother her. She decided to play him.

"Girl's gotta do what a girl's gotta do," she said, "to meet the man she wants to meet."

"And you wanted to meet me?"

Max touched his leg. "Handsome, wealthy . . . you do have some points in your favor, Mr. Sterling."

He placed a hand over hers. "Thank you for putting 'handsome' on the list *before* 'wealthy.'" Now he was the one who glanced toward the closed door. "But what do you think we should do about Marisa?"

Max moved closer. "Forget about her."

"That's an option," he said; again they were close enough to kiss. "Or . . . we could invite her to join us."

Again the air between them seemed charged, but this time in a different way, and Max forced herself not to recoil. "I don't like to share good things," she managed.

This part of the big house was very quiet. Were she and
Sterling the only ones not out front, at the party?

"Before we decide what to do about Marisa," he said, and
eased away from her, just a bit, "perhaps we should decide
what to do about *you*."

He withdrew a piece of paper from his inside jacket
pocket and dropped it on the coffee table before them—a
surveillance photo, culled from video footage, courtesy of a
security cam . . .

. . . *a picture of Max standing in the gallery of the Sterling
mansion with the real Heart of the Ocean in her hand.*

"This," he said, and he was not smiling now, "is the piece
of art I wanted you to see."

So much for disabling the video system.

He was saying, "I take it you came here tonight to . . .
what is your name, dear?"

She said nothing.

Sterling pressed on: "I take it you're here to make arrangements to return the necklace, and the Grant Wood painting
. . . correct?"

Her face blank, she said simply, "No."

"Please don't play innocent—why else would you come to
my home tonight, risking a prison sentence, going through
all the trouble of jumping the wall and skulking around like
a common thief?"

"Actually, I'm a very uncommon thief, Mr. Sterling."

His smile returned—fewer teeth, though. "That's true, my
dear—that's certainly true."

She folded her arms, Indian-style. "We could, I suppose,
arrange a price for the return of those two items. You might
be surprised by how reasonable that price might be."

His eyes tightened; he was clearly intrigued. "Try me."

She curtailed the intensity, the urgency in her voice. "Just
tell me where you got it."

"Got what, my dear?"

"The Heart of the Ocean. Tell me, and you can have it
back. . . . The Grant Wood might require some cash outlay,
but . . ."

"My dear," Sterling said. "Surely you understand that a

man who deals in the netherworld of art collecting, as I do, must protect not only himself, but his sources. Anyway, why is it any of your concern, where I got that necklace?"

"I *need* to know," she said, and this time the intensity bled through.

He considered what she'd said; then he said, "I may strike a bargain with you—but I must protect myself. Again, I must ask—why do you want to know?"

She could think of nothing else to tell him but the truth—so she did: "I'm the one who stole the necklace in the first place, from that museum in LA."

". . . I am impressed."

"I left the necklace with friends, when I skipped town. Those friends turned up dead, in the meantime—and now the necklace winds up with you. I need to know how that happened."

He seemed amused. "To avenge your friends," he said, as if this were a quaint notion.

"Of course to avenge my friends."

"And this is more important than money?"

"It is to me. Mr. Sterling . . . Jared—can we do business? Do you want your necklace back?"

"Well, of course I do . . . *gentlemen!*"

The door unlocked and Morales and Maurer stepped into the sitting room. In black suits with ties, the guards wore re-membrances of their first meeting with Max: Maurer had two black eyes and a bandage over his broken nose, and Morales sported assorted bruises. They glowered at her.

Sterling's voice turned cold. "Here's my offer: give me back what belongs to me and I won't have you killed."

"Very generous—but why should I think you'd hold up your end of the bargain?"

He smiled at her, no teeth this time; then said, "Because you have unique abilities, my dear . . . and I could use some-one of your talents on my payroll. . . . Isn't that right, boys?"

But neither Maurer nor Morales expressed an opinion.

"I fly solo," she said. "As for the rest of your offer . . . thanks, but no thanks."

"If you don't return my property, I'll see to it that your death is a prolonged, unpleasant one. If you do return my property, I'll allow you to live. Who knows? You may even change your mind about my employment proposition."

"I'll pass."

"My dear, it's the best deal you're going to negotiate. You really should take advantage of my generosity."

She almost laughed. "You really think you can make all of this fly? I mean, I have kicked the ass of both these guys and more, already."

With a shrug and an openhanded gesture, Sterling said, "That *is* true . . . but we have allies in town now; we've taken on certain . . . reinforcements. . . . Morales! Fetch our friend, will you?"

Morales nodded and stepped out of the room.

"You should have dealt with me, Max," Sterling said.

Max . . .

"How the hell do you know my name?" she demanded.

Morales came back in and took up his position to one side of the door, Maurer on the other. Moments later a third man strode in, rather tall, thin, rock-star handsome, wearing a brown leather, knee-length coat over a light blue silk shirt and black leather pants.

Kafelnikov!

Sterling said, "I believe you know my friend Mikhail."

The Russian's smile was as reptilian as his snakeskin boots. "Enjoying the party, Max?"

She flew to her feet . . . and felt the weight of a pistol barrel against her ribs.

"Now, now," Sterling said, on his feet behind her, whispering into her ear, like a lover. "Let's not be rash. . . ."

Kafelnikov and the two guards were drawing their handguns, as well. She shook her head a little. "I think I already have been . . . rash."

"So it would seem."

Even as the nose of his automatic dug into her ribs, he kissed her neck, and she felt a chill—not a good chill. "Now, my dear," he said, "I want several things from you . . . the

Heart of the Ocean . . . the Grant Wood . . . and one more item. . . ."

"That's everything," she said coldly. Her eyes were on the Russian, who was smiling at her, seemingly amused by the hatred she was glaring his way.

"*Not* everything," Kafelnikov said, and he stepped forward, a few feet from Max. "Tell us about the other one."

Max frowned. "What? . . ."

Sterling whispered lovingly: "Tell us about your partner . . . the one who broke into my place of business."

Max felt the blood drain from her face. "Partner?"

Sterling came around alongside her, the nose of the gun making the trip, too. "Don't be coy, dear—it really doesn't suit you . . . *Who is he?*"

Biting off the words, she said, "I don't know what the hell you're talking about."

"Morales!" Sterling barked. "Show her."

The guard stepped forward and handed her another security-cam picture.

This one showed a young man standing in the middle of fallen security guards. *And once again she found herself studying a grainy picture of a young man who might be her brother—Seth?* Hope leapt within her, despite her situation.

With his free hand, Sterling snatched the photo from her. "Now, dear—tell us where he is, and what the two of you have done with my property."

"Don't know the guy," Max said, with a shrug. "Sorry."

Kafelnikov laughed harshly. "I've seen you in action, Max . . . and I've seen the tape of this man, tossing cops around like dolls. If you two are not brother and sister, you at least shared the same teacher."

Max's eyes narrowed. "What makes you think we're brother and sister?"

The Russian shrugged. "You move the same, you fight the same—you move your hands, your feet, your heads the same. Either you're family or you trained under one master, most likely at the same time. Either way, you know this man. Who is he, and where is he?"

"You want to know this," Max said to the Russian, "because your business partner here got robbed . . . or is there a reward for this rebel? Maybe one for me?"

"I don't know what you're talking about," Kafelnikov said, the lie surprisingly apparent.

Max glanced sideways at her host. "Ask him about his friend Lydecker—ask your Russian pal here what kind of art Manticore's collecting."

Sterling glanced at Kafelnikov. "What's she babbling about?"

"Nothing—that's all it is . . . *babble!*"

Max was smiling, and Sterling, the two bodyguards, and even the Russian were clearly disconcerted by the absence of fear in her demeanor.

"This was a great party," she said. "Mr. Sterling, I owe you a big debt of thanks. You, too, Mikhail. I got exactly what I came for, and so much more."

"What the hell's she talking about?" Sterling demanded. *"Who is this Lydecker?"*

Sterling's attention was on the Russian, and that was where the security guards were looking, too; only the Russian's eyes were on Max, but his gun hung loosely at his side. When she hadn't struck immediately, the men's guard had flagged, got relaxed, sloppy, making this as good a time as any. . . .

She just wished she wasn't wearing these damn tight pumps.

Her hand moved so quickly, no one reacted; she twisted Sterling's pistol away from her ribs and he reflexively pulled the trigger, the slug going wild, sending the Russian and the two guards ducking for cover. She broke Sterling's ring finger, and got the gun out of his hand as he screamed in pain and surprise.

Then she took out the clip and, in one fluid move, brought the pistol up and pitched it like a ball at Maurer, just as he took aim at her. The pistol broke the guard's nose (again), turning his face into a wet crimson mask as he sagged to the floor.

She elbowed the collector in the face, stopping his screaming by knocking him cold. She moved away from the couch, the curtained window to her back, as Morales came at her with a stun rod; but she dodged, wrenching it from his grip as he swept by her, and—with a helpful push from Max that lost his balance for him—Morales tore down the curtain and crashed through the window.

Spinning, she saw Kafelnikov bring up his pistol, but as he fired, she dived. The bullet zinged through the window into the night as Max jammed the stun rod into Kafelnikov's ribs. The pistol dropped limply from his hand and he fell to the ground, unconscious.

Max stared down at him. . . .

Zack or Seth would have killed him right there, Max knew; but she was unsure whether there was any benefit in taking revenge on an already beaten opponent. She hadn't quite made her decision when gunfire ripped the room, as other members of the security force descended.

Max vaulted through the broken window, more bullets chewing the wall around her, wood and plaster fragments flying. She dropped to the ground next to the fallen Maurer, jumped up, on the run. The night was alive with the yells and screams of Sterling's guests, alarmed by the gunfire.

But by the time the guards were able to add any more gunfire to the merriment, snouts of weapons blossoming out the window, Max was long since out of range.

She couldn't risk the ferry, and didn't have a boat, so she kicked off those damn shoes and dived into the cold water. As she swam, she wondered why she'd hesitated when she'd had the chance to kill Kafelnikov.

It wasn't like her, and it certainly wasn't like her training—though the decision had some strategic merit, since the Russian was the link to Lydecker's role in the Mann's massacre. . . .

She thought about Kendra, Original Cindy, and the other "normal" people who'd come into her life . . . Normal included; maybe hanging with all these real folks all the time was making her more human.

And then she wondered whether or not being more human, more normal, was a good thing.

When she got back to her squatter's pad, dripping wet,

Kendra's frock ruined, Max was thinking of the boy who must be Seth. Now she not only needed to find him for herself, but for *him*, too.

Seth was in danger, and she didn't know how to warn him; but she'd have to find a way.

Chapter Eleven
F IS FOR FAKE

Going over the John Singer Sargent painting with a small, handheld ultraviolet device, Pepe Henderson—an art expert friend of Logan's from the Seattle Art Museum—pored over the canvas like a criminalist seeking clues. In his early forties, with a middle-aged spread courtesy of a desk job and too many fast-food lunches, Henderson was an unprepossessing professional, dark hair thinning, with thick black-frame glasses riding a round face, a button-down white shirt challenged at the belly, and black slacks that kept slipping down, revealing the kind of cleavage people do not crane their necks to see.

In a pullover sweater and jeans, apparently relaxed and centered, Logan Cale sat back in one of the two chairs that bracketed his brown sofa, the anxiety pulsing in his stomach a secret.

Three of the paintings Seth had stolen from Engidyne were spread out on the cushions of the sofa, while the other three were smoothed out on the area rug. Unstretched, the canvases had a loose quality, like animal skins, that was somehow disconcerting. The lights were low, to aid the expert in his ultraviolet testing. Logan still couldn't believe the quality of the art arrayed on and around his couch—N. C. Wyeth, John Singer Sargent, Jackson Pollock, Norman Rockwell, Charles M. Russell, and Frederic Remington . . . an amazing collection.

In his black leather jacket, blue jeans, and a gray T-shirt

that said LEXX (a reference lost on Logan), sullen Seth paced the hardwood floor just beyond the conversation area. As twitchy, as itchy, as a drug addict (Logan even wondered if the boy was low on tryptophan), Seth watched the art expert's examination of his paintings like an expectant father who'd cheerfully brought his video cam into the delivery room, only to run into a bloody C-section. . . .

"No question," Henderson said, rising, hitching up his trousers, mercifully.

"I told you they were the real deal," Seth said, coming around the sofa, cockily.

Henderson raised a hand, like an embarrassed traffic cop. "No—I'm sorry, son . . . No question it's a *forgery.*"

Eyes blazing, Seth stormed over to the seated Logan, loomed ominously over him. "What the hell . . . what kinda scam? . . . You *told* him to say that!"

Logan shook his head. "No, Seth . . . I didn't. Frankly, I don't need to scam you out of money—I *have* money." He sighed. "But I admit I was afraid they might be forgeries."

Seth pointed at the Sargent as if he wanted to shoot it. "Just 'cause that piece of shit's a fake, doesn't mean the others are, too!"

"That's true," Logan said, calming; but then added: "Still, Seth—it's hardly a good sign. Don't get your hopes up."

The art expert ambled over and joined the conversation. "Don't get me wrong, boys—it's a good job." Henderson shook his head admiringly. "As good a forgery as I've ever seen . . . but fake is fake."

"Is fake," Logan said with a nod.

"Well, what *about* the others?" Seth seethed.

"I'll need a few minutes," the expert said, and returned to his work.

Logan stood and placed a hand on Seth's shoulder; that the boy did not brush it off was a small miracle.

"Come on," Logan said, smiling a little. "We'll go into the kitchen. Get out of Pepe's hair."

"What there is of it," Henderson said good-naturedly.

"Are you *high,* Logan?" Now Seth did brush off the hand.

"I'm staying right here—your buddy could switch paintings on us."

"What with?" Logan asked savagely, gesturing all around, suddenly fed up with Seth's paranoia. "The only thing Pepe brought with him was a small case with his machine. Where do you think he would put six more fake paintings?"

"He . . . he could have 'em rolled up his pant legs!"

Henderson glanced over. "Fellas, I'll check your paintings for you, and be happy, too—but if you think I'm gonna drop trou, you got another thing—"

Logan held up a hand. "No, that's okay, Pepe . . . please get back to work." He looked at Seth, an eyebrow raised. "You ready to come back to Planet Earth?"

Seth, embarrassed, turned toward the art expert. "Listen— I didn't mean anything . . . You think they're *all* fake?"

Bending over a canvas, sharing his ass-crack, Henderson said, "The way this works is, I don't have any preconceptions. Some pretty sophisticated collectors can get fooled by fakes . . . sometimes a collection can have a forgery hanging right next to the real thing. . . . Bottom line, till I do my thing, we're all just flappin' our gums."

Logan took Seth gently by the arm. "Let's go have something to drink. . . . We'll talk."

Reluctantly, Seth followed Logan, who poured them cups of coffee in the kitchen, where they sat across from each other on stools separated by a high butcher-block counter.

His anger simmering into frustration, Seth said, "God*damn it!* Here I thought I was finally going to catch a break, for a change, have something go right, in this screwed-up life of mine."

Logan sipped his coffee and allowed the young man time to vent.

The stool couldn't hold Seth long, and soon the boy was pacing around the kitchen, pissing and moaning. Modern and airy, the room was a study in stainless steel and natural wood, with plenty of cupboard space. Logan, a neatness freak, kept this room as meticulous as the rest of his condo—reordering the chaos of the world might be beyond his control, but his living space sure as hell would do as he told it.

"I can't believe this," Seth was saying. "All that work for nothing."

"It was hardly for nothing," Logan said quietly.

"What in hell makes you think so?"

Taking a long pull from the coffee cup, Logan considered the question a moment before answering. "Think it through, Seth—Manticore gave you more than just superior warrior skills . . . you have an exceptional mind. Use it."

"Blow me."

"I'll pass," Logan said, "but thanks for the offer. . . . Look, there's only two reasons for a collector to hang fake paintings on the wall."

Seth just looked at him.

"One," Logan continued, "said collector's trying to protect his collection . . . so, he has it hidden away, somewhere."

"And hangs duplicates in their place," Seth finished.

"Yes—like a wealthy woman with a fantastic assortment of jewelry, who wears paste versions when she's out on the town."

"You think that's what Sterling did?"

"Frankly, no."

Seth frowned, but more in thought than anger, or even frustration. "Why not?"

Logan shrugged. "Our friend Jared has spent way more money for forgeries of this quality than he would have to, to just put something on the wall to fool his friends. These weren't meant as decoys, protection against home invasion; they were meant to fool everybody, even Pepe."

"Your pal Pepe spotted them easily enough."

"No—not easily . . . he had to use all the tools of his trade, exert all of his professional skills. Ask him if he would have known these were forgeries, had he just been looking at them hanging on a museum wall . . . and I think he'll say they would have fooled even him."

"But, then . . . what the hell is the point of the fakes?"

Logan's eyes narrowed. "I think Sterling was passing

these off as the originals . . . when in fact, the originals have been sold overseas."

"Why would he do that?" Seth asked, pausing in his pacing. "Doesn't he have enough money already?"

"People like Sterling never have enough money. They're always looking for more."

"Oh, but you *have* money," Seth said sarcastically, "and you would never think to scam me out of—"

"No, I wouldn't," Logan interrupted curtly. Then, wryly, he added, "But Sterling's kind?. . . . If you feel his hand in your pocket, he's not making a pass."

Seth stared at Logan, any accusation long gone. "You sound like you know something about the species."

"I do." Logan sighed. "Seen it up close and personal."

This seemed to interest Seth, who asked, "Where?" and returned to his stool.

"Long time ago," Logan said. " 'nother life."

Logan didn't want to get into an extended biography of himself and his family. Ever since his parents had died, he'd been trying to put that part of his life behind him; and he definitely didn't want to get into this discussion with Seth, a borderline sociopath who had no point of reference regarding parents, anyway.

Henderson cleared his throat by way of announcing his presence, as he strolled wearily into the kitchen, where he poured himself a cup of coffee, and pulled up a stool next to Logan.

"They're *all* fakes, aren't they?" Seth asked, his voice so subdued Logan wondered if the kid might not cry.

The art expert nodded. "Sorry, son—please don't shoot the messenger."

"Shit," Seth said. "Shit, shit, *shit!*"

Henderson sipped his coffee, sighed, and said, "If it's any consolation, these are, without a doubt, the finest forgeries I've ever come across."

"Really?" Logan asked, interested.

"Oh yeah—canvas is the right age, paint is old, properly crazed. . . ."

"What's crazy about them?" Seth asked.

"Crazed—cracked," Henderson explained. "I have no idea how anybody could pull off something so . . . sophisticated."

Logan shifted on the stool, studying Henderson the way the art expert looked at a painting. "How did you know they were fakes then, Pepe?"

Henderson's eyes opened wide, and he smirked. "I didn't—it was the UVIN that figured it out."

"You put my paintings in an *oven?*" Seth asked, frowning.

The expert shook his head, saying, "Ultra-Violet Imaging Network . . . measures a bunch of stuff, using UV rays."

Logan nodded. "And what did the UVIN tell you?"

"That despite the fact that the paint looks old and cracked, the chemical makeup is about four years old." Gesturing with his coffee cup, Henderson said, "Take the Sargent painting, for example—*Alpine Pool.*"

"What about it?" Seth asked.

"Well, the real one was painted around nineteen-oh-seven."

Hand to his forehead, as if testing for a fever, Seth stared into nowhere. "Goddamn it. I shoulda known. What a chump I am. . . ."

"Hardly," the expert said. "If I'd seen these paintings in any respectable museum or private collection, it would never have occurred to me they might be fakes."

Seth and Logan traded looks—Henderson had just confirmed what Logan had told the boy earlier.

Henderson was saying, "Remington died in nineteen-oh-nine, Russell in nineteen-twenty-six, Wyeth died in nineteen forty-five, Pollock in 'fifty-six, and Rockwell in 'seventy-eight. . . . Yet these canvases were all painted in the last three to five years."

Seth seemed to fold in on himself a little, hunkering over the counter; he looked as if he might be sick.

Henderson finished and set his cup on the counter. "Sorry I didn't have better news, gentlemen—it would have been a kick to be in the same room with the real paintings." The expert climbed off the stool and tipped an imaginary hat to his host. "I'll get my stuff together."

Now the X5 and the cyberjournalist were again alone in

the kitchen. They could hear Henderson rustling around in the living room, so Logan kept his voice low: "Seth, those paintings were a bonus—they weren't what we went in for. You *got* what we went in for. . . ."

Seth looked up, his eyes dull, lifeless. "Huh?"

"The computer disc—remember?"

The X5 said nothing.

Logan smiled tightly, and tried to keep it upbeat: "You stole the paintings as a distraction—so that Sterling would think the only reason for your break-in was to steal art. He probably has no idea that we have that computer disc."

Nodding, though rather listlessly, Seth managed, "Probably not."

"And," Logan said, "if I can break that code, we might learn something that will help us bring him—and Kafelnikov—down."

"Like what?"

Logan shrugged. "Could be anything on that disc—financial records, a tally of where the original paintings have gone, who knows? . . . Maybe even the link to Lydecker and Manticore."

Out in the living room, Henderson called, "I'm ready to take off, Logan," and Logan raised a *hold-that-thought* finger to Seth, then met the art expert at the door.

He shook hands with Henderson, saying, "I'll give you a call later."

Henderson, very softly, said, "You okay, alone with that kid?"

"Fine."

"I don't know, Loge . . . seems kinda dangerous to me."

"That's because he is."

Henderson rolled his eyes and hauled himself and the small black carrying case out of there.

When Logan returned, he said, "You'll be glad to learn all the paintings are still in the living room."

"Great. And what are a buncha freakin' forgeries worth?"

Logan stood next to the seated boy. "That's what I'm trying to explain, Seth—in terms of what we're trying to accomplish, a hell of a lot."

"Does it help me get rich?"

Logan shrugged. "Probably not. But you will have helped to stop Kafelnikov, and possibly Sterling, who is looking pretty damn dirty now."

None of this seemed to console Seth.

"Look," the X5 said, "my life comes down to this. . . . Current scenario: I'm on the run, hiding my ass, needing money all the time to do that. Worst-case scenario: Lydecker and Manticore catch up with me . . . and, since there's no way in hell I'm goin' back to Manticore alive, they kill me. Best-case scenario: I get enough money to disappear, I mean *really* disappear . . . only then can I stop lookin' over my goddamn shoulder. These paintings coulda been my *ticket.*"

Logan asked, "Are you through?"

Seth glared at him. "What do you mean, am I through?"

"With the self-pity routine? What the hell happened to the rebel who wanted me to help him take Manticore down? Manticore exposed, destroyed, Lydecker out of your life permanently . . . *that's* your 'best-case scenario.'"

Now Seth was just staring at him.

Logan met the boy's gaze, steadily, knowing he had just jumped the ass of a killing machine who could reach out and snap his neck like a twig. And, if anything had been established thus far about Seth, it was the X5's ability to perform homicide without a twinge of conscience.

Finally the silence was so terrible, Logan had to fill some of it.

He said, "You help me close down Kafelnikov, and find out where Sterling figures in this . . . and I promise, even if this lead is a cold one, you and I will find a way . . . either we'll banish Manticore from the face of this earth, or I will call on all my powers and resources to relocate you safely, in a new life."

Seth drew a deep breath, expelled it, and said, "Sorry."

"Sorry?"

"Sorry I was such a whiny candyass brat . . . what can I say . . ." The boy shrugged. ". . . shitty upbringing."

Logan risked a smile. "Yeah—somebody really spoiled you."

Suddenly Seth exploded in laughter, and Logan laughed, too; the boy extended his hand.

"It's a deal, partner," Seth said.

"It's a deal," Logan echoed.

The two men shook hands.

"Okay," Seth said, after a sip of coffee, "what about this famous computer disc?"

Logan sat down again. "Well, I've got my best cryptology program working on it. Could take ten minutes, ten hours, or ten days. There's no way to know. But it *will* work. It's never failed me yet."

"You know what?"

"What?"

"I haven't slept in four days." Seth followed this with a world-class yawn. "Can I crash on the couch?"

"No."

"No?"

"Take the guest room."

"Rad. Point the way."

Logan showed his guest to the bedroom.

Seth flopped onto the bed, saying, "Call me when your computer has good news for us."

"Will do."

"And why don't you catch some z's? You look like shit, partner."

Half a smile dimpled Logan's lightly bearded cheek. "Manticore wasn't big on tact, either, I see."

"Isn't that something you put on the teacher's chair?"

The two smiled at each other . . . and, for the first time, felt like friends.

FEDERAL BUILDING
SEATTLE, WASHINGTON, 2019

Donald Lydecker was livid.

Normally a man whose emotions were held in tight check, Lydecker—in a gray zippered jacket, black T-shirt and black jeans—stood in an FBI office in the Federal Building at Second and Madison, his temper taxed to its limits.

"You're not going to help," he said, "with a matter of national security?"

"I didn't say that," said Special Agent in Charge Gino Arcotta, seated behind a desk piled with work. "Not exactly."

Arcotta was a thin, fit man of thirty-eight, his short hair black and curly, his angular face cleanly shaven, his brown eyes alert and sharp.

"What I said," he continued, "is that I don't have any men available to assist you, right now."

"Perhaps I'm not making myself clear," Lydecker said. "This is a matter of . . ."

"National security," Arcotta said wearily, with just a touch of temper, himself. "Colonel, let me be perfectly clear. . . ."

Richard Nixon, 1968, Lydecker thought.

"This office is manned by six agents, three on days, three on nights. That's all the manpower Washington has allotted us . . . and even with that small a staff, we can't stay within our budget."

"My budget is tight, too. That doesn't mean we shirk our responsibilities."

Arcotta continued on, as if Lydecker hadn't even spoken: "Now, of the three day-shift agents, two are investigating a bank robbery across town. All three night-shift agents are investigating a kidnapping and are at this moment . . ." He checked his watch. ". . . in the sixteenth hour of their tour."

"Even one man would be helpful, Agent Arcotta."

"Colonel, the last day-shift agent is me . . . and this desk does not go unmanned; that's policy. Tell me, sir . . . where do you suppose I'm going to find agents to assign to you?"

"I can think of one place you might look," Lydecker said sweetly, and exited the office like a man fleeing a burning building.

He wasn't going to get any help on the federal level, that was obvious. His own men wouldn't be here for another twenty-four hours, due to unsafe weather conditions grounding their aircraft in Wyoming.

Well, if he couldn't get help from the feds, he'd go farther down the food chain. . . .

Twenty minutes later, he stood across a desk from a police lieutenant.

"Four men for twenty-four hours," Lydecker said. "That's all I need."

The lieutenant—balding, forty, his teeth brown from cigarettes, hazel eyes in droopy pouches from too many years on the job—said, "How about twenty-four men, for four hours? Couldn't do that, either."

Lydecker opened his fist to reveal a rubber-banded roll of bills; then he closed his fist again. "You look like a reasonable man—I can't believe that we can't reach some sort of compromise."

The lieutenant was hypnotized by Lydecker's fist, which periodically opened—as if he were doing a flexing exercise with the roll of money—to provide green glimpses.

"All I need, Lieutenant, are four men, hell, *two* men, for twenty-four hours . . . until my own people get here."

"We'd have to shake on it," the lieutenant said.

Lydecker extended the hand with the roll of money, shook with the lieutenant, and brought the hand back, empty. He tossed a card on the desk. "My hotel is on the back . . . one hour."

An hour later, in the hotel bar, Lydecker and his cup of coffee sat across a booth from two detectives and their beers; ancient Frank Sinatra ballads were filtering in over a scratchy sound system, and the smoke was stale enough to be left over from Rat Pack days, too.

The older plainclothes dick, in his fifties, looked to still be in pretty good shape, but his face was pallid, his dark eyes sad, his brown hair cut short and graying at the temples; his name was Rush, though he didn't seem to be in much of one. The younger dick, Davis, was thirty or so, with reddish hair, light complexion, and pale blue eyes.

"So," Rush said, "the lieutenant said you needed help."

"Yeah. Looking for somebody wanted in a federal matter."

"We don't usually back up 'federal matters,' Colonel. What's wrong with the FBI?"

"I heard in this town, you want something done, you go to the PD—was I told wrong?"

"Truer words were never spoken," Rush said. "Your perp got a name?"

"Sort of." Lydecker looked from Rush to Davis and back again. "Eyes Only."

The detectives exchanged wary glances.

"I need to find him."

Rush snorted. "Good luck. Give him our best."

"There's got to be a way. Look at how you people lock down sectors, those hoverdrones everywhere—"

"Colonel." Davis spoke for the first time. "We've been seekin' Eyes Only for *years* now . . . and we don't know one thing more than the day we started. He's careful, he's smart, apparently funded up the wazoo . . . and anybody who has had any dealings with him is absolutely loyal to him."

"It's like trying to get a cult member to rat out their screwball messiah," Rush said.

Lydecker twitched a nonsmile. "Well . . . there's a second suspect—*tied* to Eyes Only." He withdrew from his inside jacket pocket a handful of stills taken from the SNN video of Seth. "Recognize him?"

They each took some of the photos and riffled through them, then exchanged sharp expressions.

Perking up, Rush asked, "You know this character's name?"

"I was kind of hoping you would," Lydecker said gently. "I *know* you must recognize some of his playmates . . . those Seattle cops he's throwing around like confetti."

"Listen," Rush said, leaning forward. "All we know is this kid beat the shit out of some very good people . . . and we would seriously like to pick his ass up."

"And put it down hard," Davis added.

"Sounds like we're on the same page," Lydecker said. "But is that really all you know about this boy? You don't know *why* he got into this tussle with your brothers in blue? Convenience-store robbery? Flashing schoolkids? What?"

Rush exchanged another look with Davis, who shrugged. Then the older cop said, "Guy named Ryan Devane, sector chief, powerful guy. . . . Kid was interfering with his business."

Davis said bluntly, "Hijacking payoffs."

"Kid mixed it up with our boys," Rush said. "And you never seen anything like it . . . got away clean. And now, Devane ain't been seen in several days."

Lydecker, proud of his rebellious student, said, "Then Devane is dead. . . . This is a remarkable young man."

"Tell me about it," Davis said. "He broke my brother-in-law's collarbone."

"But nobody's found this kid," Rush said, "and believe you me, the PD looked every damn where."

"Are they *still* looking?" Lydecker asked.

Rush shrugged, shook his head; Davis, too.

"Well then," Lydecker said, sliding out of the booth, "let's get out there and start the search back up again."

Lydecker spent the next six hours with Rush and Davis. Displaying the Seth photo, offering generous bribes for any Eyes Only lead, they rousted every snitch, every lowlife, every rat bastard the two detectives had ever met (and they had met a few), with no luck. He rode in the back of the unmarked car as they continued to drive around the city.

"How the hell is this possible?" Lydecker finally asked. "This Eyes Only son of a bitch has been working in this city for *years* . . . and no one knows *anything?*"

Rush, riding up front, smirked back at his passenger. "You're gonna make me say 'I told you so,' aren't you?"

Lydecker resisted the urge to brood and thought, instead. Finally he said, "We may be going at this from the wrong angle."

"You got an angle we ain't tried?" Davis, behind the wheel, asked.

"I think so. This remarkable young man we're looking for, he's got a medical problem."

"What kind?" Rush asked.

"Seizures. Only thing that will control the symptoms is an enzyme called tryptophan. It's not a controlled substance, but a kid trying *not* to attract attention is gonna be buying it on the black market, anyway. . . . Any ideas where we might look for such a thing in your fair city?"

Once again the detectives exchanged looks, then nods.

"Sit back and chill, Colonel," Davis said. "It's across town, and'll take the better part of an hour."

On the way, Davis explained that the guy they were going to see had been busted twice in the last three years for selling controlled substances.

"And he's at large, why?"

"Guy's got a hell of a Johnnie Cochran."

Lydecker smiled at the slang term, wondering if the cop knew enough about history to realize there really had been a Johnnie Cochran back before the Pulse.

Lydecker asked, "What's his name?"

"Johan Bryant."

The unmarked car finally pulled to a stop in front of an upscale house in the suburbs, one of those retro ranch-styles the neo-affluent had been building lately. The whole street was lined with homes that probably sold for high seven figures.

"Nice digs for a drug dealer," Lydecker said.

The well-tended, sloping lawn had a NEIGHBORHOOD WATCH sign.

Rush said, "We are definitely in the wrong racket."

Nodding, Davis said, "Colonel, practically every asshole in this part of town is into some kind of crooked shit. How else in this economy could they afford pads like these?"

"Why don't you arrest them?"

"We do," Rush said. "But every mook in this neighborhood who ain't into crime is a defense attorney."

So that's what they mean by "Neighborhood Watch," Lydecker thought.

An attractive thirtyish honey-blond woman in an off-white slacks outfit answered the bell. She seemed to recognize Rush, and—without identifying herself (whether she was hired help or the man's wife or girlfriend remained a mystery)—led the little group to a large room off to the right.

The walls were pale yellow, the trim all white, the carpeting thick and heavy, also white. This might have been the living room, but Lydecker supposed it was a music room of sorts, since the only piece of furniture was a white grand piano where a man who just had to be Johan Bryant sat on the stool, his hand resting casually over the keyboard.

The man at the piano didn't rise when the trio walked in, Rush in the lead, Lydecker laying back. Tall, blond, and chiseled, Bryant might have been a member of the Hitler Youth if it hadn't been for his long hippie-ish hair ponytailed back.

"Rush, Davis—how's it hanging?" he asked, his smile wide and unrealistically white, the same shade as his white slacks; he wore a yellow V-neck pullover and sandals. A glass of clear liquid with a lemon floating in it sat on a coaster on the piano.

"I don't believe we've met," Bryant continued affably, looking past the two cops at the unimpressive figure in the gray zippered jacket.

"Not yet," Lydecker said, with a smile.

"Uncle Sam needs you," Rush said to the dealer, pointing to the colonel.

"Not the Policemen's Health and Retirement Fund, this time, huh?" Bryant said, noodling softly on the keyboard.

"Zip it," Rush said tightly.

Bryant smiled faintly, ironically.

The detectives approached Bryant at the bench. Lydecker was on the other side of Bryant; he withdrew the photos from inside his jacket. The dealer continued playing a meandering tune on the piano.

"We're trying to locate a suspect," Lydecker said. "It's not a narcotics matter."

Bryant noodled.

Lydecker said, "This individual uses tryptophan."

The dealer said, "You can get that at pharmacies."

"Pharmacies have to record sales of that nature. Customers have to sign. This individual wouldn't like that. Look at the pictures."

Bryant noodled some more.

Lydecker held one of the photos of the male X5 in front of the dealer. "Have you seen him before?"

Bryant said, "No," but he was looking at the ivories under his fingers.

Grabbing onto the man's ponytail for leverage, Lydecker shoved Bryant's face into the piano keys, making dissonant nonmusic, accompanied by a surprised, pained scream.

The woman came running, and she had a big gun in her little hand. But Davis plucked the weapon like a flower and walked her out of the room, disappearing with her.

Lydecker stepped back to allow the dealer to sit up, and compose himself; the man was touching his face—really, there were just a few cuts and welts, his forehead crying tears of blood onto his yellow sweater. Awkwardly, the dealer started to get up.

But Rush put a hand on Bryant's shoulder, holding him down. "Interview's not over."

Bryant glared back at Rush, who shook his head. Lydecker took this to mean the dealer and these cops had an arrangement . . . but this matter was not covered by it.

The dealer sat down again, his hands going automatically to the keyboard—but no more noodling.

Lydecker gave the man a handkerchief and Bryant dabbed blood from his forehead, saying to the man who'd caused the wounds, "Thanks."

"Would you mind taking another look?" Lydecker asked.

The dealer swallowed and looked at the photo Lydecker was holding up. "Yeah, now that I take a closer gander . . . turns out I have seen him before."

"Do you remember where?"

"Yeah . . . yeah, I can help you in that area. Glad to cooperate."

Lydecker twitched a sort of smile, patted the dealer's shoulder, gently. "Always a pleasure to meet a civic-minded citizen."

Bryant said, "If . . . if I tell you where he lives, will that be the end of it?"

"For you, yes," Lydecker said.

And with any luck, he thought, *for that rebel X5, too.*

LOGAN CALE'S APARTMENT
SEATTLE, WASHINGTON, 2019

Seth was still snoring on the guest room bed when Logan came in with the news.

Logan turned on the bedside lamp and carefully shook the boy to wakefulness, trying not to startle him—he would not like to be the alarm clock this sleeper took a swipe at.

"Com . . . computers come through?" Seth asked groggily, sitting up, yawning again.

"Patience has its rewards." He gave Seth a sideways grin. "So does bitchin' software."

Seth was alert, wide-awake now. "What did you find out?"

Within seconds, they were sitting in the living room, on the leather couch, Logan holding up a sheaf of papers. "When you copied that disc, my friend, you got us *everything*."

"Everything? What everything is that?"

"Smoking-gun everything." Logan tossed the papers on the coffee table. "The kind that includes dates, times, paintings, amounts . . . every damn criminal thing Sterling and Kafelnikov have been doing together."

"No shit?"

"It's all here, Seth—every sleazy transaction . . . including the next one."

Seth's eyes widened. "You know what they're going to do next?"

"*We* know, Seth."

"Where and when?"

"That's right. It's just a matter of calling the FBI now."

Seth's eyes tightened to slits. "Say *what?*"

Logan shrugged. "American Masterpieces Act violation—we'll call in the feds, have them arrested."

"Logan, you can't be serious."

"Why not?"

"Eyes Only cooperate with the feds? They're fuckin' corrupt—you always say so yourself."

"There's corruption," Logan allowed. "Widespread. But I

have contacts with honest individuals in federal law enforcement."

"Yeah, and I'll introduce you to the virgins down at the strip club." Seth shook his head. "Listen, Logan, we got the chance to do two things here. We can stop these creeps Sterling and Kafelnikov, *and* we can come away with the nest egg I need."

"The last time you 'stopped' a 'creep,' Seth . . . you killed him."

"So that's what this is about. . . . Logan, I wouldn't whack either of these guys, not right now, anyway—they're our *Manticore* connection. And anyway, Jesus! Manticore *is* the federal government—*Lydecker* is a goddamn fed!"

Logan knew Seth was right; but the blood on the cyberjournalist's hands, from their last episode together, was still clinging and damp.

"Look," Seth was saying, "we intervene when their next deal goes down, save some great slice of Americana for your conscience, Eyes Only exposes the racket with a big bad bulletin, and we help ourselves to a major contribution to the Seth Survival Telethon."

Logan, shaking his head, rose and plopped into one of the side chairs. "You lose your head again, I'll be responsible for another death . . . maybe *more* than one."

Seth leapt to his feet, gestured to himself. "You don't get it, do you? You're not responsible if I kill someone—*I* am!"

"We're 'partners,' remember?"

Seth snorted. "Well, let's dissolve that as of now. From here on out, I work for myself. When we have shared interests, you might throw me a friggin' bone."

"A bone like the details from the disc?"

"The disc *I* stole for you. . . . Logan, you can stop these guys or not—you decide."

With the biggest sigh he had ever heaved, Logan said, "All right. . . . Do what you have to do . . . short of homicide. Then you bring me the painting, and keep the cash."

"How much is that thing worth?" Seth asked, trying unsuccessfully to keep the question casual.

Logan read the sheet aloud. "*Cow's Skull Red, White, and Blue* by Georgia O'Keeffe. The buyers are Korean and the price is supposed to be a million-one."

Seth fell back onto the sofa and grinned like a kid contemplating a double-dip cone. "That'll do the trick, man. That'll do the trick."

"You've decided to disappear, then? What about Manticore?"

"Let me count my money first, and get back to you. Where and when does the deal go down?"

Logan's eyes returned to the printout. "Top of the Space Needle . . ." he looked at his watch. ". . . in about four hours."

"About time I took in the tourist sights," Seth said.

"Needle hasn't been a tourist site in some time."

"Whatever . . . meantime, I gotta get back to my crib, get prepped."

Rising, Logan faced the X5, who stood and the two men exchanged smiles that had embarrassment and maybe, just maybe, some affection in them.

"Good luck," Logan said. "Partner."

"Thanks, bro."

Seth arrived at his tiny apartment forty minutes later. Little more than a cell with a cheap blackout curtain over the single window, the apartment had a mattress, dresser, minifridge, hot plate, microwave, two chairs, card table, minuscule closet, and a small bathroom with a tub you could shower in but not bathe. A dozen or so books lay in a couple of haphazard piles near the head of the bed, mostly a mix of pre-Pulse horror fiction and weapons/martial-arts manuals.

This was, Seth knew, not quite as nice as Logan's pad.

After changing into his work clothes—black fatigues and black boots—he also laid out a black jacket, gloves, and stocking cap. The weather had turned nasty on his way home, a driving rain rolling in like it planned to stay a while.

It hadn't rained in over a week—which was a drought in Seattle—and it seemed that just when Seth needed a dark, starless night, he was going to get one. What he didn't need, though, were these relentless sheets of torrential rain. He hoped it would let up before he had to go out.

With some time left, he picked one of the books out of the pile. An old travel guide of the city, it helped him to quickly learn about the Space Needle.

Built in 1962 for the World's Fair, the Needle rose 605 feet, was protected by twenty-five lightning rods, and, at the time of its construction, was the tallest building west of the Mississippi River. Three elevators led up to the observation deck and the revolving restaurant below. One hundred feet up, the Needle had a banquet facility, and on the ground floor a gift shop. It wasn't a lot of information—the guide had been written in the heyday of the now dead tourist attraction—but it was more than he'd had.

That was when he heard the car on the street.

In this neighborhood the sound of an automobile motor was rarer than laughter—few around here could afford to own a car (Seth kept his own wheels, an old beater Toyota, off the street, hidden in a warehouse blocks away). Car motors meant cops, nine times out of ten, so the sound of one always set off Seth's mental alarms.

And when he heard the second car, he *really* knew something wasn't right. He moved to one side of the window and edged back the curtains enough to see down on the street.

Two police cars were parked diagonally, blocking the way. Just behind one of them, a third vehicle—this one a SWAT van, pulling in now—meant not only was something wrong, that something was probably him. . . .

He invested another second of watching, to get a better sense of what was coming down . . .

. . . *and saw Lydecker getting out of one of the cars.*

Seth lost another second, frozen by the sight. *How the hell had his old Manticore keeper tracked him down here?*

He grabbed his jacket, gloves, and cap, jerked open the door, and went flying up the stairs. Lydecker would have the building surrounded, but they could only work their way up from the bottom. By the time they got to Seth's place, he'd be vapor.

Slipping on the jacket, cramming his hands into the gloves, and tugging on the stocking cap, he kept running up flights of stairs. When he reached the door to the roof, he tried it and found it locked. On the other side, he could hear the rain noisily pounding on the door, anxious to get in. A howling wind cried out in protest of its own existence.

He took a step back, and threw a shoulder into it and the door gave, splintering at the jamb, lurching open while Seth jumped through, the rain slashing at him like a killer with a knife.

Turning back, he slammed the door, then picked up a stick from the roof's blacktop and jammed it under the knob.

Drenched already, he struggled to see through the downpour. He could make out the edge of the building, and sprinted there, to look across a fifteen-foot gap between his building and the next . . . a matching tenement, also six stories. Gazing down, the unyielding rain pointing the way, he saw cops and SWAT running around the building, some heading up the fire escape on that side.

Seth backed up, took a running leap, jumped the gap, landed on the other building, turning his sliding arrival into a roll, and came up running, to head for the far side of this neighboring building. Two jumps later, he was at the corner building and calmly walked, feet splashing on tar, to a rooftop door that took him down the stairs to the street.

On the sidewalk now, looking back toward his building, he saw Lydecker pounding a fist on the roof of the police car, his clenched teeth flashing in the night like tiny lightning.

It delighted Seth that he could still get the smugly self-controlled Lydecker that pissed off.

Turning, Seth started off at a slow trot. No point drawing attention to himself. Now, he just needed to put distance between himself and Lydecker's team.

On thing was certain, though: tonight would mark the last act of his new fledgling partnership with Logan Cale. Seattle was used up for the X5.

If his old commander had found him once, he'd do it again. Seth knew the man would never give up. Lydecker didn't know how to quit—it wasn't in the bastard's makeup.

The cash that would be exchanged, when Sterling and Kafelnikov's art deal went down a few hours from now, was more important than ever . . . it was a future for Seth, maybe the only one he had. . . .

Everything was riding on what happened tonight, and that was fine by Seth. The Manticore X5s had been designed for difficult missions—the greater the pressure, the better they performed.

With the possible exception of Zack, Seth felt he was the best of the X5s.

Tonight, he would get his chance to prove it . . .

. . . though he doubted his former teacher would take much pleasure out of Seth's graduation ceremonies.

Chapter Twelve

NO SALE

SUBLIME LAUNDRY
SEATTLE, WASHINGTON, 2019

In a dark T-shirt, blue jeans, and running shoes, Max sat perched on the edge of the chair across the desk from Vogelsang. The office of the goateed, overweight detective had its own unique bouquet—a distilling of egg rolls, detergent, cigarette smoke, and something that was either cleaning fluid or really rank barbecue sauce.

The funds Max was contributing to this small business were obviously not going into cleaning the place, nor for that matter was there any sign Vogelsang had upgraded his wardrobe: the private eye still dressed as though he picked his clothes at random in a very dark room . . . unless actual thought had gone into the choice of a slept-in sky-blue shirt and a pair of alarmingly bright green pants, which together turned his waistline into a bizarre, convex horizon where the sky and grass met.

"What have you found?" Max asked, not wanting to spend any more time here than she had to; she wasn't sure the peculiar aroma of this room would come off her clothes, particularly not if she used this laundromat. And she still had plenty to do yet today. The sky was threatening rain and she knew it wouldn't hold off much longer.

"I've got nothing on the woman or the Tahoe," the detective said, riffling through some papers on his desk, avoiding his client's direct gaze.

"Nothing."

He looked up and twitched a nervous smile; shrugged. "It was ten years ago. I told ya—this is gonna take some time."

"What about our badass kid?"

Vogelsang shook his head, said, "Nothing on him, either—and a contact at the PD ran the computer looking for that barcode tattoo, too. Got squat."

Max sat way forward, her eyes tight, intense. "This kid is tied to Eyes Only—and Eyes Only is somebody the cops are interested in . . . so there oughta be *something*. . . ."

"Saying he's tied to Eyes Only is like sayin' he hangs with Zorro."

"Who?"

"Pre-Pulse reference. Sorry. Damn, you *are* young. . . . Anyway, if he is working with or for Eyes Only, we'll have a damn hard time turning anything. Eyes Only is more than just a voice and eyes on some cable hack . . . it's more like a network. People who help Eyes Only, they're all loyal, and they don't talk to anybody about anything, if you're not one of them."

Max felt her hopes slipping away, like water through her fingers. She'd come into this knowing Seattle was a big city, but Vogelsang knew the town inside out; and while her brother was a trained professional soldier, so was she. Why, between the two of them, couldn't they find him?

"So you don't know anything more than when we started? What am I paying you for, again? Remind me."

With a shrug, Vogelsang sipped from a lidded cup—there was no way to tell what was inside, which was probably the idea. But something about his eyes—the way they seemed to flicker with thought, first tight, then loose, then tight. . . .

"Mr. Vogelsang!"

He almost jumped, and the cup would have spilled, but for the lid.

"You paged *me,"* she reminded him sternly. "Why? To tell me you have jack shit?"

The private eye righted the cup, then smiled in a nervous, fleeting, wholly inappropriate manner. "I guess I did find out one thing."

The hope welled within her, though she tried to keep such emotions in check. "What do you 'guess' you found out?"

". . . I'm not the only one looking for this guy."

Her eyes widened as she settled back into the chair, stunned as a clubbed baby seal. *Who else could be looking for her brother?* Two names popped into her mind: Lydecker; and Sterling . . . and then another: Kafelnikov. "How do you know?"

"It's all over the street."

Max sat forward again. "Explain."

"Pawnshop owner, name of Jacobs, he's . . . not what you would call a real upright citizen. More what you'd call . . . well . . ."

"A scumbag," she said curtly. "Hard to imagine you associating with that type. What did he tell you?"

The detective didn't argue with the characterization. "Anyway, Jacobs told me I wasn't the first guy that had come 'round lately askin' about a kid with these particular talents."

"Who *else* is looking?"

"This is where it gets . . . scary. It's somebody with a lot of grease, maybe even federal. Two bent cops . . . forgive the redundancy . . . were accompanying this character around."

"What character?"

"I didn't get a name—just a blond guy, not big or anything . . . but there was somethin' about him, Jacobs said, scared him shitless. Jacobs, y'understand, is a guy who's dealin' with the dregs every hour of every day . . . nothin' I know of ever scared Jacobs before, that's why he's able to thrive, livin' like he does, sort of on the fringes."

Vogelsang was on a nervous roll and might never shut up, and Max was listening, but her mind was working out whether the blond man was Lydecker, Sterling, or even Kafelnikov. The latter two would be bad enough, but if Manticore was on Seth's heels, Max *really* needed to get to her brother, first.

"Anyway, Jacobs said he asked around, and the two cops and the blond guy were rousting every crook on the street, from the connected ones to the crum bums . . . slappin' 'em around, when necessary, even guys that paid for protection." His concern seemed genuine; even a little of it may have been for her. "Listen, Max, we're playin' with fire—if this is *federal,* I—"

"Okay," Max said, patting the air. "Back to earth—settle."

The detective nodded and tried to regulate his breathing. He asked, "You got any idea who this blond guy might be?"

"No . . . maybe you should hire a detective to find out."

That seemed to hurt him a little. "Very funny."

"Did your friend Jacobs know anything about the kid with the barcode?"

Vogelsang shook his head. "No—but his ears are perked. I got feelers all around town on this thing."

"Good," she said, letting out a long breath. "Keep on it."

He nodded, then gave her a sheepish look. "Money's goin' fast though, kiddo."

She glared at him.

He held his hands up, as if surrendering. "What can I do? I got overhead . . . getting street info means greasing palms, and if you don't mind terribly, I gotta make a living myself."

She moved out to the edge of the chair again and gave him a cold, hard, unblinking stare. "If you want money, Mr. Vogelsang . . . you're gonna have to help me get it."

Now he pushed the air with his palms, like a bad mime fighting imaginary wind. "Whoa, whoa, whoa . . . I'm an officer of the court, y'know . . . comes with the license. I don't do crime."

She gave him an arched-brow look.

He shrugged, smirked humorlessly. "Nothing you can do time for, anyway. Guy in my line does work the gray area sometimes."

"Do tell. . . . All I need is a name."

He squinted, as if Max had gone out of focus momentarily. "Whose name?"

"Let's just say . . . speaking hypothetically, since I wouldn't want to offend an officer of the court . . . if you had a valuable piece of art, who would you go to, if you wanted to sell?"

He considered that. "I suppose this sale would have to be of a confidential nature."

She nodded.

"An off-the-books transaction."

"Don't ever let anyone tell you you're not quick."

The detective squinted again. "Large scale?"

"Oh yeah. Could keep you in egg rolls for a long time."

Sparked by this incentive, Vogelsang thought for several long, hard seconds. "Forget the guy I mentioned earlier . . . Jacobs? Large scale is beyond him. But there is one guy, and he's not far from here. His name is Sherwood."

"Where can I find him?"

"Been down on his luck, but he's good. Right now he does business in this old building off Broad Street."

This time it was Max who squinted. "Will I need an intro with Mr. Sherwood?"

"Yeah, you will."

"And who's going to do that for me?" Max asked as she rose.

Vogelsang smiled at her and rubbed his fingers back and forth against his thumb. "I maybe could be persuaded."

She leaned on the desk with both hands. "You want to keep getting paid?"

The detective switched gears. "I could call him for you, sure—sort of a favor to a good client. Referral kinda thing. Happy to do it."

"Make the call."

He did.

She listened attentively as he made arrangements with Sherwood, calling him "Woody." Vogelsang's manner was friendly enough to convince Max she wasn't the first client the detective had referred to the fence. Vogelsang assured the man these were "quality goods," that the seller was reliable, and so on.

Vogelsang covered the receiver and turned to Max. "How's an hour from now?"

"Swell," she said.

He relayed the information and nodded to her as he listened. Then he said, "I'll tell her," hung up, and gave his client detailed directions, ending with, "Third door on the right."

Max thanked him.

"So," Vogelsang said cheerfully, hands flat on his desk, "the next time I see you, you should have some cash."

"Sure," she said, exiting, throwing a blatantly insincere smile over her shoulder at him. "And the next time I see you, you should have some information."

Back at her apartment, Max changed into a black hooded sweatshirt, leather jacket and pants, to better protect her against the bad weather on its way. She collected the Grant Wood and the Heart of the Ocean (still in their zippered pouch); and then she rode the Ninja hard into the night, heading to the address Vogelsang had provided.

The rain was closing in now, as if the city was a suspect the weather was after, Max knew that the storm could erupt at any moment and, despite the zippered bag, she feared subjecting the painting to a downpour, so she pushed the bike, enjoying the engine's harsh song as she revved it up.

The first drops hit her just as she drove through the doorless entry of the building, a dilapidated three-story brick structure with most of the windows punched out and the walls starting to crumble. Only the roof seemed to be sound.

Max parked the bike, climbed off, and looked around. She stood in a wide hallway that had once had offices on either side—but now, doors were either absent or hung open, with their glass knocked out; and the Sheetrock interior walls had holes kicked in them. She could hear rats scuttling. Not surprisingly, the apparently abandoned building was dark, and if it hadn't been for her special genetics, she would have needed a flashlight to get around.

Had Vogelsang sold her out? she wondered. *Was she walking into a trap? Were Lydecker and/or Sterling and/or Kafelnikov among the rats scurrying in the darkness?*

Carrying the zippered bag like a pizza she was delivering, she crept down the hall to the third door on the right—the only closed door in the corridor. To her relief, Max saw light filtering out from underneath.

Of course, this *still* could be a trap. . . .

But caution just wasn't on her agenda, tonight. She turned the knob and walked right in.

Unlike what she'd seen of the rest of the building, this room was still in perfect shape—except for a head-sized hole on the right wall, providing an impromptu window into the next office. But the other walls were fine, the door had a lock, and an overhead fluorescent illuminated the room.

In the middle crouched a bunged-up metal desk with a TV on a crate next to it; two metal folding chairs were on the client's side of the desk. On a card table against the back wall sat a hot plate, with an open door nearby leading to a tiny bathroom. A sleeping bag, rolled up, was snugged in a corner; and the tiniest of refrigerators purred. These were spartan quarters, to say the least, but the place was spotlessly clean.

Behind the desk, his hands folded on the desktop, seated in an ancient swivel chair, was a gray-haired man of perhaps seventy with wire-frame glasses aiding lively dark eyes of indeterminate color, a neatly trimmed but thick salt-and-pepper mustache, and a long but well-tended beard every bit as gray as his hair. He wore a dark suit with a white shirt buttoned all the way up, with no tie—the suit was out of style but not threadbare. Despite the surroundings, he struck Max as both dignified and businesslike.

"Mr. Sherwood?" Max asked.

He rose, gestured to one of the metal folding chairs opposite him. "I would be pleased if you called me Woody. . . . And you're Max?"

"I'm Max," she said, and couldn't help but smile. "Interesting place of business. Do you, uh, live here as well?"

As she sat, so did he. "At the moment I do, yes. . . . Sometimes being an art speculator causes us to reevaluate our lifestyle and make certain subtractions."

"Like a bed, for example?"

He sighed, but his response seemed chipper. "I won't deny that I've had a few setbacks of late . . . but I'm just one deal away from Easy Street."

"Is that in a nice part of Seattle?"

"It's an expression, dear. Pre-Pulse."

Max thought: *I need to hang with a younger crowd.*

Sherwood was saying, "You know, dear, you're very young and quite pretty. You look healthy."

She cocked her head, narrowed her eyes. "Thanks . . . I guess. What does that have to do with any transaction we might have?"

He patted the air with one hand. "I meant nothing by it— just an observation. But the people who bring me merchandise are, by definition, thieves. The young ones are drug addicts and don't have your . . . robust glow. The older ones have a . . . hardness about them, that I hope you will never achieve."

She didn't know what to say to that; no matter: Sherwood was plowing on.

"Now I'm not saying a woman . . . a young woman . . . can't be a thief, and a good one. I've known a number, over the years. . . . The female thieves I've known have either been . . . unpleasantly hard, or, frankly, gay . . . or both."

Not knowing whether to be amused or irritated, Max said, "And you're wondering if I'm gay?"

Teeth flashed in the beard again. "My dear, at my age I'm afraid it's damn near irrelevant."

Max returned the smile. He was an engaging old boy. "Would you like to see what I have for you?"

"Oh yes," he said, with just a hint of innuendo. "I think we've had sufficient conversation to satisfy the social contract, don't you?"

She answered that with a glazed smile.

With her back to Sherwood, she slowly unzipped the bag, slipped the necklace surreptitiously into her pocket, then slid out the painting. When she turned back to him, his mouth dropped like a trapdoor.

After a long moment of staring at the painting, he asked, "Is that . . . that the *real* thing?"

"It should be." She smiled. "But I won't be offended if you want to test it."

"Please," he said.

She placed the painting on the wide desk and, from one of

the drawers, Sherwood withdrew a device that he explained was an UVIN. Then, standing at the desk, the painting like a patient on a surgical table awaiting the doctor's skills, he said, "Get the lights, would you please, child?"

Max did as the old boy requested, and the fence fired up the UVIN and ran its rays over the painting. He looked from the painting to her, his expression almost . . . alarmed; and then back down at the painting, going over it again with the ultra-violet light. A crack of thunder made her jump; heavy rain hammered at the windows and echoed down the corridor.

"My dear," he said finally, "this is indeed a genuine Grant Wood."

Trying to conceal her excitement, Max asked, "How much?"

"Normally . . ." He shrugged. ". . . six figures, easily. But you may have guessed I don't have that kind of money around here. Actually, I don't have *any* kind of money around here . . . but I know several buyers who do."

A pulse of excitement jumped in her stomach. "So—what's our next move?"

Somewhere under that beard, Sherwood had worked up a half smirk. "I suppose you trusting me, for a few days, is out of the question."

"I like you, Woody," she said. "But not that much."

"I can hardly blame you. Well, then, here's the situation. If we want to sell this beautiful painting for anywhere near its value, people are going to want to test it. To *see* it tested. . . . For that to happen, I need to have it here."

Max didn't like where this was going. "What's to keep you from screwing me?"

"Besides my age, and the price of Viagra?" He shrugged. "All I have is my word. Didn't Mr. Vogelsang vouch for me?"

"Oh, sure . . . but who'd vouch for *that* sleazebag?"

"True, true . . . but I assure you, I'm honest."

"Woody, you deal in stolen property."

"That's true, but I do it honestly."

She laughed in spite of herself. "Okay, Woody, you call me, and I'll bring the painting, and whoever wants to see it tested, can see it tested."

"That would be a workable plan," he said, "but for two things."

"Go on."

"First, my function is to buffer you from the buyers and the buyers from you—I provide insulation of sorts, should—for example—you or my client turn out to be participating in what used to be called, quaintly, a sting . . . is *that* pre-Pulse term familiar to you?"

"That one is," she admitted.

"Second, rain's coming down like a veritable son of a bitch, and you should not risk taking that painting out into it, even with that zippered pouch of yours."

Max shrugged with a knowingness beyond her years. "Maybe so, but I'm still not leaving the painting here. You have a nice line of bull, Woody, but I just met you . . . and you may be an honest crook, but you're still a crook."

He made a clicking sound in his cheek. "That is a fact . . . and this is a commission I could dearly use right now."

"Fine. Well?"

The fence let out a big sigh. "All right, little lady. Let me make a phone call. There is a client I know who would be perfect for this acquisition."

"Excellent. Tell me about him . . . or is it a her?"

For the first time, a frown creased the fence's brow. "I can't give you a name or any background—you're compromising my professional ethics enough as it is."

She said nothing; she was frowning, too.

Sherwood removed a cell phone from his suit-coat pocket. "Do I make the call? I'll do my best to get the buyer to come down right, now."

". . . Make the call."

"But you can't be here."

Now she was getting pissed. "Woody, I can't *not* be here."

Sherwood was ahead of her. "No, dear . . . What I mean to say is, you go into the office next door, you can use that hole in the wall to watch and listen." He pointed to the head-sized hole she'd noted coming in; the aperture was a foot or so behind Sherwood and would give Max the perfect place from which to monitor the transaction.

"I'd still feel better knowing who the buyer is."

"That is not negotiable, dear. I would protect you, likewise."

She rose, picked up the metal folding chair on her side of the desk, and there was a loud crack as she snapped the back off it with her two small leather-gloved hands.

Sherwood's eyes flared. "I do like an assertive female. . . . Mr. Glickman is his name, and that's all I know. He's actually another layer of insulation, the agent for a consortium of buyers. What I do know . . . and this should please you . . . is that Mr. Glickman pays top dollar, in untraceable cash . . . tens, twenties, twenty-fives . . . and he never haggles much about the price. For quality such as this, he'd expect to pay a quality price. . . . Shall I make the call?"

A tiny smile formed on her full lips as she said, "Go ahead and drop the dime."

Sherwood's smile was a delighted one. "You *do* know some pre-Pulse slang, don't you, you little vixen?"

Twenty minutes later, the rain still beating its staccato rhythm on windows, echoing down the hall like gunfire, Max and her Ninja were safely snugged in the office next door when she heard a car door slam outside. She crept to the hole in the wall and assumed a position that would conceal her and reveal the mysterious Glickman.

For his part, Sherwood didn't seem the least bit nervous, and Max realized she was no doubt not the first person to witness a transaction from this hiding place. She did wonder if the porthole had been formed by a dissatisfied client shoving the fence's head through the wall. . . .

Tucked into the shadows, Max could see through the broken-glass door frames of her private office as two men walked down the hall, passed her without looking in, and strode into Sherwood's office. The two men stayed near the door, and Max couldn't make out anything more than their shapes.

"What happened to the chair?" one of them asked, his voice sounding nasal and somehow muffled.

"Vandals," Sherwood said distastefully, as he rose, and then his tone warmed up. "Mr. Glickman, I apologize for bringing you out in such vile weather . . ." The painting was on the desk, like a colorful blotter. ". . . but, as I told you on the phone, this is a major Grant Wood."

The fence, smiling proudly, held up the Masonite board.

"It certainly is," a rather refined voice replied.

"I, uh . . . haven't met your associate. This is a breach of etiquette."

"Breach of etiquette?" another, rougher voice responded. "I can think of something worse."

An icy shiver spiked through Max: *she had heard that voice before* . . . in the foyer at Jared Sterling's mansion. One of his security team! Maurer, the black, clean-cut guard. . . .

"Something worse?" Sherwood said, clearly off-balance.

The pair stepped forward into the fluorescent's path and Max's view. In a black rain-dripping raincoat, Maurer stood on the right, his nose heavily bandaged, while on the left, the other "insulation," Mr. Glickman, stood in a London Fog, and Max recognized him, as well—his hair in the same iron-gray crew cut, the scars still on his cheeks, each about the size of a dime.

Sterling's security chief.

"I mean," Glickman said, "trying to sell back a painting stolen from my boss."

Sherwood's whole body seemed to go slack. "I . . . I . . . I had no idea. . . ."

"It was heavily covered in the media. You work in the art field. Certainly you knew this painting was Mr. Sterling's."

"But . . . gentlemen . . . I was not aware that Mr. Sterling was your client. I was under the impression you represented a consortium of overseas buyers. . . . Forgive me."

"No," Glickman said.

The security guard was reaching inside the London Fog, and Max did not think he was going for a handkerchief. She took three quick steps back, then threw herself at the Sheetrock wall. She burst explosively into Sherwood's office just as Maurer fired the first shot. Max couldn't get to him in time, but in reflexive if pointless self-defense, Sherwood lifted the painting in front of his face.

The nine-millimeter slug tore through the painting leaving

a hole bigger than a golf ball, then ripped through Sherwood's head, blowing away a piece of the old man's scalp.

"The painting!" Glickman called, in warning.

But Maurer's second shot shredded even more of the masterpiece before cleaving its way through Sherwood's chest and sending him backward, upending the chair, pitching the painting, which cracked against a wall, while the fence lay on his back, asprawl.

Max leapt, kicked, her boot connecting solidly with the bandage across Maurer's face. He screamed, dropped his pistol, and fell backward to the floor, a hand covering where the blood erupted from his nose, red streaming through his cupping fingers. Glickman had dodged when Max came through the wall, and from the sidelines fired at her, but was off-balance, and missed, the bullet burrowing into Sheetrock. She rushed him before he could get his equilibrium, ducking a wild shot, and kicked sideways, her boot slamming into the man's groin, knocking him into the Sheetrock behind him, air whooshing out of him; he slid down the wall, and his mouth was open in a silent scream.

But Sterling's security chief was no pushover, and hardly a stranger to pain; plenty of fight left in him, Glickman squeezed off another shot, this one whizzing past Max's shoulder, again thunking into Sheetrock.

On the floor near the dead fence (who was on his back staring sightlessly at the ceiling) Maurer—his hands smeared and slippery with his own blood—was scrambling for his pistol; he got hold of it, and raised it at Max, stupidly heedless of how close she and his superior were. Just as the black guard fired, Max dived out of the way and Maurer's bullet missed her and sent up a puff of pink as it punched Glickman in the chest.

The iron-haired security chief's eyes went wide with shock, and he slumped back against the wall. He looked down at his wound, then up at Maurer. His last words were a kind of cough: "You dumb fuck."

"Oh, shit," Maurer said, and brought his pistol around, searching for his target, who seemed to have disappeared.

Then Max was suddenly at his side, and grabbed his arm

and bent the elbow the wrong direction; Maurer screamed and his fingers popped open and he dropped the blood-smeared pistol. She kept going, applying torque to his shoulder as she cranked his arm around behind him.

The guard was in so much pain, he couldn't even scream.

"One question," Max said, her voice cold, hard. "Wrong answer, I break your arm." She applied a little more pressure to make her point; Maurer arched his back and groaned pitifully.

"Ask! Ask!"

"Where can I find Sterling . . . *right now?*"

He tried to twist his head around to see her, but she cranked up on the arm and his head dropped, as he yelped with pain.

"Let's have that answer," she said, and started moving the hand upward.

"Okay, okay! He's at the Needle."

Frowning, Max relaxed her grip somewhat, and with the lessening of pain, all the air went out of Maurer, who sagged; she felt if she let go of him, he'd drop like an armload of firewood.

"Space Needle?"

"What the . . . fuck other Needle . . . deal going down."

"More," she said, not bothering to punctuate her question with a ratchet of pain; the guy was cooperating now.

"The boss and that Russian, they're selling some shit to some Koreans, there. Up top."

"*Right* now?"

"Less than an hour from now . . . yeah."

Max said, "Thanks," and let go of him.

He stood there unsteadily for a second, his back to her, and he said, "I won't . . . won't cause you any trouble."

"I know," she said, chopped him across the back of the neck.

She left behind a damaged painting, a dead fence, a dead security chief, and an unconscious Sterling subordinate, who would have explaining to do about the precious painting he'd ruined and the superior he'd shot and killed.

At least Max still had the necklace in her pocket, the

precious object that had sparked so much damage and death, the weight of it suddenly very heavy. She needed this to end the cycle, or she and her brother would never be safe.

Gazing down at Sherwood, she shook her head. The old boy hadn't needed to die, but she felt no guilt or responsibility. He had chosen this path, even if he'd never made it to Easy Street. Still, she had liked the eccentric fence, during their short but significant relationship; and now Sherwood was just one more thing taken from her by Sterling and Kafelnikov, one more comrade slaughtered, like the Chinese Clan. . . .

In the office next door, she put on her amber glasses, walked her Ninja out into the hall and down to the entranceway. Then she climbed aboard, fired it up, and gunned it through the doorway into the waiting storm.

Wind-driven rain slashed at her face as she raced up Broad Street toward the Space Needle, but she didn't mind—it seemed cleansing; she wished the rain would wash away all the dirt and grime and corruption from this foul city, this fractured country. . . .

Parking in a burned-out building two blocks away, and looking up to get her bearings, she was surprised at how huge the structure looked. Naturally, she'd seen the Needle before—you couldn't live in the Emerald City and not notice the Needle—but she'd never paid much attention to it.

Over six hundred feet tall, the Needle rose like a giant metal flower. The night was so dark and the rain so dense that only during a lightning flash could she make out the crest of the building. A beacon of futuristic hope when it was built back in the '60s, the Space Needle now towered in ghostly tribute to the blight brought on by the Pulse, the skeleton of a vision dreamed in a more hopeful, naive time.

In the years since the Pulse, the downturn in the economy had brought fewer and fewer visitors to the famed tourist spot, until the restaurant had gone under, the observation deck had been closed—too many people were jumping—and the banquet facility had been forced to shutter. The structure now served primarily as a practice pad for every graffiti artist in the city, the Needle seemingly painted a hundred different shades at once; red, black, yellow, white, spray paint in every possible color had been applied somewhere on the giant building. The first-floor gift shop—its windows had long since been broken out—seemed like it would make the natural point of entry for Max.

The neighborhood around the landmark had suffered the same fate and reminded Max of vid footage she'd seen at Manticore, labeled SARAJEVO and BEIRUT. The only unbroken windows in the whole neighborhood seemed to be in the two vehicles parked in a lot at the base of the Needle, beneath a tin overhang on which rain drummed insistently. She edged closer, positioning herself behind a Dumpster at the periphery of the parking lot. From here she had a better view of the two cars.

One, a black luxury number, a Lexus, had California plates—this would be the Russian's ride; the other, an old Hummer, appeared to be a rental and reminded Max too much of her days at Manticore. Near each vehicle stood a guard; the one near the Hummer—shorter than the other guy—smoked a cigarette and strolled back and forth on the driver's side.

The other guard, near the Lexus, closer to her, leaned against the door, staring in her direction. At first, she thought he'd seen her, then she realized that he was looking at nothing, and his head just happened to be pointed in her direction. Still, as soon as she moved, he would likely see her . . . and any chance for surprise would be gone.

Behind the Dumpster, she found a rock about the size of a sugar cube and threw it down the street. The rock hit on the concrete, barely loud enough to be heard in the rain; but, to their credit, both men looked in that direction . . Max using the diversion to swing around and conceal herself in front of the Lexus.

"Hell was that?" the other man asked, his accent giving him away as Japanese.

"No idea," the guard near the Lexus said, bored. He wore a dark brown zip-up jacket and black jeans.

Closer now, Max made him as Jackson, the crew-cut wrestler from her first visit to the Sterling estate.

"Should we investigate?" the Japanese guy asked.

"Do what you want. Soak your ass. My orders are, stay put."

The Japanese guard went back around the Hummer and lit another cigarette.

Jackson was leaning against the driver's door of the Lexus, staring into space; *real ball of fire*. Max decided to take the Japanese out first. She rolled under the Hummer, and—when his pacing brought him close enough to her—she grabbed the man's ankles and flipped them up in the air. Gasping, he took the ride.

She was out from under by the time he smacked his head on the cement; sprawled there, the guard groggily lifted his head to look up at her with a glazed look, perhaps wondering if he was dreaming, such a lovely face looking down. . . .

The owner of the lovely face punched him in the side of the head and he lay back, out cold.

"You say somethin'?" Jackson asked.

When he got no answer, Jackson straightened, eyes tightening, finally interested enough to turn and look. But all he saw was Max's boots as she flew over the top of the car with martial-arts grace and dropkicked him in the face. Jackson toppled over, spitting bloody teeth like seeds, then tried to rise, clenching what was left of his smile . . . and Max decked him with a short left.

Rain drummed on the tin overhead.

Back when the Needle had been a family-fun destination, three elevators had been in service here, and though Max didn't plan on taking one, she did want to know whether or not the things were up and running. If Sterling used the Needle as a regular drop point for his dirty deals, it didn't even seem like a stretch to her that the art collector might arrange having power supplied to the building that only his people knew how to activate.

Max stepped through a broken-out window in the gift shop and surveyed the store; the only sound she was making came from the moisture dripping off her leather. Access to the power had to be on this floor somewhere. Dust blanketed the floor and the counter, too; she could make out where the cash register had been before it had been ripped out.

She paused, listened intently, heard nothing . . . and crept forward.

To the left, a doorway led to a hallway off of which were the three elevators. That hall curved back, and out of sight, so Max decided to start here. Behind the counter, another opening led to a back room. Again listening carefully, and still hearing nothing, she edged into the room—pitch-black . . . even Max had trouble seeing. After slowly scanning for any other doors, the X5 backed out into the relative light of the empty store, illuminated completely, now and then, by lightning.

Max got to one side of the store door and peered down the elevator hallway, saw nothing. Moving forward, she could make out the elevators on her right. She also could see the lighted-up floor indicator, above the elevator doors—they *were* working.

The nearest car was up on the observation deck, the other two were here at ground level. The left side of the hall had once been the glass wall of the pavilion, but now was mostly just metal framing and random shards. Six feet beyond the last elevator door, another doorway beckoned, this one with a small shaft of light shining out of it.

She slipped across the open space, peeked in . . . and saw one of Sterling's men inside the small room.

A naked lightbulb, hanging like electric fruit, provided the only light. Several large circuit boxes lined one wall and Sterling's stooge sat on a folding chair against the other wall, reading a sports magazine with a bikinied woman on the cover. This guy she hadn't encountered before, a redhead with a wide chest and a sharply angular face; he wore a zippered brown jacket and darker brown slacks.

Stepping in quickly, she said, "Can I see that when you're through with it?"

He looked up in blank confusion and she hit him with a right, a left, and another right. The magazine slipped from his hand and he and the chair tumbled; she caught them, setting both man and chair down gently, avoiding the clatter. She considered using the coil of rope on her belt to tie the guy up; but decided it might be put to a better use later on, and secured his hands behind him with his belt.

Taking the elevator up would tip them that she was coming.

She would just have to climb the stairs to the tower, where an evil prince and assorted vile advisers of his would surely await.

Chapter Thirteen
NEEDLE'S POINT

THE SPACE NEEDLE
SEATTLE, WASHINGTON, 2019

Around the corner from the elevators, Max came to a door marked STAIRWAY; it had been padlocked, but now the lock lay broken, a plucked metal flower on the detritus-strewn floor. This seemed recent work, not the ancient mischief of vandals.

She opened the door cautiously, and looked inside, up the well of stairs winding their way into darkness that swallowed them; the pounding rain echoed down like a disorganized drum and bugle corps. On the stairs themselves, however, she could easily see a pattern of wet footprints.

Seemed Max was not the only tourist who'd come to the Space Needle tonight. . . .

Gazing up into the blackness, with the drumming of rain hiding any footsteps, she had no way to tell whether the person who'd taken these stairs was half a flight ahead of her, or already long since at the top. . . .

As the storm flailed away outside, Max viewed her five-hundred-foot climb as a chance, at least, to dry out for a while. Her hair hung to her shoulders in wet clumps, those clothes of hers that weren't leather were soaked, and if she hadn't had her special gifts, she would have been freezing; all Max experienced, however, was a slight chill. As silently as possible, clinging to the outside wall of the narrow staircase (following the example of those wet footprints), Max started her ascent.

One hundred and sixty steps later, not winded in the least,

she entered a banquet room that had suffered less vandalism than the main floor, the benefit of being one hundred feet up from ground level. The lights of the city were muted by the slashing storm, but her catlike vision allowed her to take in these surroundings. . . .

The room held more tables than Max cared to count, many overturned, some still covered with white tablecloths, others covered instead with a thickness of dust. Purple chairs were scattered everywhere and any smaller items—china, silverware, water glasses, even table lamps—seemed, for the most part, long gone. The windows at this level had survived better, some but not all knocked out, normally allowing in a tiny amount of light—though tonight that meager illumination was confined to strange shadows dancing wildly in the downpour.

Listening carefully for any sign of that intruder who'd preceded her, Max heard nothing . . . only howling wind and hammering rain.

She still had a very long way to go to the top, but resisted the urge to rush, even with her superior stamina, she did not want to risk wearing herself out—after all, she could not be sure what battle awaited her at the Needle's point, and needed to be as fresh as possible after so rigorous a climb. Wasting her energy getting there could prove tactical suicide, and her next opportunity to rest would be in the skyview restaurant, four hundred feet above her. Between here and there, it was just her and the stairs . . .

. . . and, perhaps, the other "tourist" who had come up this way ahead of her.

As she continued her ascent, she considered: the only estimate she could make about what awaited her upstairs came from the size of the vehicles—the Lexus could hold six, the Hummer maybe a couple more than that. So, that was what? Fourteen guys, at the most . . . and she'd already dispatched three.

That left a potential army of eleven for her to face, assuming one of them was the person on the stairs, ahead of her. If the other stair-climber was an interloper, like herself—with an agenda as yet unknown—there could be a dozen guys . . . a dozen guns . . . waiting for her.

Before she'd started this climb, the floor indicator on the lobby level had shown the elevator stopping at the observation deck; in this weather, she wondered if the art-for-cash exchange might not have reconvened to the restaurant floor. So she prepared herself for what might await beyond the door . . .

. . . but only silence and more dust and darkness greeted her. Apparently, rain and wind or not, the deal was going down where all had agreed it would—perhaps only out in the relative open, even in a storm, could these untrustworthy men trust each other.

After these additional 640 steps and four hundred feet of climbing, even Max's genetically superior muscles could feel the burn. She paused to lean against a wall.

Now, five hundred feet above the street, the storm still raging outside, the X5 found herself in a room so dark even she had to strain to make details out of the murk. She could see elevated booths—these would have allowed even those dining in the center of the restaurant to enjoy a magnificent view of the city—and maple paneling, accented with other light woods, giving the room a classy air and probably, during the day, a natural radiance. Although covered in dust, the seat cushions revealed their original light yellow, which would have added to the daytime brightness.

She used one gloved hand to wipe sweat off her brow, her breathing easy, regulated; she felt fine, damn near fresh, ready for a final round with that last twenty feet, to end this thing, and take down Sterling and Kafelnikov . . . and maybe, just maybe, Lydecker himself. . . .

"Christ, do a sit-up once in a while, why don't you?"

It was a youngish male voice, off to her right. Wheeling toward it, she dropped into a combat stance.

From the darkness, the voice said, "And your skills are rusty as hell. . . . Damn, you didn't even know I was here."

Furious—with herself, because that voice was right—she said, "Quit the hide-and-seek, then—come on out and test my combat skills, firsthand."

The young man stepped into the shadowy light—a figure in black, from his fatigues to the stocking cap that didn't quite conceal the military-short brownish hair; the narrow, angular face, the green eyes, were the same, though he'd grown into quite a man. Max felt every muscle in her body go weak, and the climbing had nothing to do with it.

Seth.

Not Zack, but Seth . . . who had not made the escape that night, with the rest of them . . . was he Lydecker's X5? Or the rebel SNN made him out to be?

Relaxing out of her combat stance, but staying alert, Max demanded, "What the hell are you doing here, Seth?"

"I'm flattered you recognize me," he said. "Which one are you? Jondy? Max, maybe?"

"I thought you *knew* me. . . ."

"Your barcode was showing, when you leaned against the wall, sis. I'm gonna say you're Max."

She nodded, and the wave of emotion—some sort of bittersweet warmth, at being recognized by her brother—rolled unbidden through her.

Seth's eyes tightened and he pointed a gloved finger to the ceiling. "Do you *realize* what's going on up there?"

She nodded.

He was still so serious, his face a vacant mask, his eyes empty of emotion—only Zack had had a harder game face than Seth. "That's my last chance to get away from Manticore—forever."

"Get away?" she asked.

"That's right. Maybe we could go together."

More emotion surged, but she said, tightly, "How do I know you're not with Lydecker?"

The game face dissolved into confusion—hurt, sullen confusion. "Why the hell would you say such a thing?"

And now the accusation blurted from her: "When we ran, you didn't go!"

A defense was blurted back: "They *caught* me!"

"That's right . . . they dragged you back. Did you graduate with honors, bro?"

She took an ominous step toward him and he dropped into a fighting stance that mirrored her own.

But he did not attack; he said; "I escaped that same

night—two of them thought they had me, but I flipped the bastards, and got out in the confusion. I've been running ever since, just like you must have been."

Even as she eyed him suspiciously, she wanted with all her heart, every fiber of her being, to believe him. If she, and others, had escaped that night, why not him?

Despite the genetic tampering and military training, she had an impulse within her, an impulse that had been fed by Lucy and her mother (if not that terrible foster father) and, yes, by Moody and the Chinese Clan, who lay dead because of her. That impulse—which made her want to believe Seth more than she had ever believed anything—cried out for family, for someone like herself whom she could call sibling. . . .

That thought was interrupted by the squeal of tires in the parking lot below—a sound that only she . . . or someone like her . . . could hear in the squall. Responding, both she and Seth went to the edge and looked down through the slanting, slashing rain. A flash of lightning aided them, turning the world white, and they both saw the black Manticore SUVs pulling in at odd angles, TAC squad pouring out.

"Lydecker," Seth breathed.

"Damn it!" Max said, fury mingling with sorrow. "I should have *known* you were in his pocket!"

She spun and thrust a kick toward his chest, but he blocked it; she maintained her balance, but allowed him time to launch a flying kick of his own, which she expertly ducked . . .

. . . and then the two of them came up facing each other, in combat stance.

Seth was shaking his head, and his eyes seemed desperate. "Max, I swear—I'm *not* with him. I don't know *how* he found us."

Her voice dripped sarcasm: "I *bet* it's a mystery."

"Sis—we *both* need to get out of here."

She jabbed at him with a left, but he leaned back, the blow glancing off his chest, and as he went backward, he grabbed her arm, using her own momentum against her, flipping her over him onto a table that smashed beneath her impact.

As she rose from the ruins, mildly stunned, he said, "We have to get the elevators up here—that'll slow Lydecker down."

Lightning flashed through the room, and doubt flashed through Max—maybe Seth was telling the truth, after all . . .

She said, pointing to the ceiling, "No, don't do it . . . they'll see the floor indicator lights upstairs!"

That would mean any advantage of surprise would be lost, where Sterling, Kafelnikov, and their small army were concerned.

But it was too late for further discussion.

Seth had already jabbed the buttons, summoning the two remaining elevators from the ground floor up to the restaurant. She could only hope that Sterling, Kafelnikov, and their buyers weren't watching the indicator lights.

"It's worth it," Seth said, fiercely. "We can't get caught by Lydecker now."

"Or is Lydecker already in that elevator?" she said, through tight teeth.

"Damn it, sis! Grab some tables."

"Why?"

"When that elevator comes up, we'll block it open, and keep the cars up here. . . . That way Lydecker and his boys'll have to make the big climb!"

Now she was starting to believe him.

They hauled tables over, and when the bell dinged and the first elevator door opened, she paused with bated breath, waiting to see if TAC came swarming out . . .

. . . but the car was empty.

So was the second one, and they shoved tables in to wedge the elevator doors open, after which brother and sister paused to grin at each other, in a small moment of triumph.

When Seth rushed up the stairs toward the observation deck, Max hung back for a few hesitant moments. Conflicting emotions still wrestled within her; the paranoia of so many years on the run made her wonder if Seth could somehow still be working for Lydecker—could this be some sort of trap?

She didn't lag long, though. Lydecker was down there—

the blocked elevators would only delay his arrival. There was a single option left: follow Seth up to the observation deck.

Max flew up the last thirty-two stairs, burst through the door into the wind and rain on the outdoor platform.

In 1.6 seconds, Max took it all in: rain relentlessly battered the synthetic material of the steel-beamed roof of the concrete deck, which was encircled by a three-foot-high concrete wall with steel rods rising out every ten feet or so. These each contained four holes that served as eyelets for steel cables that had kept people from jumping, back when the Needle had been in business; but the cables had long ago been stolen for salvage, leaving only the low wall and the thick steel rods. Wind whipped the rain into a fury, and visibility beyond the deck itself was next to nil. The bank of three elevators came up through the middle of the Needle and opened onto the deck, in a neat row to the left of the stairway door, through which Max had emerged to see . . .

. . . Seth engaged in combat with two brawny Koreans in black raincoats, in front of the elevators!

To her right, she could barely make out Jared Sterling and another, older Korean, in tan and black trench coats respectively, their hair standing on end in the wind, as if they were terrified at witnessing the fight between the young X5 and the Korean thugs.

The tycoon held by its handle a large black art portfolio, no doubt containing some masterpiece earmarked for overseas, and the Asian's right fist clutched the handle of a briefcase . . . the two men obviously frozen in the midst of an exchange. Kafelnikov was nowhere to be seen, though he could easily be just out of sight, around either curve of the deck; and somewhere, she knew, Morales and probably several others from Sterling's security force would be lurking.

As for Lydecker and his TAC team, they would be emerging at some point—there was still one elevator to be summoned, after all, that she and Seth hadn't blocked with their tables . . . in which case, Lydecker could make his own melodramatic entrance onto this rain- and windswept stage at any moment.

Seth was uppercutting one of the Koreans, shattering the

thug's nose, a scarlet splash in the gray night; the man fell to the cement and didn't move, his dark trench coat making a black puddle. As the male X5 circled the second Korean; Max glimpsed Morales, his pistol drawn, coming around the wall of elevator shafts, unseen at Seth's flank.

Max rushed Morales, which got his attention, and the Sterling guard fired off a round at her, which she ducked, and then was all but on top of him, still low, hitting him with a straight right in the groin. Morales blew out all his breath in a howl of pain to rival the wind. As he grabbed himself with one hand, going down on one knee as if praying to her, Max batted the pistol from his other hand, like the offensive metal bug it was. Then she stood him up straight with a left to the solar plexus, headbutted him, and watched with pleasure as the hollow-eyed security man dropped backward to the deck, as unconscious as the concrete he lay sprawled upon.

Max hadn't seen it, but when Morales had fired at her, both Sterling and the Korean turned toward the shot. Each had a hand on both the briefcase and the portfolio, and the Korean apparently misread the situation as a Sterling betrayal, and tried to hold onto both items in the exchange.

When Max turned her attention to them, the two art collectors were wrestling back and forth in an almost comic tug of war, as each now tried to claim both prizes.

Seth was in the meantime mixing it up with the remaining Korean thug; he caught his opponent with a left and two quick rights, staggering the burly Korean, the man's arms dropping to his sides as if begging Seth to strike—which Seth did, leaping, kicking him in the chest. The Korean flew backward, his skull bouncing off the cement wall next to the elevators, where he slumped to the floor, either unconscious or dead.

Then Seth took off toward Sterling and the Korean buyer, only to be cut off by another pair of oversized Asians, bodyguards who had been around the far corner of the elevators and were on their way to intercede for their employer in his tug-of-war with the American art dealer.

Rain lashing, Seth was between the two Asians, keeping

them back with martial-arts kicks, when two more of Sterling's security men seemed to materialize before Max: a gangly white guy, and a compact, muscular Latino. She did a back flip, each of her feet kicking one of the men and sending them both onto their backs, apparently out.

She leapt to her feet and headed toward Sterling; but the gangly security man reached out and grabbed her ankle and brought her down, hard.

This didn't hurt Max nearly as much as it pissed . . . her . . . *off!* On her side on the damp concrete, as if doing an exercise, she kicked back, her foot taking on his face, his face losing, the nose and jaw snapping, a small crack followed by a larger one. He went to sleep, like a good boy. . . .

Only now the Latino was back on *his* feet, and obviously knew better, now, than to try to match Max blow for blow; he reached under his arm for his pistol . . . but never made it. Max sprang onto her feet, and then swung one of those feet around, connecting with the side of the face. The blow wasn't that hard—and merely caught his attention, his eyes rolling like ball bearings, but his feet staying under him. Max jumped and spun in the air, this kick practically tearing the nose off the man's face as he fell unconscious, and probably glad to be.

Sterling and the Korean collector had worked their way over to the three-foot wall that surrounded the observation deck, where the wind and rain ruled. They continued tugging back and forth on the briefcase and the portfolio, each unable to gain an advantage over the other. The sky growled at them and the wind beat on them and the rain pelted them and the deck, making their footing treacherous.

Sterling jerked on the briefcase just as he let go of the portfolio, a sudden shift that took the Korean's feet out from under him, and he pitched back against the edge and seemed to be reaching out with one hand to Sterling, even while holding on to the art portfolio with the other, his eyes pleading. But Sterling merely watched as the man tumbled over into the night, his screams barely discernible over the storm, the portfolio flapping like a big broken wing as the man fell five hundred feet to a certain death.

Coming out of her most recent spinning leap, Max caught the final moments of that confrontation, and now she whirled to find Seth, to aid him; but she saw only the two Korean bodyguards, piled on top of each other, like slabs of butcher's meat.

Finishing her pirouette, she finally saw Seth, on the move, heading for Sterling and that briefcase of money. Beyond her brother, she could see—coming around the far end of the observation deck—the Russian, his long blond hair darker and flattened by the rain, wearing a flowing long dark coat buttoned from knee to neck; the rock-star-like gangster was pointing at Seth, but not with a finger: a nine-millimeter Glock.

Seth didn't see Kafelnikov, and Max yelled a warning, but the Russian's pistol barked and a bullet tore through Seth's left shoulder, sending the X5 flying off-balance. Her brother wobbled on toward the trench-coated Sterling, who grasped a briefcase handle in one hand and held the other up as if it would stop the human freight train barreling toward him.

Sterling even shrieked, "Stop!"

As if that would do any good.

Max ran toward them, from one direction, as did Kafelnikov from the other, his pistol still raised. The Russian's second shot went wide, just as Seth was grabbing the briefcase in the hand of his good arm. But Kafelnikov's third shot caught Seth in the right calf, and the X5 pitched into Sterling, the boy's momentum carrying them both to the edge of the wall.

Executing a perfect jump kick, Max knocked the pistol out of Kafelnikov's hand and, at the same time, jarred him off-balance. Pressing her advantage, Max kicked at him again and caught him a glancing blow that sent him tumbling back. When the Russian tried to rise, she grabbed a lapel of his coat in her left hand and hit him with a hard right. His eyes closed and he sagged, the big man hanging by his coat from her tiny hand.

Dropping him to the cement, Max turned to see Sterling and Seth wrestling precariously close to the edge of the wall, wind and rain taunting them. Glad she'd held on to that rope, she grasped the coil like a cowboy prepared to twirl his lariat, and moved toward the pair. As she neared, the pair teetered, Sterling slipped on the wet cement, and they both pitched over the edge.

"Seth!" she cried.

Running to the wall, Max looked over and down to see Seth a few feet below, at the bottom of the guard wall, gripping a lip of cement with the fingers of a hand that belonged to his bad arm. His good arm held the briefcase while Sterling dangled like an earring, also clinging to the case. The howling night sky seemed to be laughing now; but the tycoon was whimpering, his eyes wide and wild, as his grip started to slip in the wetness.

Max knew she had only seconds.

She tied the rope off around one of the steel rods, then whipped it down to Seth, who was just able to let loose of the wall and grab on. Sterling yelped as he nearly dropped off, but managed to keep his hands attached to that briefcase.

"I'll pull you up!" she yelled into the wind and rain, and from below, Seth nodded—in an almost businesslike way that went back to their Manticore training—and Sterling screamed, "Hurry, for God's sake, girl—hurry! I'll pay you *anything!*"

Before Max could do a thing, however, she felt hands on her and someone lifted her bodily, swept her off her feet in a very bad way, throwing her over the side the way a kid visiting the Needle might toss a candy wrapper to earth.

Spinning in midair, Max reached out and up, grabbing blindly for the rope and instead gripping on to cloth with first one hand, then another . . .

. . . and once again she found herself hanging high above a city street, with only the lapels of Kafelnikov's jacket to keep her from falling. Her feet banged into Seth and Sterling, dangling below her, as she struggled to hang on to the Russian, who was now pressed against the wall, trying to keep from being pulled over himself. He clawed and pulled at her hands with one of his, the other tight around the grip of the Glock.

He snarled down at her: "You miserable bitch!"

Swaying, clinging to his coat, she grinned defiantly up at him, as the rain and wind had at them both. "Déjà vu all over again, huh, Mikhail?"

Now he grinned, a terrible, sadistic white smile shining down on her like a lopsided moon. "Yes—brings back lovely memories—like slaughtering your precious Chinese Clan. . . ."

The Russian was unbuttoning the coat, so he could peel it and let her plummet!

Locking eyes with Kafelnikov, she let go of one lapel; in the murk, he couldn't see her grab on to the rope with that now free hand.

"This is for Fresca," she said, ice in her voice.

He had the jacket half unbuttoned. "Who the hell is that?"

"Nobody. Just another of your victims. . . ."

And she yanked on that lapel and carried the Russian past the wall, and over her head, pitching him into the rain-tossed night.

Kafelnikov screamed the whole way down and, as a benefit of her Manticore-heightened hearing, Max was able to hear the satisfying *splat* of his landing.

She climbed the rope and hauled herself back over the wall and leaned over to start pulling the other two up. Seth remained quiet, almost placid, while Sterling was weeping, praying, and might have been wetting himself, for all she knew . . . if the rain hadn't been covering up for him.

Behind her the trio of elevators all dinged at once.

Her eyes flew to those of the dangling, wounded Seth: *they knew, the siblings knew. . . .*

Lydecker was here—he and his TAC team would be pouring out of those three elevator cars in moments!

Looking down at Seth, she saw him shake his head slowly but decisively. He didn't say, but she could almost read his thoughts: he was wounded, and couldn't escape; and he was not going back to Manticore. . . .

Was that a single tear, trailing down his face, she wondered, or just more rain?

"Sorry, Max," was all he said . . .

. . . and he let go of the rope.

Seth fell silently, bestowing the faintest smile up at the sister who reached yearningly down for him.

Jared Sterling, on the other hand, screamed and flapped his arms and hands, as if God might suddenly grant him the gift of flight; but the Almighty was apparently in an ironic mood, because all the wealthy fool got for his effort was the briefcase lid flipping open, raining money down on the parking lot.

Max turned away, before either man hit the pavement, and right now she did not relish her ability to perceive the subtleties of sound on this violent night.

A voice behind her yelled, "Freeze!"

But it wasn't Lydecker, just one of the TAC team members.

"Don't move—show me your hands. Now, now, now!"

Under other circumstances, she might have smiled, imagining the astonished expression on the squad member's face when she vaulted over the wall, and dropped out of sight, apparently plunging into the night.

Which she did. The TAC team couldn't see her snare the end of the dangling rope, swing out, then back in, through glassless windows into the restaurant below.

She landed like the cat she partially was, head up, alert— she had only seconds, now. Lydecker would be sending his men after her, some down the stairs, others down the elevators. She ran over and pushed the DOWN buttons of all three, hoping to at least slow the pursuing team, and hit the stairs running.

Her brother had given his life to avoid falling back into Lydecker's hands; she would risk hers to escape that same fate, and mourning would just have to wait.

The observation deck was like a ship plowing through a stormy sea, and "Captain" Lydecker was royally pissed.

"He jumped over the *side?*" he roared.

The soldier nodded, decked out in black fatigues with goggles, Kevlar vest, helmet, and MP7A. "But it didn't look like . . . a *him,* sir."

"What the hell are you—"

"Sir, the pictures you showed us. I was at the elevator, and he . . . or she . . . was at the wall, a girl, and with all that rain—"

Lydecker got in the soldier's face. "Mister, how in God's name can you mistake a nineteen-year-old man for a 'girl'?"

"Sir, I—"

Lydecker silenced him with a look, brushed him aside, and strode to the edge of the observation-deck wall, where the carnage below could barely be made out through the slashing rain. This would be one hell of a mess to cover up.

Then he noticed the rope, flapping in the wind, tauntingly.

He spat into his handheld radio: "TAC Five."

The radio crackled, and a voice from the ground floor said: "TAC Five."

"Anyone come down in the elevators?"

"No, sir."

"Watch them closely. We may have another X-Five on the premises. Possibly female."

". . . Yes, sir."

Lydecker motioned with his head to one of the men. "Down the rope, soldier."

The man unhesitatingly slung his weapon back over his shoulder and shimmied over the edge and down out of sight. Lydecker was roaming the observation deck now, surveying the casualties up here—half a dozen anyway. Most of them seemed alive, and were coming around, after the kind of beating an X5 could deliver. . . .

"TAC Two," he said into the radio.

"TAC Two."

"TAC Two, take half the team and search the building for our man. Possibility of a second X-Five on site, female."

"Yes, sir."

He turned to the team member nearest him. "TAC Three, dispose of the bodies and cleanse the site."

The man hesitated.

"Can't you hear me in this weather, mister?"

"No, sir. That is, yes sir."

"Then carry out your orders."

"Yes, sir."

Lydecker turned and marched back to the elevators, where another six men in combat black stood waiting. Behind him, Lydecker heard a pistol shot, then another and another.

"What's the problem?" he asked.

"The elevators, sir," one of the soldiers said. "The doors closed. . . ."

"You might trying pushing DOWN," Lydecker said through smiling teeth, though he was not at all happy. "They just might come back up."

"Yes, sir."

Something tugged in Lydecker's gut. He got on the radio. "TAC Two?"

"TAC Two. In the stairwell, sir. No sign of anyone."

"Keep looking, TAC Two. Time's running short."

"Yes, sir."

The middle elevator dinged and its doors slid open.

Into the radio, Lydecker said, "TAC Five."

"TAC Five. No movement, sir."

The other two elevators arrived, and three men got onto the cars at either side, with Lydecker flying solo in the middle one; he went down one floor and the doors opened onto the vacant restaurant—vacant, that is, but for the soldier he'd sent down the rope, who approached.

"Anything?" Lydecker asked.

The soldier pointed. "Sir, wet footprints all over the place—more than one set."

Lydecker didn't like that; what it might mean made him very unhappy. "Did you search the entire floor?"

"I followed the prints to the stairwell, sir, but some went up and some down."

Exasperated, Lydecker said, "Stay at this position."

At the lobby, Lydecker emerged from the elevator to find that the cleanup crew—in yellow TOXIC WASTE suits and carrying no weapons—had arrived. In the parking lot, they were already dealing with the splattered remains of what appeared to be four different bodies.

Several of the yellow jumpsuited Manticore specialists were scraping up parts and filling body bags. One of them broke away from the group and scurried over to Lydecker, displaying a plastic bag from the thick fingers of a yellow glove.

"You'll want to see this, sir," the yellow-jumpsuited man said, his voice muffled by his headgear.

Holding the plasticine bag up in the rain, Lydecker could see a fragment of human flesh, but nothing significant. He pulled out a Mini Maglite and took a closer look at the bag's contents: a chunk of skin with a series of black numbers, four in a row, and a barcode, the others numbers abbreviated on either end, probably from the impact with jagged concrete that had separated Seth from his head.

But even a partial number was enough for Lydecker to know they'd tagged another X5 . . . or perhaps the X5 had tagged himself.

"Good work, soldier," he said, handing the bag back to the cleanup man. "Lock that evidence away. Top security."

Colonel Donald Lydecker checked with the various TAC positions, to see if anyone had spotted anyone or anything else. That young soldier must have been mistaken: that had been Seth who went over the side, falling on his figurative sword rather than return to the Manticore fold.

His choice.

Then Lydecker got back on the radio. "All TAC members assemble at ground level—suspect has been apprehended, I repeat, suspect has been apprehended. We're going home, men. . . . Saddle up."

Another yellow-jumpsuited man approached the colonel, this time with a wallet in his hand. "One of the deceased looks to be that computer big shot—Jared Sterling."

Lydecker shook his head—*fucking mess,* he thought—and then, already weaving a new web mentally, said, "All right."

The tech returned to the gory parking lot, and Lydecker moved back inside, found a quiet, dry corner and made a cell phone call, filling in another Manticore specialist, finishing with, "Despondent over recent business setbacks, the well-known computer tycoon took his own life last night when he leapt from the top of the Seattle Space Needle."

The voice from the cell said, "We can make that happen."

"Do it—and filter the money through the usual channels."

"Yes, sir."

They wouldn't take all of Sterling's money—that might raise suspicions among certain reform-minded politicians and their liberal-press lackeys. Just a few million to make it look like things were turning sour for the art collector. Maybe they'd have to plant some drugs or incriminating photos; but the world at large would never question the not-so-tragic suicide of another poor little rich boy.

Lydecker clicked END and returned to the parking lot, to supervise. The TAC team was coming down now, and he'd get them the hell out of here, before this turned into an incident. Wouldn't do for that Eyes Only to get ahold of tonight's fun and games. . . .

Thank God the neighborhood was practically deserted, but for junkies, winos, and other riffraff, not the sort of place where anyone would call the cops over a few gunshots.

Lydecker's thoughts were interrupted by the sound—a few blocks over—of a motorcycle revving, then peeling out. When he turned his rain-flecked face toward the engine roar, Lydecker saw nothing. Something nagged at the back of his mind—that girl, that remarkable girl in LA—but he shrugged. Things were contained. And another X5 could be checked off the list.

No one would ever know what had happened here tonight. The bodies and the blood would be swept away, like the garbage they were; and the money that littered the parking lot would be taken into custody by Manticore.

Things in Seattle would soon be wrapped up. They'd be going home . . .

. . . only Donald Lydecker still had the gnawing, nagging feeling that he'd missed something, something important, that for the success of Seth's elimination, an important but unspecified failure had also occurred, making a nasty balance.

Two days later, back in Wyoming, he called a certain TAC team member into his office—the young man who had seen the X5 dive off that observation deck. Lydecker—having learned that one of the dead men was the Russian he'd aided in the Chinese Theatre massacre—wondered if Kafelnikov's presence indicated also the presence of that extraordinary young woman from the Chinese Clan, that unidentified suspected X5.

"Tell me again what you saw," Lydecker said.

The soldier, Keenan, just a kid himself (from Nebraska), wore simple black fatigues now, instead of his TAC gear. His blond hair was cut close, and he had shown nothing but loyalty to the program in his year and a half of service.

The boy was obviously considering the question carefully before risking an answer. "Sir, I saw the X5 known as Seth. He had his back to me, and—"

"No." Lydecker rose behind his desk, hands on his hips. "Don't tell me what I want to hear. Tell me the truth—tell me exactly what you *really* saw that rainy night."

Keenan met his superior's eyes. "I saw a girl, a woman really . . . with black hair, dressed in black, sir. Leather, I think. Sort of . . . motorcycle gear."

Lydecker's memory replayed the sound of that cycle revving up and taking off, a few blocks from the site. "Did you see her face?"

"Negative, sir."

"You're sure it was a female."

Nodding, Keenan said, "Yes, sir, I'm sure. She was . . ." And now he risked a tiny smile. ". . . built like a girl. Woman."

"Athletic?"

"Oh yes, and . . . nice."

Lydecker sighed. "I'm glad your faculties are so acute, Mr. Keenan . . . well done. Now . . . this stays in this room . . . between you and me."

"Yes, sir."

"Dismissed."

Keenan saluted, spun on his heels, and strode out.

Lydecker sat down, rather heavily, and thought over what he'd just heard. It wasn't completely implausible that the X5s were in contact with each other. But were they *up* to something, together?

He thought about that revving motorcycle and wondered

if he'd screwed the pooch. Maybe there *had* been two X5s in the Needle that night, Seth and one of the girls . . . Jondy, Brin, Max . . . could have been any of them. And very possibly this was the LA X5, over whom so many had died at the theater.

He would find out, when he caught up with them. He knew that someday he'd catch up with all of them.

Now, however, he was concerned that if the X5s were all communicating, maybe they were planning something, too. Maybe they were planning on catching up with him.

Shaking his head, trying to drive away the thought, he went back to work. But the notion that they might be after him as much as he was after them—that the children might come home to take revenge on their father—did not go away easily.

It never would.

Epilogue
RUMINATIONS IN THE RAIN

Rain battered the windows of the high-rise condo, as Logan stared out into the night, seeing nothing but shapes and blurs.

Ten days had passed since something had gone terribly wrong at the Space Needle, and—despite what he could only assume were Manticore's best efforts—Eyes Only had managed to piece together only a few details.

At first, Logan had thought Seth had double-crossed him, had taken the money *and* the masterpiece, and killed everyone, then disappeared across the Canadian border; that the boy's homicidal streak had combined with greed and fear to get the best of the X5.

Then Logan had started thinking about what was wrong with that scenario. Sterling's body had been found in the parking lot, yes; but there'd been no sign, living or dead, of a certain Korean art dealer, and a notorious, ambitious Russian street gang leader out of LA . . . though street rumors strongly suggested the presence of the latter.

And what of Sterling's bodyguards? Logan knew Sterling wouldn't so much as go to lunch without his muscle. Had there been a gun battle in which only Sterling himself had gone down? Or, if bodyguards had been combat fatalities (and with the X5, that would seem inevitable), why would Seth leave only Sterling's corpse to be found?

And the more Logan mulled it over, the more absurd seemed the story of a billionaire's suicide over business setbacks.

No mention, for example, was ever made of Sterling's car—where was it? Had Seth stolen it? If so, why hadn't it been found? The boy surely would have ditched it by now. And what if Seth *hadn't* stolen the car? Obviously, Sterling wouldn't have walked the twenty miles from his house to the Space Needle, just to jump off. . . .

So—how had Sterling gotten there? Where was his driver?

Spurred by these inconsistencies, Logan had started digging into Sterling's alleged financial setbacks. At first blush, every column seemed to add up; but the more Eyes Only looked, the more things appeared out of whack.

Stocks that Sterling lost money on had shown only marginal dips, far less significant than officially reported versions of the dead man's deficits. Businesses that were ancillary to his Internet company had failed, but checking their track records for the previous six months revealed each had been financially healthy until the day of Sterling's death.

So many people had their own financial woes in the economic minefield that was post-Pulse America that Logan knew no one would look very close at a calamity suffered by the wealthy likes of Jared Sterling. The country was in no mood to pity some billionaire who'd flung himself off a building at the first sign of trouble.

No, Logan told himself, no one would look into this . . . except Eyes Only. And Eyes Only knew somebody was cooking the books. The question was . . . who?

Logan had far more questions than he had answers, and whenever he spotted that pattern, his mind turned to a cover-up. And when he thought cover-up, he thought government, and when he thought government . . . in the case of a mysteriously missing X5, anyway . . . Eyes Only turned to Manticore.

He knew more about the organization now, but he still had few hard facts. Lydecker's group did, however, seem to have the kind of major clout to pull off a cover-up of this magnitude—sweeping murders under the carpet, perhaps committing more murders in the process.

But the question that nagged him was . . .

. . . *why would Manticore cover up what happened at the Needle?*

For Logan, the inevitable and rather chilling answer was: because Manticore had caught up with Seth.

This gave Logan a whole new scenario for what may well have happened at the Space Needle on that rainy, windy night . . . a scenario even more disturbing than his previous theory.

Initially he'd thought that Manticore had somehow caught up with Seth at the Needle, and captured him. Only, if Lydecker had nabbed his renegade X5, and taken him away, why had Sterling also been killed?

Not just Sterling, but the other witnesses, the Korean, the bodyguards, and God alone knew how many other un-recorded victims. . . .

But if Seth had been captured, alive . . . why kill anyone? These witnesses were involved in a crime; they could be co-erced into silence, easily enough. Sterling, Kafelnikov, and the others would have no knowledge of Manticore and the X5 program; to them, Seth would merely be an extraordi-nary physical specimen.

The only answer Logan could come up with was that Manticore had tried to intercept Seth in the midst of the art deal going down . . . and Seth had not gone quietly into that rainy night, and Manticore had been forced to kill its wan-dering son.

In front of witnesses.

Who had to die, so Manticore could cover its tracks.

The cyberjournalist turned away from the window and moved aimlessly through his rich man's apartment. He could not be sure this scenario was the correct one, but he felt cer-tain he could not be far off the mark. And it made him feel sick. . . .

Bitterly, Logan recalled how he'd lectured Seth about ethics, and yet . . . hadn't he ruthlessly, recklessly used Seth?

No matter how noble Logan's motives might be, in the end, he'd used the young X5 for his own purposes . . . which had gotten Seth killed.

If Logan Cale had helped Seth disappear, as the boy had requested, instead of recruiting him to help in the Eyes Only crusade, maybe the young man would be plotting his next revenge against Manticore from somewhere remote and safe, like the small town near the Arctic Circle where he'd sent the lab tech, Ben Daly.

Logan fell heavily onto his bed, on his back, and took off his glasses, resting them on the nightstand and closing his eyes, pressing a thumb and forefinger to the inner bridge of his nose.

Sleep would not come easily tonight . . . or any other night, not for a very long time. The guilt he felt for getting Seth killed would gnaw at him like a small, voracious animal, always there, chewing him up inside. When sleep did come, it would only be after considerable reflection on the memory of Seth, and speculation on whether Logan had himself tumbled into the ends-justify-the-means abyss.

A few months from now, Logan Cale—Eyes Only— would meet another X5, recognizing a young woman's superior feats as those of a Manticore soldier . . . with the barcode to match.

But his sense of guilt over the death of one of her sibs would prohibit Logan from immediately confessing his "crime" to her. He would work with her, collaborate with her as he had with Seth, in the pursuit of Eyes Only's crusade . . . though always filtered through what he had learned from his first unhappy experience with an X5.

The second X5 would be beautiful and trusting of him, and—as he fell in love with her—Logan's secret would turn dark and even fester; but he wouldn't tell her, for fear of driving her away.

It would be a very long time before she learned his secret . . . and when she finally did, it would come at a terrible time in both their lives, with a potentially damaging cost.

Tonight, however, Logan Cale's major problem was getting some rest. He opened his eyes and stared at the ceiling. Sleep tonight would indeed be a long time coming.

THE SPACE NEEDLE
SEATTLE, WASHINGTON, 2019

The rain rivaled that other night, not so long ago, when so many had died here.

Max wasn't sure what had drawn her back to this place, with its awful memories. She sat, hugging her knees, rain drops pearling off black leather, her hair turning into thick wet braids, baring the barcode on her neck, her impassive face streaked with what might have been tears . . . but was just precipitation.

She'd climbed all the way—not just to the observation deck, this time, but farther, to the hard curved metal of the top. She sat up there now, the wind whipping her, a punishment that seemed strangely pleasant on this dark night, the city's scattered lights like fallen stars before her.

Max would reflect here, in the days and months and years to come, on many things. Sometimes she would still be perched there, when dawn came.

Was she wrong, she wondered, to want to find her real family? These surrogate families hadn't worked out so well—the Barretts, an abusive father, an enabling mother, and yet another lost sister; the Chinese Clan, with Moody and Fresca and the others, where she had perhaps felt the most at home, until her mentor's life of crime, and her own Manticore-haunted past, had led to slaughter.

Of course, she was making a new family now, with Original Cindy, Kendra, Herbal, Sketchy, even Normal . . . the whole Jam Pony gang. Max hoped she would not endanger them, too; she would do her best to protect them from the darkness that followed her . . .

. . . but they would never be her only family, her real family. She had connected with Seth for such a short, even tragic time; and yet making that link had been a revelation to her. *She had to find her brothers and sisters.* They were out there, her siblings, out in that world somewhere, stretching endlessly before her from her Space Needle roost; and she would just have to keep on searching.

How could she not? Lydecker surely would.

Max smiled and shook her head, flinging water, but not noticing. She had come out of all this with only one tangible thing—the Heart of the Ocean, a blue stone so hot, so precious, she had almost been unable to fence it. What she finally wound up with was a nice wad of cash . . . about enough to keep Vogelsang on the job for another month or two.

Now that the violence was over, the Needle had a stately silence—not to mention a fabulous view—and she could reflect, in this terrible yet somehow sacred place, where her brother had died. She would come here, from time to time, to think . . . and to be with Seth.

MAX ALLAN COLLINS has earned an unprecedented eleven Private Eye Writers of America "Shamus" nominations for his historical thrillers, winning twice for his Nathan Heller novels, *True Detective* (1983) and *Stolen Away* (1991).

A Mystery Writers of America "Edgar" nominee in both fiction and nonfiction categories, Collins has been hailed as "the Renaissance man of mystery fiction." His credits include five suspense-novel series, film criticism, short fiction, songwriting, trading-card sets, and movie/TV tie-in novels, including *In the Line of Fire, Air Force One,* and the *New York Times* bestseller *Saving Private Ryan.*

He scripted the internationally syndicated comic strip *Dick Tracy* from 1977 to 1993, is cocreator of the comic-book features *Ms. Tree, Wild Dog,* and *Mike Danger,* has written the *Batman* comic book and newspaper strip, and the miniseries *Johnny Dynamite: Underworld.* His graphic novel, *Road to Perdition,* has been made into a DreamWorks feature film starring Tom Hanks and Paul Newman, directed by Sam Mendes.

As an independent filmmaker in his native Iowa, he wrote and directed the suspense film *Mommy,* starring Patty McCormack, premiering on Lifetime in 1996, and a 1997 sequel, *Mommy's Day.* The recipient of a record five Iowa Motion Picture Awards for screenplays, he wrote *The Expert,* a 1995 HBO World Premiere; and wrote and directed the award-winning documentary *Mike Hammer's Mickey Spillane* (1999) and the innovative *Real Time: Siege at Lucas Street Market* (2000).

Collins lives in Muscatine, Iowa, with his wife, writer Barbara Collins, and their teenage son, Nathan.

ENGINEERED TO BE THE PERFECT SOLDIER.

UNLEASH HER THIS FALL ON YOUR PLAYSTATION®2 AND XBOX.™

JAMES CAMERON'S

DARK ANGEL™

HTTP://DARKANGEL.SIERRA.COM